"It's not ... breath aw... y

"Noah—"

He eased forward slowly, giving her ample time to stop him. "I can't pretend you don't stir something in me, Callie. And I sure as hell can't pass up this opportunity."

Her mouth felt soft beneath his as he caressed her uninjured cheek. Keeping his touch light, he coaxed her mouth open and slid his tongue in to meet hers.

Callie pulled back and brought her hand to her lips. "Noah, we can't do that."

"Pretty sure we can and did."

"You don't need this complication on top of caring for me, and I can't afford to be sidetracked by you and your charms...and those kisses."

He couldn't help but grin. Apparently he'd found just the thing to distract her.

HOLLYWOOD
HOUSE CALL

BY
JULES BENNETT

Published in Great Britain 2013
by Mills & Boon, an imprint of Harlequin (UK) Limited,
Eton House, 18-24 Paradise Road, Richmond, Surrey TW9 1SR

© Jules Bennett 2013

ISBN: 978 0 263 90623 3
ebook ISBN: 978 1 472 01182 4

51-0613

Harlequin (UK) policy is to use papers that are natural, renewable and recyclable products and made from wood grown in sustainable forests. The logging and manufacturing processes conform to the legal environmental regulations of the country of origin.

Printed and bound in Spain
by Blackprint CPI, Barcelona

National bestselling author **Jules Bennett**'s love of storytelling started when she would get in trouble as a child and would tell her parents her imaginary friends were to blame. Since then, her vivid imagination has taken her down a path she'd only dreamed of. And after twelve years of owning and working in salons, she hung up her shears to write full-time.

Jules doesn't just write Happily Ever After, she lives it. Married to her high school sweetheart, Jules and her hubby have two little girls who keep them smiling. She loves to hear from readers! Contact her at authorjules@gmail.com, visit her website, www.julesbennett.com, where you can sign up for her newsletter, or send her a letter at PO Box 396, Minford, OH 45653, USA. You can also follow her on Twitter and join her Facebook fan page.

For my husband, who thinks I'm beautiful
whether I'm wearing a formal dress, jeans and boots
or lounge pants. I love you with all my heart.
Thank you for showing me the beauty of love.

One

"I want your body."

Callie Matthews jerked around to see her boss, her very sexy Hollywood-plastic-surgeon boss standing only a few feet away in the foyer of his office. When he reached behind his back, the lock to the front door slid into place with a quick flick of his wrist.

"Excuse me?" she asked, thankful the office was now closed.

A naughty grin spread across Noah Foster's face, showcasing that killer smile that never failed to make women weak in the knees as their panties were dropping. Granted, her panties had always remained in place, but still…

Mercy, she was so shallow, because if he so much as crooked a finger for her to follow him into the break room and…

"Hear me out," he said, holding his hands up. "I know you want to catch your big break by acting—"

O-kay. So they obviously weren't having the same thoughts about him wanting to tear off her underwear in the break room. Such a shame.

"But," he went on, oblivious to her naughty thoughts, "I have a proposition for you."

Those last three words were like music to her ears. That break-room fantasy might come true after all.

"I have an upcoming ad campaign I'd like you to model for."

She shook her head. "I'm sorry. What?"

Model? The chubby teen that still lived inside her nearly laughed. But Callie had long since left that girl behind in Kansas.

Noah moved toward her, never taking his gaze from hers, never breaking that signature smile. "I'd like you to do the modeling for the ad to launch my new office across town."

Callie came to her feet and moved around the desk. "Obviously, you haven't thought this through."

He raked his eyes down her body, sending all kinds of yummy thoughts swirling through her overactive imagination. "Oh, but I have. And it's you I want."

Oh, baby. If only those words were used under different circumstances.

"You have tons of clients you could use," she told him as she turned and marched down the hall to the lounge to retrieve her purse. "Besides, I've never modeled."

Like most transplants to L.A., Callie had come eager to be the next actress that would make Hollywood directors and producers sit up in their chairs and take notice of her remarkable talents. Unfortunately, her agent couldn't get her any auditions that weren't embarrassing. So far she'd done a commercial for zit cream and one for STD meds. Yeah, not the claim to fame she'd been hoping for. But she had to start somewhere, right?

Wait, maybe that whole STD thing was why Noah wasn't so interested in seeing her outside the office. He did know that was purely acting…didn't he? She was free and clear in that department, especially considering her lack of sexual experience. Not that she was a virgin, but she might as well be for the two pathetic encounters she'd had.

"I just want a few pictures of you, Callie." Noah followed her and rested an impressive broad shoulder against the door-jamb. "The ads we're going for will showcase the natural side of surgery, how to stay young and fresh."

Callie mimicked his action and crossed her own arms over her chest and leaned against the counter. "But other than that minor chin scar you did microdermabrasion on, I haven't had anything else done. Isn't that false advertising?"

"Not at all," he argued. "If you had never been a client, then that would be false advertisement. But you're perfect, Callie. You're beautiful, the camera will love you, and you'll be on billboards across town. Tell me you don't want that kind of exposure."

Well, this *was* a giant step up from zit cream and STDs.

"You think this will help with my acting?" she asked.

He shrugged. "It can't hurt."

There was a role coming up in an Anthony Price film that she would give anything for, and her agent had yet to get her an audition. But maybe if she had the right connections…

"I have a proposition to throw back at you," she countered.

Dark brows drew together as his eyes narrowed. "You make me nervous when you get that look. Last time you had a lightbulb moment we ended up with a cappuccino machine in the break room that shot mystery liquid all over the walls and the floor."

She waved a hand through the air. "Minor technical difficulty."

He sighed. "Let's hear it, Callie."

"You talk to Olivia Dane about getting me an audition for this upcoming film of Anthony's and I'll pose for you."

If Noah called the Grande Dane of Hollywood, who just so happened to be their number-one client and mother to the hotshot producer on the new film Callie was aching to get a part in, Callie would forever be grateful.

"I'm not asking you to have her give me a part," she went on when he was silent. "I just want an audition to show them what I can do."

God, she hated to sound as if she was begging, but, well... she was. She'd come to L.A. to pursue a dream, not to get this close and have a door slammed in her face.

Callie believed in fate and it was no coincidence she worked for the same plastic surgeon who catered to all of the needs of the most recognized woman in Hollywood.

"Please," she said, offering a sweet smile.

His brows tipped down as he tilted his head. Damn, he had that George Clooney sultry look down pat.

"Your agent can't get you an audition?" he asked.

Callie shrugged. "She claims this isn't the right role for me. But I can't prove myself if I don't get the chance."

He reached out, placed those large, masculine hands on her shoulders and all sorts of happy tingles spread through her. Mercy, she wanted those hands on her without the barrier of clothing.

One dream at a time, Callie.

"Your agent has been in this business for a while," he told her, his voice softening as if he were trying to explain something to a toddler. "Maybe she knows what she's talking about."

"I don't see how it would hurt," she insisted. "If I don't get it, I'm no worse off. But there's that chance I could land this and launch into something I've been dreaming of my entire life."

Dark gray eyes searched her face. "I can't call her. I know how bad you want this, but I couldn't live with myself if I threw you into a lifestyle that isn't as glamorous as you think it is. You haven't been in town that long, Callie. Why don't you ease into this? Anthony Price is a big deal."

No matter how sexy Noah was, she refused to let him ruin her dream. "Fine. I'll get this audition my own way."

He dropped his hands and placed them on his narrow hips. "Let your agent do the grunt work, Callie. Stars weren't born overnight.

"You're a beautiful woman. You won't have a problem getting attention."

Something very warm spread through her at his declaration. To think a man like Noah Foster thought she was beautiful, a man who created beauty for a living, was one of those compliments she'd keep locked away in her heart forever.

"I'll give you fifty thousand dollars to pose."

Callie froze at his abrupt offer. "Fifty thousand? Are you out of your ever-lovin' mind?"

He chuckled. "You know, when you're shocked, your accent becomes really strong."

"I don't have an accent," she told him. "And get back to that offer. Are you kidding me?"

His smile faded. "I don't kid about business or money."

Fifty thousand could go so far. Her parents needed a new roof desperately and she could buy them a second car, something reliable. God, how could she turn down this offer?

As she ran through the pros and cons—and there were definitely more pros—Noah's eyes studied her in that way that always made her nervous. For one thing, he was a Hollywood surgeon to the stars and she always felt as if he was analyzing her. Another reason was because, well, she found her boss drop-dead, curl-your-toes-into-the-carpet sexy. Why on earth the man was still single was beyond her.

Maybe he slobbered when he kissed—that was a total turn-off. Or maybe he was terrible between the sheets.

As she studied him, she knew there was no way a man like Noah Foster would be a slacker in the sack. The man exuded sex appeal, and he looked so amazingly perfect with clothes on she couldn't even imagine what he did to a birthday suit.

Noah offered that killer, dimpled smile as if to reassure her of her future. He was not fighting fair with those damn twin dimples, and she had a feeling her resolve was going to crumble about as fast as her panties would drop if he'd offer that break-room fantasy of hers.

Yeah, she knew she couldn't turn down that money. As much as she'd wanted him to talk to Olivia, she was grateful for the fact he had so much confidence in her to offer such a large amount.

"I'll do the ad," she told him. "If you're sure my look is what you want plastered on billboards."

Crazy thought, but whatever he wanted. He was the one paying.

"You're exactly the look, Callie. I want to capture that youthfulness, that innocence."

Callie laughed. "I'm not that innocent."

"You moved here less than a year ago and you grew up in the Midwest." His lids lowered slightly over those dark eyes as he leaned forward just enough to get into her personal space. "You're practically still a virgin."

Callie's mouth went dry because the word *virgin* instantly brought to mind sex, and the word *sex* hovered in her mind while Noah stood this close with his bedroom eyes locked onto hers.

"I assure you, I'm not a virgin."

Shut up, Callie.

"Good to know," he told her with that cocky grin. "But I'm glad you've given in to the pictures."

"Have you ever had to fight for anything you want or do you just flash that smile?" she joked.

Something dark passed over his face; his smile faltered, and he swallowed. But just as quick as it came, it passed. "You'd be surprised by what I've had to fight for and what I've lost."

None of her business, she told herself. Everybody had a past, and just because he was a rich, powerful surgeon didn't mean he'd had it easy. But this was the first glimpse she'd had of any kind of pain hidden behind that billion-dollar smile.

She wasn't a virgin.

Noah inwardly groaned. Callie Matthews might not be a virgin in the sexual sense, but she was certainly very innocent because if she had any clue where his thoughts traveled when he thought of her, she'd be suing him for sexual harassment.

He refused to be so clichéd as to date his receptionist, but damn if he didn't want to see her on more personal, intimate terms. He'd played with fire when he'd cornered her two days ago in the lounge. When he'd moved in closer to her, he'd noticed her bright green eyes widening, the way she kept nervously licking her lips...those sexy, naturally full lips that begged to be kissed. His female clients paid a small fortune for a mouth like Callie's.

Noah eased back in his office chair. She'd be coming in any moment and he intended to keep their relationship professional. No more touching, no more getting pulled under by her hopeful eyes and childlike dreams.

If Callie had any idea what she was in for in this Hollywood wannabe-actress cycle, she'd run back to that cornfield she came from. It wasn't all glitz and glamour. There was no way in hell he'd see another woman he cared about fall to the dark side of Hollywood.

The scars from his fiancée were still too fresh, too deep.

And between the house they'd shared that he had to go home to every day and her ailing grandmother he cared for, Noah had a sickening feeling those wounds would never heal.

And Callie reminded him so much of Malinda sometimes it hurt to even think of the bright way his fiancée used to light up over her future career. Callie was Malinda all over again... only this time he refused to get attached.

He raked a hand through his hair, trying to rid himself of the nightmare that still plagued him.

His fiancée had meant everything to him. He'd have done anything in his power to save her. But he'd failed. He'd failed the one woman he'd loved with his whole heart, the one woman he'd wanted to spend the rest of his life with. Noah refused to ever let his heart become entangled again. He honestly didn't think he could afford another crushing loss.

So there was no way he could talk to Olivia about this role for Callie. He was actually using the modeling as a way to keep her from slipping into a darker world that Callie had no clue about. If he could keep her satisfied with the money, the attention from modeling, perhaps she'd reach those stars in her eyes. Maybe she'd let go of this movie-star fetish.

He had to intervene and do something. And no, he didn't care that he was being devious. He couldn't stand by and watch another innocent woman fall victim to the ugly side of the industry.

Because he already had a nugget of worry where his beautiful, naive receptionist was concerned. He knew what he paid her, but he also knew she was always scraping by. Those few commercials she'd done surely hadn't sucked her into the dark world he wanted to keep her from...had they?

Cynicism had never been part of his life until he'd lived with an addict, and he hated that negative vibe that always seemed to spread through him.

The back door to the office opened and shut. He heard

heels click down the tiled hallway, then slow at his office. Noah smiled at the vision that stopped just outside his door.

"Everything okay?" Callie asked, clutching her purse to her shoulder and her lunch bag with the other hand.

"Of course. Why wouldn't it be?"

She gave him a sideways look and a half grin. "Because you're never in the office before me."

That vibrant blue dress hugged her body in a professional yet sexy way, and Noah had to force himself to keep on track and not think about what it would be like to peel that garment down her body...or to think of how she managed to fit anything beneath it. She either had on a thong or nothing. If she was going commando... God, he couldn't go there.

"I had some things to do before my first client showed," he told her, trying to stay professional. "There's a little boy who was recently scarred due to a house fire and might be referred to me. I actually just hung up with a colleague about some options for this boy."

"I remember that referral." Callie smiled wider. "That's what makes you an awesome doctor. I was so excited when you agreed to take on his case."

Noah didn't want her to look at him like some type of savior. And he sure as hell didn't want to get emotionally involved with a child. Children were vulnerable creatures by nature and he worried that his heart simply couldn't take that level of commitment again.

"The boy's aunt is a good client and she asked if I'd look at him. That doesn't mean I can make him perfect. I just have to wait a few weeks because his wounds are still fairly fresh."

"You're at least giving him a chance and hope," Callie told him, still smiling and still looking at him as if he was more than just a doctor. "That in itself is so much, Noah. Don't downplay your talents."

"I'm not, but I'm going into this realistically. There may be nothing I can do, but I'll do everything in my power to help."

Most doctors had a God complex; Noah liked to think he was not one of them. He knew his abilities, his limitations. But he never backed away from a challenge, and he certainly wasn't about to turn away a ten-year-old boy, no matter if the aunt was a client or not. Noah would try to help a burned child regardless of who called.

"You're quiet," he told her. "That means you're thinking. Should I be nervous?"

A wide, vibrant smile spread across her face. "Well, I have news since we talked the other day about the audition."

Oh, no. That smile could only mean one thing....

"I got a call!" she shouted. She stepped farther into his office and dumped her items in the chair across from his desk. "Isn't that awesome? My agent called me when I was on my way home yesterday and said she was able to get me an audition for this Monday."

A dreaded sense of déjà vu spread through him.

"I'm happy for you," he lied. "Make sure you call Marie to see if she can fill in for you."

"I will." She smiled, then looked down, brought her hands up to her face...and burst into tears.

What the hell?

"Callie?"

He moved around his desk to get closer to her. What had just happened? One second she was beaming with joy and the next she was sobbing into her hands.

"Callie?" he repeated softly. "You okay?"

She swiped her damp cheeks and shook her head. "I'm so sorry, Noah. It's just..."

Those moist eyes turned to him, and even with the smudge of mascara, she was still amazingly stunning.

"You wouldn't understand," she told him.

Wouldn't understand? Understand what?

"I've wanted a break and this is it," she told him through a hiccup. "Once I called Olivia—"

"Wait." He held up a hand. "You called Olivia?"

Callie sniffed and nodded. "Yesterday morning. I was calling to remind her of her Botox appointment next week. I just had to take a chance and ask her about an audition. The worst she could've said was no."

Un-freakin'-believable. This was not happening.

"She was impressed with my initiative and said she'd see what she could do." Callie smiled through the tear tracks. "And my agent called last night, so it's a done deal."

He truly didn't think she knew what she was asking for. In Callie's starstruck mind, she probably had this image of Hollywood as all about red carpets and cocktail parties.

But right now she looked so happy how could he not act supportive? She had no family nearby and she'd only talked about her neighbor a handful of times, so he didn't even think she had too many friends. He'd be a total jerk if he didn't at least show some support. Damn the gentleman-like qualities his mother instilled in him.

"I can't believe you used a patient contact," he said. "Don't you think that was overstepping a bit?"

Callie shrugged, but her smile remained. "No. I've become friendly with Ms. Dane. I don't think I abused my power, and I can honestly say I'd do it again, Noah."

He studied her and knew she was fighting for a dream she believed she deserved. He could forgive her anything when she smiled at him that way.

"That's great, Callie." He even gave her his own smile to show her he was happy, then pointed toward her face. "You may want to touch up your makeup before the patients arrive."

Callie gasped, reaching up to pat beneath her eyes. "Oh,

no," she cried when she glanced at her black fingertips. "I'm sure I look like a mess."

"There's nothing you could do that could diminish your beauty."

Without thinking, he reached out to wipe away the tear tracks on her porcelain cheek. As the pad of his thumb slid across her skin, her breath hitched, her eyes held his. How had they gotten this close? Had he stepped toward her or had she come to him?

Her damp eyes dipped down to his lips, then back up.

What he wouldn't give to pull her against him and taste those full lips. Just once. Would that hurt anything?

Oh, yeah. Their working relationship.

"I better go clean up," she told him, backing away and gathering her things from the armchair beside him. As she turned to walk away, she glanced back over her shoulder. "Thank you, Noah. It means a lot to have someone cheering me on."

And now he was a damn hypocrite. But what should he have done when she'd been all teary and smiling? Shot down her dreams right in her face? Showing support and being supportive were two different things...weren't they?

And what the hell had he been thinking? Touching her, complimenting her and getting into her personal space so that he could see the dark green rim around her irises and become spellbound by her fresh, floral scent that always seemed to hover around the office.

She'd already been looking at him as if he was some saint. He didn't want that. He wanted Callie, but not on a deeper level than the physical. Anything else would be insane. But his hormones weren't getting that message.

Damn it, he had to gain some control. Beautiful women were his bread and butter, but there was something so innocent, so vibrant about Callie that he found intriguing. She wasn't jaded or bitter like most women he knew. And perhaps that was why he found her so fascinating and why he wanted to keep her that way.

Now, if he could just remember that professional relationship they had, maybe he could stop imagining her naked and wrapped around him.

He couldn't get too close to Callie. He'd sworn to never get involved with anyone again. Besides, she worked for him. Wasn't that reason enough to keep his distance?

Damn if he didn't want to seduce her. He'd never experienced such a strong sexual pull with a woman. And all the signs were there that she was just as attracted.

But he had to keep his distance. There were too many similarities between Malinda and Callie. The stubbornness, the stars in their eyes, the naive way they went after their goals. Not to mention that fiery-red hair and that porcelain skin. Noah couldn't let his heart get mixed up or broken again. But he also couldn't stand by and watch Callie ruin her life.

He'd stick close to her to make sure she didn't make any life-altering decisions that could destroy her.

God help him for the torture he was about to endure by making Callie Matthews his top priority.

Two

Callie's hands were literally shaking. Was this really happening? Was the door of opportunity finally opening for her? Granted she'd been in L.A. a little less than a year and most people took much longer, if ever, to get the audition that would launch their careers.

But Callie had not only gotten the audition nearly two weeks ago, she'd completely nailed it. And her agent had just called to inform her she'd landed the part. It wasn't huge, but she had lines and three scenes with the lead actors. Now she just had to prove herself, make that role shine and wait for other opportunities to come her way.

She squeezed her steering wheel and let out a squeal as she drove toward Noah's office. She couldn't get there fast enough to tell him the good news. Today was her half day to work, so Marie would be there, too, to share in her good news.

This was it. She was finally going to put the old Callie to rest and have everything she'd ever wanted. She'd landed the part; next she would pose for some pictures for Noah and get the money to help her parents in a major way. God, they'd be so happy for a little more security in their lives, and she couldn't wait to be the one to give it to them.

Her whole life she'd been overshadowed by her siblings—her übersmart brother, who was about to graduate college after attending on a full academic scholarship, and her homecoming-queen sister. Callie had been the average middle child. Because she hadn't excelled at sports, academics or popularity, she was most often forgotten. Well, no more being overlooked...by anybody.

Callie knew she looked like a complete moron driving down the road with a wide grin on her face, but she didn't care. For an overweight girl who'd come out of Kansas with big dreams, she'd finally gotten the break of a lifetime.

All her college years of hard work, dieting and exercising before coming to L.A. had paid off. Her goal of becoming an actress was within her reach. That chubby teen in her mind could just shut up because that naive girl with low self-esteem didn't exist anymore.

Callie shoved aside the humiliating years of her past and focused on the happiness she felt now. No way would she let those old insecurities and her school days of being bullied and made fun of come into play. This was her moment to remember, her moment to shine in the glorious fact that she was going to be in the next Anthony Price movie.

Callie pulled up close to the office and barely got her old Honda in park before she was out and racing across the parking lot. Thankfully it was almost lunchtime and the last of the clients should be finishing up before the office was closed for an hour break.

When she entered the cool, air-conditioned building, Marie, the fill-in receptionist, greeted her.

"Hey, Callie," the elderly woman greeted, a smile beaming across her surgically smooth face. "Someone looks very happy today."

Callie couldn't hide her excitement. "I got the part," she all but yelled. "I can't believe it. I got it."

Marie jumped up from her chair, came around the desk and threw her arms around Callie.

"I'm so excited for you," Marie said as she squeezed her.

"You may not be excited when I have to quit once filming starts." Callie eased back. "You'll be swamped with extra hours."

Marie laughed. "I'll make sure he hires someone else, though no one could replace you."

The compliment warmed Callie. "Is Noah wrapping up back there?"

Marie nodded. "Mrs. McDowell is getting her stitches out and then he'll be all done. Go on back to his office, and I'll make sure he knows you're here."

"Don't tell him the news." Callie shifted her bag higher on her shoulder. "I want it to be a surprise. Actually, don't even tell him I'm here. You can just let him know someone is in his office."

Marie giggled. "I like how you think. I'll make sure he goes straight there."

Callie turned to the right, toward Noah's office and away from the patient rooms. She couldn't wait to tell him, to share her excitement and accomplishment.

She went in and took a seat behind his desk in the big, over-size leather chair. Maybe it was not professional to get cozy at his desk, but she honestly didn't think he'd mind. Easing her bag to the floor beside her, she crossed her legs and waited.

She'd tried to call her parents on her way here, but the phone had been disconnected…again. She couldn't get that fifty thousand fast enough. She'd buy the new roof, a reliable new car and prepay some of their utilities for a few months.

With her father still laid off from the chemical plant and his unemployment long since run out, Callie's mother was pulling double shifts at the local grocery store to make ends meet…and they weren't meeting very well.

Guilt ate at Callie. How could she spend all the money she made on herself when her parents were facing such desperate times? She knew families all across the country were struggling, but it was hard to see the ones she loved fall on hard times.

Besides, she'd do something for herself with the money she made from the movie. God knew she could use a new car, as well. Her poor Honda needed to be laid to rest years ago. She couldn't wait to go car shopping. To find something that really said *I've arrived*.

Before her thoughts turned too shallow and she could imagine the color of the car she'd look best in, Noah stood in his doorway. She didn't give him an opportunity to speak before she jumped from the chair and screamed, "I got the part!"

Noah froze for a moment as if to process her words, then he crossed the room and she suddenly found herself coming out from behind the desk, meeting him halfway and being enveloped in a strong, masculine hold.

Oh. My. God.

Had she known he felt this good, this…hard all over, she would've insisted on good-morning hugs every day he came into the office—a much better pick-me-up than coffee. When you could feel a man's rippled muscles beneath his clothing, you knew there was some mighty fine workmanship beneath that cotton.

Noah eased back, keeping a firm grip on her bare biceps. "You seem really happy."

"I've never been happier," she told him, the thrill of her phone call still running through her.

"Then I'm excited for you," he said, letting his hands fall away.

"I feel like celebrating."

He laughed. "Don't celebrate too much and forget the photo shoot in the morning."

Callie smiled. "I know when it is. I'll be there."

Noah studied her face, and Callie refused to look away. When a man like Noah Foster held your gaze, you didn't want to focus your attention on anything else.

"What do you say to dinner to celebrate?" he asked suddenly.

"Dinner?"

Noah's rich laughter washed over her...and she was still tingling from his touch. "Callie, I understand what it's like not to have your family here. Someone needs to share this time with you."

Callie recalled him saying some time back that his family lived in Northern California. Other than that, the topic had been off the table, so she'd assumed that meant for her not to ask any questions about them. But that didn't stop the questions from whirling around in her mind.

"When should we go?" Callie asked, knowing there was no way she would turn down personal time with Noah.

"How about after work?" he suggested, sliding out of his white lab jacket and hanging it on the back of his office door. "Our afternoon is light. We may even get out early."

Callie glanced down at her clothes. While she might look fine, she'd want to freshen up.

"You could leave your car here," he continued. "I'll drive."

Callie wasn't going to turn that offer down. This might not be a date, but it was as close as she would get to dating her hunky boss—though she wasn't under any delusions that Noah would fall for her type. Though so far, from what she

could tell, he didn't have any particular type. So why hadn't he ever asked her out?

Oh, yeah. She worked for him.

So what? This was L.A. Did a code of ethics really matter in a land full of sin and silicone? Either something else held him back or he simply wasn't attracted to her. Either way, she had her work cut out for her if she wanted to pursue anything beyond a professional relationship with him. Granted, she had her sights set on her career, but she could so carve some time out of her day for scenery like Noah Foster. And she knew he wasn't a long-term type of guy, so really, what could the harm be in getting to know each other on a personal level?

"Where will we go?" she asked, following him out of his office and down the hall toward the break room.

He threw a killer smile over his shoulder. "You pick. It's your night, Callie."

She mulled it over, thinking of where she'd always wanted to go but never could justify going alone or paying such high prices. This milestone really deserved to be done up right.

Then she remembered the one place she'd always wanted to go but never got a chance.

She offered a wide grin. "Oh, I have the perfect place in mind."

Of all the restaurants Callie could've picked in L.A., Noah couldn't believe she'd chosen this one. A pizza place with games that spit out tickets so you could pick out prizes at the end. On a Friday night this place was crazy with kids running amok, screaming, laughing and waving their generic prizes in the air.

And Callie seemed to be fitting right in.

This was not what he'd envisioned when he'd told her to choose a place. But she'd laughed as she'd smacked the mole heads that kept popping up through holes, and she'd been a major sharpshooter at the "shooting range." Now she was off to a driving game while he stood fisting a wad of bright yellow tickets.

Bright yellow. If Callie Matthews was a color, she'd be yellow. The woman was always happy, always bubbly and never failed to take him by surprise.

And he hadn't necessarily lied when he'd told her he was happy for her. Seeing her beaming from ear to ear had stirred something in him. While he still wasn't thrilled at the possibility of her innocence being shattered, he couldn't let her celebrate alone.

Her sweet naïveté was getting to him. And she had no idea the power she was holding over him.

His cell vibrated in his pocket and he slid it out, smiling when he saw the number.

"So you are alive," he said in place of a traditional hello.

"Kiss ass."

Noah laughed at his best friend and Hollywood heartthrob, Max Ford. "When a whole week goes by and I know you're not filming, I have to assume you're either dead or getting some serious action. Glad to know you're still with us."

"Oh, I'm alive," Max assured him. "Where are you? It sounds like you're at a kid's birthday party."

Noah glanced around the open room where kids ran from game to game, parents chasing to keep up with the chaos. His gaze circled back to Callie and he watched her steering intensely at the racing game.

"You wouldn't believe me if I told you."

"You're moonlighting as a clown for kids' parties, aren't you?" Max joked. "I'm not sure the ladies will go for the Bozo wig, pal."

Noah laughed. "Did you call to annoy me or do you have a point?"

"I wanted to know if you were free tomorrow. Haven't seen you for a while. Thought we could get together."

Callie jumped from her racing chair and grinned like a kid as the machine spit out another row of bright yellow tickets. Her enthusiasm was contagious, and he found himself standing in the middle of the room with a silly grin on his face. When was the last time he truly grinned because he wanted to and not because he felt forced to please his current company?

"Actually, tomorrow is the photo shoot for the ads for my new office," Noah told him. "But I should be free in the evening if all goes as planned."

"I thought you were still looking for a model."

When Callie turned and caught his eye, he motioned that he was stepping outside. She nodded and moved on to another game.

"Callie is doing it for me," Noah said, walking toward the door to move farther away from the noise.

"Callie Matthews? Damn, she's hot. How did you manage that? Has she done modeling before?"

Once outside, Noah took a seat on the bench next to the door. "No, but I'm trying to watch out for her. She's got stars in her eyes, man. And she just got a pretty good-size role in a new Anthony Price film."

"Noah, you can't save everybody," Max told him with a sigh. "You've got to let go of the past."

"Easier said than done."

"Had any more offers on the house?" Max asked.

"Just the two."

"Which you turned down?"

Noah rubbed a hand over his head and glanced through the door to see Callie smiling while tackling another game. "Yes. I turned them down."

"And you're still going to see Thelma every day?"

Noah's chest tightened. "I'm all she has."

"She's not even your family, Noah. You have to let go. I understand she's Malinda's grandmother, but you've been paying her assisted-living bills for a year now. She has Alzheimer's. She won't know if you don't show up. You've got to bury the past."

He sighed. "I'll bury it when it's time."

"Good," his friend said. "You can start by asking Callie out on a date. She'd be perfect."

"I'm not asking her out," Noah replied. At least, he wouldn't ask her on a *real* date.

"Great. Then you won't mind if—"

"Yes, I would mind." Noah cut him off. "You've got enough on your plate without adding Callie to the mix."

Max's laughter nearly vibrated Noah's phone. "You can't keep dibs on her and not do anything about it. You're both adults. If you want to go beyond business and get personal, what's stopping you?"

"She's the best receptionist I've ever had. I'd like to keep her for a while."

"She'll probably be leaving when she starts acting, anyway, so why not just go for it now instead of torturing yourself?" Max asked. "You know you've thought about it."

Thought about it, fantasized about it. Had taken the proverbial cold showers to prove it.

Noah came to his feet, glancing inside at Callie, who was looking toward the doors, probably looking for him.

"Listen, I need to go," Noah said. "I'll call you tomorrow and let you know what time I'll be free."

After sliding the phone into his pocket, he went back inside. Callie's smile across the crowded room did something funny to his chest...something he'd rather not explore.

"I'm ready to cash in my winnings," she told him, holding up her tickets. "I've got a hundred here and I think I gave you a hundred. Let's go see what I can get."

Noah followed her as he pulled her tickets from his pocket. He still couldn't believe this was her idea of celebrating. She certainly wasn't like all the other women he knew. Their idea of celebrating would be to head to the most expensive restaurant and try to get into his bed afterward…not that he ever complained about those nights.

But Callie was different—a fact he'd known from the first day of working with her. She was like a breath of fresh air. He never knew what to expect from her, but he knew it would be something great.

After she chose her prizes—a hideous monkey with tie-dyed fur and a flower-shaped eraser—he escorted her to the car and drove back to his office. Even though she was fairly silent during the ride, she was beaming from ear to ear.

"You had a good time."

It wasn't a question, more like an observation.

"A blast," she told him. "I'd always wanted to go to a place like that as a kid."

He threw her a glance as he pulled up beside her car. "Why didn't you?"

Callie's smile faltered, and she toyed with the ear on the monkey. "I didn't have a very pleasant childhood. And that's the best way I can put it."

Noah put the car in Park and turned to face her. "I'm sorry, Callie. I didn't mean to pry. You've worked for me for a while now and I don't know much about your life before you came here."

She attempted a smile, but her sad gaze met his. "I'd rather focus on my life here than back home."

Wherever she came from, whatever she experienced must be painful because the L.A. Callie was a bright, bubbly woman who didn't care to let everyone see how positive she was about life.

"I can't thank you enough for everything, Noah." She

reached out, placed a hand on his forearm. "You don't know how much I value our friendship. At least, I like to think we're friends."

"We are," he said, cursing his voice when it cracked like some damn adolescent.

Her dainty, warm hand on his arm really shouldn't turn him on, but he'd been intrigued by her for a while now.

"Good," she said, smiling wider. "It's nice to know I have people I can count on."

She leaned over and gave him an innocent, simple peck on his cheek, but as she pulled back, her face remained within a breath of his and she locked eyes with him again. He froze and was surprised when she placed a softer kiss on his lips, hesitating as if waiting for approval.

"I'm sorry," she whispered. "Was that unprofessional?"

"Not as much as this."

He cupped the side of her face and claimed her lips.

Three

Callie knew on some level this was wrong—that would be the professional level.

But on a personal, feminine level, kissing Noah Foster was so, *so* perfectly right. There was no way she could not respond to such a blatant advance.

His thumbs trailed along her jawline as he shifted and changed the angle. Mercy, this man could kiss her lips and she felt it all the way down to her toes...not to mention all the important spots in between.

Callie grabbed hold of his biceps as the glorious assault on her mouth continued. This attraction wasn't new on his side or he wouldn't be devouring her mouth in such a way that had her limbs trembling and her thighs clenching.

But before she could bask in the fact this was the best kiss she'd ever experienced, Noah pulled back.

"God, Callie," he all but growled. "I'm—"

"No." She shook her head, putting a bit of distance between them so she could look in his eyes. "Don't say you're sorry."

His eyes searched hers, that warm gaze dropping to her lips before coming back up. "I wasn't. I was going to say I don't know what came over me, but that would be a lie. I've wanted to do that for some time."

The revelation wasn't surprising, but she was a little taken aback that he admitted it. Which brought to mind the all-important question: Why hadn't they locked lips before now? Had she known he had such…talents, she would've taken charge months ago.

Okay, well, maybe she would've held back since he was her boss, but she definitely would've fantasized about it more.

"So have I," she admitted.

The corners of Noah's sexy, and she could now add tasty, mouth lifted. "But you work for me."

"So now what?" she asked. God, that sounded lame. "I mean, I don't have to quit, do I?"

"Do you want to quit?"

Callie quirked a brow. "Don't answer my question with a question."

"Just trying to figure my way around this…."

She grinned. "By this, you mean the fact that I want you?"

He studied her face. "Yes."

Callie's hands slipped from his thick arms. "I won't lie about my feelings, Noah. If that makes you uncomfortable…"

"I'm not uncomfortable," he told her. "I won't deny the sexual tension between us."

The chubby girl who still lived deep inside her couldn't believe this was happening. The new Callie, the one who took charge of her life and made things happen, knew this was a moment she'd remember forever.

Noah Foster, one of the sexiest men she'd ever met, was admitting he was sexually attracted to her.

"I don't do relationships, but I can't deny the chemistry is strong here. I've never been in this situation before, and I'm trying to keep this simple."

Intrigued, and a little surprised that he inadvertently admitted that she had the upper hand here, Callie grinned.

"And what situation is that?" she asked. "Making out in your car with an employee?"

With a sigh, Noah turned in his seat, laughed and shook his head. "You're not going to make this easy, are you?"

"What's that?"

Throwing her a glance and a wicked sideways smile, he said, "Oh, now you're going to answer a question with a question."

"Touché."

"How about we go on a date and see where this leads?" he asked. "Since the attraction is mutual, I don't see why we couldn't."

Callie's belly quivered. She had no doubt that if they went out they'd probably continue where they left off with that kiss. Because a kiss that held those kinds of promises was just a stepping-stone straight to the bedroom. The possibilities thrilled and aroused her, but she also had to be realistic. She didn't want to cause any awkward moments in the office. Though right now she was feeling anything but awkward.

"Tell you what." She shifted sideways and smiled. "When I start filming, I'll go on that date, but not before I quit my job. Deal?"

His eyes roamed over her face, pausing on her lips, then back up to her eyes. "I already told you I can't do a relationship, anyway, so it doesn't matter when to me. I'd rather see you outside the office now, but that's because I'm not a patient man."

She laughed. "Boy, you really lay on the charm, huh?"

He shrugged. "I won't lie. I worry about you getting mixed

up in this Hollywood scene so fast." He blew out a sigh, not wanting to scare her. "I know it's not my place, but..."

"I'll be fine, Noah," she assured him. "This is what I've always dreamed about. There's no need to worry."

He looked out the windshield and off into the distance. "You have no idea," he murmured.

He'd initially worried about exploring his attraction to Callie because he was her boss, but if he kept her close, maybe then he could also keep her safe. He knew he couldn't save everyone. He hadn't been able to save Malinda, but he damn well couldn't watch another woman get hurt if he could prevent her downfall. If he could only save one woman, he wanted it to be Callie.

Callie gathered her things, including that heinous monkey, and tugged at the door handle. "I better get going. Thanks again for everything."

Before she exited the car, she leaned in and kissed him. Not a friendly peck, but a soft, open-lipped kiss right near the corner of his mouth.

Oh, yeah, it was going to be a long, long wait for that film to start shooting next month.

Noah paced, checked his watch and paced back the other way. He not only had to get this shoot over with, he needed to run by the assisted-living facility to check on Thelma. He wasn't happy with the afternoon nurse and he wanted to pop in unannounced. And then he planned to meet up with Max.

"Listen, Noah, I can only give about five more minutes," the photographer told him. "Then I'm going to have to re-schedule. I have another shoot later this afternoon I need to set up for."

Hands on his hips, Noah stopped and nodded to the photographer. "I'm sorry, man. I've tried her cell several times.

This isn't like her to be late or blow off a job. She's very professional."

They hadn't been out late the night before, but had she gone back out? Flashes of Malinda making promises to show somewhere flooded his mind. He'd usually found her at home, strung out and totally out of touch with reality.

He hated to think the worst of Callie, but he'd been lied to and deceived for so long before Malinda's death that it was just hard to trust anymore. Added to that, he wondered where Callie put all her money. She always packed her lunch and drove a clankity, beat-up old Honda. He hadn't seen any signs of drug use, but most new users didn't use all the time, and the signs were slow in coming. Besides, just how well did he know Callie aside from at the office? For all he knew, she partied all weekend.

The image of Malinda just before her death, dark eyes, pale skin and sunken cheeks, still haunted him and he'd hate to see the vibrant Callie Matthews fall into that dark abyss.

Callie had always been a professional, though, and she had never been late for anything. She was a bright spirit and he wanted to believe deep in his heart she was an innocent. Something was wrong.

He pulled his cell from his pocket and tried calling again while the photographer started taking down his equipment. A sinking feeling settled deep in his gut each time her chipper voice mail clicked on.

He'd left enough messages and texts, so he hung up and slid the phone back into his pants pocket.

"I'll pay you for your time today, Mark," Noah said. "Can we go ahead and reschedule for next Saturday? Same time?"

Mark nodded. "Sure thing. And don't worry about paying me today. Things happen."

Noah helped Mark carry the lighting and some other equipment to his waiting car. By the time all of that was done and

Mark had left, almost another hour had passed and still there was no word from Callie.

If he weren't so worried, he'd leave her be. She was an adult, after all. But there was a niggling feeling in the back of his mind that something wasn't right. Whether she was hung over or had been in an accident, he didn't know.

Before he stopped at the assisted-living home, Noah thought he should at least drive by Callie's place to check on her. She was, after all, alone in L.A. with no family here and no roommate. He just needed to make sure she was okay.

Endless possibilities flooded his mind. As morbid thought after morbid thought raced through his head, his cell rang. Panic filled him instantly, but relief slithered through. Hopefully that was Callie on the other end ready to apologize for being late.

But when he glanced at the caller ID and saw Private Caller, his hope died. He punched the button on his car to put the call on speaker as he drove down the freeway toward her apartment.

"Hello?"

"Mr. Foster?"

Not recognizing the voice, he answered, "Yes."

"This is Marcia Cooper. I'm a nurse in the E.R. at Cedars-Sinai Medical Center. We have a Miss Matthews, who was brought in to us. We tried calling one of her neighbors, but we couldn't get her. Callie suggested we try you next."

Fear gripped Noah, but if she'd mentioned his name and number she was at least coherent. "Is she all right?"

"I really cannot discuss her condition over the phone," the nurse told him. "Are you able to come in?"

"I'll be right there."

Noah pushed the pedal farther, weaving in and out as best he could with the thick afternoon traffic. The thought of Callie hurting in any way made his stomach clench. He'd only known her to be vivacious, full of life and always smiling.

He understood the nurse was not able to disclose any information due to privacy laws, but knowing Callie was in the E.R. and not knowing her condition scared him more than before he'd gotten the phone call. Did she have a cut that just needed stitches? Had she fallen and hit her head? Had she been attacked?

Damn it. Where had she been when she'd gotten hurt?

A vision of his late fiancée crumpled on their bedroom floor flashed through his mind, but he quickly blocked the image. He couldn't travel down that path. Right now, Callie needed him.

Noah parked in the doctor's lot, thanks to his pass. He had privileges at several L.A. hospitals, including Cedars-Sinai, thank God.

He ran into the entrance and quickly made his way to the Emergency Department.

"Noah."

He turned to see Dr. Rich Bays, an associate he knew quite well, coming toward him.

"You here for a patient?"

"Yeah," Noah said. "Callie Matthews. Are you treating her?"

Rich nodded. "I am. She's in room seven."

"How is she?"

"I'll fill you in as we go to her room." Rich motioned for him to walk with him. "She has a deep facial laceration that extends from her temple down to her mandible and a fractured right clavicle. The CT scan should be back anytime and I'll be in to let her know what it says. From what I'm told of the car accident, she's very lucky things aren't worse."

Deep facial laceration. As a plastic surgeon, he'd seen some severe cases, but he didn't even want to think how serious Callie's case was because whatever was wrong, he would fix it.

"Is she being admitted for observation?" Noah asked.

Rich nodded. "For the night. Even if the scan comes back clear, she was unconscious when she was brought in." Dr. Bays stopped outside the glass sliding door. "And when she goes home, she'll probably need help."

Noah nodded. "I'll make sure she's cared for."

No doubt Callie would brush off the help, but he wasn't letting her go through this alone. Either she'd stay with him or he could stay at her apartment.

Another thought slammed through him. How would this affect the role she'd just landed? Didn't filming start soon?

God, he hadn't wanted her to get the part, but he sure as hell hadn't wanted her injured or scarred. Did she even know the severity of her wound? The broken bone would heal, but the injury to her face…

A deep laceration could take a year to heal, depending on the tissue that was damaged. Possible surgeries filled his mind. No matter how many she needed, he would be the one seeing to all of her medical care.

He needed to assess her injuries before he jumped to any conclusions. She might not be as bad as he was imagining… or she could be worse. That sickening knot in his stomach clenched so tightly he thought he'd be sick.

Noah knew one thing for certain, though. No other plastic surgeon was going to be putting his surgical hands on Callie. He'd do the job and make sure it was done right. Perfection in the O.R. was his life and he'd settle for no less with Callie.

"She's in here." Rich nodded toward the closed door. "I'm going to check to see if that scan is back yet. I'll be back as soon as I learn anything."

"Thanks, Rich."

Noah steeled himself for what he'd see on the other side of

the door and privacy curtain. He told himself that as a doctor he'd seen it all, but the thought of Callie wrapped and damaged scared him on a level he didn't think still existed after he'd faced the hell he'd gone through in the past two years.

He wasn't going to lie, wasn't even going to try to deny the fear that coursed through him and nearly had a choke hold on him.

Too many times he'd seen Malinda at her worst. But he'd never seen Callie as anything but bright, smiling and joyful.

He knew he needed to be strong for Callie so he took a deep breath, eased open the door and stepped in. When he pulled aside the thick curtain, his knees nearly buckled. Her whole face, save for her eyes and mouth, was wrapped in white gauze, her hair puffed out in a matted mess around it. Her arm was in a sling to protect her broken collarbone. She looked so frail, so lifeless lying there.

He had to mentally distance himself from this or he'd never be strong enough to help her. Damn it, he had to be a friend first, not a doctor, not a boss and certainly not a wannabe lover.

As he eased closer to the bed, her eyes shifted to lock onto his.

"Hell of a way to get out of the photo shoot," he said, trying to lighten the moment.

"God, Noah," she whispered. "I'm sorry. So sorry. I was on my way to the shoot and a truck came out of nowhere.... I don't remember anything between seeing a semi and waking up here."

She started to weep and Noah's heart constricted. Other than the happy tears in his office, he'd never seen her cry, had never seen anything from her but smiles and happiness—which was why he'd considered her the color yellow. Cheerful and sweet.

He wondered if she'd seen her face or if Rich had told her how bad the injuries were.

The doctor in Noah wanted to demand to see her chart so he could review it, but she needed to be consoled, needed to know everything would be all right. Because no matter what care she needed, he'd see to it himself. And he didn't mean hire a nurse. He'd literally see to her every need personally. Even if he had to refer his clients for the next few weeks to a colleague, he would do everything in his power to make her comfortable and secure.

"Callie." He moved over to the edge of the bed, taking her good hand in his. "There's absolutely nothing to apologize about. Nothing."

"I'm sorry to have to bother you, but I didn't know who else to call when my neighbor wasn't home," she told him, trying to turn her head away.

"I wouldn't be anywhere else." He squeezed her hand. "What can I do for you?"

She tried to shake her head, wincing at the obvious pain.

"Just try to relax." He stroked the back of her hand with his thumb. "I'm not going anywhere, Callie."

"I'll be fine," she assured him, but her voice cracked as tears filled her eyes again. "I know they're keeping me to-night, but I'll have my neighbor take me home when I get re-leased tomorrow. You don't have to stay."

"I'll leave if you really want me to, but when you're dis-missed, I'm taking you home with me."

She slid her hand from his and tried to roll over, only to gasp when she realized she'd rolled onto her bad side.

"Easy, Callie. Don't be so stubborn. You're going to need help, and since I'm a doctor, I think the best place for you is with me."

She didn't respond. Silence filled the room and Noah knew

she didn't want his help. Too bad. He wasn't going to leave her like this.

"Do you want me to try your neighbor again?" he asked. "You can give me the number."

"No," Callie said softly. "I don't need a babysitter. I know I need someone, but…God, Noah, I don't want to be here. I don't *want* to need someone."

Before he could say anything further, Rich stepped into the room and slid back the curtain.

"CT scan looks good," he said. "But I'm going to go ahead and get a room ready for you just for overnight observation. You were unconscious when you were brought in and I'd feel more comfortable monitoring you for a bit. You should be able to go home in the morning. Have you thought about who can help you there?"

"I'll manage," she told him, still keeping her face turned to the far wall.

"Miss Matthews, I can't let you go without knowing you'll be taken care of."

Noah shot Rich a look and whispered, "I'll take her."

Rich merely nodded and left the room.

"I'm not going to stay with you," Callie said. "I'll be fine at home."

"Then I can stay with you," he told her, trying not to get angry over her stubbornness.

"I know I should have someone to help, but I'll call my neighbor or you if I absolutely have to. I want to be alone."

Noah refused to back down. "Well, that's too bad. I'm going to help you, Callie, whether you want it or not. So you can decide right now if you want to be difficult or if you want to cooperate. The end result will be the same."

Slowly, she turned to face him. "End result? And what is the end result, Noah? That I'll never be able to start filming this movie? That my dream was just pulled out from under me? They won't wait on me to heal, if I ever do heal. I'll never be the same."

God, he hadn't wanted her to do the film, but he'd certainly never wished for anything bad to happen to her. And if he hadn't insisted she model for him, she wouldn't be in this damn bed wrapped up and broken.

Sobs tore through the room and Callie pounded the bed with her left fist. "Don't you see, Noah? The end result is that my life and everything I've ever worked for were just taken away."

Noah took her hand once more and laced his fingers with hers. "I'll make this right, Callie. No matter what I have to do, I'll make you whole again."

Four

And how the hell could he ever come through with a promise like that?

He wasn't God. He was a surgeon.

Unless scars were covered by skin grafts, they were permanent. The odds were in his favor that he could minimize the appearance, but what were the odds she'd be happy with even a minor scar? True, he'd been able to nearly rid her of the one on her chin with microdermabrasion, but it had been so minimal to begin with.

But he'd be a fool to believe that she'd be able to go after just any part. She was right in admitting her opportunities had just diminished, but he would still do everything he could to make her feel beautiful again, to make her confident enough to pursue that dream.

Right now, though, he had another obligation he needed to tend to.

Noah hated the mixed emotions flooding through him.

He hated that he was now torn between his present and his past. He wanted to stay with her, but he had to get to the assisted-living facility.

He left Callie resting, as well as she could, considering, and headed out the door. If he hadn't needed to see the afternoon nurse Thelma had been complaining about, he wouldn't have left Callie's side…no matter what she said.

For all he knew, the afternoon nurse was perfectly fine. After all, Thelma did have Alzheimer's and still believed her granddaughter and he were engaged to be married. Noah had never told her any different. Why upset the poor woman when she wouldn't remember it the next time he went to see her?

As he walked up to the front doors of the facility, he pulled his cell from his pocket and dialed Max. Of course the call went to voice mail because the man was rarely available. One of these days he was going to get really burned-out on work.

"Hey, Max," Noah said after the beep. "I can't make it tonight. Callie was in a pretty bad accident so I'll be with her. Text or call when you get a chance."

He slid the phone back into his pocket and entered the glass double doors. An elderly lady greeted him. It was the same white-haired lady who sat by the door every time he came to visit Thelma. Supposedly, the woman was waiting on her husband to come pick her up, but Noah had been told the lady's husband had passed away over ten years ago.

Alzheimer's was a fickle bitch and it sickened Noah that so many people were affected by it. As always, he smiled to the lady and made his way down the narrow carpeted hallway.

Thelma's room was the last one on the left, and as usual, her door was closed. According to Malinda, she'd never been much of a social butterfly even before the disease. Since Noah never knew Thelma before she got sick, he had only Malinda's opinion to go on.

Noah tried the knob, not surprised to find it locked. Tapping his knuckles against the wood door, he called out. "It's Noah, Thelma."

After a moment, he heard shuffling from inside the room before there was a soft click and the door eased open.

Her short silver hair was matted on one side and in the back—a sure sign she'd been asleep in her recliner again.

"How are you feeling today?" he asked, stepping into the room that inevitably was hotter than Satan's personal sauna. Why did the elderly need their heat on full throttle in the middle of summer?

"A little tired today," she told him, moving across the room to her old green chair positioned in front of the TV. "You caught me in the middle of my soaps."

Noah laughed as he eased behind her to turn the heat down. His shirt was already sticking to his back.

"I won't stay long," he promised as he took a seat on the edge of the bed that faced her. "Did you have lunch?"

She stared at him, those blue eyes full of doubt and confusion. "I believe so. Can't recall what I had. Let's see…ham sandwich? No, that wasn't it. Chicken soup. I think."

Noah nodded like he always did. He knew she wouldn't recall, but he was buying some time until the nurse was due in.

"Where's Malinda today?" Thelma asked, her eyes widening and a smile spreading across her face. "I want to hear all about the wedding details."

This was never an easy topic to broach. Not only because he still felt that emptiness Malinda had left in his life, but because he hated lying to this sweet woman, even if she wouldn't remember the truth. Even with the disease robbing her memory, Thelma knew there was a void in her life.

"She couldn't come today," he said honestly.

"That girl works too hard," Thelma replied as she pulled the handle on her recliner. "You tell her that her grandmother wants to see her. I have some wedding ideas I want to discuss with her."

Noah nodded and smiled as always. Though the smiling was costing him. He hated standing there discussing a wedding that would never be, to a woman who was dead, with someone who wouldn't remember this conversation five minutes later. But Thelma still had hope shining in her eyes and he wasn't about to take away the one thing she held on to.

"I'll be right back, Thelma." He moved to the door and propped it open. "I'm just going to step outside your room to look for someone."

She didn't answer, but her soap opera had come back on and she had that tunnel-vision look as she smiled at the characters on TV.

Noah moved into the hall to look for the nurse. Thelma's pills were supposed to be distributed with her breakfast and lunch and just before bedtime. But a few of her prescriptions hadn't been refilled on time and Thelma had claimed she didn't recall seeing the nurse at lunchtime very often. Thelma's fading mind might be to blame, but he couldn't take the chance that she wasn't getting the best care.

When Noah saw the nurse in question come out of a room down the hall, he hurried to catch up with her.

"Excuse me, Lori."

She turned and smiled. "Yes, Mr. Foster?"

"I was wondering if I could speak to you about Thelma."

The nurse nodded as her eyes darted down the hall toward Thelma's room. "Of course. Is something wrong?"

"Has she had her pills today?" he asked.

"She's had all of the medication she gets on my shift. Why?"

He hated to think this nurse wasn't doing her job, but he would keep a closer eye on the meds and make sure Thelma was getting her daily doses.

"No reason. Just making sure," he said with a smile. "She forgets and tells me she hasn't had any."

Lori nodded and patted his arm. "It's the disease. Robs their minds. I assure you she's being taken care of."

"Thanks. That's good to hear."

She dropped her hand. "If you'll excuse me, I need to see to another resident."

As she scurried off, Noah had that gut feeling that always settled deep within him whenever Malinda would lie to him about where she'd been. He wanted to believe Lori, but he wasn't naive. He would keep his eye on her and make more appearances in the afternoon during lunch breaks. No matter the cost, he couldn't let his late fiancée's grandmother down. He was all she had left.

More than likely Lori was clean, but that cynicism ran deep and he had major issues taking someone's word at face value.

As he went back to spend a few more minutes with Thelma, he checked his watch. He didn't want to be gone from Callie very long. No matter how stubborn she was going to be during this process, he could be more so.

No matter what it took, he'd see Callie through her recovery, and if he had to lock her inside his house to do it, then so be it.

One woman was not only hurt on his watch, she'd died. He'd damn well never let that happen again. No matter how he had to rearrange his life.

And beyond the guilt lay an attraction that he couldn't fight. But what scared him the most was that he didn't know if he even wanted to.

Waves of emotions flooded through Callie as she settled into Noah's luxury SUV. Her body ached all over from the accident yesterday, but the physical pain was nothing compared to the emotional pain of having her dream of becoming an actress destroyed. She'd never act or model for Noah and she'd never get that money to send home.

She'd never be able to play her role in the Anthony Price movie, which would start filming next month. Her face was all bandaged up, but she'd seen the damage beneath. She knew the ugliness that waited for her on the other side of the white gauze. The role of a royal beauty couldn't be played by a woman who looked like an Egyptian mummy.

All those thoughts whirled around in her mind, bumping into each other and exacerbating her nausea, brought on by meds.

"Whatever is going through your head, get it out." Noah brought the engine to life and pulled from the curb of her apartment complex, where they'd stopped to pick up her things on the way to his place. "As a doctor I know the impact positive thinking can have on recuperation. You have to stay focused on the good here, Callie."

She turned her head to look out the window. "Just drive."

"You can talk to me, you know."

Callie fought back tears. The man was relentless. He'd come back to her room yesterday and stayed overnight with her as if she was some invalid or small child who couldn't look after herself. He kept trying to get her to open up, to talk to him as if he was some shrink. All she wanted was to be left alone. She didn't want to talk about her problems. Would that put her face back to the way it was? Would opening up make it so she would be able to film the movie she'd worked so hard to get? Granted, she hadn't been in L.A. for long, but she'd used connections and fought for what she wanted.

Added to that, would talking get her fifty thousand to help support her family?

No. So she wasn't going to waste her time pouring her heart out. Yes, she was bitter, and yes, she was going to lash out at whoever tried to pry inside her heart right now. She just didn't have that chipper energy she was known for. She feared she might never be that happy girl again. Even the spark of attraction they'd had before was out of her reach. And there wasn't a thing she could do about it.

"Have you called your family?" he asked as he maneuvered through the traffic.

"No."

Their phone was probably still shut off, but she would send her brother a text in a few days. Even though he was away at college, he usually went home on weekends if he was able to get off work from his part-time job.

On the other hand, she might not text him at all. Why would she want them to know she'd failed? She'd been so, so close and had lost it all. She refused to text her sister, whom she rarely talked to, anyway. The woman was too busy with her perfect family in Texas to be bothered with helping.

She tried to swipe at the moisture in her eyes, reaching up with her right arm.

"Ouch. God," she groaned.

"Take it easy." Noah reached over and patted her leg. "I know it's habit to use your right arm, but try to hold it still. The more you rest it, the sooner it will heal."

"I don't care about my arm," she told him. "That's the least of my concerns."

He drove for a moment before breaking the silence again. "This will get better, Callie. I know you don't see that proverbial light at the end of the tunnel, but it's there. We need to give this some time."

"We?" she mocked. "I'm positive your career will go on, Noah. You have everything you could ever want."

His hands tightened around the steering wheel. "We all have our own hell, Callie. I've just learned to live with mine."

Callie doubted very much his *hell* was life-changing. He probably had to pay more property taxes or didn't get invited to some of his clients' glamorous parties. No matter what the so-called darkness in his life was, Callie knew it couldn't compare to having her dreams slide through her fingers like sand. She'd held that reality for such a short time and now she would have nothing to show for it.

"I don't mean to argue with you," he told her softly. "I'm here to help you and that's exactly what I'm going to do."

"I still don't think staying with you is the answer," she told him.

"If you have a better suggestion, I'm all ears."

She sighed and ignored the twinge of pain in her shoulder at the deep breath. "I hate being someone's responsibility and an inconvenience."

"Callie, you're neither of those things. If I didn't want to help, I wouldn't have volunteered. Besides, you need assistance and I'm a doctor. You're getting the best free of charge."

She never dreamed if she ever got an invitation to Noah's Beverly Hills home it would be for him to play doctor in the literal sense. There would be no way he'd ever want to date her now. What man would find a woman with a slash down her face attractive? She hadn't even talked to Noah about surgery, but she highly doubted she'd ever look the same again.

She'd worked in his office long enough to know that scars could never be fully removed—minimized, yes, but it would still be there. Even with microdermabrasion or, God forbid, a skin graft, there would still be a slight imperfection on her face. And Noah Foster was used to perfection—that was his job, for crying out loud.

She rested her head against the back of the seat and let the silence of the car surround her. She didn't feel like chitchatting, didn't feel like thinking positively as he'd suggested. Surely she was entitled to a pity party, right? Entitled or not, she was throwing one for herself. Hopefully, when they arrived at his house, he'd leave her alone to wallow in her misery.

A short while later he pulled into a gated drive, rolled down his window and punched in a sequence of numbers until the wrought-iron gate slid to the side, allowing them through. A large, two-story, beige stucco home, with white trim and white columns surrounding the arched entryway, took center stage in the circular drive. Noah hit the garage-door opener and eased the car inside.

"I'll come around and help you out."

Since Callie didn't have the energy or the will to fight, she allowed Noah to escort her into the house. Normally she would've taken the time to marvel at the spacious, pristine kitchen, but she just wanted to go to her room...wherever it was located.

"You'll be upstairs with me." He led the way as he rolled her small suitcase behind him. "I meant, beside me."

Fantastic. Now she was not only in his house out of pity and obligation, she was going to have to sleep with one wall separating them. As if any lingerie would override her mummified state. Sheer material was sexy...sheer gauze, not so much.

"I can show you where your room will be, then you can do what you want." He moved up the wide, curved staircase that circled around a low-hanging chandelier. "I can fix lunch while you unpack, if you'd like."

Once at the top of the steps, she stopped. "Noah," she said, waiting until he turned. "You don't have to do this. Other than changing my bandages and helping me with basics because of my collarbone, pretend I'm not here. You don't have to feed me or entertain me."

He left the suitcase and stepped toward her. Placing his hand on her good shoulder, he looked into her eyes. There was that mesmerizing gaze that had made her toes curl, her belly tingle, so many times. And now was no different. But in so many ways, the important ways, this instance was nothing like the others.

The last time he'd touched her and looked into her eyes. he'd kissed her with so much passion, so much desire....

"Pretending you're not here would be impossible," he told her, holding her gaze. "I know you aren't comfortable, but it's me, Callie. We've worked together long enough, and went quite a big step beyond friendship in my car the other day, that I'd hoped you would be comfortable here. This doesn't have to be difficult. Let me care for you. Please."

She couldn't keep looking at him. She almost felt like a kid, like if she looked away, maybe he couldn't see her. Her eyes darted to the V in the neck of his black T-shirt.

"What are you thinking right now?" he asked.

With her one working shoulder, she shrugged beneath his touch.

He took his free hand and tipped her chin up so she was looking at him once more. "Talk to me, Callie. I won't let you go through this alone, even though you want to."

Blinking back tears, she sighed. "I just don't know how you can look at me like that."

"Like what?"

"Like...like you care for me."

His head tipped to the side as he smiled. "Callie, I do care for you or you wouldn't be here. You're hurt and it's my fault."

Confused, Callie stepped to the side, away from his touch. "What do you mean, your fault?"

"If I hadn't asked you to model, you wouldn't have been on that freeway and you wouldn't have been in the accident."

She hadn't thought it possible to hurt more, but pain sliced through every fiber of her being. His declaration just proved she was at his house, under his care, because he felt pity. And not just pity, but obligation and guilt, and not because they'd begun something in the car the other day.

She closed her eyes, forcing the tears back until she was alone. "Just show me to my room. I'm tired."

He looked as if he wanted to say more, but after hesitating a brief moment, he nodded and moved farther down the wide hallway. Callie prayed her collarbone would recover fast so she could go home.

For so long she'd been such a fighter. But right now, she wasn't so sure she had any fight left in her.

She wanted to have something to push toward, to look forward to after her healing was over. But she knew the odds of living out her dream had more than likely died the second her car slammed into that semi. And Callie would replay that hellacious moment in her head over and over until she died. Of that she was dead sure.

She headed to bed, praying somehow things would look better in the morning.

Five

Noah put the towels away in his master suite and glanced at the small picture of Malinda and him during one of their earlier, carefree times that sat on a shelf beside the window. This was the only picture in the house he hadn't stored in a box on a shelf in the back of his closet. One last reminder of the happiest moments of his life.

He still had a closet full of clothing from Malinda's job as a personal shopper; most of them still had tags. But for some reason he still couldn't let go.

Some reason? No, he knew the reason. How could he let go? If he let go of the past, he'd be finalizing the fact that he had failed the one person he'd loved more than life itself. If he severed all ties with that portion of his life, the finality of the truth would settle in deeper, and quite possibly cripple him.

He just couldn't bear to face the truth. Not only was Malinda gone, he hadn't been able to do anything to stop her swift spiral down to the depths of her drug overdose.

And Callie thought he knew nothing of hell on earth? He lived it every single day. The reminder of the life he thought he'd have with Malinda was always in the forefront of his mind. Between the picture he just couldn't take down and tending to Thelma's needs, the past just wouldn't let him go. He was caught in the vise of this damn nightmare and he had no way of getting out and moving on. And he feared he'd always be on this roller-coaster ride of emotions.

As he moved into his bedroom, he sighed. He was getting frustrated with Callie and he didn't want to go all alpha male on her and take over, but he would if he saw she wasn't taking care of herself. Stubbornness had no place in the healing process.

Since they'd arrived, she hadn't come out of her room. He'd asked her about eating and she'd claimed she wasn't hungry and just wanted to rest. Well, that was nearly five hours ago.

Now it was time for her medicine, so she was going to have to open the door and let him in. She had to eat something because she couldn't take these heavy pain meds on an empty stomach or she'd feel a whole lot worse. He'd also apply more ointment to her face, though that was really just an excuse to get close to her.

Callie's self-esteem and bubbling energy seemed to have been a casualty in the accident, and he intended to make them come back to life. More than likely that would take time, but Noah couldn't watch another woman destroy herself whether it be via drugs or depression.

As a doctor, he'd vowed to protect and heal people. But as a man, he just couldn't sit by and see Callie beat herself up and let her anger and frustrations fester. If she didn't open up, she might end up worse than she was now.

And yeah, the irony of him thinking someone needed to open up was not lost on him. Looked as if the pot and the kettle would be spending a lot of time butting heads over the next few weeks.

Noah kept Callie's medicine in his room so he could have easy access, but also so it wouldn't be with her. The risk of her becoming addicted was too great. He would let her have the prescription painkillers for the next two days, but after that it would be over-the-counter meds. He needed to wean her off the narcotics.

Just the thought of Callie hooked on painkillers sickened him. But the fact they were back in his house only made him have flash upon flash of another woman, another drug.

Of course, before Callie's accident he'd wondered where all her money was going and he'd even considered the possibility of her using, but he wanted to dismiss those tainted thoughts. His past with Malinda just made him skeptical, and where Callie was concerned, he had a gut feeling what he saw was what he got. Perhaps that was why he found her so refreshing. She'd never tried to be fake and she tended to wear her heart on her sleeve.

Grabbing the antibiotic and the mild painkiller from the top of his chest of drawers, he headed next door to her room. There were five spare bedrooms in his house and for some reason he'd chosen to put her right beside him.

There were so many underlying reasons. He'd told her it was because he wanted to be near in case she needed help, but in actuality, he wanted to be close because this was Callie, and he'd envisioned something more intimate between them. He had ever since she'd come to work for him six months ago.

Now, though, his rational mind told him he had to put that desire on a back burner. It wasn't that the accident had diminished his attraction; he simply realized the timing was off. The man in him, however, could hardly ignore the desire he felt for her.

And now that she was under his roof, he could choose to

either be a man and potential lover or be her doctor and caring friend.

His sense of responsibility made that decision for him.

With the bottles in one hand, he tapped on her door with the other.

Callie looked away from her breathtaking view from the window seat toward the door when Noah knocked. He'd been trying to get her to come out, but she just wasn't in the mood. Besides, this bedroom was the size of her apartment and the view of the pool complete with waterfall and hot tub was rather relaxing to stare at.

"I'm fine, Noah," she called without getting up.

"I need to look at your bandage and I have something for your pain."

Of course he would have to come in. She glanced down to her less-than-sexy attire of black yoga capris and a T-shirt. She only had one arm through because she refused to call for Noah to help her dress. At some point, she feared she'd have to suck it up and let him assist her.

She crossed to the door and pulled it open to see Noah leaning against the doorjamb holding a small container with gauze, tape, ointment and pills. His eyes raked over her appearance.

"Why didn't you tell me you needed help dressing?"

She tilted her chin up. "Because I didn't."

"Don't start this arrangement off by being stubborn and ridiculous."

Instead of retorting, because it would just cause an argument, she eyed his inventory.

"I was just dismissed this morning," she told him. "Surely this doesn't need to be looked at already."

"I want to make sure there's enough antibiotic on it. If it gets too dry, the scar can be harder to repair."

Callie rolled her eyes. "You're not actually thinking this is repairable, are you? I know the odds, Noah."

Noah sat his stuff down on the desk a little harder than he should've and Callie jumped.

"Listen to me," he said, taking her by her one good shoulder. "I am going into this with a positive attitude and you need to, as well. Until or unless I see that your scar is indeed irreparable, we will approach this as if everything is going to be fine. Understand?"

Callie refused to allow the warmth of his strong hand to seep in any farther than her T-shirt. She couldn't let that fantasy of the two of them together come into play just because she was staying at his house...especially because she was staying at his house and he was taking care of her.

"If you want to stay optimistic, go ahead." She stepped away and walked over to the window seat she'd just vacated. "I'm going to be a realist here and try to come up with a plan B."

"What do you mean, plan B?" he asked.

Callie leaned her back against the warm glass and pulled her knees up to rest her feet on the cushion. "I can't very well model for you, act or work in an office that promotes beauty and perfection. And going back home to Kansas is even more depressing, so I need to figure out where to go from here."

Noah crossed the room and took a seat beside her. "The modeling and the acting might be out for now, but who said you can't work in my office? I certainly never said, nor did I imply, that you were going to be replaced. God, Callie, did you think because you have an injury that I'd ask you to leave? I'm sure Marie will be more than happy to cover for you until you're ready to come back to work. Besides, with the other office opening there will be plenty of work."

Callie stared back into those dark, sexy eyes. "I wasn't talking about when my arm heals, Noah. Do you really want your clients to see this ugly, marred face as soon as they come in the door?"

Noah slid a stray hair behind her ear and ran a fingertip down her uninjured cheek. "What I want my clients to see is a woman with a bubbly personality who will put them at ease and make them feel welcome. That's why I hired you to begin with."

Callie rolled her eyes. "Don't lie to me."

"I'm not lying, and I'm not going to let you stay in this room until you're healed to your perfect standards."

"That day will never come," she muttered.

Noah came to his feet and took the hand on her good side. "Come with me."

Callie hesitated until she realized Noah was relentless and he wouldn't back down. The sooner she played his little charade, the sooner he'd leave and she could go back to her self-imposed solitary confinement.

He led her to the adjoining bath and stood her in front of the mirror that spread across the entire wall behind the double sinks. Yeah, as if she wanted to be shoved in front of a mirror.

"Noah, I don't think—"

"Look," he demanded. "Turn and look at your uninjured side."

She moved her head so she could see her smooth, perfectly intact face void of any makeup, marks, scars.

"Now turn and look at the other side."

With a sigh, she turned until she saw that hideous bandage that mocked her and the dreams she'd lost.

"Does this exercise have a point?" she asked.

His eyes met hers in the mirror. "You're the same person, Callie, from the left or the right. Whether you have a bandage, a scar or flawless skin. What you have going on here on the outside doesn't make a difference to who you are on the inside."

Callie laughed because the only other option was to puddle to the floor and cry. "Do you hear yourself? You make your living off making people beautiful and perfect and you're lecturing me on what's on the inside?"

He turned her to face him, but he didn't back up. His strong, hard body held hers against the counter of the vanity. How many times had she wished for a moment like this? How many fantasies had she conjured up after that heated kiss in his car? If only she'd acted on that kiss and taken what he'd been obviously willing to give. But now she'd never know. She'd never have that intimacy with Noah because she wasn't the beautiful woman she used to be. Plain and simple.

"I know you, Callie," he said, holding her gaze only inches away. "I know what you have inside. You're capable of so much more than giving up."

"I'm not giving up," she defended. "I'm taking a break. Of all the times I looked ahead to see my dreams and the obstacles that could get in my way, this was never, ever a thought in my mind."

"Okay, so you've been blindsided." He pushed away that annoying strand of hair that kept sliding from behind her ear. "Don't let this define you. Don't let your insecurities take over and alter your direction in life."

That overweight teen from Kansas started to rear her ugly head. And at this point in time, Callie would almost rather turn back into the chubby, insecure girl she once was as opposed to the woman who might never reach the one goal she'd had her whole life all because of one marred cheek.

"You have no idea what insecurities I hold, Noah. The person who worked for you isn't the same person I used to be."

"The person who worked for me is the real you," he told her. "I don't care who you were before or who you think you are now. I can tell you're a fighter, Callie. I wouldn't admire you so much if you weren't."

Callie's breath hitched. Noah's face was so, so close to hers. Two days ago she would've taken this opportunity and kissed him, not caring about the possible rejection because she would've been confident in his participation.

But now she wasn't even going there. Besides the fact that her whole face was still very sore, she didn't think kissing a mummy was on Noah's Bucket List.

"I agree this is a major speed bump on your path to getting what you want," he went on as if he had no clue where her thoughts were going. "But I'm not going anywhere and we'll get through this. When you're ready for surgery, we'll explore our options on how to make this as quick and efficient as possible."

Callie shook her head. "I don't have that kind of money, Noah. Reconstruction is very expensive. I work on the statements, remember?"

"I'm my own boss. Remember?" he asked with a slight grin. "I meant it when I said I'd stand by you, Callie. I will make sure you have the best reconstruction—and that means me. I won't trust another surgeon to your needs."

"Do I have a say in the matter?"

He shrugged. "Did you want another doctor?"

"Of course not, but don't steamroll me." She sighed, looked up into his eyes and continued, "Why are you taking me on as a charity case? I couldn't possibly repay you."

He took her good hand and held it between his two warm ones. "I'm not looking for payment of any kind. I just want to see you happy. I want to see you reach that dream you so deserve, and I want to make sure you know that I'm here for you and that someone cares enough to look after you."

Callie's eyes filled with tears, and she cursed that constant state of vulnerability she'd felt in the past twenty-four hours. Still, no one had ever said such things to her before.

"I don't deserve you as a friend," she whispered. "I'm

going to be a complete jerk during this process. I'm pretty angry and I don't want you to bear the brunt of that anger. I can be my biggest cheerleader, but I can also be my own worst enemy."

"I'm not worried about myself." He placed a kiss on her forehead. "And I'm not worried about you, either, because I'm not going to let you beat yourself up for something that wasn't your fault."

She leaned into his touch, not caring if she appeared defenseless or weak. Right now she was both and there was no point in hiding the fact.

"I just keep replaying the accident in my mind," she admitted as she sniffled against his shirt. "I saw all the brake lights. I started to get over and that semi literally came out of nowhere."

His hand roamed up and down her back, his chin resting on her forehead. "You don't have to relive it now, Callie. You're safe."

Safe? She'd had nightmares last night while she'd been in the hospital; surprisingly her cries hadn't woken Noah up as he'd slept in the chair near her bed. She prayed the dreams wouldn't visit her again tonight.

"It's impossible not to replay it," she told him, lifting her head to look back into his eyes. "My life changed in literally seconds. There were so many cars in the accident. I heard there were no fatalities, but I feel as if a portion of me died."

"You can't mean that." He cupped her jaw and leaned down closer to her face. "Don't even think like that."

His face was a breath away and he was so angry. She'd read somewhere that passion and anger were similar and one could change to the other in the blink of an eye.

But she was a fool for thinking of passion and an even bigger fool for believing Noah would take this moment and turn it into something sexual.

The muscle ticked in his jaw and Callie knew he was angry so she just nodded.

"I'll go get the supplies."

He stalked out and Callie sighed as she sagged back against the counter. This was going to be a long six weeks of recovery.

Six

Callie took a seat on the small stool in front of the vanity. She wanted to get this doctor/patient time over with. Their bonding moment wasn't something she was comfortable with because she certainly didn't want to give him any more ammunition to fuel his pity.

She'd not only been so close to her dream of landing a role, she'd finally gotten Noah Foster to see her as a desirable woman. Now she didn't even want to know what he thought when he looked at her.

"Sorry." Noah came back in with supplies and a shirt. "I ran to my room to grab this for you."

She eyed the shirt and glanced up at him. "A shirt?"

"It's a button-down," he explained. "You can't keep your one arm tucked beneath a T-shirt for six weeks. This way you won't have to lift your arm over your head. You can just slide it through the sleeve."

That would be more convenient, but if she needed to change, then...

"I can help," he offered.

"No." She sat up in her seat, eyes on him. "I can do it."

"You're going to be stubborn, aren't you?" he asked. "I've seen naked women before."

"Not this naked woman."

His eyes roamed over her, then back up. "Do you think the way we were headed a few days ago that I never would've gotten you naked, Callie?"

Chills spread over her; her skin tingled. She knew exactly where they'd been heading.

"Do you think I wanted to just kiss you like that and leave it?" He stepped closer, just enough for her to have to tilt her head up to keep hold of his warm gaze. "I don't choose lovers on a whim."

"Noah..."

He held up a hand, took a step back and shook his head. "Sorry. That was completely out of line. Let's see what your face looks like."

Callie released the pent-up breath she'd been holding.

Going to his knees on the plush carpet, he slowly eased the surgical tape from her face and below her jaw to examine the wound. "Sorry, I know that pulls."

"It's okay."

She closed her eyes, not because of the pain, but because she couldn't bear to see his face when he looked at her injury. She hadn't let him look at her wound in the hospital. She'd been poked enough, and the last person she wanted playing doctor was her very attractive boss.

Biting the inside of her lips, Callie waited in the silence for anything. A hitch in his breath, a mutter of curse words. Anything to indicate his thoughts.

After a moment without the bandage, she finally opened her eyes, but didn't look at him. "Be honest. I can handle it."

"I'll fix this," he replied, his voice thick.

Callie eased around to look him in the eye. "That's not what I asked. How bad is it? If I were your patient, what would you tell me?"

His eyes met hers. "You *are* my patient. This will take some time. I can't tell you for certain because of the swelling, but if the tissues beneath aren't too damaged, then we have good odds of minimal scarring. I will do everything in my power to make that happen."

Callie held his gaze. "You don't have to do this, Noah."

"I don't trust your care to another surgeon."

"I didn't mean the surgery," she corrected. His face was so close to hers now, but if she thought she was hideous before with her bandages, she was certainly grotesque now without. "I mean take care of me. I know I need someone. I just don't want to be a burden for you."

A smile flirted around his kissable lips. "We've been through this. I'm a doctor and I'm your friend. If I didn't want to help, I wouldn't have offered."

"But you offered out of pity," she told him, hating that damn word and all the emotions it stirred within her.

"I offered because I don't want to see you suffer and I want to make sure you get the proper care." He sighed and turned to grab the ointment. "Now, are you going to let me help or are we still going to argue over the living arrangements for the next several weeks?"

Callie tried to grin, but her face was too sore. "I guess you can win this round."

"You should know by now that I win all the rounds," he told her with a full-fledged, double-dimple grin. "As a doctor and a man."

Callie had to look away. She couldn't fall under his spell

even more than she already had. She couldn't keep wishing for things that could never be because she didn't think she could handle any more letdowns.

First things first. Her love life would have to be put on hold…again. She needed to climb back up and see what happened after she recovered and had surgery on her face. Then, maybe, if all worked out she could circle back around to where she and Noah had left off making out in his car. That is, if he hadn't moved on. What were the chances of him staying single for weeks, months?

In fact, his personal life seemed to be very hush-hush, so it must be busy. Anytime she had tried to bring it up to Marie, she'd gotten the message clearly: his love life was off-limits. But Callie couldn't imagine what a sexy, young plastic surgeon would keep so secretive.

Noah put away all the supplies once he was done changing Callie's bandage. She'd taken her medicine and had asked for some privacy. He was all too happy to oblige.

He shouldn't have forced his way into her room to change that bandage. She would've been fine until tomorrow, but he just had to see how she was doing. The doctor in him knew she was fine, but the man in him, the man who was filled with guilt, had to keep his eye on her to make sure she was okay.

As he started to head back downstairs, he passed by her room and heard the hiss of water running.

What the hell?

He knocked on her door, but got no response. Surely she wasn't actually trying to shower or take a bath. Was she?

He tried her knob, and when it turned beneath his hand, he eased the door open and called her name. "Callie? Everything okay?"

She didn't answer, but the sound of the Jacuzzi tub filling with water filtered through from the attached bath.

Damn fool woman. How could she do this on her own with that arm in a sling? Not to mention she couldn't get her stitches wet.

He walked to the open bathroom door and sucked in a breath. Callie stood with her back to him wearing only thin satin panties and her T-shirt, which she was trying to wrestle up her body.

When she cried out in pain, he stepped forward. "Callie, stop."

She jerked around, her eyes wide. "What are you doing in here?"

"I heard the water and thought you'd need help." He willed his eyes to stay on her face and not travel down the path of her toned, tanned legs or to the triangle of pink satin between her thighs. "What the hell are you doing trying to have a bath alone?"

"I thought if I soaked for a while it might help the soreness."

He leaned over and turned the faucets off so he didn't have to keep talking over the water. "It will, but you can't do this on your own, remember? That was the whole reason for having someone care for you."

She eyed the tub, then him. "There's no way you're going to help me take a bath."

The image nearly killed him.

"I need to at least help you out of that shirt and underwear."

He resisted the urge to swipe his damp hands down his jeans. He was a doctor, for crying out loud. He'd seen more naked women than Hugh Hefner, and here he was in his guest suite afraid to see Callie in nothing but a tan. But no matter the near-naked women he'd seen in his office, none of them had been Callie. None of them conjured up emotions, feelings…hormones…the way Callie did.

"Don't make this uncomfortable, Noah." She tried to pull

the hem down lower, hiding her flat stomach and the flash of a jewel in her belly button. "I can take a bath. It may be hard, but I won't overdo it."

"Nothing has to be hard. That's the whole reason you're here."

God, this was infuriating. He stepped forward and reached for the hem of the shirt, but Callie stepped back.

"Noah, I can't do this." Her bottom lip trembled and her eyes filled with tears that nearly dropped him to his knees because he couldn't handle seeing her so hurt. "I'm a horrifying sight, I have bruises all over me and I'm stuck here until I can be alone. Added to that, I can't let go of the memory of us kissing and it's really making staying here, being so close to you, difficult. Please, I'm begging you, let me have what little pride I have left."

Shocked at her declaration, he remained silent. The woman was blunt, truthful, and he admired the hell out of her.

"You can stay in the bedroom. I'll close this door and if I need something I promise to yell." Her chin tilted up as she blinked away the tears. "Can we agree to that?"

Damn, he admired her stubbornness. He had to admit that if the tables were reversed, he'd be pissed to have his independence taken away.

Noah nodded. "I'll be right outside that door, Callie. Be careful not to get the bandage on your face wet or move your arm too much. You can bend at the elbow, but don't lift the entire arm up."

Callie smiled through her watery eyes. "I'll be careful."

Hesitating only a moment, Noah reluctantly left the room and shut the door. With just that piece of wood between them, he leaned against it and closed his eyes.

Callie was so much like Malinda. So strong-willed, so independent and stubborn. Why was he attracted to that type?

And that was just their personality. He didn't even want to

think how their physical attributes were similar. Same long, dark red hair, same milky skin tone.

He could admit to himself that when he'd hired Callie, her looks were just another reason. After all, Malinda had only been gone six months and this was just one more way he could hold on to her.

But the longer Callie worked for him, the more he could see the differences between the two women. Callie laughed more, smiled when she spoke and truly had a gift for making a room brighter simply by walking into it.

Noah listened, waiting for her to call for him, praying she did all the while praying she didn't. He'd go in there in a second if she needed him, but first he'd have to turn on doctor mode. If he went in there as a man—a man attracted to a woman—he'd be a complete jerk and forget about her injured body and take his fill of looking at her, touching her and quite possibly kissing her breathless as he had the other day. God, he wanted his mouth on her again.

And didn't that make him all kinds of a fool for having these thoughts about an injured, vulnerable woman?

He heard the water slosh and his mind filled with the erotic image of her settling into the oversize garden tub.

"Turn the jets on," he yelled through the door. "That will help ease the soreness."

As if he needed another image of her relaxing, now he pictured her with her hair spilling down around her, her head tipped back against the porcelain as the jets brought thousands of bubbles up to the surface.

His phone vibrated in his pocket, but when he checked the caller ID and saw it was his Realtor, he shoved the cell back in. He wasn't in the mood to hear another piddly offer on the house they were trying to sell. The other two offers were laughable; he wasn't selling this home just to get rid of it and he sure as hell wasn't selling it at a loss.

Malinda had chosen this Beverly Hills mansion when they'd decided to move in together. Noah had a home on the other side of town, but this was closer to where she was working as a personal shopper until she caught her "big break." In love and naive, Noah agreed to move, but he loved his other house so much, he held on to it and rented it out.

He still had that home he could go to, but he just couldn't say goodbye to the memories he and Malinda had made here...the happy ones.

Noah swallowed the lump of guilt that always settled in his throat when he thought of how he should've seen the signs of her abuse earlier. How he should've done something...anything. He was a doctor, for pity's sake. His job was to fix people, but the one person he'd loved and had planned to spend his life with he had failed and she had paid the ultimate price.

"Noah?"

He jerked against the door and opened his eyes. "Yes?" he called back.

"Um, it's hard to wash my hair with one hand."

Oh, Lord. He was going to have to go back in there—where she was naked, wet and needy. Noah took a deep breath and shoved aside the man who had wanted Callie's sexy body for months now and he slid his doctor persona into place.

You're a professional, damn it. Act like one.

"Need help?" he asked, gritting his teeth.

"Please."

One simple word. It meant so much and he knew she'd put her pride and dignity aside.

He eased the pocket door open and entered the steamy room.

"I'll need another towel," she explained. "I wanted to cover up so this wouldn't be any weirder."

He glanced her way and sure enough she had draped the

large white bath towel across her. It was tucked beneath her armpits and floated down across her tanned thighs.

He knelt down beside the tub. "Just sit up a tad."

Taking the shampoo bottle, he squeezed a generous amount into his palm and lathered his hands together. When he finally started rubbing his fingers through her long, silky strands, she moaned.

"God, it always feels so good when someone else washes your hair," she said. "I can scrub and massage all day, but it's just not the same at all."

So had her previous boyfriends done this for her? If she was his, and this was the type of thankful reaction she gave, he'd sure as hell wash her hair every damn night.

"I actually tipped the shampoo guy at the salon two weeks ago even more than usual because he massaged my scalp longer."

Noah felt like an idiot. Maybe she wasn't talking about past boyfriends at all. Noah would pretend she was just discussing the salon and not potential foreplay with other men.

"Hang on, I'll grab something to rinse it with."

He came to his feet and shook off the suds into the tub. Beneath the vanity he found a small, plastic pitcher his cleaning lady always used to rinse the shower and tub when she cleaned. He squatted back down and dipped it into the water and began rinsing her hair. Time and time again he dipped and poured. He'd run his hand through her hair to see if he still saw suds, but even when they were long gone, he kept rinsing and running his hand through her long, crimson strands.

The way they splayed across her damp, bare back was sexy. The way she moaned the entire freaking time he washed her hair was sexy. And the fact she sat inches away from him totally naked was beyond sexy. *Torturous* was more the word. He'd never imagined if he ever got the chance to see Callie naked she'd be broken and battered and vulnerable. And in this tub alone.

"Um, Noah?" she peered over her shoulder at him. Water droplets clung to the edge of her thick, dark lashes. "It's rinsed by now, isn't it?"

He squeezed the pitcher in his hand, surprised it didn't pop out and shoot across the room.

"Yeah," he replied, his voice huskier than he would've liked. "It's clean."

Her eyes darted to his mouth, and she might as well have touched him below the belt with her bare hand because the effect was the same. He was hard in a second.

"Thanks," she told him, her eyes locked onto his. "I can take it from here. But if you could get me a dry towel…"

A droplet of water slid down her forehead and Noah reached out and thumbed it away. But he didn't remove his hand. He cupped her cheek and stroked her soft, dewy skin.

"It's not often someone takes my breath away," he whispered. "Hardly ever, actually."

"Noah—"

He eased forward slowly, giving her ample time to stop him. "I can't ignore this," he told her. "I can't pretend you don't stir something in me, Callie. And I sure as hell can't pass this opportunity up."

Her mouth opened beneath his as he caressed her uninjured cheek. Keeping his touch light, he coaxed her mouth open and slid his tongue in to meet hers.

Another of those soft moans escaped her and Noah found it damn hard to resist the urge to haul her out of that tub and find the nearest flat surface.

Callie pulled back and brought her hand to her lips. "Noah, we can't do that."

"Pretty sure we can and did."

"No, I mean, we can't do this." She waved her good hand

between them. "You don't need this complication on top of caring for me, and I can't afford to be sidetracked by you and your charms and those kisses. You make me all muddled and I can't think when you touch me."

He couldn't help but grin. At least she wasn't crying or angry over the accident. Apparently he'd found just the thing to distract her. But at what price? Now he was more tortured than ever. But sacrificing himself for her was a no-brainer. He'd do anything to make her smile again, make her whole again.

"Glad I could take your mind off your problems for a moment," he told her.

Callie eased back into the tub. "Did you kiss me because—"

"No." He held up a hand. "Kissing you had nothing to do with this accident. I kissed you before and I plan on kissing you again. One has nothing to do with the other. I like kissing you, Callie. And if it helps, I can barely think when your mouth is on mine, so this sexual attraction goes both ways."

She closed her eyes. "But I just don't think this is right, Noah. I don't want you to feel because we're thrown together like this it means that we should be intimate."

Noah came to his feet, pointing down to his bulging zipper. "You think this didn't happen before you came here? I assure you, many times at work I'd have to go to the restroom or my office and close the door and recite the Gettysburg Address to get my mind off you."

Callie raised her brows as her gaze darted from his erection to his face. "You did not recite the Gettysburg Address— Are you admitting that you've wanted me for a while?"

"Yes, I did and yes, I am."

Callie adjusted her wet towel. "Well, um, that's… I can't think right now, Noah. You caught me at a weak moment and

I'm on drugs. Is this how you get women into your bed?" she joked.

The band of guilt around Noah's chest tightened. He turned toward the linen closet and grabbed another towel and sat it on the edge of the garden tub.

"Get dressed and we'll see about dinner."

And before he could get too wrapped up in his past or his present, Noah fled the room like a child who was scared of the boogeyman. Because, let's face it, that boogeyman that kept chasing him was himself. No one else was to blame for the death of Malinda.

Seven

Callie tried, she really did try to put on a bra, but it just wasn't going to happen. It wasn't as if her B-cup breasts needed restraints, anyway. She certainly wasn't some busty Playboy type and she wasn't saggy, thank God, so fighting with a bra was not only painful, it was also insane.

Okay, so that was the only perk—bad pun intended—of being injured.

Well, unless she counted the bath she'd just somewhat shared with Noah. The bath *and* the kiss. Mercy, her entire body had heated.

But what on earth had happened afterward? He'd gone pale before he'd grabbed her towel and demanded she dress. She knew he hadn't gone far, in case she needed him, because she could hear him out in the bedroom talking on the phone. She actually had heard him shout to someone about the price being set to sell and he wasn't "giving the damn thing away." Apparently, he was trying to sell his home and not having much luck.

God, what she wouldn't give for a home like this. Her entire threadbare apartment could fit in the guest suite.

After she carefully got into the button-down shirt Noah had loaned her, she used her good hand to pull on a pair of cotton shorts.

She glanced into the mirror. Her hair hung in long, crimson-colored wet ropes, her face was pale, patched and swollen, she wore a blue dress shirt that was so large the shoulder seams nearly hung to her elbows, and she had on hot-pink shorts. Yeah, she wasn't going to be winning any fashion awards with this hot mess.

Realizing she was fighting the proverbial losing battle, Callie grabbed her sling and went into her temporary bedroom. Noah was standing by the window looking out into the yard, his hands fisted at his sides.

"Everything okay?" she asked.

He turned and for a brief second she saw pain lurking behind those stunning gray eyes. He quickly covered the emotions with a smile. "Great. Need help with that?" he asked, nodding to her sling.

"Yeah, I didn't think I could reach and fasten it."

He closed the gap between them and moved her hair out of the way to slide the strap around her neck.

"Sorry," she told him, tilting her head to get her hair out of the way. "I couldn't pull it up or comb it. I'm afraid it's going to be quite a mess until I can use my arm again."

Noah stepped back. "I can comb your hair, Callie. I could probably pull it up, too, but I can't guarantee how good it would look."

Callie stared up at him. For some reason the image of a man combing a woman's hair had always seemed sexy to her. She and Noah had shared an intense moment in the bathroom, so adding hair into the mix wasn't going to do any more damage to her hormones. She didn't think she could want this man any more than she already did.

"If you don't mind." She went to her bag and pulled out a wide-toothed comb. "Use this. My hair is pretty tangly."

He motioned for her to sit on the bed, and once she was settled, he took a seat behind her. His knees rested on either side of her hips and she tried to block out the fact they were both on the bed, she wasn't wearing a bra and they'd just had a major intimate moment in the bathroom.

"It helps if you go in sections," she told him, trying to reach back and part her hair with her left hand. "Otherwise it's more of a mess."

"I think I can figure this out," he told her. "Just tell me if I hurt you."

Yeah, as if she'd tell him that. She didn't want to give him a reason to stop or move away. He combed with ease, taking small sections at a time. Normally when Callie combed her hair she gave it several yanks and if the tangle didn't come free, then the entire knot of hair broke off, but she was surprised and turned on even more at the care Noah was using.

His body seemed to be all around her. Those strong thighs rubbed against her sides as his knees eased forward, his hands in her hair, occasionally brushing against her neck and her cheek as he combed out the tangles.

"I heard you on the phone," she said, trying to ease the sexual tension. "I didn't mean to eavesdrop, but you seemed upset. Anything you want to talk about?"

His hands stilled in her hair a second before he spoke. "Just something I need to deal with that I'm not sure I'm ready for."

"Are you selling your house?" she asked, tracing her fingertip along the damask pattern of the silk comforter.

"Trying to."

"You have somewhere else you'd like to live?"

"I have another house on the other side of town." He shifted his weight on the bed and moved to work on the other side of her hair. "I had been renting it out, but I'm thinking of moving back in there. It's sat empty for a few months."

"Why not sell that one and stay here since all of your stuff is here?"

Noah cleared his throat. "Are you feeling better since your bath?"

O-kay. Apparently, that was a touchy subject.

"That wasn't subtle." She didn't mind stepping into his personal space. After what they'd shared during her bath, personal space seemed to have gone by the wayside. "You seem upset and I'd like to help."

"I know. There are just some things I'm not comfortable discussing with anyone."

There was a story there, but in all honesty, it wasn't her place to pry.

"So are you feeling less sore?" he asked again.

"I'm still sore, but I feel much more relaxed."

"That's good." He eased off the bed and came to his feet. "Where's a rubber band?"

She pointed to her overnight bag. "In there. I have a small travel bag sitting on top. Rubber bands are in that."

He unzipped her bag and grinned. "You're a reader?"

She glanced over to see him holding a mystery. "I love it," she told him. "Nothing like escaping your problems and reading about someone else's."

Noah laughed. "Too bad that's not possible in real life."

She wanted to question him but realized that was prying again, so she remained silent and waited for him to come back with a band.

"How do you want it?" he asked.

Glancing over her shoulder, she laughed. "Seriously? You tell me it won't look good and you think I'll give you specifications? I'm just happy you combed it and it won't look like a nest."

He gathered the sides back and pulled her hair together in the middle at the nape of her neck and wrapped the band around her hair. "I think we'll do the most basic. By the time these weeks are over I may have you wearing a French twist."

"You know what a French twist is?" she asked, surprised.

"I'm not a moron," he joked. "Just because I know the term doesn't mean I know how to do one. But maybe I'll look up hairstyles since I'll not only be your doctor, I'll be your beautician, as well."

Callie laughed, came to her feet and stared down at him. "Yeah, if this plastic-surgeon gig doesn't work out, you can add stylist to your resume. I'll be a reference for you."

He grinned up at her and her heart flipped. She didn't want to enjoy being here this much, because this was temporary. Not only that, if she liked it, she'd have to think of the reason she was actually staying here, and it wasn't pleasant.

"Are you hungry?" he asked as his eyes floated down from her face, landed on her perky nipples and back up.

Oh, she was hungry, and she had a feeling he wasn't just referring to food, either.

She cleared her throat. "I could eat."

"Let's head down to the kitchen and see what we can find."

Yeah, getting out of this bedroom was an excellent idea. Her hormones had obviously not taken a hit in the accident, because they were working just fine.

Noah pounded his heavy bag and tried to block out the image of last night when Callie came from the bathroom, skin still dewy, wet hair clinging to her—no, his—shirt, making the material thinner, making those unconfined breasts all the more enticing…

These next few weeks were going to kill him. Literally flat-out kill him.

As if his sexual pull for her hadn't been strong before, now being under the same roof with her was really testing his willpower.

She'd been here such a short time and already she'd left her mark. Her floral scent filled every room, making him realize having a female in his home was a major milestone.

Callie was the first woman Noah had brought home since the death of Malinda. He'd been on a few dates, but he'd never brought another woman here. This was the home he'd planned to share with his wife, and bringing other women here just didn't seem like the right thing to do.

But Callie's situation was different and he refused to feel guilty for helping a friend...even if she was a friend he was fighting an attraction to. Fighting and failing.

The burn in his knuckles with each punch only helped slightly to keep his mind off the fact his house wasn't selling, the fact that Thelma might or might not be getting the proper meds, and the fact that his new housemate was sexy as hell and walking around wearing his shirt, no bra and shorts that showcased her tanned, toned legs and dainty feet with pink, polished toes. Even the bandage, sling and spattering of purple bruises didn't diminish her beauty. Oh, all of that dulled the light in her eyes, but he'd find a way to put it back.

His cell rang, cutting off the image of Callie parading barefoot through his home as if she belonged. Yanking off his boxing gloves, he moved to the weight bench and grabbed his phone.

"Hello."

"Hey, you busy? You sound winded."

Noah took a seat on the bench and rested his elbows on his knees. "Beating the heavy bag. What's up, Max?"

"Calling to check on Callie. How's she doing?"

Noah sighed. "She's only been here a day. Her injuries were making her sore yesterday, and this morning when she woke she was pretty stiff."

"And you stayed home to play doctor?" Max joked. "Sorry, bad pun. Seriously, dude, are you staying with her today?"

Noah nodded as if his friend could see. "I actually rescheduled all of this week's appointments. I wanted to be able to stay with her for a while until I could see how she was getting along."

"You can't keep your eye on her all the time, Noah." Max hesitated before going on. "You also can't blame yourself for her condition."

"I can do whatever the hell I want," Noah countered, ready to defend his actions. "I won't have another woman suffer when I can prevent it."

Max sighed. "I won't argue with you about this again. I just called to see if you'd like to get together for a cookout or something. I want you to meet Abby."

"Abby?" Noah laughed. "Weren't you just dating someone else?"

"Not dating…"

"Forget it," Noah said. "Bring whomever you want, but let me get back to you as to when. I don't want to make Callie uncomfortable."

He had a feeling the last thing she'd want was visitors, especially a woman of Max's choosing, because if Max was "dating" someone, she more than likely would show up with three things: silicone, implants and a spray tan.

"You know, why don't you just come over?" Noah asked. "I'd love to meet your new friend, but maybe not with Callie around. She's pretty vulnerable right now."

"Sure. I understand. Why don't I come over tomorrow night with some steaks and we can just grill out?"

"I'll run it by Callie, but I'm sure it'll be fine."

"Just text me and let me know what's going on."

"Will do."

Noah hung up and grabbed a towel off the bar to wipe his head and chest. He'd pounded the bag for nearly thirty minutes and before that he'd run five miles on his treadmill. Normally he'd run outside, but he didn't want to leave Callie in case she needed something.

No matter what Max said, Noah knew Callie was his responsibility. She'd been in that accident because of him and she was going to get the proper care because of him, too. It was the least he could do.

Fantasizing about her, thinking about her in a sexual way was not going to help matters. He needed to keep in mind what happened last time he lost himself to a woman who had stars in her eyes.

No, this time he would remain professional. He was one of the best plastic surgeons in L.A., damn it, and he needed to remember that and keep his hormones in check.

He'd just come to his feet when he felt Callie step into the room. He couldn't explain it, but suddenly there was this... presence that had him turning.

She stood leaning against the doorjamb with her good shoulder. "I was wondering if I could use your computer. I forgot to bring my laptop."

He took in the sight of her still sporting his shirt, the one she'd slept in, and those damn sexy legs peeking out beneath little shorts, and like a hormonal, stuttering teenager, he merely nodded.

"Is something wrong?" she asked.

Yeah, something was wrong. He was getting confused between being a man and being a doctor, not to mention the fact he was torn between being dutiful and giving in to his most basic of desires.

"Just trying to finish my workout," he told her, coming

off a little more agitated than he meant to. "I'll be done in a minute."

She straightened. "I won't bother you again."

Turning, she eased back down the hall and disappeared around the corner. Great, now he'd upset her and made her feel worse. As if she needed to feel worse. The woman had lost her dream job, her independence and the simple life she was used to, and he'd growled at her simply because he had a hard-on that he couldn't keep under control.

Well, whose fault was that?

Noah shoved his hands back into his boxing gloves. He wasn't done with that heavy bag. As long as his past demons were chasing him and his present situation was joining in, he needed to punch out some of his anger and frustrations.

Eight

Callie booted up the computer that sat in a small nook off the kitchen. She'd just wanted to look for some online work she could do until she felt comfortable facing the world again. There was no way she could go back to the office looking like a constant work in progress, and there was certainly no way she could go to a casting call, unless they were doing a horror film.

But she wasn't going to focus on what she couldn't do. In order to get back on her feet, she needed to focus on what she could do. Noah wanted to see that old Callie back, so she was going to try.

There were no guarantees, but she had to do something positive. That was the only way she could get out of this house. So far she'd been here for nearly twenty-four hours and she'd had enough of the roller coaster of humiliation and desire to last her a lifetime. Between the bath, the hair and just now seeing him in all his shirtless, sweaty glory, she knew she needed to get some distance.

No, it wasn't smart to try to leave, but if she could find something to do from home using a computer, surely she could stay by herself. She wasn't an invalid; she just had problems getting dressed and bathing. If she worked from home, she wouldn't have to worry about all that.

But even if Noah insisted she stay, she still felt she needed to pay her way somehow. Not to mention the fact she couldn't just take a break from her income. Not only did she have bills to pay for herself, she needed to send some money back home so her parents' phone could be turned back on.

She did have a tiny bit left in savings and she probably should keep it since her future was so unclear, but she couldn't stand the thought of being out of touch.

After a few clicks, she'd taken money from her account and put it into her parents', which she had access to. Then she sent an awkward, left-handed text to her brother so he could get the message to their mom and dad.

Callie did several searches, hoping with her teaching degree she could find something. Maybe online tutoring. That would be ideal.

She'd come to L.A. in the hopes of not using her teaching degree because she'd been so afraid she'd get stuck in a rut. At least as a receptionist, she'd known she wouldn't feel guilty leaving that job when she caught her big break. Working with kids, she would've gotten attached and been worried about leaving midyear.

Thankfully, she'd worked part-time in a dentist's office back home, so she'd had a little experience to get her this job with Noah.

"What are you doing?"

Callie jumped and turned in her chair. Now Mr. Sweaty Rippling Muscles stood just behind her and she hadn't heard him come in. Lord, it was hard to focus when that chiseled, delectable body was staring back at her.

"Looking for an online job," she told him, forcing her eyes to stay locked onto his.

"What the hell for?" he asked, taking his small white hand towel and mopping his forehead. "Is this your way of turning in your resignation?"

Callie came to her feet and winced. The soreness was so much worse today. But she didn't think another intimate bath encounter was such a good idea.

"I didn't figure you'd want a mummy for your receptionist," she told him, easing back down onto the chair because it was much more comfortable than standing in pain. "Besides, I'm not sure I'll be comfortable around too many people once this bandage comes off."

"How much pain medication have you had?" he asked.

"Enough that I shouldn't feel like this," she told him. "But I guess it would be worse if I hadn't taken those two pills."

"Two?"

"One wasn't cutting it and I just took another before I came to find you. It should kick in soon, I hope."

"I had them in my bedroom."

"I know. They were sitting on your dresser so I grabbed one."

And forced herself not to stare at his bed and wonder...

Okay, so she'd stared and fantasized, but only for a few minutes.

The muscle in Noah's jaw ticked. "You can't take any more medication without asking me first. You only needed one."

"You're not the one in pain," she retorted. "I am and I needed another. You're not my mother."

"No, I'm your doctor and I will flush those pills next time you pull a stunt like that."

Callie had never seen him angry. Frustrated, agitated and

annoyed, yes, but never this angry and never directed toward her. He was practically shaking with waves of fury.

"Okay, okay. Calm down," she told him, holding her hand up. "I'm hoping when it kicks in I'll feel like resting. I didn't sleep too well last night."

"Why didn't you come get me?"

Callie laughed and leaned back against the seat. "What for? Just because I was up didn't mean you had to be. Nothing you could've done."

"You wouldn't have been lonely."

Yeah, she would've. Because no matter what he would've done or said, she would've known he was only sitting with her out of guilt and pity. She'd take loneliness any day over that.

"I was fine. Tired, but fine."

He stared at her for several long moments before he glanced beyond her to the screen. "You're not seriously going to leave the office, are you?"

Callie nodded. "I think I should. It's not fair to you for me to take time off until I heal, and I can't afford the break in income."

"I can help you financially until you're back to work, Callie. I don't want to lose you."

He didn't want to lose her. That warmed her in so many ways, but he wasn't talking on a personal level. More than likely he didn't want to train anyone to fill her shoes and Marie couldn't do both offices.

"Marie, I'm sure, would fill in until you found someone," she told him, only to be rewarded with a scowl.

"I need to call her anyway to let her know how you're feeling because she left me a voice mail."

Callie shook her head. "Talk to her all you want, but I won't be coming back, Noah."

"I need you, Callie."

She jerked up out of her seat, standing literally toe-to-toe with him. The elbow of her arm in the sling bumped against his hard abs.

"You need?" she mocked. "Let me tell you what I need. I need to go back in time, I need to not have this new life I'm adjusting to and I need to get my independence back. Your needs are irrelevant at the moment."

Noah stared at her, his eyes holding on to hers, and Callie wondered if she'd totally overstepped her bounds shouting at not only her boss that way, but also the man who was putting aside his life to help her recover.

She closed her eyes and sighed. "God, I'm sorry. That was really cruel of me to say and very selfish."

Noah's strong hand cupped her cheek. "It's okay. You're entitled to be upset, to hate me, this situation, your life. I'm tough, Callie. I can take it."

She lifted her lids, though her eyes burned with unshed tears. "But you shouldn't have to take it. I just get so frustrated when I look at long-term goals because I can't even put my own clothes on, for pity's sake."

His thumb stroked across her cheek as he glanced down to her lips and back up to her eyes. "I don't mind, Callie. I know it's upsetting to lose your independence, but there's nothing about helping you that bothers me. What does bother me is how hard you are on yourself."

"I just want to be whole again," she told him. "But that may never be."

He wrapped an arm around her waist, tugging her in closer. "It will be if I have anything to say about it."

His lips came down on hers in a powerful yet tender way. Callie froze for a second, but then slid her hand up his bare, sweaty arms. That hard body pressed against hers, combined with his musky scent from his workout, made her moan as his lips continued to claim hers.

She squeezed his thick biceps, making sure to keep her

body angled so she could still get the maximum benefit of rubbing against his even while protecting her arm.

His lips were just as gentle yet demanding as the other night. He nipped at her and pulled her bottom lip between his before he eased back.

Noah rested his forehead to hers and sighed. "I won't apologize for that, Callie. I just can't control myself sometimes around you. I know you're here to heal, not to get mauled, but you do something to me."

"Yeah, you do something to me, too," she admitted.

That something was tying her up in knots and leaving her confused. This man could have nearly any woman he wanted and he was standing in his kitchen—wearing only gym shoes and running shorts with those glorious sweaty pecs on display—and he was kissing a broken woman. That made no sense.

"I can't help but feel you're recovering from something, too." She searched his face. "I may be far off the mark, but sometimes you get this look in your eyes like you're hurt. I've seen it when we discussed the house and when you think I'm not looking."

His eyes closed for the briefest of moments before he opened them and sighed. "I'm going to hop in the shower. Think about what I said and don't start looking for another job just yet."

Callie nodded, unable to form a coherent thought after that kiss and his intense stare as he totally dodged her analysis. Which just proved she was more than likely accurate in her assessment.

Someone or something had a hold on him. He had a past that haunted him and she had a sinking feeling in her stomach that he was waging an inner war with himself. One second he was kissing her like he needed her air in his lungs and the next second his eyes held pain and doubt.

This was so much more than casual. Casual was what had almost transpired before the accident. What was happening now was something even he couldn't explain. Were these higher levels of emotion stemming from their living arrangements? Were they growing closer without even trying, simply because of the accident?

"Oh, I almost forgot. Max called and wanted to know about coming over tomorrow and grilling out. I told him I'd run it by you."

Callie tilted her head. "You don't have to run anything by me, Noah. This is your house."

"I didn't want you to feel uncomfortable."

Nearly every conversation with this man left her heart melting more and more. The way he'd put every single one of her needs first made her wonder what it would be like if he cared for her beyond friendship, beyond the path that was leading them to intimacy.

"I'll be fine," she assured him. "It'll be nice to have something to look forward to."

"I'll let him know." He kissed her forehead. "Now I'm going to take that shower."

After Noah walked away, she sank back into the chair and replayed his previous words. More than once he'd admitted that she affected him. More than once they'd shared heated stares and all-too-brief kisses. But what did all of that mean? Where did he want to go from here?

Callie didn't know, but she did know that she needed to be on her guard where her heart was concerned. She couldn't focus on healing if she was worried about what those kisses meant and what his true feelings were.

She wanted so badly for him to open up and let her in even though his past wasn't her business. And he probably wasn't opening up about this past because they both knew she wasn't going to be part of his future.

* * *

Noah hung up the phone and slid his cell back into his pocket. This evening was going rather smoothly. He and Callie had shared a nice meal on the patio and they'd chatted about mundane things, and he was sure to steer the topic far away from anything sexual because it was all he could do to sit there and watch her as a doctor should watch a patient.

But that kiss in the kitchen earlier had been anything but professional. For the life of him, though, he hadn't been able to stop and he didn't care about the consequences. With her parading around in his oversize shirts… His gut clenched just thinking of it. Now when he went to wash them, they would have Callie's scent all through them.

His emotions were a jumbled, chaotic mess. He'd told himself in the beginning to just be a friend or a doctor, to distance himself from her emotionally. But the more Callie was around him, the more he found he wanted to be around her. So, okay. Sexual chemistry was definitely one thing he could handle. But they hadn't had sex.

Where the hell did that leave his emotional state? Because right now he truly had no clue how to feel or act with her.

He'd been taken so off guard when Callie had mentioned something hurting him, something that still had a hold on him. She'd been spot-on and that fact made him very uncomfortable. Was he that transparent? After a year of living without Malinda he'd thought he'd taken control of his emotions.

Yes, Callie had initially reminded him of Malinda, and even so, he'd believed they could have a short, no-strings affair. But he knew better now. He didn't want his past and present to collide. He was doing all he could to keep from claiming Callie in his bed. Getting wrapped up in another vulnerable woman was not a good idea, especially when that woman could get under his skin as Callie seemed able to do, but his hormones weren't getting that message. He could handle sex, if that was all there was to this relationship, but he had a feeling Callie was thinking of much more…especially now that they'd played house for a few days.

He rubbed the back of his neck and headed back inside. Callie had already gone in, but when his real-estate agent had called, he'd stepped out onto the shaded patio. There was a buyer interested in looking at the house tomorrow afternoon and Noah had agreed to a time. Now he had to get Callie out of the house and maybe persuade her to have a picnic or something in the park. She wouldn't be a fan of going out in public so soon, but there was no other choice.

Noah found her sitting in the living room fumbling left-handed with the remote.

"Let me get that," he told her as he stepped down into the sunken living area. "What do you want to watch?"

She shrugged. "Doesn't matter. I was looking for a good movie, but you have like two thousand channels and I wasn't even sure where to look."

Noah laughed and flopped down beside her. "Name a movie you'd like to see and I'll put it on for you."

She pursed her lips and wrinkled her nose as if in thought. "Hmm…how about *Blackhawk Down?*"

Surprised, Noah grinned. "Really? Why that one? I would've pegged you for a romantic-comedy type."

She shook her head. "Growing up I was a daddy's girl and whatever he watched, I watched. He was a war-movie or Western guy, so that's my thing. Besides, after really researching films and sinking my teeth into the fact that's what I wanted to do, I appreciate all the special effects more."

He placed his hand on her leg. "I'm sorry, Callie."

"It's okay," she told him, her eyes on his hand on her bare thigh. "We're moving forward. Let's just concentrate on right now. Okay?"

He squeezed her leg and went to search for the movie before his hand got a mind of its own and started wandering.

"Sure, come in and hit three buttons and make it look simple," she joked once the movie appeared on the screen. "I was in here for fifteen minutes and got nowhere."

"It's my TV." He grinned and caught the wide smile on her delicate face. "I pretty much know how to work it."

As the movie's opening music started, he propped his feet up onto the squat table in front of him. "So, you liked Westerns and war movies as a kid. Tell me what else you liked."

Callie eased back against the arm of the sofa, sitting somewhat sideways. Noah reached over and slid a hand beneath her thighs to bring her legs up and over his lap. He didn't know why he did that, but he wanted that additional innocent contact with her. Granted, this wasn't so innocent considering where his thoughts were heading.

"Well, I wasn't really popular in school so I was more of a homebody."

Noah jerked back. "Not popular? How is that possible? You're outgoing, not to mention stunning."

He cringed at the same time she did and he knew he'd chosen the wrong words.

"Damn, Callie. I just keep digging that hole deeper." He shook his head and met her gaze. "Even though you've had this setback, you're still beautiful to me."

She smiled and rested her head on the back cushion. "That's okay. It's not your fault. It is what it is."

"I plan on taking you to the office next week if you don't mind."

Her eyes widened. "What for?"

"A minor microdermabrasion. Your stitches will come out and I'd like to start removing some of the dead skin a little at a time and take this process slowly so we can insure the best results."

Callie smiled. "That would be great, Noah. The sooner I can see what I'm dealing with, the better."

Pleased with her eagerness, he settled deeper into the cushions and rested his arms on her legs. "So, what did you do at home since you didn't participate in school activities?"

"My dad found this old pool table at a yard sale and worked to clean it up. We loved that thing. Every night my brother and I would bet who would win. I beat him nearly every time."

Noah laughed. "I can see that. You're a fighter."

Her eyes held his. "You're right. Sometimes I forget that." She offered a smile.

"You're entitled to, but just make sure you don't lose it."

"I won't."

Her eyes darted to the big screen as the movie began. He watched her for a moment before he, too, rested his head against the back of the couch and slid his hand down to one of her dainty feet. He began massaging one foot, working her arch, her heel, each of her tiny toes.

She let out a slight moan and he smiled as he picked up the other foot. As she watched her movie, her body relaxed and Noah kept right on massaging her. He wanted her to stay relaxed, wanted her to stay comfortable.

By the time the movie was about halfway through, Noah glanced over and found her asleep. He'd stopped massaging her a while ago, but apparently she'd settled into this state of comfort and let her guard down.

With her slinged arm resting on her stomach and her other arm behind her as a pillow, she looked so innocent, so young. She had bluish circles beneath her eyes and he knew she hadn't been sleeping well. She was worried about her prospective career and he'd be lying if he didn't agree that her future in the movie industry was unstable.

But he also hadn't been lying when he said he'd do everything in his power to make her whole again. He'd make damn sure she had the best treatment and care she needed, and he'd be with her every step of the way.

He slid a hand over her foot, over her ankle and along her shin. She was so soft, so smooth. His hand glided back down as his groin tightened.

God, what a jerk he was sitting here getting hard and stroking a sleeping woman. Seriously? Had it come to that because he couldn't just admit how much he wanted her and instead let fear prevent him from acting on his emotions? Had he turned into a voyeur?

Her lids fluttered and Noah watched as she awoke and her gaze met his. Slowly she pulled her arm from behind her head and extended it before laying it across her stomach.

Darkness had long since settled, and the only light came from the big flat screen hanging on the wall across the room. Her face glowed in the subtle light and Noah couldn't stop from reaching out and taking her hand, stroking it with his thumb.

He shifted, placing a knee on the couch between her legs and easing up over her. Keeping his movements slow, he waited for a sign of fear or doubt from her, but the way that pink tongue came out to lick her lips was all the indication he needed. That and the heavy rise and fall of her chest as her breathing quickened.

Reaching for the buttons on his shirt, which she wore so much better than he ever did, he slid one button, then another, then another open until he reached where her sling lay. Her tanned, flat abdomen stared back at him; her belly button held a small blue stone twinkling in the low light.

His hands gripped her waist as he leaned down to kiss her stomach and let his tongue flick the gem. She felt so smooth beneath his lips, he moved lower. Once more he glanced up at her to see her staring back at him, her face flushed, her breathing heavy. How could he not move forward with this?

He might regret it later, but he'd had regrets before. And now he wanted to taste Callie the way he'd been fantasizing about for months. This was nothing more than physical. He wouldn't let it be.

With both hands, he slid his fingers inside the waistband of her shorts and eased them down. He stripped them all the way off and flung them aside. Staring down at her plain pink cotton panties was more of a turn-on than if she were lying here in a red teddy. She was simple, she was real, she was wearing his shirt and for now she was his.

He skimmed a finger across the top band of her panties, then slid his fingers along the elastic that hugged her thighs. She was already hot and wet. For him.

Easing the moist fabric aside, he slid one finger into her heat. Her body arched up as she dug her heels into his couch. Slowly in and out he worked her until she was rocking her hips and gripping the cushion with her good hand.

Perfect. Just how he wanted her.

He dipped his head and slid his tongue over her, pleased when she cried out. He spread her legs farther with his shoulders and kept hold of the panties with one hand while his mouth and other hand continued to assault her.

Her moans, her heavy breathing, her tilted hips against him had him working harder to bring her pleasure.

And he didn't have to wait long. Her body arched, froze and she gasped. Noah stayed right with her until she stopped trembling.

"That was the most erotic thing I've ever seen," he whispered as he let her panties slide back into place.

Her eyes found his and a slight flush crept over her cheeks. "Um...watching a movie isn't what it used to be," she joked.

He put his arm along the back of the couch and leaned toward her face. "You don't have to be embarrassed or uncomfortable."

Her eyes darted to his groin. "Speaking of uncomfortable…"

Noah smiled. "Yeah, it is, but that was all for you. I've been wanting to do that for some time."

Callie tried to ease herself up, but before she had to struggle, Noah offered a hand and pulled her up with her good arm.

"You can't just stay like that," she said, pointing to the obvious. "I want to—"

He placed a fingertip over her lips. "I know you want to, and believe me, so do I. But this isn't the time."

Callie's heavy-lidded eyes darted to the floor as she nodded. Damn, he hadn't meant it that way.

"Hey," he said softly, taking her chin in his hand and forcing her to look at him. "This has nothing to do with you physically. I just think you've been through enough and I hadn't exactly planned on seducing you in my home."

Her eyes studied him. "It's okay, Noah. You're right. This isn't good timing and you obviously have something in your past you're still working through."

He dropped his hand and sat back. "You know nothing about my past, Callie, so you'd best not bring it up again."

She sighed as she sat back against the arm of the sofa. "I was just making an observation. That's all."

Noah cursed and came to his feet, raking a hand through his hair. "No, I'm sorry. There are just some topics that I cannot talk about with anyone, and my past is one of them. I'm still sorting through some rough things, but that's really none of your concern and has no place here."

God, he was such a liar. No place here? Didn't he carry those demons around with him everywhere? Didn't he put them down beside him in bed each night? Hadn't they brought him to Callie and inadvertently led to her accident? How the hell could he say they had no place when in fact they had every place imaginable in his life right now?

He looked back down at her, clad in nothing but his shirt, which was unbuttoned from her rib cage down, exposing those soft panties he'd just been inside.

"I have someone coming to look at the house tomorrow. I'd like to take you out—"

"Noah," she started, but stopped when he held up his hand.

"I know you're not comfortable," he told her. "But I was thinking of just going to the park for a picnic in the shaded area where no one is lingering. Or we could visit my friend Max."

"The movie star?" She laughed. "Yeah, like he wants me in his house."

"Actually, he's called to check on you," Noah told her, turning to face her fully and placing his hands on his hips. "He's one of my best friends, and if you're not comfortable with the picnic, we can hang at his place for a few hours. He won't mind a bit."

"Of course." She tried to button the shirt with only one hand. "This is your house and you're putting your life on hold for me. I'm being a jerk trying to get picky about where I go. Actually, we can go to my place if you want. I could grab some more things and get my mail, check my messages."

Noah nodded as he sat on the edge of the couch and slid her hand aside so he could adjust the buttons.

Why hadn't he thought of her place? Maybe because that was just another level of Callie he was afraid to enter. While she was here, on his turf, he was fine. But if they went to her place, he would be so out of his territory....

"That will be fine," he conceded. "We can pick up some lunch and eat at your apartment. The real-estate agent is coming at noon, so I'd say we need to be gone by eleven-thirty."

"I'll be ready," she informed him. "But, um…are you sure you're okay?"

He cocked his head, and when her eyes darted to his lap, Noah laughed.

"I'm okay," he assured her. "I promise this isn't my first hard-on and it won't be my last where you're concerned."

Nine

Callie was so confused. She wanted to read more into last night's little escapade, but how could she when he'd only been on the giving end and not the receiving?

Had to be out of pity. But what man did that? She'd never known a man to put her sexual needs first. Of course, she hadn't had that many lovers by which to judge.

Mercy, she was beyond confused.

As Noah wove his way through the streets toward her apartment, she was trying to recall if it was clean. Oh, well, too late now, and it wasn't as if she had a cleaning service to come in and take over.

He pulled up in front of her building and came around to help her out.

"My key is in the side pocket of my purse," she told him, holding her bag with her left hand while he dug out the keys.

Noah unlocked her door and ushered her in. "While you

gather more things, I'll get the food from the car and meet you in the kitchen."

Callie nodded and headed to her room. With her right arm snug against her body thanks to the sling, she had to tug on drawers with her left hand, one side at a time until they sprang free.

She grabbed more underwear, because she just couldn't bear to ask Noah to wash hers, a few more shorts and the few button-down shirts she owned. As much as she liked wearing his, she knew she couldn't go on like that the whole time she was with him.

She tossed all that she wanted onto the bright orange comforter and went in search of a tote. She had a slew of tote bags from various pharmaceutical companies when sales reps came into the office.

She found a bag and began putting her items into it and hoisted it up onto her good shoulder with only a slight wince as she pulled too hard and jarred the broken collarbone.

She needed another pain pill, but she was afraid to ask Noah after his reaction the other day.

After placing the bag by the door, she turned to see Noah at her two-seater table spreading out their Chinese food containers.

"Smells great," she told him. "I've been craving Moo Shu Pork for a while."

He smiled and looked up at her. "We just had it in the office two weeks ago."

Callie shrugged. "Then I've been craving it for two weeks. Seems like so much longer. I could eat this stuff every day."

He pulled out their egg rolls and turned toward the kitchen. "What do you want to drink?"

Callie moved past him. "I can get it, Noah. It's my apartment. Let me."

"No, you sit. I can get the drinks."

She sighed. "You're not going to let me win this little argument, either, are you?"

He grinned and that damn head tilted sideways as if he just knew his charm would win any battle he fought.

"Fine. I'll take some ice water. I can't imagine there's much else in there. I was due to go to the store after the photo shoot."

The photo shoot. At least she could say the words now without breaking into a crying fit or turning into a total bear and growling at everyone. Well, not everyone. Just Noah.

"It's no problem. Water is fine with me, too." He came back to the table with two bottles of water and unscrewed hers for her. "Eat up."

"You don't have to tell me twice."

They ate in silence, but something kept digging at her curiosity and she wanted to approach it. Even if he'd told her to back off.

"Why sell the house if you don't really want to?" she asked.

His fork froze at his mouth before he dropped it back into the box. "What makes you think I don't want to sell?"

"Because I've seen your face when you talk about the house being for sale and I saw your face when you told me the real-estate agent was coming by today. You're not happy about this decision, so why make it?"

Noah sighed and eased back in his seat. "Part of me needs to, but the other part of me is afraid to."

Well, that revelation shocked her. Noah Foster afraid of something? She'd seen the sadness and occasional darkness in his eyes, but she'd never believed he'd admit to fear.

"Then why the rush?" Callie asked. "Wait until you're not afraid anymore."

"I have a feeling that fear will never go away. It's just something I need to do."

"Does this have anything to do with that past you don't want to discuss?"

His lips thinned as he eased forward in his seat and grabbed his fork. "Leave it, Callie. You're purposely dancing on shaky ground."

She crossed her legs and sat back in her creaky chair. "So you can pry into my life and make me face my fear, but I can't do the same to you?"

"We don't share the same fears," he told her. "Not even close."

"Really? Why don't you try me?"

"I don't want to try you," he told her, his hands on his hips, his lips thin. "This is not up for debate."

"I don't find it fair that you can dig into my life, my personal space, and then tell me that a part of you isn't up for discussion." She remained in her seat because as much as she wanted to stand up and shout, at least one of them needed to remain calm. "I thought we were moving toward something, Noah."

"We have a sexual attraction, Callie. I'm not looking for more, and honestly, I wasn't even looking for that."

"Okay, no need to be so blunt," she told him, trying to hide the hurt. "I'm just trying to help you. You know, like you're helping me?"

"I'm helping you as a doctor."

Okay, now she did come to her feet. "Really?" she asked, resting her good hand on her hip. "So what happened on your couch last night was, what? You playing doctor?"

"Don't make this into something it's not."

"And what is that? I don't even know what the hell is going on because you're so closed off."

"I have to be closed off," he retorted, his voice booming. "You don't know the pain I went through, the pain I still live with."

"No, I don't because you won't let me. You are always flirty, always eager to make me happy, but you're miserable, Noah. I can see it now that I've spent more time with you."

"You think you know me because you shared a few nights in my house and worked for me for a few months? Because we shared an intimate evening? There's so much, Callie. So much in my heart, in my life, that you don't know."

"Then tell me so I can help," she pleaded. "This can go both ways, you know. Keeping your hurt or anger bottled up can't be healthy."

"Maybe not, but talking about it also makes it…"

"What? Real?"

He closed his eyes and sighed. "I just want it to go away."

"Yeah, I know how you feel." She'd give anything if this living nightmare she was in would vanish. "Please, Noah, let me in."

"You want in?" He opened his eyes, met hers, and she was surprised to find not only anger lurking in those mesmerizing gray eyes but also unshed tears. "Getting in would mean more than I can give right now, Callie. Trust me, you don't want to live my hell."

She tilted her chin and stepped closer. "I don't want to live mine, either, but I am."

Callie's cell chimed through the room, cutting the tension with the upbeat ringtone.

She crossed the room and rummaged with her left hand through her purse. She glanced at the screen and sighed.

"Hi, Amy," she greeted her agent.

"Just calling to check on you. How are you feeling?"

Callie glanced over her shoulder to Noah, who was staring back at her. He could be part of her private life and she couldn't be part of his?

She turned her back and walked to the front window. Her apartment wasn't big, but at least moving away would give off the silent hint that he wasn't welcome to listen to her conversation.

"I'm getting better every day," Callie responded, trying to sound upbeat.

"I just want you to know that the role has been recast for the Anthony Dane movie." Amy paused before lowering her voice. "I'm so sorry, Callie. I didn't want this to happen, but there was nothing we could do. They start shooting next month."

Callie swallowed the burn in her throat and bit her lips to keep from crying. "Um…it's okay. I mean, it's not, but like you said, there's nothing that can be done."

Callie watched as a couple pushed their baby stroller down the street and as a little boy rode by on his bike. Life went on for everyone else while her world had crumbled. She didn't know if she had the strength to build it back up again.

"I'm here," Amy went on. "As long as it takes to get you back to your old self, I'll be here, Callie. I have faith in you."

Callie blinked back the tears. "Thanks. Listen, I need to go. We'll talk later."

Callie ended the call before her emotions exploded. She hated crying on the phone. Who wanted to listen to a blubbering mess on the other end? After sliding the phone into the pocket of her capris, she put her left hand over her eyes and willed the inevitable crying jag away. But it was a moot point because the second she felt Noah's strong hand on her shoulder, she fell back against that hard, sturdy chest and lost it.

He didn't say a word, but he did turn her so she was facing him. She leaned against him, her face against his chest. She was probably going to soak his shirt, but she couldn't stop the tears any more than she could change her fate.

His warm hand roamed up and down her back as he rested his chin on top of her head. Callie knew as soon as she looked up at him she'd see pity, and that was the last thing she wanted. Right now she just needed to get this cry out of her way. Of course, she'd been saying that a lot lately. But she just couldn't help it.

"I knew the part wasn't mine anymore," she whispered against his chest. "But it still hurts to know I've officially lost it."

"There will be others, Callie," he told her softly. "If Anthony Price wanted you once, he'll look at you again."

She eased back and shook her head. "He wanted the flawless Callie. I doubt he'll have use for a scarred Callie. Men can pull off imperfections and Hollywood thinks it's rugged and sexy. A woman has to be regal and flawless at all times to be considered."

Noah nodded. "I won't lie, that's pretty accurate. But I also know you're a fighter and I know I'm a damn good surgeon. Together we won't let this dream of yours disappear."

She studied his face. "I still don't understand why you're so hell-bent on helping me. Yes, I worked for you and I know we shared some...moments, but you're putting your life on hold. Why?"

He reached up and stroked her good cheek. "Because I can't sit back and watch someone I care about suffer. I couldn't live with myself if I didn't try to make your life better."

Callie jerked back. "You care for me?"

Noah stepped forward. "It would be impossible not to feel something more than friendship toward you, Callie. I've tried to ignore the sexual pull, but after tasting you last night, I've been unable to think of little else."

"But just a moment ago you were so adamant about this thing between us being nothing."

Holding her with his mesmerizing gaze, he said, "That's because I wanted to ignore this pull, but when I hold you, I can't lie. My actions betray me."

Shivers raced over Callie's body. "This timing isn't the best, Noah. Especially since you're struggling with...whatever."

"As much as I wish we could explore this, I'm afraid I just can't go into something with you when I don't even know what demons you battle or what my future holds."

He picked up her hand and kissed her knuckles. "Then we'll take this slow. I never back away from what I want, Callie, and I want you. In my bed."

"Well, that was blunt."

"And honest," he told her. "I'm done lying to you, to myself. I guess I'm learning you need to take what you want when you want it because it could be gone in an instant."

She listened to his tone grow almost angry, yet nostalgic.

"Noah, I can't be a replacement for whatever happened to you. You act as if I'm plan B in whatever went wrong in your past. That's not how I want to live. I'll never play second to anything or anyone."

"And you shouldn't have to," he told her, stroking her cheek. "But I want you to know where I stand and why I'm so adamant about being with you again."

Callie leaned into his touch. "I'd be a fool to lie and tell you I haven't thought about you, fantasized about you. But right now the last thing I feel is sexy."

He stepped back and nodded. "You can't help how you feel, but know this. I find you damn sexy, Callie. No matter what you look like on the outside. To me, you're a sexy woman because of your kick-ass attitude and your personality. I know that's unusual for a man to say, but it's true. *Sexy* doesn't have to mean *flawless*."

Callie laughed. "I hope you're not going to use that for your new ad slogan."

The corners of Noah's mouth kicked up. "No, that's for your ears only."

"Then I won't tell anyone," she replied, but her smile faded. "Noah, I know this probably doesn't need to be said, but—"

"No, it doesn't." He cut her off. "I don't want to hear it."

She looked down at her feet, then back up beneath her lashes, afraid to fully look him in the eyes. "I'm sorry I let you down for the new ads."

Noah closed that final sliver of space between them and took hold of her face with both hands, careful of where he touched her right side. "Listen to me and look me straight in the eye. I don't care about the ads. They will go on and something else will work out. Those ads are the last thing I'm worried about right now."

"I realize you're not worried, but your new office is supposed to open in a couple months and you didn't have anything else planned."

"No, I didn't," he agreed, smoothing her hair off her forehead and away from the bandage. "But I also know that something will come to me, and the ad agency I hired is on it. We're looking at a few options, but nothing is final. We may not use a model now. We're looking at something simple with a catchy slogan."

"You're so good to me," she whispered. "Even though I've done nothing but bring you misery, you're amazing. Don't think I'm not grateful. Even when I yell at you and cry, I'm still thankful to have you in my life."

Callie wrapped her arms around his waist and hugged him, because she'd just seen another flash of fear, of angst, spear through his eyes, and she didn't want to get into another argument on whether or not he should open up to her. One day soon, she vowed, she'd get those demons from his closet and then she could help him bury them where they belonged.

Ten

She'd hidden long enough.

Callie hadn't lied when she told Noah that he didn't need to worry about her and to have his normal life with his friends over. This was his house and she was his guest.

But Noah's best friend was the hottest actor in Hollywood and here she looked like Frankenstein's project gone awry.

Callie took a deep breath and smoothed down the simple backless sundress she'd snaked up over her body. But she'd be lying if she tried to pretend she didn't love wearing Noah's soft cotton shirts, because even though they'd been laundered, they still had the very sexy masculine scent of his cologne. And once when he hadn't been looking, she totally turned her nose straight into the collar and took a long, deep inhale.

Just because she was battered and vulnerable didn't mean she didn't still have needs, emotions and a craving for the man.

Callie moved down the wide hallway leading to the patio

doors off the kitchen. Before she stepped outside, she stopped to admire the fine scenery the two men on the patio made. They were opposite in so many ways, yet both of them were so sexy that a woman couldn't help but notice them.

Noah had that dark hair, sultry smile and bedroom eyes. Clichéd as it sounded, the description fit him perfectly. The man always had those heavy lids that screamed *Do me, baby*.

Max, on the other hand, had that messy dark blond hair that never quite seemed fixed but worked for him and his carefree ways. He was quick to smile and always flashed those dimples. He'd starred in so many films recently, Callie would be fooling herself if she didn't admit she was jealous of his string of luck.

No. She was not going to let her thoughts ruin Noah's company or his day. She was a guest. She didn't have to stay out and socialize the whole time, but she did owe it to Noah not to sit inside and pout like a child.

She pushed the door open and stepped out onto the warm stone patio. She hadn't bothered with shoes since she was just going to be by the pool.

"I hope you like your steak still mooing on your plate," Max said with that signature smile. "Noah here likes to barely get them warm before he pulls them off."

"You're just cranky because Abby had to cancel at the last minute and you're dateless." Noah flipped the large hunks of meat and closed the grill lid. "I'll have you know I have had those on there for ten minutes."

Callie smiled. "I'd prefer mine to be dead and not still bleeding."

Max laughed. "Take yours off and leave mine and hers on. I'll man the grill."

Noah turned to his friend, using his tongs as a pointer. "No one mans my grill but this man."

Laughing, Callie moved to the steps of the pool and eased

down onto the top one to put her feet into the refreshing, cool water.

"I'm sorry about the movie, Callie."

She jerked her attention to Max, who was also coming to sit on the top step with her.

"Thank you. It's been…hard to digest."

Max nodded. "I imagine. I can't compare my experience to yours, but I was turned down for a role I wanted once. It was the one role I knew would really launch my career."

Intrigued, Callie shifted to face him better. "Really?"

"I was overlooked because of my height."

Callie knew Noah was taller, but she'd never thought of Max as short by any means.

"Your height?"

"The producer wanted someone well over six foot and I'm just at six even. I didn't figure a few inches would make a difference. Apparently, I was wrong."

Callie extended her legs and swirled them around the water. She hadn't known how Max got started in the industry. He seemed to have just exploded onto the screen.

"Looking back, I'm thrilled I didn't get that role," he went on. "That movie ended up tanking in the box office and the part I would've played was cut out except for a few scenes."

Callie rested her feet back on the smooth step and leaned back onto her good hand. "Wow. I had no idea."

His eyes met hers and Callie could easily see why all the ladies swooned over him.

"Every actor has a story, Callie," he told her with a soft smile. "We don't always jump straight into stardom, and we fight to get where we are. And if Anthony Price wanted you in this film, I can guarantee you he will look at you again."

Callie shook her head. "I'm not so sure."

"I am," he told her with confidence. "I know Anthony and

he's a great guy. They have so many makeup artists and tricks they can pull to make that scar disappear."

If only it were that easy....

"But I'd have to go into a casting call looking like this," she told him. "That's a strike against me."

"Perhaps," he agreed, resting his muscular arms on his legs and leaning forward. "But your acting skills will override any scar. They'll see your talent and know any good makeup artist can fix that."

More hope bloomed within her and she so wanted to believe every word he was saying.

"If you two are done, these steaks are officially dead," Noah called from the other side of the patio.

Max came to his feet, extending his hand to help her up, and smiled. "He gets grouchy when I tell him how to cook."

Callie laughed. "If you hadn't, I would've."

"Fine, then," Noah mocked as he set the platter of meat on the patio table. "Next time you two know-it-alls can make me dinner while I sit by the pool."

Callie shrugged. "Fine with me, but I'm not a good cook, so you're just punishing yourself."

Max laughed. "Yeah, well, I'm an excellent cook. That's how I was raised. My parents own a large chain of restaurants on the East Coast."

"And how are you still single?" she joked, taking a seat.

Max threw her a smile. "I'm having too much fun."

Noah served the steaks and brought out some potato salad and drinks. Callie was thankful for this break in her new daily life of worrying and wondering about her future. Not only was this a great distraction, the uplifting words from Max really made her feel as if something in the future could open up for her. It might not be for a while, not until after Noah performed surgery or whatever he had in mind, but at least there was that proverbial light at the end of the tunnel and it was calling her name.

The following week brought Callie even more happiness. The stitches were out and her first microdermabrasion treatment was over. Callie hoped to God she was on the road to recovery.

She'd stayed at the office because Noah had a few patients to see and Marie had needed to leave early to get her granddaughter to a doctor's appointment. So here she sat in the receptionist's chair like she had so many times before. Only, all those other times she hadn't been so self-conscious.

Marie had simply hugged her and with tear-filled eyes declared how happy she was that Callie was back and looking beautiful. Callie knew the woman was just being kind and Callie didn't correct her about being "back."

Noah was finishing up with the final patient and Callie couldn't wait to get back home, or to Noah's home, where she felt safe, all tucked away from Hollywood's critical eye.

When the phone rang, Callie swiveled around in her cushy chair and picked up the receiver.

"Dr. Foster's office."

"Hello, my name is Mary Harper and my son, Blake, has an appointment next week. I was just calling to see if there were any cancellations before then."

Callie pulled up the screen with the appointments and scanned through. She knew Noah's schedule was pretty tight considering he'd taken off so much and had cut back on his workdays to be home with her, but she looked, anyway.

"I'm sorry, Mrs. Harper, but I don't see any. Is there any way I can take your name and number and we can call you if something opens earlier?"

The lady on the other end sighed. "That would be wonderful. Blake is so anxious to see the doctor. He's afraid to go back to school until his face and arm are better."

Callie knew this must be the ten-year-old boy Noah spoke of a couple weeks ago. The little boy who'd been burned. Noah was doing this appointment as a favor to a client. She knew he didn't usually take on children or burn victims, though not because he wasn't capable. Noah was one of the top surgeons in the country, but he tended to specialize in breast augmentations, face-lifts and other enhancement procedures on women.

Callie glanced at the screen again, feeling even guiltier for keeping Noah from helping this boy who had such high hopes. Callie understood those hopes.

"Mrs. Harper," Callie said, "could you bring Blake in tomorrow at five?"

"But I thought—"

"I think one more patient at the end of the day won't overwork Dr. Foster too much, and since this is the consultation, it won't be a long appointment."

Mrs. Harper burst into tears and instantly Callie teared up. "You don't know what this means to us," the woman said. "Truly. You don't know how thankful I am you can fit him in sooner. I just want my son to have a little hope. We'll be there."

Once Callie hung up, she added the last appointment. If she had to come to the office herself and stay by Noah's side then she would. There was no way she could sit in Noah's lavish home being babysat by the doctor when he was needed here so much more. There was a boy afraid to go to school, afraid to see his friends, all because he was imperfect.

The irony was not lost on her and she prayed the young boy would find the courage to go back to school, even if his scars couldn't be healed.

When the last patient came out, Callie was all ready to

take her chart and file it. Thankfully, the woman didn't have
a co-pay, so she breezed right on out the door. When the busty
blonde had checked in, Callie had had her head down looking at another chart, so she'd bypassed the whole awkward
situation of seeing beauty staring her in the face.

God, she didn't know how long she could continue to work
here. There was no way she could dodge all the beauty that
came in and out the door.

Once the client was gone, Callie locked the front door and
set the alarm for the front of the building. After turning off
the lights for the waiting room and shutting down the computer, she went to Noah's office.

"You ready to go?" he asked her as he shut down his own
computer.

Callie nodded. "Yeah."

He glanced up at her, his brows drawn. "Something
wrong?"

"I just got off the phone with Mrs. Harper. Blake will be
here tomorrow at five."

Noah shook his head. "His appointment is next week. I'll
be home with you tomorrow afternoon."

Callie crossed her arms over her chest. "No. Tomorrow at
five you and I will both be here. If you can't leave me at home
to take care of myself, I will come with you. He needs to be
seen. Needs to know that there's hope for him."

Noah crossed the room and stood within inches of her,
making her tilt her head to meet his eyes.

"Of course there's hope," Noah told her, cupping her cheek.
"I plan to do everything I can for him. I can't imagine how
he must feel. He's been away from school for so long, first
because he needed to stay away in case of infection and now
because he feels he would get made fun of. His feelings must
be all over the place."

Callie nodded. "I know they are," she whispered.

Noah stroked her smooth, unmarred cheek and laid a gentle kiss on her lips. "You're amazing, Callie."

"Why?"

"To stay here, to come back tomorrow in order to help a young boy. You just amaze me over and over."

Callie shook her head. "Noah, if I can help this one boy have something to cling to, something that will give him the inspiration to believe that he's the same kid with or without the burns, then my staying here is totally worth it."

"He's the same kid, huh?" Noah asked with a slight grin. "Sound like something I told you before?"

Callie shook her head. "This is a kid, Noah. I'm not the same person now. Something changed in me, something I'm not sure I'll ever get back."

Her heart clenched when he pulled her against him, careful of her shoulder, and lightly touched his lips to hers.

"You'll get it back," he murmured against her mouth. "We'll get it back."

How could she not cling to his strength, his faith? How could she give up when Noah was giving all he had for her?

Callie knew that if a little boy had faith, and Noah had this grand amount of confidence, she should feel the same. Fate might have taken her off her path, but she was on a new path now, and the decisions she made would alter the next course she took.

Callie waited in Noah's office while he had the consultation the following day with Blake. She didn't want to see the young boy, didn't want to be reminded that people had worse problems than her. She knew that. She even felt guilty for her self-induced pity parties. But she just couldn't see Blake, though she was eager to hear Noah's prognosis.

Thankfully, Marie was heading up the reception desk and Callie could hide back here. She didn't want to be out front again for a while, though now that her stitches were out and the bandage off, she didn't feel as much like Frankenstein, but she still had a sling and a long, red scar on her face.

Callie glanced at the clock and wondered what her parents were doing. She hadn't told them about the accident. She still didn't want to, but they were her parents and she'd always prided herself on her honesty.

She pulled her cell from her pocket and resigned herself to the fact she'd probably be having one of the most depressing phone conversations ever.

Her parents' phone rang and she tightened her grip on her cell.

"Hello."

"Mom?"

"Callie? Darling, it's so good to hear from you."

Her mother's smile sounded in her tone and Callie could picture the woman standing by the stove cooking, as she often did.

"I didn't expect to catch you home, Mom. Are you not working today?"

Erma Matthews sighed. "Well, they had to cut my hours back at the grocery, so I'm only doing single shifts now."

Callie closed her eyes, rubbed her temple and eased back in Noah's cushy leather office chair. "I'm so sorry, Mom. I assume since the phone is back on you got the money from the account."

"Yes, honey. Thank you. I just hate you're spending your hard-earned money on us. Hopefully, your father will find something soon. He's actually got a job interview in two days at a factory about an hour away. It would be a commute, but the pay is even better than what he was making before the layoff."

A sliver of hope slid through her. "That's wonderful, Mom."

For a moment, silence entered their conversation. Callie toyed with the dark buttons on the brown leather chair, knowing she was going to have to come clean.

"Mom, I need to tell you something and I don't want you to worry."

"What's wrong? Are you all right? You can't tell a mother not to worry and expect her not to, Callie."

Callie swallowed and eased forward in the chair, resting her elbow on the desk while holding the phone to her ear on her uninjured side.

"I was in an accident a couple weeks ago. But I'm fine," she quickly added. "I have a broken collarbone and I had some stitches, but I'm fine."

"Good heavens, honey. Why didn't you text your brother and have him tell us?"

Shame. Humiliation. Risk of sounding like a failure.

"I didn't want you all to worry. But because of the timing of the accident, I won't be able to fulfill my role in the Anthony Price movie I told you about."

"Oh, honey." Erma's tone softened and Callie imagined that tilt of the head most mothers got when they felt a twinge of regret. "I'm so sorry, sweetheart. I know how much you wanted that."

Wanted? No. She craved it, ached for it.

"There will be other roles," her mother assured her. "What's meant to be is what will happen."

"Listen, Mom," Callie said, trying to hold back tears, "I'm at the office and I need to go. I just wanted to touch base and let you know what was going on."

"I'm so glad you called. I love you so much."

"Love you, too, Mom."

Callie disconnected the call, calling herself all kinds of coward for not disclosing the full extent of her injuries. But she just couldn't. She'd left her mother with the hope that there would be more roles, more movies. But the reality was there probably wouldn't be.

A moment later, Noah stepped into the office and hung his lab coat on the back of his door. Without a word he moved to the desk, opened the side drawer and pulled out his keys.

"I'm ready."

Callie watched as he walked out the door and turned to head out the back way.

Um…okay. Apparently, something was wrong, but since he was already walking away, she couldn't ask.

She nearly chased him out the back door and into his car, which he had already started. After getting in and barely having time to put on her seat belt, she glanced over.

"I assume Marie will lock up?"

Noah nodded and maneuvered into traffic.

"Would you like to tell me what happened to make you so upset?"

"No."

He didn't look at her, didn't elaborate, simply drove toward his home. Callie knew when to keep her mouth shut, though she hated that he was obviously at war with himself and it didn't take a genius to figure out it more than likely had something to do with the young boy he'd just had a consultation with.

Callie only prayed that the boy and his mother hadn't left on the same upsetting note that Noah had.

By the time they pulled into his garage, the tension was thick and Callie thought it best if she just went into the house. If he wanted to talk, he would. Though she wasn't counting on it. He was closed off when it came to anything personal.

Before she could grip her door handle, he turned off the ignition and slammed his palm onto the steering wheel with a loud thump.

"Damn it."

Callie sat still, waiting to see if he was going to open up and vent.

"I don't know if I can do this, Callie." Noah stared straight ahead to the white garage wall. "I can't work on that little boy and not get attached."

Callie bit her lip, not wanting to interrupt.

"He sat there looking at me with all that hope in his eyes and I want to deliver on promises his mother has made to make him well again. I want to be the hero he seems to think I am."

Callie reached over, touched his arm. "Then what's stopping you?" she asked.

"What if I fail?"

Noah turned, meeting her gaze. And there was that pain she'd seen a glimpse of before. Now it was raw, no longer hiding, and he wasn't trying to keep it under control.

"I refuse to fail another person, Callie."

Another person? Who had he failed before?

"Noah—"

He got out of the car and went into the house, slamming the door as he went. Callie sighed and rested her head against the leather seat. The man was going to break. If he didn't open up soon, he was going to shatter, and then all of his secrets, all of his feelings, were going to be laid open for all to see and there would be nothing he could do about it. She prayed that he'd let her help, but he was too stubborn, too strong-willed.

Ironically, some of those qualities that annoyed her she could relate to all too easily.

Eleven

Over a week had passed since the showing of his home and Noah still couldn't call his real-estate agent back with an answer. Yes, the amount the newlyweds had offered was very close to the asking price and higher than any other offers, but he just couldn't bring himself to make that call and get the ball rolling.

Added to that, he'd talked with colleagues about Blake's case and met with the little boy and he was certain he was the best one for the job. But the thought of being the one that little guy pinned his hope on was almost more than Noah thought he could bear. He was still dealing with Callie and all that hero worship she had in her eyes when he discussed her healing process. Both Callie and Blake were looking for something within Noah that he just didn't know if he could give.

For right now, though, he needed to take a step back from being a doctor. He needed to get back to being Callie's friend and letting his workload ease from his mind for just a bit. And he knew just the thing to get them back on friendly footing. He'd had something delivered earlier today and he couldn't wait to show Callie.

She'd laid back down for a nap just after lunch when she'd taken a pain pill. She hadn't had one in a while, but he knew she'd been in pain. She'd been trying to work on her arm exercises even when he'd told her to take it slow.

That pain medication always made her so tired and Noah encouraged her to sleep because resting would help her body heal faster, as well.

She'd taken her sling off today and had promised to go easy on her arm, but he would be keeping a close eye on her. He'd done the microdermabrasion last week and he was hoping to do more next week. If he could work on her wound as often as medically possible, perhaps her healing time would lessen and her scar would not be so visible.

It was so hard to shut down his doctor mind-set. Right now, though, he had something else in mind. Something fun.

He wanted to show Callie her surprise, but she was still asleep. He walked into the kitchen and saw the painkiller bottle on the counter. A sick feeling overcame him. For so long he'd lived with bottles floating around...usually empty ones that had just been prescribed only days before.

But this sick feeling didn't stem from his past; it came from the fact that Noah knew he hadn't left the bottle out when he'd given her a pill earlier that morning. He glanced at the clock on the stove and knew it was just now time for another pill, so why was this bottle out?

He twisted the cap off and counted the pills. It was two short compared to what should've been in there.

She'd taken that extra one the other day, which meant she'd taken another one today At this point, she shouldn't be taking two pills in the same day. Her pain had to have significantly lightened, so she should be able to get by with just an over-the-counter medication.

He'd thought he could leave them out and not treat her like a child. Apparently, he was wrong.

Not taking any more chances, Noah put the lid back in place and gripped the bottle as he set off for her bedroom. By the time he reached the second floor, he was angry, upset and feeling a little betrayed. If she was lying to him, he wasn't going to help her anymore. He couldn't live like that again. Not to mention the fact he couldn't be her doctor if she wouldn't follow orders.

He eased the door open and saw her lying on her side, her hands tucked beneath her uninjured cheek. The covers had been kicked off and she'd opened her window to let the afternoon breeze blow in. Crimson strands danced around her shoulders and her breathing was slow, soft.

Moving into the room, he placed the bottle on the nightstand and eased down onto the edge of her bed. The movement caused her to stir and soon her lids fluttered open until she focused on him. She looked like she had the other night, just before he'd made love to her with his mouth. So much for putting distance between them.

"Did you take a pill without telling me?" he asked, not even trying to hide his irritation.

She blinked, eased up onto her side and looked him in the eye. "I took one just before I lay down. I think I overdid it with taking my sling off. I only did a few more exercises than usual with my arm, but it started hurting more than it had been."

He picked up the bottle, marched into her adjoining bathroom and flushed the pills. When he came back out she was on her feet and angry.

"Why did you do that?" she cried.

"Because I'm afraid you'll get hooked. These are highly addictive. And I told you if you did that again I'd flush them."

Callie laughed. "I won't get addicted, Noah. I took a pill only a little before it was due. I'd had the other one in my system for over six hours. It's not like I was going to OD."

Even the term made him ill. The image of how he'd found Malinda was embedded in his head for the rest of his life. He found himself instantly seeing Callie that way and the thought made him want to vomit.

"If you're going to stay in my house and allow me to be your doctor, you will do exactly what I say, when I say it, or I won't help you anymore. I thought we'd already settled this."

Callie stepped back, blinking. "Wow. Um…okay. Calm down. I promise not to do anything else without asking."

He stared at her for several seconds. He needed to get a grip.

What he really needed to do was remember this wasn't Malinda and he truly didn't believe Callie had a drug problem. He needed to lighten up before he drove her away. Then what good would he be to her?

God, his past had consumed him and overtaken his emotions, fueling his anger. Callie still had nearly a whole bottle of pills, and if this were Malinda, that bottle would've been gone within a few days. Callie had been here a few weeks.

He took a deep breath, trying to erase the previous images of fighting with Malinda.

Remembering the surprise, he told her, "I had something delivered and I was hoping you'd be awake when it came, but you slept through it all."

She tilted her head and grinned. And just like that she'd forgiven him for bursting in and yelling at her. Yeah, she was quite different from Malinda.

"What is it?" she asked, smile beaming. "Did you get a dog? I've always wanted a dog like the one I left back in Kansas."

He laughed. "Um, no dog. This is something else you left back in Kansas."

Her brows drew together and she shook her head. "My old beat-up Jeep with the broken horn and busted grill?"

Taking her hand, he pulled her toward the door. "Just follow me and stop guessing. You're taking the fun out of the moment."

She shuffled her bare feet along behind him as he led her down the stairs and through the wide hallway toward the back of the house where he had a game room.

When he entered the room, he flicked the light on and stepped aside so she could see.

"Oh, my God," she squealed. "Noah, you didn't!"

Seeing her reaction was so worth paying extra to have the pool table delivered and set up so quickly. "I'm a fan myself and had thought of adding one to the game room, so when you mentioned it, I knew I needed to get one. Max and I used to play in college."

She stood staring and he almost felt a fool at her silence, so he kept rambling.

"Of course, we played while killing a case of beer and talking about women."

Her eyes darted to his and she smiled. "It's nice you two are still so close."

"He's like family," he told her.

She moved farther into the room and ran her hand along the green felt of the pool table. "It's going to be hard to do this with one bad arm."

Stepping closer to her, he grinned and rested a hip on the table beside where her delicate hand roamed. "That's what I'm here for, isn't it? To assist you with things you can't do?"

Her body visibly shivered and he was glad he had that effect on her, because she sure as hell had some amazing sort of power over him.

"Are we going to play now?" she asked, her voice husky.

Noah knew an opportunity when he saw one. Even though he knew in his mind he needed to be her doctor and friend above all else, his libido wasn't receiving that memo. Damn, he wanted her. She was still all rumpled from sleep with her dark crimson hair tumbling around her shoulders, her face free of makeup and the oversize shirt of his hanging nearly off one slender shoulder. He knew beneath that well-worn cotton she wore no bra, because since that first day with her bath, she hadn't asked him to put one on her. She wore these tiny little denim shorts with the frayed edging flirting with her bare thighs.

He assumed she'd managed the zipper and button them without his assistance.

"Yeah," he told her, keeping his gaze on her lips. "We're going to play now."

Callie started to ease forward, but Noah stepped back and cleared his throat. "I'll get a stick."

God, could there be more metaphors between sex and a game of pool? He'd never been turned on playing before. Then again, he'd been playing with Max or other guys from college and they were too busy trash-talking and comparing their previous dates.

Callie maneuvered the balls into the triangle while he chalked up the tip of the stick. "I'll stand behind you," he told her.

She stayed against the table and smiled. "I'll have to push with my left arm, if you can reach around and hold it with your right."

"Gladly."

He was torturing himself. Actually, he'd been torturing himself since he'd completely overstepped his patient/doctor bounds on his sofa the other evening, but that was uncontrollable and he'd gotten swept into the moment.

He slid the stick between her waist and her left arm. She grabbed the back of it and shifted her body. Noah wrapped his right arm around her and was careful not to touch her shoulder.

His face was mere inches from her mass of subtle curls. Inhaling, he pulled in a tropical, fruity scent that always seemed to surround Callie, filling his home with her signature intoxicating scent. He eased a bit closer until his mouth was at her ear, her hair tickling his lips.

"Lean into it," he whispered as he eased her body down his own.

Her body bent at the waist and Noah went with her. Together they leaned over the table and he eyed the cue ball.

"Relax," he whispered. "You're breathing hard. Take your time. Focus on what you want to happen."

Damn. If he didn't keep his mouth shut he was going to start pitching a tent in his jeans, and wood behind a zipper was never comfortable or concealable.

"I've done this before, you know." She tilted her head to look at him over her shoulder, but when she did, her mouth brushed against his jaw and he had to steel himself not to turn and take advantage of her lips.

"But it's been a while," he reminded her. "I'm just here to help you remember how everything works."

"Oh, I think I remember," she said with a sultry smile.

Noah swallowed. She was good at this, the flirting and sassy talk she'd done before her accident. She was slowly coming around to her old self.

"Hold the stick firmly," he told her, holding his left hand over hers on the stick. "Don't rush it. Practice stroking it and not letting it go too early."

For pity's sake, shut up, Noah. Why was he using a game of pool as a pathetic form of foreplay? If he wanted her so badly, why was he making himself miserable by holding back? He'd already admitted to her that he wanted her in his bed. There was no going back on that. Sex was simple. It was all that other emotional garbage he couldn't and wouldn't deal with or allow himself to get wrapped up in.

"I got it," she told him and pushed the stick forward until it hit the cue ball into the other balls, sending the various colors rolling around the table.

Two stripes sunk instantly.

"Good job," he told her as he stood up. And yup, there was that pressure against his zipper. *Well done, Noah. Well done. Way to avoid getting an erection.*

"If you thought that was good, you're going to be really impressed," she told him as she rounded the table. "In fact, I think I can take you without your help and using only one arm."

Impressed and intrigued, he crossed his arms and smiled. "Then let's see it, hotshot."

She proceeded to show him just how amazing she was at this game and he was damn glad his friends weren't here to see it. Max would give him hell for losing so easily.

By the time the game was coming to a close and she was ready to sink the eight ball, Noah had had more than enough of seeing her bent over the table wearing those little shorts and his shirt. In the two weeks she'd been at his house, he never got tired of seeing her wearing his shirt. He loved the way it hung on her, occasionally giving him a glimpse of a swell of her breast or the curve of her slender shoulder.

Before she could sink that last ball and totally embarrass him, he snagged an arm around her waist and pulled the stick from her hands. "I think you've shown off enough."

Her gasp of surprise quickly turned into a wide grin. "Sore loser, Noah? I'm not surprised. You're very competitive, but I hate to break it to you. I own this game."

He laid the stick across the end of the table and used both

hands to span her narrow waist. "Yeah, well, there's something else I'd rather own right now."

That smile of hers faltered as she bit her lower lip a second before licking them. Her hand came up to his shoulder, slid around his neck and toyed with the ends of his hair on the nape of his neck.

"I'd swear you planned this, but you had no idea I was getting this table."

Her brows drew together. "Planned what?"

"Those shorts," he told her. "Bending over the edge of the table to take your shots and throwing your rear in my face at every opportunity."

"I certainly had no clue you'd be getting this," she defended. "Besides, it was you who practically dragged me out of bed."

Noah inched closer, pulling her lower body taut against his. "I should've kept you there."

His mouth slammed down onto hers and she responded in an instant. Her body arched against his and he palmed her lower back while his other hand slid up to thread his fingers through her hair.

Her tongue invaded his mouth and Noah nearly sank to his knees. This woman knew how to take as much as he was willing to give. With one arm banded around her waist, he hoisted her up onto the edge of the pool table and stood between her legs. He pulled her forward a tad to stay as close to him as possible. He wasn't about to let her get away, not when he'd been denying himself for so long.

Keeping his mouth locked on hers, he reached between them and slowly unbuttoned each of the buttons, one agonizing hole at a time.

She pulled her mouth from his. "Pull the darn thing."

Noah laughed. "It's my shirt."

"Buy a new one."

"As you wish."

He gave a yank and the last of the buttons scattered across the hardwood floor. Easing the shirt off her shoulders, Noah kept his gaze on her chest. He was a guy—where else was he supposed to look?

"You're magnificent," he whispered. "Don't look away, Callie."

She shook her head. "I'm not. I just… It's hard to have you look at me like this. I mean, you create beauty for a living and I'm just…me. Flawed, but even before nothing special."

He took her face in his hands and kissed her softly before pulling back. "Listen to me. I'm sure as hell not comparing you to anyone. I want you, Callie. You. Because I'm attracted to you. It's that simple."

She reached with her left hand and palmed his cheek. "Then don't let me complicate things with talking, because I'm about to explode."

As if he needed any more of an invitation. He peeled his shirt off and flung it to the side and quickly pulled off his jeans and boxers—but not before grabbing a condom from his pocket and tossing it onto the table.

Callie's eyes widened and he couldn't help but laugh.

"I'm optimistic," he defended with a grin.

"I'm glad, but I'm more shocked at you," she told him, her face turning a cute shade of pink. "It's just…wow. If I were you I'd totally walk around naked and stare at myself."

Noah kissed her. "Shut up, Callie. Let me show you what else we can be doing."

He unfastened her shorts, and with her help of rocking from side to side, he eased them along with her panties down her toned legs before dropping them to the floor.

Noah stepped back to look at her, and even though he knew she was uncomfortable, he wanted her to get comfortable with the fact he enjoyed looking at her.

* * *

Callie wished he'd do something. The way he kept looking at her was making her nervous. He might say he wasn't comparing her to patients, and that was probably true, but he had to at least be comparing her to his past girlfriends, who were no doubt model-perfect.

"Noah?"

"I just wanted to see you. All of you."

He stepped forward again and wrapped his hands around her waist, helping her to ease forward on the table. One hand slid between them to her heat and Callie spread her legs wider. When he parted her, stroked her, she felt unable to stay upright anymore, and she leaned back on her good hand to expose herself more to him.

"That's it," he whispered. "Relax."

He lifted her feet one at a time to rest on the edge of the pool table as he continued to stroke her. When she was splayed before him, he slid one finger inside and started to move slowly in and out. Her hips lifted, needing more, silently begging for more.

"Slow down," he told her. "We've got time."

She looked up at him and saw that he was smiling. He was enjoying her torture. But she wasn't going to beg. He'd like that too much.

She lay back all the way on the table and closed her eyes. Let him take his time with her. She wasn't about to complain.

The sound of the condom wrapper filled the room and she waited with eager anticipation.

With his hands on either side of her inner thighs, he eased her open even more, and she braced herself as he slid into her.

She reached her left arm up and he grabbed it, pulling her back up so her torso met his, causing him to sink fully into her. Her hard nipples rubbed against his coarse hair, his hard chest, and she groaned as he started moving within her.

His hand remained on the small of her back, guiding her body against his, keeping it where they both wanted it.

His other hand clutched the nape of her neck as his mouth captured hers again. His tongue swept through her mouth, mimicking the actions of their bodies. Callie had never felt so much of a man from her head to her toes and all delicious points in between the way she felt Noah.

His breathing quickened as did his rhythm. Callie clutched his shoulder as she kept her body flush against his. His lips left her mouth, but he rested his forehead against hers. Eyes shut, jaw muscle ticking, Noah groaned.

Knowing she could bring him to the point where he looked as if he'd burst was all the initiative she needed to let go. Her body clenched around his as her ankles locked behind his back, her knees digging into his sides.

Noah's head tilted back as his body slammed into hers one last time and then froze as he released. She held him until they stopped trembling, until her body had chilled and he eased back.

With a wry grin, he brushed the hair away from her face. "This was the best addition to my house I think I've ever added."

Twelve

Noah walked down the hallway of the assisted-living facility toward Thelma's room. Her door was slightly ajar and he eased it all the way open to find her sitting in her favorite recliner, asleep. Her color wasn't too good today and it wasn't the first time he'd noticed she was looking more run-down.

As a doctor, he knew she probably didn't have much time, but as the one person who was the closest thing she had to family, the thought seeped into his heart and left a gap that he feared might never close. This was just another piece of Malinda he couldn't hang on to. Not that he wanted to hang on to those nightmare memories, but he wanted desperately to cling to the good times, the dreams they'd shared before drugs murdered their life together.

Noah eased into the room and closed the door. The slight click of the knob had Thelma stirring. She looked up at him and smiled.

"I didn't know I was going to have such a handsome visitor today. What's your name, honey?"

He laughed. Apparently, she wasn't lucid today, but he found it kind of cute at her age she still had that flirty spunk left in her.

"It's Noah, Thelma." He took a seat in the small wooden armchair next to hers. "You remember me. I'm engaged to Malinda. Your granddaughter."

She studied his face for a moment and he didn't think she'd register the names, but finally a slow smile spread across her wrinkly face. "Oh, my beautiful Malinda. Why isn't she here? Is she working?"

"No, she couldn't make it today."

Thelma's smile held. "Well, can you tell her to stop by? I miss seeing her. She's all I have left of my own daughter."

Noah knew Malinda's mother had been gone several years before he'd met Malinda, and Noah hated that Thelma was struggling with that pain all over again. Every time her memory was jogged, she had to relive losing her daughter all over again. There was no way he could tell her about Malinda. He'd let the woman go on believing.

"I'll see what we can do," he assured her. "But I want to know how you're feeling."

Thelma shrugged. "I'm okay. Um...could you call Malinda? I'd really like to talk to her."

That was a first. Usually he could dodge the question of bringing her in, and she'd never asked him to call her.

"She's busy today," he lied. "I promise she misses you, too."

Thelma nodded and grabbed his hand between her frail ones. "She's such a sweet girl. And to be engaged? I bet she's so happy. I can't wait for the wedding. I know my Malinda. She'll be a beautiful bride."

Noah swallowed the lump that crept up with the image.

Yeah, she would've been a beautiful bride. A beautiful wife. Had she stayed clean.

"She always played dress-up when she was little," Thelma went on. "She wanted to be an actress and she would dress up in different costumes and show off. Most of the time she played a bride and would come down the stairs with a pillowcase on her head as her veil."

Noah could easily picture a young Malinda playing dress-up. Acting had been her thing for as long as he'd known her. And eventually that was what killed her.

And he was shocked to realize that for the first time since he'd been coming here alone, the memories didn't hurt nearly as badly. He knew Callie coming into his life was easing that hurt, that guilt. Little by little, Callie was making his life better.

"Did you eat breakfast today?" he asked her, silently pleading for her to dodge the topic.

She pursed her lips and let his hand ease away from hers. "Hmm…I'm sure I did, but I can't recall what it was. Fruit, maybe?"

Because so many patients with Alzheimer's forgot to eat, he wanted to make sure she was getting enough calories. "How about if I get you some juice and yogurt?"

"I don't think I have any," she told him.

He moved to her small fridge in the kitchenette and opened it. "I brought a few things over the other day. You have yogurt or cheese and crackers. What would you like?"

"The yogurt, please."

He put it on the small tray and set it on her lap, then went back to get her some juice. He'd wait until she ate and drank it all. He knew it wasn't much, but it was something and he'd been asking the staff to watch her at meals to make sure at least half her plate was clean.

Even as she ate her yogurt, she kept bringing up Malinda. Noah merely nodded and smiled.

But it was so hard to picture Malinda, not because she'd been gone a little over a year, but because when he imagined anyone, it was Callie whose image appeared in his mind.

Guilt slid through him. Did that mean she was replacing Malinda? Could he truly be that heartless? Or was his mind telling him to finally move on, to let go of something, someone who would never be his?

Every time he thought of Callie, the same erotic visual flooded his mind from last night. Callie leaning over his new pool table. Callie spread out on the pool table. Callie wrapped around him on the pool table. He hadn't wanted to let her go when she'd gone up to bed alone.

God, he honestly hadn't meant to cross the line from doctor to man with her, but there was nothing he could've done to stop it. He'd seen the inevitable coming and had warned her, and himself, what to expect, but he'd never expected their uniting to be so powerful, so...memorable. So, yeah, apparently he was replacing Malinda, but not in his heart. He didn't even know if there would ever be room for another woman to fill that gaping hole.

But Callie's warmth and sweet spirit, which was slowly easing back, made him think things he probably shouldn't. And he'd gotten so used to her being in his home, always there when he thought of her. He could admit to himself how much he enjoyed her company on a personal level...sex aside.

Thelma laughed and brought his attention back.

"What?" he asked.

"You have the most peaceful smile on your face," she told him. "I've seen that look. You're in love."

Noah started to deny it, but Thelma assumed he'd been thinking about Malinda—the woman he had been completely in love with.

He just laughed instead of commenting. What could he say that wouldn't be a bald-faced lie?

"I remember when I fell in love with my William." She took a sip of her juice and grinned. "He was the most handsome man ever. Almost as handsome as you."

"Thanks."

"My granddaughter has good taste," she told him. "We don't pick out the ugly ones, but we definitely make sure they're gentlemen, too. I know you're going to treat my Malinda right, like a good husband. Caring for her and providing for her, that's what she needs. She's vulnerable at times, but you're a strong man. I'm so happy she found you."

Noah came to his feet. He couldn't sit here any longer and listen to her go on and on about what a good provider and caring man he was. He wasn't any of those things or Malinda would still be alive.

"Thelma, I have a meeting and need to be going, but I promise to come back tomorrow." He took her tray and set it in the kitchenette. "Is there anything else you need before I go?"

She smiled up at him and shook her head. "Just make sure to bring my Malinda by and tell her I love her."

Noah nodded, kissed her on the cheek and left. Good God. He couldn't keep doing this. How did he release this guilt of letting down not only Malinda, but Thelma? He was a fake, sitting in there smiling, laughing with his dead fiancée's grandmother.

He was a doctor, a profession known for healing people, but right now he felt like a complete failure. And he'd failed the one woman who loved him. He refused to fail Callie, too.

Callie slid her cell back into the pocket of her shorts and resisted the urge to throw something or just break down and cry. When she'd called her mother to see how her parents were,

Callie knew something was wrong. After getting her father on the phone, he claimed a storm had come through and torn off a piece of their roof. He'd put a tarp over it and was hoping to be able to at least patch just that part even though they couldn't afford to do the entire house just yet.

Life was fickle. Either everything was puppy dogs and rainbows or blow after blow kept knocking you down.

On a sigh, she walked down the hall of Noah's house toward the workout room. It had been a while since she'd been on the treadmill because she'd been so afraid to jar her shoulder. But if she just put the setting on a fast walk, she wouldn't be bouncing so much, and honestly, it wasn't hurting at all today. Besides, she really needed that stress reliever so she could clear her mind.

She assumed Noah wouldn't mind if she used this room. He'd never said otherwise.

Callie entered the gym and smiled. The man had thousands of dollars of equipment in here and all she'd ever seen him use was the heavy bag in the corner. She moved to the bag and used her left hand to give it a bit of a shove. Yeah, no wonder they were called heavy bags. And no wonder Noah's arms looked so, so fine. They'd felt pretty fine, too, beneath her fingertips as she'd gripped them while—

She closed her eyes and sighed. What was she doing? Seriously. She was living in her boss's home, letting him care for her, getting intimate with him all the while knowing he wouldn't commit to her beyond the present. He'd said as much, and to be honest, she didn't want to be with someone in a committed relationship when they were holding so many secrets inside. Secrets that were obviously still very painful. So painful he couldn't even mention them.

Or maybe that was the problem. Maybe he just didn't want to mention them to her.

"You look like I feel."

Callie jerked her head up and looked in the mirror-lined wall to see Noah's reflection as he stood in the open doorway. He looked ready for a workout with his running shoes, knit shorts and no shirt. The tattoo of a dragon slid over his shoulder and down onto one pec. He only had one tattoo, but that piece of art really showcased some nice, well-toned muscles.

"Bad day?" she asked, still looking at him in the mirror since he remained in place.

He nodded. "I just got back from the assisted-living facility."

"You go nearly every day. I never wanted to pry, but…do you have a family member there?"

"You could say that. We're not blood related, but I'm all she has."

A piece of Callie's heart melted. Did the man have any flaws?

"Is she worse?" Callie asked. "Sorry, not my business. You just look…worried."

He ran his hands over his face and sighed as he moved into the room. "She's got Alzheimer's and some days are worse than others. She keeps wanting to see her granddaughter."

"What's wrong with that?"

Noah rested his hands on his hips. "Her granddaughter passed away a little over a year ago."

"Oh, God. That's terrible. What happened?"

Noah glanced to the floor and shook his head. "A senseless accident that should've been prevented."

Alarm bells went off in her head. Was this "accident" the cause of the nightmare that plagued his life?

"Can you avoid the topic with her?" Callie asked.

"I've tried. Every time I visit, I dodge it, but that's the one thing she's noticed is missing from her life. Of all the things she's forgotten, she's never forgotten Malinda."

"Families have strong bonds," she murmured. "Some stronger than others."

Noah tipped his head. "Everything okay back home?"

She wasn't ashamed of her background, but she'd never really gotten into the whole situation about how her father lost his job and her mother had to take on an extra one. There was no need to pull out the "I was a poor kid" card. She didn't want pity from anyone. For any reason.

"Not really," she told him honestly. "I may have to go home for a few days."

His brows drew in. "What's wrong?"

Callie shrugged, not wanting to get into too many details because she'd bet every dollar left in her checking account that he'd never had to worry about his electricity or water getting shut off.

"Just some issues I need to deal with and I can't do it from here. Not sure what I can do while I'm there, but I just can't ignore my parents when they need help."

Noah crossed the room and held her gaze in the mirror. "Is there anything I can do?"

"No, but thanks."

He studied her as if he knew she was hiding something. "I can come with you. I'm not sure what's going on, but I'd like to help."

Okay, she'd known he was very generous, very caring, but to offer to fly to Kansas to help people he didn't know with a situation he knew nothing about? God, he really was the proverbial knight in shining armor.

But the last thing she wanted was for him to see where she grew up, because it was the polar opposite of this cushy twelve-thousand-square-foot home.

"You don't need to come," she told him. "You have work and you've taken off enough time to be with me."

"And a few more days won't matter."

She smiled. "Really. I'll be fine and I'll only be gone a couple days. You won't even miss me."

He looked as if he wanted to argue, but then he glanced down to her shoulder.

"How's the collarbone?" he asked.

Apparently, he was very good at reading women and knew when not to start an argument, but she had no doubt he'd get back on the topic of her home life soon...just as she would circle back to his issues, as well.

She lifted her arm until she felt pain. "Feeling much better. It's healing quicker than I thought it would."

"That's because the more it's immobilized, the quicker it can heal. Plus, you're still young and fit. That always helps."

"Maybe being cared for by the best doctor in town helps, too," she told him with a smile.

He returned her grin and stepped forward, coming up directly behind her. "Are you flirting with me?" he asked.

Callie smoothed her hair back from her forehead and shrugged. "What if I was?"

Sliding an arm around her waist and pulling her back against his hard body, Noah leaned down to her ear, all the while keeping his eyes locked on hers in the mirror.

"Then I'd have to do something about that," he whispered. "Are you looking for something beyond flirting?"

Warmth spread through her body at his words, his presence. "Maybe we've both had a bad day. It's never too late to turn it around."

His hand spread across her flat abdomen; his pinkie finger dipped into the waistband of her shorts. "I'm all for making your day better."

He snaked his hand up her shirt, his fingertips grazing the bottom of her breast and sending shivers through her. "Are you sure you can handle everything? I have a feeling this could take a while."

Callie dropped her head back to his shoulder and groaned as his finger and thumb found her nipple. "I'm sure," she murmured, unable to really think, let alone form more than a two-word sentence.

Before he could make good on his promise to improve her day, the doorbell rang.

Noah froze and cursed in her ear. "I'll kill whoever is at the door and be right back. We'll bury the body later."

Laughter bubbled up through Callie as she stepped forward. "Go answer it. It's not like I won't still be here when they leave. I sleep here, remember?"

His eyes darkened as he narrowed his gaze on her erect nipples, which were apparent through the cotton shirt.

The doorbell chimed again and he growled, "I'm so not in the mood for visitors."

Callie looked down at the bulge in his shorts. "Why don't you let me get it while you start reciting the Gettysburg Address again? That should help you...settle down."

As she walked from the room, Noah's bark of laughter trailed down the wide hallway. No matter that her day wasn't what she wanted it to be; Noah always managed to make her smile. She only hoped she could do the same for him. If she did it enough, maybe she could help him get past whatever it was that plagued him.

Callie glanced out the sidelight and saw Max. There wasn't a woman in Hollywood, or most of the world for that matter, that didn't love Max Ford. The man was not only one of the best actors in the business; he was drop-dead, curl-your-toes, giggly-schoolgirl gorgeous. But while Callie didn't deny the fact he was a very sexy piece of scenery, he didn't give her those flutters like Noah did.

Oh, God. She knew she'd been infatuated with Noah and enjoyed the sex, but...flutters? Was she feeling something more for her boss, caregiver, lover?

Shoving aside the epiphany and fear, she pulled open the door.

Max's eyes were shielded by a dark pair of sunglasses and he wasn't smiling. The man was always grinning, even when he talked; that was all part of his charm

"What's wrong?"

"Is Noah here?"

Callie stepped aside. "He's in the gym. Everything okay?"

Without an answer, Max took off down the hall, and Callie didn't know whether she should follow. This really wasn't her business, but at the same time she knew Noah had had a rough day and she didn't want him to have to receive more bad news. Whatever it might be.

But as she walked down the hall toward the gym, she heard the word *cancer* and froze. Did Max have cancer? She tried not to eavesdrop…okay, she didn't try, but she felt guilty for it and that was close enough. As she went to the door, she heard Max say *mother* and that was all she needed to hear to realize this was not her place.

Poor Max. He'd looked helpless when she'd opened the door and she'd never seen him look anything but charming, sexy and smiling.…

She made her way to the office where Noah had told her she could use his desktop computer instead of the laptop in the kitchen nook. The office was dark with navy walls, exposed walnut beams overhead and on the floor, but it was the floor-to-ceiling windows behind his desk that really opened up the room.

If she was serious about not working for him, she really needed to start looking to branch out somehow. Perhaps with her teaching degree she didn't have to limit herself to public schools. She could teach at handicapped schools or even work in an office at a school. The possibilities were there; she just had to explore them.

More than that, though, she needed to look at her life differently now. As much as she wanted to get her face back to normal, to get her life back to where it had been, she had to face the reality that this might not happen. Ever.

Noah had mentioned considering surgery soon and the thought terrified her. Oh, she wasn't afraid of pain, not to her face, anyway. She was terrified of the pain in her heart she'd endure if the surgery failed. She just couldn't get her hopes up.

She logged on to the internet and looked at job postings for the schools in the surrounding area, shocked to see how many there were. She could even go a bit farther out of L.A. There wasn't anything holding her here anymore.

First she'd have to write up a really nice résumé, and then she'd have to see if Noah would write her a letter of recommendation.

She eased back in the leather office chair and sighed. There was a major part of her that wanted to toss that computer across the room, but this life she now faced was her fault. She'd been so wrapped up in wanting to be the next big star that she'd never planned for anything else.

Oh, her parents made her get an education, but she'd never even created a résumé using that degree because she never thought she'd need it. Callie had never had any intention of becoming a schoolteacher.

Good thing she'd listened to her parents.

She reached up, lightly touching the imperfection down the side of her face. She tried to avoid mirrors, and since she was temporarily living with a man, that wasn't too hard, because they weren't all over the house. But there was one on the far wall by the entry to the office. The mirror was actually rather large and Callie figured Noah's interior designer probably put that there so the light coming in the windows across the room would bounce off the mirror.

Callie eased from the seat and made her way over. She

wasn't scared, not like she'd been those first few days of look-ing at herself after she'd get out of the shower. There was no surprise that was going to be waiting for her once she saw her reflection.

She approached the mirror and sighed as she closed that final distance. The ugly red, puckered line running from her temple down to her jawline, thankfully missing her eye, stared back at her. Callie turned slightly to take a better look. She supposed it was looking better, but not nearly what she wanted. Even if she parted her hair on a different side and covered the scar for casting calls, she'd have to let it show at some point. Not all roles would have her hair down, clinging to the right side of her face.

She reached up gently, using her right hand, and traced the jagged line. Her shoulder was healing beautifully and was al-most as good as new. Her face…well, that was still something Noah didn't discuss too much and she didn't know if he just didn't want to upset her or if he was afraid to tell her the truth.

She chose to believe the latter even though she'd never taken him for a coward.

Noah stepped into the room and came to stand behind her. "Staring at it will not make it go away," he told her.

"I know." Callie nodded, holding his gaze in the mirror. "How's Max?"

"Scared, worried. His mother has cancer."

"I heard him tell you that, so I decided to leave you two alone."

Noah rested his hands on her shoulders and eased her against his chest. "That means a lot to me that you knew we needed that time alone."

Callie drew her brows together. "Of course you needed to be alone. He's your best friend and he's dealing with life-altering news."

He stared at her in the mirror and sighed. "I've just never

known anyone like you, Callie. In the office you were an awesome employee and someone I wanted to know better, but now that I've gotten to know you even more, I can honestly say you're amazing."

Compliments made her uncomfortable, so she didn't reply.

"I'm glad you're here," he whispered as he slid her hair aside and kissed the side of her neck. "And I'm positive we were working on something very encouraging before that doorbell rang."

Shivers slid through Callie's body as she relaxed fully against him. "You've had such a stressful day, Noah. Why don't you let me—"

"I know exactly what you can be doing and it involves silence," he whispered against her ear before he placed a warm kiss in that very delicate, erotic area.

"What are we doing?" she asked.

"I'm about to get you naked."

She sighed and smiled. "I mean, what are we doing? Is this a relationship or are we just having a good time?"

He froze, bringing his eyes up to the mirror. "I can't answer that right now, but I can tell you I'm happy when you're with me and I'm happy you're here. Not with the circumstances, but I like having you in my house."

She didn't say anything, wasn't quite sure how to respond to his lack of commitment.

"I'm sorry," he told her. "I just can't give you more right now."

Callie smiled. "It's okay. You're honest. I'd rather that than you telling me what you think I want to hear."

"Are you done talking?" he asked, the corners of his mouth tilting up.

Callie grinned. "I'm done. Now, what were you about to show me in that workout room before Max came?"

"I was about to show you how good we are together."

Callie tried not to let those promising words into her heart, but she couldn't keep them back. He'd turned them loose and like an arrow, they shot straight to the target.

But she knew he didn't mean that like it sounded. She also knew they *were* good together and she wanted to explore the possibility that this might not be as temporary as either of them had thought.

Noah's talented lips cruised from her mouth down her throat and into the V of the oversize shirt. She loved wearing his shirts, always having that little piece of him right next to her bare skin at all times.

She gripped his shoulders as he undid each button and slid the garment off and to the floor.

In seconds, he'd turned her to face him and crushed his mouth onto hers. Chest to chest, she arched against his warm body, thankful he'd been about to work out and he'd forgone the shirt.

Without breaking the kiss, he shoved her shorts and panties down. She helped by wiggling until they were at her feet and she flicked them aside with her toes. She helped rid him of his shorts as well after he'd kicked off his tennis shoes.

"I love the way you taste," he murmured against her lips. "I can't get enough."

Neither could she.

He bent and scooped her up in that romantic gesture she'd only seen on TV or read in books. And when he sat her on the edge of his desk, she grinned up at him.

"We never make it to a bed."

He smiled. "I have six bedrooms and they're all too far away."

Callie looped her good arm around his shoulders and gripped his neck as she slid her body forward, closer to his. She wanted him so badly. She'd never felt this way before.

Never known she could lose control so quickly or fall so hard for one man.

But there was no lying to herself anymore. The way he looked at her, cared for her and cherished her made her realize she was totally in love with Noah Foster.

The thought terrified her. Could she seriously risk her heart, her emotional state, on another dream that might not come true?

But for right now, she wanted him and she would take what she could get.

"Condom?" she asked.

He rested his forehead against hers. "In my bedroom."

She bit her lip and said, "I'm clean, Noah. I've only been with two people other than you and I've always used protection. Plus, I have an IUD."

His lips pressed to hers. "I've always used protection, too, but this is your call."

Without using words, she gave him her answer when she locked her ankles around his back. As he drove into her, he slid one hand behind her back and another hand beneath her hair, bringing her mouth to his.

Their bodies moved so beautifully together, Callie knew this man was the one for her. Perfection didn't happen with anything in life, but this coming together was as near to perfect as she could get.

With her ankles secure behind him, she arched farther, pulling him deeper and moaning into his mouth as her climax edged closer.

Noah's body quickened as he tore his mouth free. He rested his forehead against hers and their gazes locked for a second. In his eyes she saw not the pain that usually hid there, but something deeper. Something she doubted he knew he felt.

For that one brief second, she saw love.

Callie's body quivered as she let her orgasm roll through

her. Noah's body tightened with hers and he squeezed his eyes shut.

He might not want to admit or even acknowledge what had just happened or what he'd been feeling, but Callie knew in her heart that Noah was falling for her. Now she just had to make sure whatever hell his past kept him in didn't break either of them.

Thirteen

Callie felt like a little girl again. As she pulled her rental car into the drive of her Kansas home, all her childhood memories flooded her.

Sure enough, a giant blue tarp covered the roof at the end of the house, right over where her bedroom used to be. Of course that was where the roof would choose to blow off. Fate wasn't being kind lately and this was just par for the course.

Mentally, Callie gave fate the one-fingered salute and laughed—it was either that or cry at the image of rainwater filling her bedroom, making even her past life a mess.

As she exited the car, her mother and father came out onto the porch and all that worry with the roof, with the accident and the lost movie part were pushed to the back of her mind. She'd missed them. Even though she hadn't grown up with the best of everything, her parents had always been there. Even when she'd felt fat and like an outcast, her parents had urged her to better herself, always seeing the brighter side of her.

Callie dropped her bag on the ground beside the steps and reached for her mother with her left arm. When her father moved in for a hug on her right side, Callie stepped back.

"Sorry, I'm still a little sore from the broken collarbone." She tried to smile, but both her parents zeroed in on her cheek. "It's not as bad as it looks. Just healing kind of ugly."

Her mother teared up. "Oh, baby. I'm so sorry you were hurt."

Callie waved it off because she did not come home for pity; she came to help and that was precisely what she'd concentrate on.

"I'm fine. Really. Noah has plans to fix this once it's ready for surgery." Not that he could make her perfect again, but she doubted her parents knew that. "So, what's the cost of the roof going to be?"

Her father sighed. "A buddy I used to work with said he could help replace it, but the materials are still costly. We're hoping to just get that side done for now, but another bad storm and the rest could go."

Bad storm? In Kansas? Yeah, the chances of that were well over 100 percent.

Callie nodded. "Then we'll find a way to get this done," she told them. "I have a little money left. Not much after my plane ticket, but I'll make some calls and see what I can do."

Her father wrapped his arm around her. "Honey, we didn't expect you to rush home. There's nothing you can do that I couldn't do."

"True, but I feel better knowing I'm here helping you guys."

Her father stared down at her and then smiled. "You always were such a fighter and so determined. I'm glad you're home, Callie."

Yeah, that was her. Determined and a fighter. Too bad she'd

been sitting around wallowing in self-pity over this accident. But now she'd at least feel as if she was helping.

And she wasn't even going to ask if her sister had helped. More than likely she didn't even know how bad off Mom and Dad were.

"Let's get inside and catch up," her mother said, reaching for the bag. "I want to hear all about Hollywood and the glamorous things you've seen."

Okay, that was a topic she could definitely discuss because the things she'd seen in that office were fodder for girlie gossip and she could use the laughs with her mother.

The trip alone would be good for her. She needed time away from L.A., from Noah. And spending the evening with her mother was the perfect way to help her clear her mind.

Callie had forgotten how much she missed home-cooked food. Her mother had made biscuits from scratch and gravy with eggs and sausage. There was nothing like a meal full of carbs and calories to have her slipping into a state of euphoria while snuggled on the old, comfy couch watching television—an old war movie, of course.

Her mother sat beside her, and her father had planted himself in his recliner. Yeah, this was the simple life she both did and did not miss. It was nice to come home and get back to the simplicity, but at the same time, Callie knew she did not want to grow up and live in a small town where the most exciting thing in the evening was watching the news or doing crossword puzzles.

The doorbell cut through the room, causing the three of them to turn their attention toward the front door.

"Wonder who that is," her father mumbled as he went to the door.

Callie remained in her seat as her father flicked the dead bolt and opened the door.

"Excuse me, sir."

Oh, God. She knew that voice.

"I'm looking for Callie Matthews."

She jumped to her feet, pulled her T-shirt down and stepped up beside her father. "Noah! What are you doing here?"

Dear Lord, she wanted the earth to open up and swallow her, but at the same time she was so shocked at his presence she didn't know how to act. Inside she was jumping up and down with joy that he'd taken the initiative to come all the way here, but she didn't want him to feel obligated to help her.

"Noah?" her father asked, opening the door wider. "This is the doctor you work for?"

Callie nodded, keeping her eyes fixed on Noah, who looked so…down-to-earth in his worn jeans, tennis shoes, plain gray T-shirt and a bag slung over his shoulder. If she didn't know he was a top Hollywood surgeon, she'd guess he lived right here in Kansas.

"Come in, come in," her mother chimed from behind her. "Don't leave the poor man on the porch."

Callie glanced around to the tidy, yet very well-worn living room. Nothing matched and all the furniture was from her childhood. But she refused to be embarrassed about her humble beginnings. This was the life she knew before meeting him, and while she might not want to be at this point anymore in her life, she wasn't ashamed, either.

"I thought I could help." Noah set his bag on the floor by the door. "Since you wouldn't let me come with you, I thought I'd surprise you."

Callie laughed. "I'm surprised, all right. I assume you looked up my emergency contact on my file at work to get the address?"

Noah smiled and that high-voltage smile was all Hollywood and should've been in front of cameras instead of hiding behind a surgical mask.

"I tend to get what I want," he told her, holding her gaze for a brief moment. Then he turned his attention to her father and held out his hand. "We haven't been properly introduced. I'm Noah Foster."

"Jim Matthews," her father said, pumping Noah's hand. "And this is my wife, Erma."

"Pleasure to meet you," Noah told her parents. "I don't want to intrude, so after I talk with Callie for a bit, I'll just find the closest hotel. But I meant it when I said I could help."

"You'll not stay at a hotel," her mother scolded. "We may be down a bedroom because of the roof, but we still have the bedroom in the basement. You're more than welcome to stay here. Are you hungry? We just had dinner and there's some left over."

Noah shook his head, smile still in place. "No, ma'am. I grabbed something when my plane landed."

As Noah charmed her parents, Callie stood frozen. Noah Foster was in her living room talking to her parents as if he belonged here.

Her father's voice broke into her thoughts. "Callie, honey, why don't you show Noah the bedroom he can use downstairs?"

"Of course." She moved around the group and headed down the narrow hallway. "Come on, Noah. We can talk down here."

She opened the basement door and flicked on the light to descend the steps. Once she hit the bottom, she turned on another light that illuminated the bedroom.

"It's pretty bare," she told him when he joined her. "We don't usually have company. My bedroom is out of commission, so I'll be taking the couch."

He jerked his head toward her. "Couch? I'll just go to a hotel, or I can take the couch."

Callie shook her head. "Don't be silly. You're here and this room is all yours...unless you want something fancier."

Noah dropped his bag on the worn carpet and stepped closer. "Callie, I think you know me well enough by now to realize that I'm not a snob. I didn't fly all this way to be pampered or treated like a socialite. I came to help you in any way I can. I know you are here to help your parents. I care for you and I'm here for you. Don't shut me out because you're ashamed of where you came from."

Callie looked away, unable to hold his gaze.. He tapped beneath her chin with his finger until she looked up at him.

"Now, instead of the couch or the hotel, why don't we just share this room?"

"Because I'm not shacking up with you while my parents are in the same house."

Noah laughed. "You think they are unaware that you're not a virgin?"

"I'm sure they know I'm not, but still."

He quirked a brow. "Still what? I want you in bed with me, Callie. We can...talk. That way tomorrow we will be ready to tackle whatever needs to be done."

On a groan, Callie reached up with one hand and toyed with his dark hair. "I can't believe you flew all this way to help me when you don't even know what you're helping with."

He shrugged. "I assume it has something to do with that big blue tarp on the house?"

"Yeah." She sighed. "The storm the other night took off a portion of the roof that was over my bedroom."

"So they need a new roof? What's the cost?"

"Dad has a friend who will help him replace the roof, but the materials are still so costly." Callie dropped her hand and picked up Noah's bag, placing it on the small dresser. "I plan to go to the bank tomorrow to see about a small loan to help them. I'm not sure if I can get one, but I know that my credit is better than theirs, and with my dad still unemployed—"

"You need to relax," he told her. "This will all work out. Why don't you go take a bath and read a book? I know you love to read."

Callie smiled. "I would love to go be lazy for a few minutes, but I'm not leaving you alone with my parents."

He moved toward her, wrapping his arms around her waist. "Why? Afraid they'll pull out the baby pictures or embarrassing school photos?"

"To be honest, yes." She slid her hands up his arms. "You wouldn't recognize the girl I used to be."

Noah's lips softly touched hers before he pulled her into a warm embrace. "I'm sure the same loving, caring, bright spirit would be looking back at me in those pictures."

Callie inhaled the sexy, masculine aroma that she'd become familiar with since being with Noah. "You may be surprised."

"I promise not to look at any pictures," he told her, easing back. "Now, go relax in the tub and grab a book. Your parents and I will be just fine."

Callie hesitated, but she was tired, and if she was going to actually sleep down here with Noah, she'd at least like to freshen up first.

Lord help her. Noah must really care for her to show up like this, but she feared reading too much into this surprise. No matter her feelings, she couldn't assume he felt the same.

Noah had set his plan in motion and now all he had to do was wait for Callie to come back downstairs. After a brief yet detailed talk with her father, Noah was ready to enjoy his time with Callie. Alone. Naked.

While he'd been upstairs he'd seen a few random snapshots of the family over the years. He had to assume the overweight girl in the photos was Callie because the tall blonde certainly wasn't and the only other kid in the pictures was a boy. No wonder she said he wouldn't recognize her. She was quite heavy, but she'd still been beautiful and that smile had been just as radiant.

He heard Callie upstairs in the kitchen speaking with her mother, but couldn't make out the words. After about an hour, she came down wearing an old, baggy T-shirt and a pair of boxer shorts. She was the sexiest sight he'd ever seen.

"I wasn't expecting a sleepover," she explained. "I knew I had old clothes here, so I didn't pack pajamas."

Noah remained seated on the edge of the bed. "Don't apologize for being you, Callie."

"These were some of my fat clothes," she told him, holding on to the newel post. "Since you're here, you might as well know more about me and why I fought so hard to get out of this town."

Noah waited because he could see her searching within herself to find the courage to speak up. He was surprised at how deeply he wanted to get to know her.

"I was quite overweight growing up," she began. "I wasn't popular, I didn't feel like I belonged, especially being a middle child, and I knew I would leave this town as soon as possible.

"I used to watch old movies while all the other teenagers were at parties or ball games. I would fantasize about being a star, wonder how awesome it would be to make a name for myself."

Callie sat on the bottom step. "My parents were adamant I get a college education. Through financial aid I got my bachelor's in Early Childhood Development, but I knew I didn't want to be a teacher. I wanted to be an actress. I also knew that with my appearance, Hollywood wouldn't look twice in my direction."

The picture she was painting made Noah's heart ache for

her. He was getting a glimpse inside this little girl's dream and the woman who had to face reality.

"The entire time I was in college I worked out and ate right," she went on. "By the end of my four years, I was a totally different person. And after I graduated, I continued to work for the college in the office until I could save enough money to move to L.A."

Her eyes drifted across the room to his. The entire time she'd been talking she'd focused her attention away from him, as if she was afraid to see his reaction.

"Why are you acting worried and ashamed of what I may think?" he finally asked. "Does it truly matter what I think, Callie? Or anyone else for that matter? All this story does is prove to me that you're a fighter."

She shrugged. "That may be, but fighting won't change anything now."

Noah came to his feet, crossed the room and took hold of her hands until she stood in front of him. "You may be right, but if you want a job in the movie industry, then you'll get one. You just have that personality. It's like mine. No matter the odds, we don't back down from what we want."

Callie studied his face. "What odds were ever stacked against you?"

He wasn't ready to open up about Malinda so he decided to share a different problem. "I can't live up to this hero-worship status that Blake has me at," he explained, baring a piece of his own fears. "No matter how I go about performing surgery on this little guy, he's still going to have scars, and the harsh truth is, kids will be kids and he will probably be stared at when he goes back to school. I can only minimize the damage."

But Noah would give anything to be able to make the child perfect again. And Callie.

Callie stroked his cheek. "You're doing all you can and he

sees that. His mother sees that. Any improvement will make him happy. You need to believe that."

Noah grabbed her hand, kissed her palm and tugged her against his chest. "What I believe is that I need you. Here. Now."

She wrapped her arms around his waist and her floral aroma from her soap or shampoo enveloped him. He'd warned himself not to get too involved with this woman, yet when he knew she was worried for her family and needed to take off halfway across the country, he hadn't thought twice about joining her.

The fact that he was in deeper than he'd ever imagined scared him, but he wouldn't let fear override the need, the passion and the special bond he shared with Callie.

Callie's mouth hovered over his. "Make love to me, Noah."

He didn't need any more of an invitation.

Callie woke to the sound of pounding and banging and glanced to the bedside clock.

Nearly ten? She rubbed her eyes and looked again. She'd never, ever slept this late. The opposite side of the bed was empty, and when she ran her hand over the sheet, she found it to be cold, which told her Noah had been up for some time.

After she changed into jeans and a more fitted T-shirt, she flipped her head upside down so she could pull her hair up without reaching so far.

No one was in the house so she assumed they were all outside with the commotion. But the sight she saw when she stepped off the porch was one she'd never forget for as long as she lived.

Not only was her father up on the roof with his friend who'd offered to help, her brother was there and…Noah? For real? The man had a steady hand with a scalpel and a syringe full of Botox. He didn't go around wielding hammers.

But he did look mighty fine with his sweat-stained gray T-shirt and muscles flexing as he pulled off the old shingles and tossed them into the yard.

He caught sight of her and smiled. It was the same smile he'd given her as they'd made love, the same smile she noticed he seemed to keep in reserve for just her...because there was heat and, dare she hope, promise behind that grin.

"Morning, sis," her brother greeted. "What happened to your face?"

Callie sighed. Apparently, her parents hadn't said anything to him. "Car accident."

Her brother nodded and went back to ripping off shingles and tossing them. Apparently, a twenty-two-year-old didn't think twice about her accident or the impact it had on her life.

"Did we wake you?" Noah called down from the roof.

Callie shielded her eyes from the bright morning sun. "I should've been up before now. Can I talk to you just a moment when you can take a break?"

Noah laid his hammer on the roof and climbed down the ladder.

"Don't keep him too long," her father shouted down. "We don't have all day. Your doc has to leave for the big city tomorrow."

Callie smiled at her father, grabbed Noah's hand and took him around to the side of the house.

"What in the world is going on?" she asked.

"If you'll let me get back up there, a new roof is going on."

Callie propped her hands on her hips and rolled her eyes. "Obviously, but where did the miracle funds and materials come from, and more important, why didn't I know you could play carpenter, too?"

Noah slid an arm around her waist. "Ready to see me in my tool belt?"

Trying to hold back a smile, and failing, she placed a hand

on his chest. "Simmer down, lover boy. I didn't know you knew how to replace a roof."

He shrugged. "I don't, but I can follow directions and they need the help."

Callie's heart clenched. As if she hadn't already been head over heels, the man's simple declaration reached in, grabbed her heart and took it all for himself.

"Where did that truck full of new shingles come from?" she asked, trying not to put her heart on her sleeve.

"I called the local home-renovation store last night, put everything on my credit card and asked for immediate delivery."

Flabbergasted, she gripped the arm that he still had locked around her waist. "How did you know what to order and when did you do all of this?"

"I talked with your father while you were in the shower and he told me what was needed."

Callie quirked a brow. "My father just let you, a stranger to him, come in and pay for all of this?"

Noah's eyes softened. "I may have mentioned we were closer than employee/employer and I had no real family of my own and I wanted to help."

Tears lodged in her throat as wave after wave of emotions slammed into her. Gratitude and love played the biggest role.

"I can't even…" Callie turned her head, swallowed back tears and met his gaze again. "I can't begin to tell you what this means to me, to my family."

Noah swiped her damp cheek and kissed her gently. "I didn't want this to happen. This relationship we have. I fought against it, but you do something to me, Callie, and when you need anything, I want to be the one who provides it for you."

Oh, God. Did he mean…

"I'm glad I could help," he went on. "But I do have to get back to L.A tomorrow. I plan to meet with Blake very early Monday morning so we can go over his pre-op plan."

Callie nodded, cupped Noah's face and slid her lips over his. "Get back to work."

As he walked away, Callie couldn't help but wonder where his feelings had landed him. Did he love her and was just afraid to say it?

She knew one thing for sure, though. When they got back to L.A. they had a major talk in their future.

When she'd first had her accident she thought for sure all was lost, but in some weird, twisted way, had this damage to her life opened her eyes wider to what was really important? Had this tragedy brought her and Noah together more strongly than would have been possible before?

For the first time in weeks, Callie had a new hope for her future, and that fighter in her was back full force.

"Callie."

She glanced up to see her mother coming around the side of the house.

"Hey, Mama."

Erma smiled. "Why don't you come inside with me and we can start preparing a nice, big lunch because our men will be ready to eat in a couple hours?"

Callie shook her head. "Oh, Noah's not my man, Mom."

Reaching out, her mother smoothed her hair off her forehead and nodded. "Oh, he is. You wouldn't have slept downstairs with him and he wouldn't be here helping if he weren't yours. Besides, I saw the way he looked at you. That man has much more than lust in his eyes, Callie Ray. He has love."

Callie stared at her mother, unable to speak. Love? Dare she hope?

"Now, come on in," Erma said, looping her arm through Callie's. "And tell me all about your hunky doctor."

Fourteen

Noah had taken off as much time as possible and Callie's
arm was healing nicely, though he still managed to find reasons to assist her and he was pleasantly surprised she let him.

But he'd gone back to work today with his regular hours
and the load was full, which meant he left the office later
than he wanted to. Marie was wonderful, but he missed seeing Callie's bright, chipper smile at the front desk.

Truth was, he missed Callie. Period. Their relationship
had changed the last time they'd been intimate. A change
he wasn't ready for and certainly couldn't define. But there
was another level of trust, of caring. And that was a place he
couldn't visit, couldn't think about and couldn't get wrapped
up in. This had to be just sex.

Tonight, though, he had a surprise for his houseguest.

When he finally pulled into his garage, he nearly sighed
with relief. He loved his job, truly he did, but after two and a

half weeks of staying home with Callie, he found he'd spoiled himself.

He was anxious to see Callie's reaction to her gift. Though the pool table might have been his best gift ever, he was still eager to see how she would react to something more…personal.

When he stepped into the house from the garage, he didn't spot her right away.

"Callie?" he called as he walked through the foyer and headed up the stairs.

He didn't find her in the living room or her bedroom. Curious, he went outside, and sure enough she was lounging by the pool wearing a loose halter top and matching shorts. The sun had kissed her skin, and her nose was a subtle shade of pink. He assumed she'd put her antiobiotic ointment on her scar, so she should be fine, but if she turned red, he'd have to get her inside.

"Getting some sun?" he asked, coming to sit on the foot of the chaise longue.

She'd been reading and she put the book across her stomach. "Trying to. I was starting to look pretty pale."

His eyes traveled down her legs and back up. "Looking pretty good to me."

With a soft smile, she eased forward. "How was your first full day back to work?"

"Everyone asked about you," he told her. "They all wanted to know when you were coming back. I told them I wasn't sure."

Callie sighed. "Why didn't you just tell them the truth? I'm not coming back."

"You might. The only person stopping you is you."

She motioned to her face. "No, this is stopping me."

"A scar?" he asked. "You would be so surprised at how many people will be glad to see you and that you're healing.

Please, at least try to come back for one day a week and we'll go from there."

Callie glanced out to the waterfall trickling into the pool. "I'm not sure, Noah. I don't even want to go out to the grocery store, much less work in an office full of beautiful people."

Noah took her hand, pulled her to her feet as he stood. Her book fell to the stone patio.

"Wait," she told him before he could pull her away. "I'm not saying that to anger you, really I'm not. I just don't want you to think me working in your office is a long-term thing or something I'll be comfortable doing. Even if I did come back for one day a week, I still wouldn't be staying there."

He admired her—how could he not? But he was so damn tired of her thinking her beauty was superficial.

"I want to take you somewhere."

She started to protest, but he held up his other hand. "I promise no one will see you, but even if they did, they'd think you were beautiful just like I do. You don't even need to change."

She slid into her flip-flops and followed him through the house and to the garage.

"But aren't you tired?" she asked as they got into the car.

"Not too tired for this."

Somehow they'd arrived at a deeper emotional relationship than just colleagues or friends. He didn't know where it would lead, but it was past time she learned a bit more about him, about why he was so adamant that she realize beauty was from within and there was so much more to life.

He hit the freeway and blended into the thick traffic, all the while hoping he didn't infringe on some unspoken code of plastic-surgeon ethics.

Callie wasn't going to believe his platitudes just because he kept preaching them. She needed a visual and he planned to give her just that.

"Where are we going?"

He threw her a sideways glance and a smile. "I knew you couldn't just sit back and enjoy the ride."

"Well, you're right. So, where are we going?" she repeated.

"We're going to a place that will remind us both of how something good can come out of a bad situation."

Callie sighed and leaned against the door. "I'd rather be home."

The word caused a tightening in his stomach that caught him off guard. By *home,* she meant his house, not her apartment.

He didn't comment, didn't really know what to say, but he was glad she was comfortable and felt as if she could call that her home.

But she'd still never been in the bedroom that he'd shared with Malinda.

He pulled into a familiar subdivision and found the place he was looking for.

"Here we are," he told her as he shut off the car. "Come on in."

Callie looked at the stone-and-brick home that was obviously fairly new and beyond gorgeous. Then she jerked her gaze back to his.

"Wait," she said, reaching for his arm. "Come in? Who lives here? You said I didn't have to see anybody."

"I own this house," he told her before he got out. "This is the one that has sat empty."

Callie opened her car door and followed Noah up the thin steps to the front door with a small stained-glass window adorning the top.

He unlocked the door and gestured her in first.

"Noah, this house is stunning." She moved through the open floor plan, trying to take in the giant room all at once. "I love how this is all so cozy, yet open."

There was a tall stone wall only a few feet wide that was
the center of the main floor and somewhat separated the living area and the dining room and kitchen. Water trickled
down the stone, making her instantly relax. The neutral colors weren't masculine or harsh.

She turned back to him. "This house is so different from
your other one."

He nodded. "That's because I had this one built to my
specifications after my first house on this property nearly
washed away."

"Washed away?"

He motioned for her to enter the living area on the other
side of the stone waterfall.

"This was the first house I purchased after I started my
practice." He pointed to a picture on the end table. "I lived
here about five years before flooding took it. I remember
thinking that I had nothing but an empty, muddy lot."

Callie stared at the photo, trying to even fathom a house
simply washing away.

"I didn't realize there was a flooding problem out here."

He came to stand beside her. "The drainage isn't great, so
if it rains too much, too fast, we have floods."

She turned to face him. "I know you're trying to teach me
a lesson here, but I'm not getting it."

His bright eyes bored into hers as he rested his hands on
her shoulders. "I had an ugly thing happen in my life and I
had a choice of whether I wanted to let it consume me and
feel sorry for myself or if I wanted to take control of my life
and turn this unwelcome disaster into something positive."

Callie glanced to the picture and back to him. "Are you
comparing me to this house?"

He turned her body to face the stone centerpiece again
and eased her closer.

"That stone was all I had left when my home was destroyed," he told her. "I used all I had to rebuild my life. But I not only rebuilt it, I made it better."

His words hit her straight in her heart. She wanted to rebuild her life, truly she didn't want to be that person who sat around and cried for herself, but she had no clue how to rebuild.

"If I thought I could take my life and make it better, Noah, I would."

He eased her back around to face him as he gathered her into his warm, caring embrace.

"It will be better." He kissed the top of her head and eased back. "The microdermabrasion went well and we can do another soon. I've talked with a few colleagues and we all seem to think that will make a tremendous difference over the next few months until we can further explore surgery options…if we even have to go that route."

Callie tensed. "Really? You think surgery may not be needed?"

"The swelling is gone in the tissues beneath the laceration and the wound isn't as deep as we'd first thought. The healing is looking remarkable."

Tears burned Callie's eyes. "I want to hope, Noah. I don't even mind surgery. I just want to be me again, but I'm afraid."

Noah tilted her face up to his and captured her lips. Softly, lovingly he coaxed her lips apart and showed her how he felt.

"I'm not afraid, Callie," he whispered. "I'm excited for your future. This is going to work and we are going to battle it together."

She lifted her lids and looked him in the eye. "You're always such a confident doctor."

"I won't lie to you," he told her, still framing her face with his hands. "It will take time. But I believe we can really make this minimal. The wound itself isn't as bad as I'd first thought."

Callie nodded and smiled as a tear slid down her cheek. Noah swiped it away with the pad of his thumb.

"I trust you."

She slid her arms around his neck and toyed with the ends of his hair. His hands spanned her waist as he pulled her fully against him.

"I want you," he murmured. "In my house, with the sunset coming in that window. I want you, Callie."

Shivers slid over and through her body at his honest, raw words. "Then have me."

Noah captured her mouth again and walked her back to the living area, where he eased her down onto the cushy chaise. Noah pulled his polo off, flinging it to the side.

Callie stared up at him in all his golden, muscular glory. As he finished undressing, her heart picked up just a bit faster and her body quivered with anticipation. Each time they were intimate, each time they took their relationship to another level, she wanted to know where this was headed. But right now she only wanted one thing. Noah.

With ease, she took off her halter top, exposing her bare breasts to his appraisal, and tossed the unwanted garment to the floor with his clothes. Noah held his hand out and she took it as he helped her to her feet. After sliding out of her shorts and flicking them off to the side with her toe, she moved to mold her body against his. She never got used to how amazing that initial contact felt. Never got over that first feeling of how right it was being with Noah.

Callie threaded her hands through his hair and pulled his mouth down to hers. Noah's strong hands covered her back, his fingertips gripping her. Her breasts flattened against his chest, her hips bumped his. And it was still not enough. Not close enough, not emotional enough. She wanted more.

"Noah," she whispered against his lips. "I need you to know—"

"Shh." He nipped at her lips again. "Later."

Callie wasn't sure if she should tell him she was in love with him or if fate had just saved her from making a fool of herself. But when his hands came down to grip her rear and lift her off the floor, she didn't care.

Noah eased a knee onto the chaise and he slowly laid her down, never breaking their contact. He didn't want to break this bond, didn't want to ruin this perfection. If he could crawl inside this moment in time and live here forever, he would. Right now, at this second, he was happier than he'd been in a long, long time. He owed Callie so much for showing him how to live again. This little trip to the old house wasn't just an eye-opening experience for her; reality had also slapped him in the face. He'd come to the conclusion that no matter what he'd lost, he could still make that decision to move forward or let the past consume him.

And right now he was making the decision to make love to Callie in his living room.

"I want you. Here. Now."

And that was all Noah needed to hear before he slid into her, without the barrier, without anything between them, just like the past two times.

But this time was different. He'd laid his heart out there for her to see and that vulnerability could get him hurt again. But he couldn't stop this emotional spiral he was on when it came to Callie and her sweet, sometimes innocent ways.

His body moved over hers, but he was careful to hold himself up on his elbows. He didn't want to crush her, but seeing her look up at him, with all the trust and love in her eyes...

Love?

Yes. When he looked at her, he saw love. And if he were honest with himself, he'd seen it in Kansas, too.

Noah kissed her, unable to look into those expressive eyes

for another moment, because what if she could read his? What would she see?

His tongue mimicked their bodies as he increased the pace and her ankles locked together behind his back.

Before he could think too much about what he'd seen, her body tightened around him, causing him to lose control and give in to the pleasure that only Callie could provide.

As his body settled half on hers, half off, he tried to shut out the fact that every time he closed his eyes and thought of a woman in his life, Malinda wasn't even in the mental picture. Callie filled his mind. She was filling his bed, his house, and he feared she'd fill his heart if he let her.

Fifteen

Callie ran her fingertips up Noah's back, but she had a feeling he'd fallen asleep. His breathing had slowed and his body had relaxed against hers some time ago. And even though her belly growled, she didn't care. The sun had set and they were lying in the dark, completely naked, and she finally saw a sliver of hope in this darkness she'd been living in. Could they have a future together? He seemed to not even worry about her looks, the scarring.

Admitting to herself that she was in love with Noah didn't frighten her or make her wonder about their future. He might not admit he had feelings for her, but she knew in her heart that he felt something beyond friendship or he wouldn't be so giving, so patient and caring with her. He'd totally put all her needs first for the past several weeks, even choosing to take care of her over going into the office.

The man who was known for dating a different woman nearly every night and during the day making his clients perfectly beautiful was now devoting all of his time to her. Callie knew he had deep feelings for her, but she also figured that past, and that photo in his room, kept him from moving forward. She only hoped he'd open up to her, let her further into this world of his she so desperately wanted to be part of.

But she wouldn't be that clingy woman, wouldn't be the one who put her heart out there with the possibility it could get stomped into unrecognizable pieces.

"Thelma," Noah murmured in his sleep. "Don't. Please."

Callie sat up, shifting Noah's body a little more off her and onto the oversize chaise. She looked down to his tortured face, his brows drawn together, his jaw clenched.

"No," he cried. "Don't worry."

Callie shook his shoulder. "Noah. Noah, wake up."

He muttered something else she couldn't quite make out and the intense look on his face tore at Callie's heart.

Shaking him harder with one hand, Callie tapped at his cheek with her other. "Noah. You're dreaming."

His lids fluttered open, his eyes darted to hers, held there, and then he closed his eyes again.

"Damn," he whispered.

Callie wasn't sure how to proceed on this shaky ground, but she wasn't backing down.

"Care to tell me what just happened?"

Noah shook his head, running a hand down his face. "Just dreaming about Thelma."

Callie nodded. "I got that. Who is she to you?"

His gaze met hers. "She's the lady at the assisted-living facility I visit."

Noah got up, walked naked through the room and rummaged around to find his pants, using only the pale glow of the distant city lights cutting through the windows.

Callie eased back on the chaise, hoping he'd elaborate

more, needing to understand why this woman who wasn't even a blood relative was in his nightmares.

"So, how does she have such a hold on you?"

Noah pulled up his dress pants, leaving them unbuttoned, and rested his hands on his hips. Callie watched as he struggled with himself. He lowered his head between his shoulders and rubbed the back of his neck.

"It's a long story, Callie, and one I'm just not comfortable getting into."

Hurt filled her, tugging at her heart she'd so freely given to him.

"I'd like to think we are here for each other, Noah. I want to help, but you won't let me in."

He turned to face her, that look of torment still all over his face. "If I could let anybody in, Callie, it would be you."

Callie came to her feet. That declaration was bittersweet. She knew he wanted to open up, but something in his past simply wouldn't let him, and he was hanging on to whatever it was that was not healthy for him or this relationship they were starting.

"Can I come with you?" she asked, placing her hands on his shoulders.

"To see Thelma?"

Callie nodded. "She's obviously very important, Noah. I'd like to be there for you."

"That's not a good idea," he told her.

"Why not?"

His hands slid around her waist. "Because she's confused. She won't know who you are."

"If she's got Alzheimer's, then she won't even remember I was there." Callie squeezed his shoulders and slid her hands up to frame his face. "I want to be there for you, Noah. You've done so much for me. Please, let me do this for you."

His lips softly slid over hers before he leaned back and smiled. "Can you go tomorrow?"

"I'd love to."

Noah's nerves kept him up most of the night.

Since it was Friday, he had taken half a day off after doing some minor in-office surgeries. Now he and Callie were traveling to the assisted-living facility. He only prayed Thelma didn't start rambling about the wedding.

"I should warn you that Thelma may flirt with me."

Callie laughed. "Then she's sharp if she's flirting with a hot guy."

Noah reached over, gripped her hand. "Just don't get too jealous."

Once they arrived at the facility, Noah led the way to Thelma's room. As usual, the door was closed and locked. Noah knocked and waited.

Soon the door eased open and he reached over, gripping Callie's hand. She squeezed back, silently supporting him.

When Thelma saw him, then looked beyond and saw Callie, her whole face lit up.

"Malinda! My Malinda!"

Thelma reached out, pulling Callie beyond Noah and into a full embrace.

A feeling of dread overwhelmed him. He hadn't even thought that Thelma would mistake Callie for Malinda. Yes, the two had the same dark red hair, but he'd spent so much time with Callie lately he'd forgotten the similarities.

This was a bad, bad idea and nothing good would come from these next few minutes. He prayed to God again that Thelma didn't mention the wedding.

"Come in, come in." Thelma eased back. "I'm so glad you two are here."

Noah followed the ladies into the sweltering room. Once

again, he turned the heat down...way down. Because with his nerves, he was already sweating.

"I can't believe my Malinda is finally here," she gushed. "You're such a beautiful sight, my dear."

Callie glanced to Noah as if silently asking him to intervene.

"Thelma," he began. "This—"

"Is such a surprise." Thelma reached out for Callie's hand and squeezed. "I've been waiting for you to come." Thelma's eyes narrowed on Callie's face. "Darling, what happened?"

Callie's eyes sought Noah's again and he stepped forward. "She was in an accident, but she's fine. Just a cut."

Yeah, more lying to keep an old woman happy and worry-free.

"Oh, are you all right?" Thelma asked, searching Callie's face.

Callie offered a smile. "I'm fine. How are you doing?"

Thelma laughed. "I'm old. That's about it. I've been waiting for you to come. I can't wait to hear how the wedding is coming. Noah has told me very little. I want to hear more details from the bride-to-be."

"Oh, we're not engaged," Callie said. "We—"

Noah rested a hand on Callie's shoulder in the silent gesture for her to stop talking.

"Thelma loves to talk weddings, but I'd rather discuss how you're feeling today," he said, turning to Thelma. He had to change the subject.

Thelma waved a hand in the air. "I'm fine. I already told you. I'd much rather discuss the wedding of my beautiful granddaughter." Thelma pushed out of her recliner. "Hold on just a moment. I have something for you."

Callie turned to Noah and whispered, "Who does she think I am?"

Swallowing, Noah replied, "Her granddaughter."

"Were you engaged to this person?" she whispered be-tween gritted teeth.

Noah could only nod. He was a coward. He was a jerk. Was he going to regret bringing her here, finally opening up to her in his own way?

Perhaps subconsciously he'd brought her here as a way to tell her. Callie deserved to know, and there was no easy way to break the news about his past.

"Here we are," Thelma stated as she came back with a photo. "I've had this here for a long time and I love looking at it, but I think maybe you could put it in your new home together."

Noah barely caught a glimpse of the photo as it passed from Thelma's hand to Callie's. And with that simple ex-change, he knew any hope he'd had of not sharing the full truth with Callie was gone.

Callie looked down at the photo and nearly choked on in-stant tears that filled her. Noah had not only been engaged, but he'd been engaged to a woman who looked very similar to her.

Noah's arm was wrapped around the shoulders of this Ma-linda person and they were both smiling into the camera with their heads tilted toward each other. Callie wanted to tear it up, throw the confetti pieces into the air and run like hell out this door.

But because Thelma was looking at her with such hope and admiration, Callie smiled. "Thank you. This is wonderful."

"I'm giving this to you and hopefully you can give me an-other photo of the two of you, but this time I'd like one from the wedding."

Callie nodded. "Um, I'm not feeling so well."

Noah tried to put an arm over her shoulder, but Callie stepped aside. She didn't want him to touch her.

"Oh, darling," Thelma said with a frown. "Are you all right?"

"I'm just tired, I think. Would you mind if we discussed the wedding another time?"

"Of course." Thelma looked to Noah. "Get her home and take care of her."

"I intend to," Noah told her. "It was good to see you."

"Please, come back soon," Thelma said with a smile. "I miss seeing you both together. It just warms my heart."

Callie accepted the hug from the frail woman and managed not to burst into tears at the innocent endearment.

When they got back in the car, Callie didn't even know where to begin. The hurt was so deep, so all-consuming, she feared she'd break into a million pieces before she learned the full extent of his lies.

"You were engaged to her granddaughter?" Callie asked.

Noah sighed. He didn't start the car, didn't even turn to look at her...which should've told her the amount of guilt he carried.

"Yes."

She closed her eyes. "And you didn't think to mention that to me? Or the fact we have similar features?"

"Honestly—"

Callie laughed and glared at him. "Yes, Noah. Let's try for honesty."

Now he did turn to face her and Callie had to steel herself against the pain in his eyes.

"I didn't think you needed to know," he told her. "I didn't want my past to play a part in my present."

"Or your future?" Callie mocked. "Or did you not see me in your future, Noah? Did you think when I was healed I would just go back to my apartment, forget how good we were together and you could go on your way, too? Because I for one had envisioned more for us than just a few intimate moments. You met my family. You acted as if what we had was so much more. Was it all a lie? A way to pass the time until you got over your fiancée?"

"I never acted with you, Callie. And I never told you this was long-term."

That knife he'd stabbed her with slowly turned. "You never told me any different," she whispered through tears. "And your actions sure as hell told me what you were afraid to admit was in your heart. Apparently, you're still a coward."

But she would not cry. She'd hold on to this last bit of dignity she had.

"What happened to Malinda?" Callie asked, almost not wanting to hear the answer.

Noah's eyes hardened as he held her gaze. "She died of a drug overdose a year ago."

Of all the things she'd imagined him saying, that hadn't even made it on her list.

"She wanted to be an actress," he went on. "She wanted that big life she'd always dreamed of, and before I knew what was happening, she was hooked on drugs. Painkillers. I tried to get her help. She even went to rehab twice, but checked herself out both times."

Callie listened, knowing this confession was costing him, but right now they were both bleeding out for the other to see.

"I should've seen the signs earlier, should have done more. But in the end, I failed her."

Callie's heart broke for the man, the doctor who thought he should save everybody. But her heart also broke for herself at the realization of what he was *not* saying.

"So, was I the charity replacement?" she asked. "You couldn't save her so you thought you'd save me?"

Noah's gaze darted away, then came back. "I didn't see it that way, but probably in the beginning, yes. I didn't want to fail someone I cared about."

"Care about?" she cried. "You didn't care about me, Noah.

You cared about redeeming your flawed image of yourself. You cared about that damn ego and didn't once think about how this would hurt me, humiliate me. Did you think we'd just be intimate and I wouldn't fall for you? That I wouldn't start thinking long-term thoughts about us?"

She'd come this far, might as well rip the rest of the Band-Aid off.

"Did you think I wouldn't love you?" she whispered, no longer caring that tears had slid down her cheeks. She held his gaze, wanting him to see how he'd damaged her even more.

"I wish you'd never offered to help." Callie swiped at her unscarred cheek. "I would've much rather been on my own than know I was a fill-in for someone else."

He started to reach for her, but she shrank back against the door. "Don't even think of touching me."

Noah dropped his hand and nodded. "I didn't mean to hurt you, Callie. You've come to mean more to me than I wanted."

"If that were true, you wouldn't have used me as a replacement or tried to hide your past." She refused to listen to another lie or another excuse. "Take me home. And by *home,* I mean my apartment. You can bring my other things later and leave them on the stoop. I don't want to see you again, Noah."

"Callie, you can't mean that."

Her eyes slitted. "Oh, I mean it. And consider this my notice for the office. Effective immediately."

Sixteen

Noah moved through Callie's room. Her bed was rumpled where she'd slept, his shirts she'd worn were folded and lying on the trunk at the end of the bed. Her sandals were strewn around the room, and the second he stepped in here, he was enveloped by her sweet, floral aroma.

Noah gripped the edge of the dresser and closed his eyes. He'd majorly botched up everything he ever had with Callie. By protecting his heart, he'd completely crushed hers. What kind of man did that to an already vulnerable woman?

He glanced into the adjoining bath, his eyes instantly falling onto the tub where he'd helped her with her hair that first day. It was only six weeks ago, but so much had happened since then.

Aside from her quick healing, she'd opened up emotionally, she'd fought to not let her accident ruin her, he'd met her family and instantly felt a connection to them when they welcomed him into their home.

But the main thing that had happened was his heart had been taken over. Noah had sworn when Malinda died that no one would ever fill that void...and no one could. But he realized now that Callie found a new place in his heart to reside and she wasn't replacing Malinda at all. What he found with Callie was new, fresh and so real he didn't know why he hadn't seen it until that hurt, anger and despair flooded her eyes along with tears.

It was those tears that nearly killed him. He was the cause of those tears. He did this to her and he would have to be the one to fix it.

As a surgeon, he knew all too well that fixing things wasn't always simple or easy. But it was worth the time and effort.

And Callie Matthews was worth everything he had in him to give. He wasn't letting her go that easily.

Noah pulled his cell from his pocket and called his Realtor. This was just the first step in getting her back. For good.

Callie went right to work on her computer trying to find another job. At this point, she knew she couldn't be picky.

Noah had dropped her off that morning and here it was near dinnertime and he still hadn't brought her stuff. If he thought she'd be coming back, he was a total moron.

She'd cried in the shower until the water ran cold, then pulled on a blousy, sheer yellow top over a white tank and denim shorts. At least she could look cheerful even if she wasn't feeling it.

Callie had been on her laptop the past few hours because searching for work was productive and at least keeping her mind focused on something other than the fact that another fantasy, another dream had just been taken away by fate.

Callie refused to believe coming to L.A. was a mistake. She did love the town, and after going home, she knew for sure that being in the city suited her.

There were several tutoring jobs that she could start immediately and that would be good money until she could figure out what else she needed to do. She wasn't giving up on acting. Even though Noah had lied to her, Callie firmly believed what Max had told her about Anthony looking at her twice and she knew a makeup artist could work with her face.

She refused to let fate take control of her life. She'd let herself grow dependent on Noah by living with him, falling in love with him and focusing more on him than on her questionable career. And now she had to refocus on her original goal—acting.

But since she'd quit her job, she needed immediate funds that would keep a roof over her head, not to mention pay for the expense of the microdermabrasion. Perhaps she could take out a loan.

Someone knocked on her door and Callie froze. If that was Noah, he could just drop the stuff off and be on his way.

"I need to talk to you, Callie."

She closed her eyes and sighed. Might as well get this over with because her neighbors didn't deserve the bellowing.

Crossing the room, she jerked open the door. "What?"

His eyes raked over her body and she refused to allow the tingle to creep through and spear her heart anymore.

"Where's my stuff?" she asked, noting he held nothing and there was no luggage on the stoop.

"I want to take you somewhere," he told her.

She folded her arms over her chest, as if that would keep more hurt from seeping in. "You've got to be kidding me!"

"Just one hour, Callie. That's all I'm asking for, and at the end of that hour if you don't want to see me again, I'll walk away."

It was so tempting to slam the door in his face, but she couldn't do it. As much as she hated liars and deceivers, she wanted to know what he had in store for her.

"One hour," she told him. "No more."

His shoulders relaxed as he blew out a breath. "Thank you."

She grabbed her keys and her purse by the door and locked it behind her. By the time she was seated in his car, she wondered if she'd made a mistake. Now that she was in his presence, would she crumble and believe every word he said? She didn't want to be that woman who believed liars and found excuses to take them back.

"You look beautiful," he told her as he pulled out of her apartment complex.

"Don't. I don't need the pretty words."

"That time we went to celebrate your role, and you were standing there holding those yellow tickets, I thought of you as the color yellow," he went on as if she hadn't said anything. "I know it sounds stupid, but you're always so vibrant, so alive, and that smile you had on your face as you held that insane amount of tickets, I just thought if Callie were any color, it would be yellow."

She glanced down to her yellow top and closed her eyes. "What do you want from me, Noah?"

"A fresh start?"

Callie glanced across the spacious SUV and stared at him. "What?"

"I called my real-estate agent and accepted that last offer on my house. I'm moving back into my old house."

Her heart clenched as she fisted her hands in her lap to keep from reaching for him. "That's great."

"And I have a proposition for you, but you can take time to think about it."

Intrigued, and angry at her crumbling defenses, she asked, "What is it?"

He spared her a glance as he came to a red light. "I want

you to still model for me. I've made a decision on the new office I'm opening."

Reaching across, he took her hand and squeezed it. "I'm going to make it a surgical center for victims who have been scarred or burned."

Callie jerked her hand back, bringing it to her mouth in an attempt to hide her quivering chin. "Noah…"

He pulled ahead when the light changed and then turned into the pizza place where they'd "celebrated" weeks ago. Once the car was in Park, he faced her, taking both of her hands now.

"You've taught me so much, Callie. You can't know how you've opened my eyes to what's important." His eyes filled with unshed tears. "After meeting your family, learning even more about you and knowing how hard you've fought for what you want, I know that you are the woman I want in my life. I want your drive, your determination…your love."

Callie shook her head. "You don't mean that. You just see me as another woman who left you."

"You and Malinda may have similar appearances, but that's where the similarities stop. You have my heart, Callie, in a way I don't think she ever did. Yes, I'll always have a piece of me that loves her, but what I feel for you is so big, so beyond anything I've ever known. I can't give you up and I won't let you give up on us. Not when we're so close to perfection."

Callie glanced to the restaurant, saw all the kids inside playing games, getting tickets and running around with smiles.

She wanted to believe every word he said. She firmly believed that if he didn't truly love her, he wouldn't have acted so fast after she left. He wouldn't have sold his house, wouldn't have shown up at her door ready to fight for what they had.

She glanced back to him. "What are we doing here, Noah?"

His smile widened. "Celebrating."

"What are we celebrating?"

He reached behind her seat and pulled out the ugly monkey she'd won weeks ago. "It's not a ring, but I'm hoping you'll celebrate spending our lives together. Forever."

Callie looked at the pathetic stuffed animal and smiled through tears. "God, that was so romantic and silly at the same time." She laughed.

"What do you say we go in and win more ridiculous stuff to put in our house?"

She threw her arms around his neck and held tight. "I can't think of anything else I'd rather do."

Noah eased back, framed her face and kissed her lips. "I love you, Callie Matthews."

She saw the truth in his watery eyes. "I love you, too."

* * * * *

Madison entered the dining room

wearing a slim black skirt that came right above her knees, conservative heels and a simple white blouse. But Sheikh Zain knew better. That professional, prim and proper persona only served to conceal the daring beneath her cool exterior. He'd wager his kingdom that she had on a pair of brightly colored panties.

A richly detailed fantasy assaulted him, one that involved sitting beside her and running his hand up the inside of her thigh and—

"Where would you like me?"

He thought of several answers, none of them appropriate. "Are you referring to the seating arrangements, or do you have something else in mind?"

THE RETURN
OF THE SHEIKH

BY
KRISTI GOLD

Published in Great Britain 2013
by Mills & Boon, an imprint of Harlequin (UK) Limited,
Eton House, 18-24 Paradise Road, Richmond, Surrey TW9 1SR

© Kristi Goldberg 2013

ISBN: 978 0 263 90623 3
ebook ISBN: 978 1 472 01183 1

51-0613

Harlequin (UK) policy is to use papers that are natural, renewable and recyclable products and made from wood grown in sustainable forests. The logging and manufacturing processes conform to the legal environmental regulations of the country of origin.

Printed and bound in Spain
by Blackprint CPI, Barcelona

Kristi Gold has a fondness for beaches, baseball and bridal reality shows. She firmly believes that love has remarkable, healing powers and feels very fortunate to be able to weave stories of love and commitment. As a bestselling author, a National Readers' Choice Award winner and a Romance Writers of America three-time RITA® Award finalist, Kristi has learned that although accolades are wonderful, the most cherished rewards come from networking with readers. She can be reached through her website at www.kristigold.com or through Facebook.

To all the readers who continue to embrace the
romance genre through your belief that love
has the power to conquer all.
You are appreciated more than you know.

One

The moment Madison Foster exited the black stretch limo, a security detail converged upon her, signaling the extreme importance of her prospective client. The light mist turned to rain as she crossed the parking lot. One massive guard was on her right, a somewhat smaller man at her left, while two other imposing goons dressed in dark suits led the way toward the Los Angeles high-rise. A few feet from the service entrance, she heard a series of shouts and camera shutters, but she didn't dare look back. Making that fatal error could land her on the cover of some seedy tabloid with a headline that read The Playboy Prince's Latest Paramour. And a disheveled presumed paramour at that. She could already feel the effects of the humidity on her unruly hair as curls began to form at her nape beneath the low ponytail. So much for the sleek, professional look. So much for the farce that it never rained in sunny Southern California.

When the guards opened the heavy metal door and ushered her inside, Madison stepped carefully onto the damp tile surface as if walking on black ice. Couldn't they see she was wearing three-inch heels? Clearly they didn't care, she realized as they navigated the mazelike hallway at a rapid clip. Fortunately they guided her into a carpeted corridor before she took a tumble and wounded her pride, or worse. They soon reached a secluded elevator at the end of the passage where one man keyed in a code on the pad next to the door.

Like a well-oiled human machine, they moved inside the car. Madison felt as if she were surrounded by a contingent of stoic man-crows. They kept their eyes trained straight ahead, not one affording her even a casual glance, much less a kind word, on the trip to the top floor.

The elevator came to a smooth stop a few moments later where the doors slid open to a gentleman dressed in a gray silk suit, his sparse scalp and wire-rimmed glasses giving him a somewhat scholarly appearance. As soon as Madison exited the car, he offered his hand and a hesitant smile. "Welcome, Miss Foster. I'm Mr. Deeb, His Highness's personal assistant."

Madison wasn't pleased with the "Miss" reference, but for the sake of decorum, she shook his hand and returned his smile without issuing a protest. "It's nice to meet you, Mr. Deeb."

"And I you." He then stepped aside and made a sweeping gesture to his right. "Come with me, please."

With the guards bringing up the rear like good little soldiers, they traveled down the penthouse's black marble vestibule beneath soaring, two-story ceilings. As a diplomat's daughter and political consultant, she'd been exposed to her share of opulence, but she wasn't so jaded she couldn't appreciate good taste. A bank of tall windows revealing the Hollywood Hills drew her attention before her focus fell on the polished steel staircase winding upward to the second story. The clean lines and contemporary furnishings were straight out of a designer's dream, but not at all what she'd expected. She'd envisioned jewels and gold and statues befitting of royalty, not a bachelor pad. An extremely wealthy bachelor's pad nonetheless. Only the best would do for Sheikh Zain ibn Aahil Jamar Mehdi, the crown prince of Bajul, who'd recently and unexpectedly become the imminent king, the reason why she'd been summoned—to restore the tarnished reputation of the man with many names. In less than a month.

After they passed beneath the staircase and took an immediate right, Madison regarded Mr. Deeb, who also seemed bent on sprinting to the finish line. "I'm surprised the prince was willing to meet with me this late in the evening."

Deeb tugged at his tie but failed to look at her. "Prince Rafiq determined the time."

Rafiq Mehdi, Prince Zain's brother, had been the one who'd hired her, so that made sense. Yet she found Deeb's odd demeanor somewhat disturbing. "His Highness is expecting me, isn't he?"

They stopped before double mahogany doors at the end of the hall where Deeb turned to face her. "When Prince Rafiq called to say you were coming, I assumed he had spoken to his brother about the matter, but I am not certain."

If Rafiq hadn't told his brother about the plan, Madison could be tossed out before her damp clothes had time to dry. "Then you're not sure if he even knows I'm here, much less why I'm here?"

Blatantly ignoring Madison's question, Deeb pointed to a small alcove containing two peacock-patterned club chairs. "If you wish to be seated, I will come for you when the emir is prepared to see you."

Provided the man actually decided to see her.

After the assistant executed an about-face and disappeared through the doors, Madison claimed a chair, smoothed a palm over her navy pencil skirt and prepared to wait. She surveyed the guards lined up along the walls with two positioned on either side of the entry. Heavily armed guards. Not surprising. When a soon-to-be-king was involved, enemies were sure to follow. She'd initially been considered a possible threat, apparent when they rifled through her leather purse looking for concealed weapons before she'd entered the limo. She highly doubted she could do much damage with a tube of lipstick and a nail file.

Madison suddenly detected the sound of a raised voice, though she couldn't make out what that voice might be saying. Even if she could, she probably wouldn't understand most of the Arabic words. Yet there was no mistaking someone was angry, and she'd bet her last bottle of merlot she knew the identity of that someone.

Zain Mehdi reportedly didn't know the meaning of restraint, evidenced by his questionable activities. The notorious sheikh had left his country some seven years ago and taken up residence in the States. He'd often disappeared for months at a time, only to surface with some starlet or supermodel on his arm, earning him the title "Phantom Prince of Arabia."

That behavior hadn't necessarily shocked Madison. Many years ago, she'd met him at a dinner party she'd attended with her parents in Milan. Back then, he'd been an incurable sixteen-year-old flirt. Not that he'd flirted with her, or that he would even remember her at all, a gawky preteen with no confidence. A girl who'd been content to blend into the background, very much like her mother.

She didn't do the blending-in thing these days. She intended to be front and center, and if she managed to succeed at this assignment, that would prove to be another huge feather in her professional cap.

When the doors opened wide, Madison came to her feet, adjusted her white linen jacket and held her breath in hopes that she wouldn't be dismissed. "Well?" she asked when Deeb didn't immediately speak.

"The emir will see you now," he said, his tone somewhat wary. "But he is not happy about it."

As long as she had the opportunity to win him over, Madison didn't give a horse's patoot about the prince's current mood. "Fair enough."

Deeb opened the door and followed her inside the well-appointed office. But she didn't have the time—or the inclination—to study the room further. The six-foot-plus man leaning back against the massive desk, arms folded across his chest, his intense gaze contrasting with his casual stance, now captured her complete attention. Publicity photos—or her distant memories—definitely didn't do Zain Mehdi justice.

With his perfectly symmetrical features, golden skin and deep brown eyes framed by ridiculously long black lashes, he could easily be pegged as a Hollywood star preparing to play the role of a Middle Eastern monarch. Yet he'd forgone the royal robes for a white tailored shirt rolled up at the sleeves and a pair of dark slacks. He also wore an expression that said he viewed her as an intruder.

Madison tamped down her nerves, shored up her

frame and faked a calm facade. "Good evening, Your Highness. I'm Madison Foster."

He studied her offered hand but ignored the gesture. "I know who you are. You are the daughter of Anson Foster, a member of the diplomatic corps and a longtime acquaintance of my father's."

At least he remembered her father, even if he probably didn't remember her. "My sincerest condolences on your loss, Your Highness. I'm sure the king's sudden passing came as quite a shock."

He shifted his weight slightly, a sure sign of discomfort. "Not as shocking as learning of his death two weeks after the fact."

"The emir was traveling when his father passed," Deeb added from behind Madison.

The sheikh sent his assistant a quelling look. "That will be all, Deeb. Ms. Foster and I will continue this conversation in private."

Madison glanced over her shoulder to see Deeb nodding before he said, "As you wish, Emir."

As soon as the right-hand man left the room, the sheikh strolled around the desk, dropped down into the leather chair and gestured toward the opposing chair. "Be seated."

Say please, Madison wanted to toss out. Instead, she slid into the chair, set her bag at her feet and made a mental note to work on his manners. "Now that we've established you know who I am, do you understand why I'm here?"

He leaned back and streaked a palm over his shadowed jaw. "You are here at my brother's request, not mine. According to Rafiq, you are one of the best political consultants in this country. *If* your reputation holds true."

If his reputation held true, she had her work cut out for her. "I've worked alongside political strategists in successfully assisting high-profile figures with public perception."

"And why do you believe I would need your assistance with that?"

Okay, she'd draw him a picture, but it wouldn't be pretty. "For starters, you haven't been back to Bajul in years. Second, I know there's concern that you won't be welcomed with open arms when you do return to assume your position as king. And last, there is the issue with the women."

He had the gall to give her a devil-may-care grin. "You cannot believe everything you hear, Ms. Foster."

"True, but many people believe what they read. Therefore, it's imperative we convey that you're focused on being an effective leader like your father."

His smile disappeared out of sight. "Then I am to assume you wish to mold me into the image of my father."

She found the comment to be extremely telling. "No. I want to help you build a more favorable image of yourself."

"And how do you propose to do that?"

Very carefully. "By reintroducing you to your people through a series of public appearances and social events."

He inclined his head and studied her straight-on. "You intend to invite the entire country to a cocktail party?"

She could now add *sarcastic* along with *sexy* to his list of attributes. "The social events would be private. I'll include only those in your close circle of friends and your family, as well as members of the governing council. Possibly a few foreign dignitaries and politicians and perhaps some investors."

He grabbed a pen from the desktop and began to turn it over and over. "Go on."

At least he seemed mildly interested. "As far as the public appearances are concerned, I have a lot of experience with speech writing," she said. "I'd be happy to assist you with that."

He frowned. "I have a graduate degree in economics from Oxford and I am fluent in five languages, Ms. Foster. What makes you think I cannot compose my own speeches in an articulate manner?"

Nothing like stepping on his royal pride. "I'm sure you're quite capable, Your Highness, which is why I said I'd *assist* you. What you say and how you say it will be extremely important in winning over the masses."

He tossed the pen aside and released a gruff sigh. "I have no reason to engage in political maneuvering. In the event you haven't heard, my position is already secure. I was chosen to be king, and my word is the law. I *am* the law."

"True, but when people are happy with their leader, that makes for a more peaceful country. And we have less than a month before your official coronation to change your country's opinion of you. During that time, we'll cover all the details, from the way you speak and act to the way you dress."

He sent her a sly, overtly sensual smile. "Will you be dressing me?"

The sudden images flitting around Madison's mind would be deemed less than appropriate. They even leaned a little toward being downright dirty. "I'm sure your staff can assist you with that."

"It's unfortunate that's not among your duties," he said. "I would be more inclined to agree to your plan."

As far as she was concerned, he could put that cha-

risma card right back into the deck. "Look, I realize
you're used to charming women into doing your bidding, but that tact doesn't work with me."

He gave her a skeptical look. "If I decide to accept
your offer, would you be willing to stay on after the
coronation?"

She hadn't expected that question. "Possibly, if you
could afford to keep me on staff. My services aren't
cheap."

He released a sharp, cynical laugh. "Look around,
Ms. Foster. Does it appear I'm destitute?"

Not even close. "We can discuss the possibility later.
Right now, we need to concentrate on the current issue
at hand, if you're willing to work with me."

He studied the ceiling for a moment before bringing
his gaze back to hers. "The answer is no, I am not willing to work with you. I am quite capable of handling
my own affairs."

She wasn't ready to give up without pointing out
the most major concern. "Speaking of affairs, I'm also
skilled when it comes to dealing with scandals, in case
you have any of those little sex skeletons hiding in a
closet."

His expression turned steely as he stood. "My apologies for wasting your time, but I believe we are finished now."

Apparently she'd hit a serious nerve, and yes, they
were definitely finished.

Madison came to her feet, withdrew a business card
from her bag and placed it on the desk. "Should you
change your mind, here's my number. I'll let you break
the news to your brother."

"Believe me, I have much to stay to my brother," he
said. "That is first on my agenda when I return to Bajul."

She'd like to have front row seats to that. She'd also like to think he might reconsider. Unfortunately, neither fell into the realm of possibility at the moment. "I wish you all the best for a smooth transition, Your Highness. Again, let me know if you decide you need my services."

After slipping the bag's strap back on her shoulder, Madison covered her disappointment with a determined walk to the door. But before she made a hasty exit, the sheikh called her back. "Yes?" she said as she faced him, trying hard not to seem too hopeful.

He'd rounded the desk and now stood only a few feet away. "You've changed quite a bit since we first met all those years ago."

The fact he did recall the dinner party, and he hadn't bothered to mention it before now, thoroughly shocked her. "I'm surprised you remember me at all."

"Very difficult to forget such an innocent face, ocean-blue eyes and those remarkable blond curls."

Here came the annoying blush, right on cue. "I wore glasses and braces and my hair was completely out of control." Which had all been remedied with laser eye surgery, orthodontists and flat irons.

He took a few steps toward her. "You wore a pink dress, and you were very shy. You barely glanced my way."

Oh, but she had. Several times. When he hadn't been looking. "I've since gotten over the shyness."

"I noticed that immediately. I've also noticed you've grown into a very beautiful woman."

Madison barely noticed anything but his dark, pensive eyes when he walked right up to her, leaving little space between them. "Now that we've established my transformation," she said, "I need to get to the airport so I don't miss my flight to D.C." She needed to get away from him before his extreme magnetism commandeered her common sense.

"I do have a private jet," he said, his gaze unwavering. "You are welcome to use it whenever it is available. If you plan to travel to the region in the future, feel free to contact me and I'll arrange to have you transported to Bajul. I would enjoy having you as my guest. I could show you things you've never seen before. Give you an experience you will not easily forget."

She'd enjoy being his guest, perhaps too much. "You mean an evening trek by camel, or perhaps on the back of an elephant, across the desert? You'll feed me pomegranates while we're entertained by dancing girls?"

He looked more amused than offended by her cynicism. "I prefer all-terrain vehicles to camels and pachyderms, I detest pomegranates, but dancing would be an option. Between us, of course."

She didn't dare dance with him, much less take a midnight ride with him in any form or fashion. "As fascinating as that sounds, and as much as I appreciate the offer, I won't be traveling outside the U.S. now that I won't be working with you. But thank you for the invitation, and have a safe trip home."

This time when Madison hurried away, the future king closed the doors behind her, a strong reminder that another important career door had closed.

However, she refused to give in to defeat. Not quite yet. As soon as the sheikh returned home, he might decide he needed her after all.

He greatly needed an escape.

The absolute loss of freedom weighed heavily on Zain as the armored car navigated the steep drive leading to the palace. So did the less-than-friendly reception. A multitude of citizens lined the drive, held back by the guards charged with his protection. Some had their fists raised in anger, others simply scowled. Because of the bulletproof glass, he couldn't quite make out what they were shouting, yet he doubted they were singing his praises.

Rafiq had suggested he return at night, yet he'd refused. He might be seriously flawed, but had never been a coward. Whatever he had to endure to fulfill his obligation, he would do so with his head held high and without help.

He thought back to Madison Foster's visit two days ago, as well as her intimation that he might be considered a stranger in a familiar land. He'd come close to accepting her offer, but not for those reasons. She'd simply intrigued him. She'd also forced him to realize how long it had been since he'd kept company with a woman. Yet she would have proven to be too great a temptation, and he could not afford even a hint of a scandal. If they only knew the real scandal that had existed within the palace gates, a secret that had plagued him for seven years, and the primary reason why he'd left.

As the car came to a stop, Zain quickly exited, but he couldn't ignore the shouts of *"Kha'en!"* He could not counter the claims he'd been a traitor without revealing truths he had no intention of disclosing.

Two sentries opened the heavy doors wide, allowing him to evade the crowd's condemnation for the time being. Yet the hallowed halls of the palace were as cold as the stone that comprised them. At one time he'd been happy to call this place home—a refuge steeped in lavish riches and ancient history. Not anymore. But he did welcome the site of the petite woman standing at the end of the lengthy corridor—Elena Battelli, the Italian au pair hired by his father for his sons, despite serious disapproval from the elders. Elena had been his nursemaid, his teacher, his confidante and eventually his surrogate mother following his own mother's untimely death. She'd been the only person who understood his ways, including his wanderlust.

As soon as Zain reached her, Elena opened her arms and smiled. "Welcome back, *caro mio.*" She spoke to him in English, as she always had with the Mehdi boys, their "code" when they'd wanted to avoid prying ears.

He drew her into an embrace before stepping back and studying her face. "You are still as elegant as a gazelle, Elena."

She patted her neatly coiffed silver hair. "I am an old gazelle, and you are still the charming *giovinetto* I have always adored." A melancholy look suddenly crossed her face. "Now that your father has sadly left us, and you are to be king, I shall address you as such, Your Majesty."

"Do not even think of it," he said. "You are family and always will be, regardless of my station."

She reached up and patted his cheek. "Yes, that is true. But you are still the king."

"Not officially for another few weeks." That reminded him of his most pressing mission. "Where is Rafiq?"

She shrugged. "In your father's study, *caro.* He has spent most of his time there since…" Her gaze wandered away, but not before Zain glimpsed tears in her eyes.

He leaned and kissed her cheek. "We shall have a long talk soon."

She pulled a tissue from her pocket and dabbed at her eyes. "We shall. You must tell me everything you have been doing while you were away."

He didn't dare tell her everything. He might be an

adult now, but she could still make him feel like the errant schoolboy. "I look forward to our visit."

Ignoring his bodyguards and Deeb, Zain sprinted up the stone steps to his father's second-floor sanctuary and opened the door without bothering to knock. The moment he stepped inside, he thought back to how badly he'd hated this place, plagued by memories of facing his father's ire over crossing lines that he'd been warned not to cross. King Aadil Mehdi had ruled with an iron hand and little heart. And now he was gone.

Zain experienced both guilt and regret that their last words had been spoken in anger. That he hadn't been able to forgive his father for his transgressions. Yet he could not worry about that now. He had more pressing matters that hung over his head like a guillotine.

His gaze came to rest on his brother predictably seated in the king's favorite chair located near the shelves housing several rare collections. The changes in Rafiq were subtle in some ways, obvious in others. He wore the kaffiyeh, which Zain refused to wear, at least for the time being. He also sported a neatly trimmed goatee, much the same as their father's. In fact, Rafiq could be a younger version of the king in every way—both physically and philosophically.

Rafiq glanced up from the newspaper he'd been reading and leveled a nonchalant look on Zain. "I see you have arrived in one piece."

He didn't appreciate his brother's indifference or that he looked entirely too comfortable in the surroundings. "And I see you've taken up residence in the king's official office. Do you plan to stay here indefinitely?"

Rafiq folded the paper in precise creases and tossed it onto the nearby desk. "The question is, brother, do you intend to stay indefinitely, or will this be only a brief visit?"

Zain's anger began to boil below the surface as he attempted to cling to his calm. "Unfortunately for you, as the rightful heir to the throne, I'll be here permanently. I've been preparing for this role for years."

"By bedding women on several continents?"

His composure began to diminish. "Do not pretend to know me, Rafiq."

"I would never presume that, Zain. You have been away for seven years and I only know what I have read about you."

At one time, he and Rafiq had been thick as thieves. Sadly, that had ended when his brother had sided with their father over their differences, leaving brotherly ties in tatters. "I left because our father placed me in an intolerable position."

"He only wanted you to adhere to the rules."

Outdated rules that made no sense in modern times, yet that had only been a small part of his decision. If Rafiq knew the whole story, he might not be so quick to revere their patriarch. "He wanted me to be exactly like him—unwilling to move this country into the millennium because of archaic ideals."

Rafiq rose slowly to his feet and walked to the window to peer outside. "The people are gathered at the gates, along with members of the press. One group demands an explanation as to why their new king deserted them years ago, the other waits for the wayward prince to explain his questionable behavior. Quite the dilemma."

"I will answer those questions in due time." Those that needed answering.

Rafiq turned and frowned. "Are you certain you can handle the pressure?"

If he didn't leave soon, he could possibly throw a punch, producing more fodder for the gossip mill. "Your lack of faith wounds me, brother. Have you ever known a time when I failed to win people over?"

"We are not children any longer, Zain," he said. "You can no longer brandish a smile and a few choice words and expect to prove you are worthy to be king."

He clenched his fists now dangling at his sides. "Yet our father chose me to be king, Rafiq, whether you agree or not."

"Our father believed that designating you as his successor would ensure you would eventually return. And in regard to your current status, you have yet to be officially crowned."

Zain wondered if his brother might be hoping he would abdicate before that time. Never in a million years would he do that. Especially now. "That should be enough time for a seamless transition." If only he felt as confident as he'd sounded.

"There will be serious challenges," Rafiq said. "Our father worked hard to maintain our status as a neutral, autonomous country. Our borders are secure and we have avoided political unrest."

"And we will continue to do so under my reign."

"Only if you can convince your subjects that you have their best interests at heart. Any semblance of unrest will only invite those who would take advantage of the division. That is why I urge you to consider working with Madison Foster."

He should have known it would come back to her. He'd had enough trouble keeping his thoughts away from Madison without the reminder. "Why do you believe her input would be so invaluable?"

"She has been extremely successful in her endeavors," Rafiq said. "She has taken men with political aspirations and serious deficits and restored their honor."

He was growing weary of the insults. "So now my honor is in question?"

"To some degree, yes," Rafiq said as he reclaimed the chair. "What harm would there be in utilizing her talents? Quite frankly, I cannot believe you would refuse the opportunity to spend time with an attractive woman."

As always, most people assumed he had no other concerns than his next conquest. Of course, he couldn't deny that he'd considered the advantages of having Madison involved in his daily routine. Yet that might be dangerous in the long term, unless he wanted to prove everyone right that he could not resist temptation. "Again, I do not wish or need her help."

Rafiq blew out a frustrated sigh. "If you choose the wrong path, Zain, there will be no turning back. If you fail to win over your subjects, you will weaken our country, leaving it open to radical factions bent on taking advantage of our weakness. Is your pride worth possible ruin?"

Zain thought back to the angry voices, the accusations he'd endured moments ago. He hated to concede to his brother's demands, but he did recognize Rafiq's valid concerns. He would find a way to maintain his pride and still accept Madison's assistance—as long as she understood that he would remain completely in charge. Considering the woman's obvious tenacity, that could be a challenge. But then he had always welcomed a good challenge.

If bringing Madison Foster temporarily into the fold kept Rafiq off his back, he saw no harm in giving it a try. "All right. I will give it some thought, but should I decide to accept her assistance, I will only do so if it's understood that I'll dismiss her if she is more hindrance than help."

"Actually, the agreement is already in place, and the terms of her contract state she cannot be dismissed on the grounds of anything other than gross misconduct. That would be my determination, not yours."

Contract? "When did she sign this document?"

"After she contacted me to report on your initial meeting. She is bound to stay until after your coronation, but she insisted on a clause that allows her the option to leave prior to that time should she find the situation intolerable."

His own brother had tied him to a liaison against his will. However, that did not mean he had to be cooperative. "Since you leave me no choice, my first official edict states you will be in charge of the arrangements to bring her here."

Rafiq sent him a victorious smile. "You may consider it done."

As fatigue began to set in, Zain loosened his tie and released the shirt collar's top button. "We'll continue our conversation over dinner." He suddenly remembered he hadn't seen any sign of his youngest brother. "Will Adan be joining us?"

"Adan is currently in the United Kingdom for flight training. He will be returning before the coronation."

Zain couldn't mask his disappointment. "I've been looking forward to seeing him and catching up on his accomplishments. But it's probably best we have no distractions when you bring me up to speed on the council's most recent endeavors."

Rafiq cleared his throat and looked away. "We will not exactly be dining alone."

"Another member of the council?"

"No. A woman."

Zain suspected he might know what this was all about. "Is this someone special in your life?"

"She has no bearing on my life."

He internally cringed. "If this is the beginning of the queen candidate procession, then I—"

"She is not in the market to be your wife."

He did not appreciate his brother's vagueness. "Then who is she, Rafiq?"

"Madison Foster."

Two

"Do you always insist on having your way?"

Startled, Madison shot a glance to her right to discover Zain Mehdi standing in the doorway, one shoulder leaned against the frame, his expression unforgiving on that patently gorgeous face. "Do you always barge in without knocking?" she asked around the surprise attack.

"The door was ajar."

She turned from the bureau, bumped the drawer closed with her butt and tightened the sash on the blue satin robe. "Really? I could have sworn I closed it before I took my shower. But I suppose it could have magically opened on its own, since Arabia is well-known for its magic."

He ignored her sarcasm and walked into the room without an invitation, hands firmly planted in the pockets of his black slacks. With those deadly dark eyes and remarkable physique, the Arabian king could pass for an exotic male model—a model who sorely lacked good comportment.

He strolled to the open armoire to inspect the row of suits, skirts and slacks that Madison had hung only moments before. "As I predicted. Conventional clothing."

His audacity was second only to his arrogance. "It's known as business attire."

"Attire that conceals your true nature," he said as he slid his fingertips down the side of one beige silk skirt.

She couldn't quite explain why she shivered over the gesture, or the sudden, unexpected image of experiencing his touch firsthand. "What do you know about my true nature?"

"I know your kind." He turned and presented a seriously sexy half smile. "Beneath the conservative clothes you wear colorful lingerie."

Lucky guess. "That's a rather huge assumption."

"Am I wrong?"

She refused to confirm or deny his conjecture. "Don't you have some royal duty to perform? Maybe you should have all the locks checked on all the palace doors."

He took a few slow steps toward her. "I'll leave as soon as you tell me why you're here when I made it quite I clear I do not need your help."

She was starting to ask herself the same question. "Your brother's convinced that you need my help."

"Rafiq isn't in charge of my life, nor is he in charge of the country. I am, and I can handle the transition on my own without any assistance."

Oh, but he did need her help, even if he wouldn't admit it. Yet. "From what I witnessed during your arrival, it appears the people aren't welcoming you with open arms."

His expression turned to stone. "As I told you before, Ms. Foster, they have no choice. I am this country's rightful leader and they will have to learn to accept it."

"But wouldn't it be more favorable if you had the blessing of your country's people?"

"And how do you propose to assist me in winning their approval? Do you plan to throw me a parade along with the international cocktail party?"

She mentally added *cynical* to the *sexy* thing. "I suppose we could try that, but a parade isn't successful unless someone shows up. I have several ideas and I hope that you'll at least give me the opportunity to explore those options with you."

"Ah, yes. The social gatherings where you'll be parading me in front of dignitaries."

"We nixed the parade, remember?"

Amusement called out from his dark eyes. "I am still not convinced that you will make an impact on my acceptance."

Time to bring out the legal implications. "As I'm sure your brother told you, the contract states I'll be here until the coronation, whether you choose to work with me or not. Of course, I can't force you to cooperate, but it would be worth your while to at least make the effort."

He seemed to mull that over for a minute while Madison held her breath. "All right. Since you are protected by a legal document, and I've been stripped of my power to dismiss you, I will cooperate on a trial basis. But that cooperation hinges on your ability to meet my terms."

She should have known he'd have an ulterior motive behind his sudden change of heart. "And what would those be?"

His smile returned, slow as a desert sunrise. "I'll let you know in the upcoming days."

Something told Madison his terms could be somewhat suspect. Still, she was more than curious, as well as determined to win him over. "Fine. We can begin tomorrow morning."

"We can begin tonight after dinner," he said, followed by a long visual journey from her neck to her bare feet. "I personally have no objection to your current attire, but something a little less distracting might be more appropriate."

She'd basically forgotten what she was wearing— or wasn't wearing for that matter. "Since I've spent a good deal of time attending state dinners, I know how to dress properly."

He rested one hand on the ornately carved footboard. "This isn't a diplomatic affair, Ms. Foster, only a casual meal."

She felt somewhat uncomfortable having him so close to the bed. "Will both your brothers be dining with us?"

"Only Rafiq. Adan's currently away on a mission."

She was disappointed she wouldn't meet the youngest Mehdi son. "Diplomatic assignment?"

"Military. He's testing a new aircraft."

"That's right. I'd read somewhere he's a pilot."

"Adan's affinity for danger is second only to his appreciation of beautiful women," he said. "He will be greatly disappointed if he does not have the opportunity to meet you."

Maybe it was best if baby brother stayed away for as long as possible. Two womanizers under one roof could be too much to handle. "Will he be back for the coronation?"

Zain pushed away from the bed, allowing Madison to breathe a little easier. "As far as I know."

She hugged her arms closer to her middle. "I'll meet him then."

"If you are still here," he said.

He wasn't going to get rid of her that easily. But she did plan to dismiss him for the time being. "Since it's getting late, I should probably get dressed now."

"Yes, I suppose you should," he said, a hint of fake disappointment in his tone. "I wouldn't mind seeing you in the black dress you have hanging behind your business suits."

He'd been more observant than she realized. "I'll decide what I'm wearing after you're gone."

"You should definitely consider the red lingerie."

Madison didn't understand his fascination with her underwear, or how he'd correctly guessed her fondness for red silk, until she followed his gaze to some focal point at her hip. When she looked down, she saw her bra strap hanging from the closed drawer like a crimson snake in the grass. She quickly stuffed it back inside before pointing toward the door. "Out. Now."

"Dinner is at five-thirty sharp. Do not be late," he said as he walked out the door and closed it behind him.

The man's overbearing behavior equaled his fortune, but he had a thing or two to learn about Madison's determination. She didn't appreciate his observations, even if he had been on target when it came to her clothing. Still, no sexy, bossy sheikh—even if he happened to be a king and her current employer—would dictate her choice in panties. In fact, Zain Mehdi would have nothing whatsoever to do with her panties. And the next time she had him alone, she planned to set him straight about what she expected from him. Namely respect.

The sudden knock indicated she could have an immediate opportunity to do that very thing. On the heels of her frustration, she strode across the room, flung open the door and greeted the offending party with, "More commentary on my underwear?"

When she saw the demure lady with silver hair and topaz eyes standing in the hallway, Madison realized she'd made a colossal mistake. Yet she couldn't seem to speak around her mortification.

"I'm Elena Battelli," the woman said as she extended her hand. "And I am not concerned with your undergarments."

She accepted the gesture and attempted a self-conscious smile. "I'm Madison Foster, and I'm so sorry. I thought you were—"

"Prince Zain, of course."

Realizing her state of undress had only compounded the erroneous assumptions, Madison hugged her arms tightly around her middle. "I know how this must look to you, but His Highness accidentally walked in on me."

The woman sent her a knowing look. "Prince Zain never does anything accidentally."

She wouldn't dispute that point. "Regardless, nothing inappropriate occurred."

"Of course," Elena said, her tone hinting at disbelief. "Do you find your accommodations satisfactory?"

Who wouldn't? The massive marble jetted tub alone was worth any grief Zain Mehdi could hand her. "Very much so, thank you."

She took a slight step back. "Good. Dinner's at six."

"Prince Zain told me five-thirty."

"I am afraid you've been misled," Elena said. "Dinner is always served at 6:00 p.m. That has been the designated time since I've been an employee."

Madison saw the woman as the perfect resource for information on the future king. "How long ago has that been?"

She lifted her chin with pride. "Thirty-four years. I arrived before Prince Zain's birth to assume my role as his *bambinaia,* or in English, his—"

"Nanny," Madison interjected, then added, "I speak Italian. I studied abroad in Florence my sophomore year in college."

Elena's expression brightened. "Excellent. I am from Scandicci."

"I visited there a few times. It's a beautiful place. Do you go back often?"

All the joy seemed to drain from Elena's face. "Not as often as I would like. My life is here with the royal family."

A royal family with adult sons who no longer needed a nanny. A keeper, maybe, but not a nursemaid. "How do you spend your days now that the princes are grown?"

"I am basically in charge of running the household while waiting for my opportunity to raise another generation of Mehdi children."

Madison didn't quite see Zain as father material, an opinion she'd keep to herself. "I'm sure you gained invaluable experience with Prince Zain."

"Yes, yet clearly I failed to impress upon him the merits of self-control when it comes to the opposite sex. Otherwise, he would not be interested in your undergarments."

They shared in a brief laugh before Madison revealed her opinion on the subject. "I assure you, Prince Zain will not be commenting on my personal effects if I have any say in the matter."

Elena presented a sly smile. "A word of advice. Prince Zain is a good man, yet he is still a man. What he lacks in restraint, he makes up in charm. Stand firm with him."

With that, she walked away, leaving Madison to ponder exactly what the future king might have up his sleeve when he'd told her the incorrect time for dinner. She highly doubted he'd forgotten standard palace protocol in spite of his lengthy absence. Perhaps he was simply trying to throw her off balance in order to be rid of her.

Too bad. She would definitely stand her ground with him from this point forward. And as far as dinner went, she'd ignore his edict and show up when she darn well pleased.

She was fifteen minutes late, yet Zain wasn't at all surprised. Madison Foster possessed an extreme need to be in control. Granted, he had the means to break down her defenses, and he was tempted to try. Nothing overt. Nothing more than a subtle and slight seduction designed to make her uncomfortable enough to bow out and return to the States where she belonged.

However, she could very well turn the tables by responding to his advances. Possible, but not likely, he decided when she entered the dining room wearing a slim black skirt that came right above her knees, conservative heels and a simple white blouse. A blouse sheer enough to reveal the outline of an equally white bra, most likely in an effort to prove her point. But he knew better. That professional, prim and proper persona only served to conceal the daring beneath her cool exterior. He'd wager the kingdom she had on a pair of brightly colored panties. Red panties.

A richly detailed fantasy assaulted him, one that involved sitting beside her and running his hand up the inside of her thigh and—

"Where would you like me?"

He thought of several answers, none of them appropriate. He chose the least suggestive one. "Are you referring to the seating arrangements, or do you have something else in mind?"

She approached the table and sent him a false smile. "Let me rephrase for the sake of clarity. Where do you want me to be seated?"

Zain gestured to the right of where he was positioned at the head of the lengthy table. "Here." He waited for her to slide into the chair before he launched into his reprimand. "You're late."

She made an exaggerated show of checking her watch. "Actually, I'm fifteen minutes early, since it seems, according to Elena, dinner is and always has been at six."

He'd been betrayed by his former governess and longtime confidante. "Now that I will soon assume my rightful role as king, dinner will be at five-thirty."

She folded her hands atop the table, her gaze unwavering. "I suppose having your first royal edict involving dinnertime is preferable to, oh, say, changing the entire governmental structure."

"That will be my second royal edict."

She looked sincerely confused. "Are you serious?"

He smiled. "Not entirely, but I do plan to implement some much-needed change."

"Change cannot occur until you are officially crowned, brother."

Zain pulled his gaze from Madison to see Rafiq claiming his place at the opposite end of the table. "As disappointing as it might be to you, *brother,* that will happen in a matter of weeks. In the meantime, I plan to outline those changes to the council later this week."

Rafiq lifted his napkin and placed it in his lap. "I have no designs on your position, Zain. But I do have a vested interest in the direction in which you plan to take my country."

He fisted his hands on the heels of his anger. "*Our* country, Rafiq. A country that I plan to lead into the twenty-first century."

Madison cleared her throat, garnering their attention. "What's for dinner?"

"Cheeseburgers in your honor."

When he winked, she surprisingly smiled. "I was truly looking forward to sampling some Middle Eastern fare," she said.

"We're having the chef's special kebabs," Rafiq said. "You will have to excuse my brother's somewhat questionable sense of humor, Ms. Foster."

After shooting Rafiq an acid look, Zain regarded Madison again. "I believe you'll agree that a questionable sense of humor is better than no sense of humor at all."

She shifted slightly in her seat. "I enjoyed meeting Elena. Will she be joining us?"

"Not tonight," Rafiq said as one of the staff circled the table and poured water. "She has some work to attend to, but she sends her apologies."

"She works much too hard," Zain added. "I plan to put an end to that and soon."

Rafiq leaned back in his chair. "I am afraid her work will not let up until after the coronation and the wedding."

"Wedding?" Madison asked, the shock in her tone matching Zain's.

"And who is the lucky bride?" Zain asked, though he suspected he knew the answer.

"Rima Acar, of course," Rafiq said. "We will be married the week before the coronation."

Zain wasn't at all surprised by the news his brother was going through with the long-standing marriage contract. He was surprised—and angry—over the timing.

"Is this wedding a means to detract from my assuming my rightful place as king?"

"Of course not," Rafiq said. "This wedding has been in the planning stages for years. Almost twelve if you consider when Father and the sultan came to an agreement."

"Ah, yes, the age-old tradition of bride bartering." Zain turned his attention back to Madison, who seemed intent on pushing fruit around on her plate. "We are destined to choose a wife from the highest bidder. Someone who will give us many heirs, if not passion."

"As you, too, had your bride chosen for you," Rafiq added.

Madison's blue eyes went wide. "You're engaged?"

"Not any longer," Rafiq said. "Zain's intended grew tired of waiting for his return and married another."

He had thanked his good fortune for that many times over. "Her decision was for the best. I refuse to wed a woman whom I've never met, let alone kissed." He leaned forward and leveled his gaze on his brother. "Have you kissed Rima? Have you determined there will be enough passion to sustain your marriage? Or do you even care?"

He could see the fury brewing in Rafiq's eyes. "That is none of your concern. Passion is not important. Continuing the royal lineage is."

"Procreating would be rather difficult if you cannot bear to touch your wife, brother. Or perhaps you will be satisfied with bedding her only enough times to make a child, as it was with our own parents."

"Do not believe everything you hear, Zain. Our parents had a satisfactory marriage."

Rafiq—always their father's defender. "Satisfactory?

Are you also going to dispute that the king played a part in our mother's—"

Rafiq slammed his palm on the table, rattling the dinnerware. "That is enough."

Zain tossed his napkin aside and ignored the woman setting the entrée before him. "I agree. I have had enough of this conversation." He came to his feet and regarded Madison. "Ms. Foster, my apologies for disrupting your meal."

Without even a passing glance at his brother, Zain left the room and took the stairs two at a time. He had no doubt that after the display of distasteful family dynamics, he would have no need to seduce Madison Foster. She would most likely be taking the first plane back to America.

With a plate balanced in her left hand, Madison knocked with her right and waited to gain entry, affording the king the courtesy he hadn't shown her earlier that afternoon.

"Enter" sounded from behind the heavy wooden door, the gruff, masculine voice full of obvious frustration.

Madison strode into the room, head held high, determined not to show even a speck of nervousness, though admittedly she was a little shaky. More than a little shaky when she met his stern gaze and realized he didn't look at all thrilled to see her.

She set the plate on the desk and sat across from him without waiting for an invitation. "Elena sent you some pasta and the message that if you don't eat, you'll be too weak to rule."

He didn't bother to stand. Instead, he stared at her for a few moments before he pushed the offering away. "You may tell Elena I will eat when I'm hungry."

She'd been stuck in the middle of one argument too many today. "You can tell her. Right now, we need to discuss your upcoming plans."

He leaned back in the brown leather chair and tented his hands together. "I assumed you would be well on your way home by now."

"You assumed wrong. I'm determined to see this through."

"Even after we aired our family grievances at dinner?"

He had a lot to learn about her tenacity. "I've heard worse, and now I'd like to ask you a few questions."

"Proceed."

She would, with caution. "Do you have a strategy for overcoming your playboy reputation?"

"My reputation has been overblown, Ms. Foster."

"Perception is everything when it comes to politics, Your Highness. And believe what you will, you're in a political battle to restore your people's faith in you. You've been gone almost ten years—"

"Seven years."

"If you were a dog, that's equivalent to almost fifty years." And that had to be the most inane thing she'd said in ages, if ever. "Not that you're a dog. I'm only saying that seven years is a long time in your situation."

He hinted at a smile. "Do you own a dog?"

"Yes, I do. I mean, I did." Clearly he was trying to divert her attention from more pressing concerns by using her former pooch. "Could we please get back on point?"

"Yes," he said. "The point is I am quite capable of overcoming my exaggerated reputation by demonstrating there is more to my character."

He was so sure of himself. So sexy in his confidence, and she hated herself for noticing. Again. "Can you really do that? Can you persuade the world you're a serious leader when you can't even convince your own brother you're committed to your duty?"

His dark eyes relayed an intense anger. "What did Rafiq tell you when I left the table?"

Not as much as she would've liked. "He only said that he's worried you'll take off again if the pressure becomes too great."

"Despite what my brother believes, I am not a coward."

"I don't think anyone is calling you a coward." She sighed. "Look, I realize you have a lot of pride, but you might want to give up a little and realize you need someone in your corner. Someone who can serve as a sounding board during this transition."

"And you are that someone?"

"I can be. And if you'll allow me to use my connections, I can help establish some allies, and every country needs those. Even small, autonomous countries. I also still contend that you could use some help with your public addresses." When he started to speak, she held up her hand to silence him. "I know, you have a degree and you're intelligent and articulate, but I don't see the harm in brainstorming content."

"I still see no reason why I would need to consult anyone on what I wish to say or how I wish to say it."

She was making no headway whatsoever. "What about the press? Wouldn't you like to have someone serve as a buffer to make certain they convey the proper message?"

"I have Deeb for that."

Deeb had about as much personality as a paperweight. "But if you show the world that you have a woman at your side, and one you're not engaging in a torrid affair, that would send a clear message you're not the player everyone believes you to be."

He studied the ceiling and remained silent for a few seconds before he brought his attention back to her. "Should we proceed, I have to be assured that whatever you might hear or might learn within these sacred walls will not be repeated."

Madison sensed impending victory, and possibly some serious secrets. "You can trust me to maintain confidentiality at all costs. But I have to know if there's a scandal that could surface in the foreseeable future."

"Not if I can prevent it. And at the moment, that is all you need to know."

Madison could only hope that he might eventually trust her enough to confide in her. Otherwise, she couldn't prepare for the worst-case scenario. "Fine. Then you agree to accept my help?"

He streaked a palm over his shaded jaw. "For the time being, and as I stated earlier, you must agree to my terms."

Clearly he needed to maintain control. She'd give him a little leeway for now. "Fine. Perhaps now would be a good time to spell out your terms."

"If I disagree with your advice, you'll refrain from arguing," he said.

That could prove to be a challenge. "Okay."

"You will consult me before you plan your soirées, and you will let me approve the guest lists."

Considering his lack of popularity, it could prove to be a short list. "Fair enough."

"And you will adhere to my schedule, which means I will decide the time and the place for our meetings."

"I assumed your study would be the most appropriate meeting place."

"It might be necessary to find a more private venue."

Now she had her own terms to present. "As long as it's not your bedroom."

He smiled. "You're not the least bit curious about my royal quarters?"

Oh, yes, she was. "No. Anything else?"

He feigned disappointment. "I'll let you know as soon as I've determined what I expect beyond what we've already discussed."

Talk about being vague. But she'd accept vague as long as she could continue as planned. "We'll go over your upcoming schedule in the morning, Your Highness, and plan accordingly."

"Call me Zain."

Her mouth momentarily dropped open over the request. "That's a bit too informal, don't you think?"

"When we're alone, I want you to call me by my given name. Otherwise, our agreement terminates immediately."

What kind of game was he playing? Only time would tell, and Madison hoped she didn't find herself on the losing end.

She came to her feet and tugged at the hem of her blouse. "Whatever floats your boat, *Zain*. Now if you'll excuse me, I'm going to my room to relax."

"You are excused. For now."

Madison had only made it a few steps toward the door before Zain uttered the single word. "Black."

She turned and frowned. "Excuse me?"

"You're wearing black lingerie."

Did the man have X-ray vision? "Why are you so fascinated with my underwear?"

His grin arrived slowly. "Am I correct?"

She folded her arms beneath her breasts. "That's for me to know—"

"And for me to find out?"

She should've known he'd been in America long enough to learn all the little sayings. "That's for me to know, period. Anything else? Or would you like to discuss *your* royal underwear?"

His grin deepened. "I have nothing to hide."

That remained to be seen. She intended to leave well enough alone before she was tempted to abandon the good-sense ship. Before she gave in to the tiny little spark of awareness or the slight full-body shiver brought about by his deadly smile. "I'm going now."

He finally rose from the chair. "I suggest you watch the sunset from the terrace outside your room. I'll have Elena send up some of her special tea to help you relax."

She'd be more relaxed as soon as she got away from all his charisma. "What kind of tea?"

"I'm not certain," he said as he strolled toward her and stopped only a foot or so away. "I've never tried it. I do know it is formulated to help a person sleep."

She'd probably have no trouble sleeping the moment her head hit the pillow. "Thank you, and I'll see you in the morning."

"You're welcome." He reached out and pushed a strand of hair behind her ear. "If the tea doesn't help you sleep, my room is next door to yours. Feel free to wake me."

"What for?" As if she really had to ask.

"Whatever you need to help you relax."

She suddenly engaged in one heck of a naked-body fantasy that made her want to run for cover. "I assure you I won't need anything to help me relax."

"Let me know if you change your mind."

"I won't be changing my mind." She turned toward the door then faced him again when something dawned on her. "By the way, if all this innuendo is some ploy to scare me off, save your breath. I've been propositioned by the best." And the worst of the worst.

He looked almost crestfallen. "I'm wounded you would think I would resort to such underhanded tactics."

Maybe she had overreacted a tad. Some men just happened to be blessed with the flirtation gene. "My apologies if I'm wrong about your motives."

"Actually, you are correct," he said. "That was my original plan. But you have bested me, so I promise to behave myself from this point forward."

She had a hard time believing that. "Well, in case you should get any more bright ideas, just know it will take more than a few well-rehearsed, suggestive lines to send me packing. I've spent many years studying human nature, and I know what you're all about."

He braced a hand on the doorframe above her head. "Enlighten me, Madison."

The sound of her name rolling softly out of his mouth, his close proximity, was not helping her concentration. "You use your charm to discourage perceived threats to your control, and to encourage the results you wish to achieve, namely driving people away. But beneath all that sexy macho bravado, I believe you're a man with a great deal of conviction when it comes to his country's future. Am I correct?"

"Perhaps you are only projecting your need for control on me. I believe at times giving up control to another is preferable. Have you never been tempted to throw out logic and act on pure instinct?"

Her instincts told her he wasn't referring to a professional relationship. "Not when it comes to mixing business with pleasure, if that's what you're asking. Don't forget we're trying to repair your reputation, not enhance it."

He had the nerve to show his pearly whites to supreme advantage. "Sometimes the pleasure is worth the risk."

"I thought you promised to behave."

He straightened and attempted to look contrite. "My apologies. I was momentarily struck senseless by your analysis."

Before she was momentarily struck stupid and kissed that smug, sexy smile off his face, Madison made a hasty exit.

She hadn't lied when she'd admitted she'd been propositioned before. She *had* lied when she'd claimed she hadn't been tempted to cross professional lines, because she had—the moment she'd reunited with Zain Mehdi.

Three

Perception is everything...

Zain had to agree with Madison on that point. He'd always been perceived as a man with a strong affinity for attractive women, a fact he could not deny. Yet that standing had provided the means to carry out his covert activities over the past seven years, and earned him the Phantom Sheikh title. His absence had always been blamed on a lover, and most of the time that had been far from the truth. *Most* of the time. He hadn't been celibate by any means, but he had not had as many affairs as what the media had led people to believe. If he had, he would have been perpetually sleep deprived.

He also recognized that giving in to temptation with a woman like Madison Foster—an intelligent, beautiful and somewhat willful woman—could possibly lead to disaster. Still, he wasn't one to easily ignore temptation, even if wisdom dictated that he must. And at the moment, Madison looked extremely tempting.

Zain remained in the open doorway to his suite in order to study her. She stood at the veranda's stone wall, looking out over the valley below, her golden hair flowing down her back. She'd exchanged her conservative clothing for more comfortable attire—a casual gauze skirt and a loose magenta top that revealed one slim, bare shoulder. He didn't need to venture a guess as to the color of her bra, since she didn't appear to be wearing one. That thought alone had him reconsidering the merits of wisdom.

Zain cleared his throat as he approached her, yet she didn't seem to notice his presence. Not until he said, "It's a remarkable view, isn't it?"

She sent him a backward glance and a slight scowl. "Why do you keep sneaking up on me?"

He moved beside her, leaving a comfortable distance between them. "My apologies. I did not intend to startle you. I only wanted to make certain you have everything you need from me."

She faced him, leaned a hip against the wall and rolled her eyes. "Are we back to that again?"

"My intentions are completely innocent." Only a half-truth. He'd gladly give her anything she needed in a carnal sense.

She took a sip from the cup clutched in her hands. "Sorry, but I'm having trouble buying the innocent act after your recent admission."

That came as no surprise to Zain, and he probably deserved her suspicions. "I will do my best to earn your trust." He nodded toward the cup. "I gather that's Elena's special tea."

"Yes, it is, and it's very good."

"Do you have any idea what might be in it?"

She lifted that bare shoulder in a shrug and took a sip. "I suspect it's chamomile and some other kind of herb. I can taste mint."

He turned toward her and rested one elbow on the stone barrier. "Take care with how much you drink. It could be more than tea."

"Too late. This is my third cup, and do you mean alcohol?"

"Precisely."

"Is that allowed?" she asked.

"Elena is free to do as she pleases, as is everyone else in the country, within reason. We've always had a spiritually, economically and culturally diverse population, due in part to people entering the borders seeking—"

"Asylum?"

"And peace."

She turned back to the view and surveyed the scene. "Then Bajul is the Switzerland of the Middle East?"

"In a manner of speaking. I might not have agreed with all my father's philosophies, but I've always admired his determination to remain neutral in a volatile region. Unfortunately, the threat to end our peaceful coexistence still exists, as it always has. As it is everywhere else in the world."

She took another drink and set the cup aside. "The landscape is incredible. I hadn't expected Bajul to be so green or elevated."

"You expected desert."

"Honestly, yes, I did."

Another example of inaccurate perception. "If you go north, you'll find the desert. Go south and you'll find the sea."

She sighed. "I love the sea. I love water, period."

He took the opportunity to move a little closer, his arm pressed against hers as he pointed toward the horizon. "Do you see that mountain rising between two smaller peaks?"

She shaded her eyes against the setting sun. "The skinny one that looks almost phallic?"

That made him smile. "It is known as Mabrúuk, our capital city's namesake. Legend has it that Al-'Uzzá, a mythological goddess, placed it there to enhance fertility. Reportedly her efforts have been successful, from crops to livestock to humans."

"Interesting," she said. "Do people have to go to the mountain to procreate, or does it have a long radius?" She followed the comment with a soft, sensual laugh. "No pun intended."

Discussing procreation with her so close only made Zain's fantasies spring to life, among other things. "I suppose it's possible, but that's not the point I was trying to make."

She turned and leaned a hip against the wall. "What point were you trying to make, Your Highness?"

She seemed determined to disregard his terms. "Zain."

Madison blew out a long breath. "What were you going to say before the topic turned to the baby-making mountain, *Zain?*"

He liked the breathless way she said his name. He liked the way she looked at the moment—slightly disheveled and extremely sensual. "I was going to point out that beyond the ridge there are two lakes. Perhaps I'll take you there in the near future."

"That would be nice, as long as you don't expect any baby making."

He certainly wouldn't mind making love to her in the

shadow of the mountain, or perhaps in the lake. Without the resulting baby, of course.

He forced his thoughts back to business matters. "My intent would be to show you the key to Bajul's future."

"What would that be?"

"Water."

She appeared to be confused. "For a fishery?"

"Food and water are commodities in the region," he explained. "We have more rain than most, and our lakes have deep aquifers. They also have the capacity to sustain our land for many years to come, and that means bountiful crops and livestock. Those commodities could serve as an export for countries that suffer shortages as long as we make certain we protect our resources. My plans include exploring innovative and eco-friendly ways to treat and preserve the water from the lakes."

She laid her palm on his arm. "That sounds like a wonderful plan, Zain."

The simple touch sent a surge of heat coursing through his body. "That plan will not come to fruition unless I can convince the council it's our best recourse as opposed to oil."

She unfortunately took her hand away. "But you'll have your brother's support, correct?"

If only that were true. "He'll be the hardest to convince. He will most likely side with the council and suggest drilling as soon as possible. I refuse to allow that unless we have exhausted all alternatives."

"I don't understand why the two of you seem to butt horns at every turn."

This would require more than a brief explanation, yet he felt she had the right to know. "Most believe that the crown automatically passes to the firstborn son. In my family's case, the reigning king can designate a successor, and he designated me, not Rafiq. My brother has resented that decision for years."

She shook her head. "I guess I assumed Rafiq was younger, although he does seem older in many ways. Not in appearance, because the resemblance between the two of you is remarkable. But he's very stoic."

"He's thirteen months older," he said. "And he is serious about preserving traditions that should be deemed obsolete in this day and time."

"I take it you're referring to arranged marriages."

Unfortunately, that was one change he wasn't prepared to make, even if it impacted his own future. "The tradition of selecting a bride with a royal heritage is necessary. Only a member of royalty can understand the royal life."

"Of course, and keeping the blood blue must be very important."

He ignored the bitterness in her tone. "I know how antiquated it might sound, but yes, that does hold some importance."

"Then why did you give your brother such a hard time about it?"

"Because I do not believe in committing to someone if you haven't explored an intimate relationship prior to committing to marriage. I would never have bought my Bugatti without test-driving it first."

Her eyes went wide. "You're comparing a woman to a car?"

"No. I am only saying that sexual compatibility holds great importance in a marriage, or it should. How will you know you are compatible in that regard unless you experience intimacy before you make a commitment?"

She looked skeptical and borderline angry. "In my

opinion, sex shouldn't carry too much weight. As they say, passion does have a tendency to fade."

"You sound as if you speak from experience. Have you been married?"

"No, but I was in a long-term relationship, and he's the reason I no longer have my dog."

"So you parted because of a canine?"

She briefly smiled. "We were the cliché. He wanted a house and kids and to live in suburbia, while I wanted a career in the city."

"And you have no desire to have a family?"

An odd and fleeting look of pain crossed her expression. "I have no intention of giving up my career for a man. My mother fell into that trap with my father."

Her past obviously was as complex as his. "That wasn't the life she chose?"

She downed the rest of the tea. "Oh, she chose it, all right. She gave up a career as a medical researcher to globe-trot with her diplomat husband. I've never understood how someone could claim to love someone so much that they'd set their aspirations aside for another person."

"Perhaps it all goes back to shared and sustained passion."

She released a sarcastic laugh. "Sorry, but I just can't wrap my mind around that. In fact, I don't even want to think about passion and my parents in the same sentence."

Her skepticism both surprised and intrigued him. "Have you never experienced a strong passion for someone?"

"As I've said, it's overrated."

Apparently she hadn't been with the right man. A man who could show her the true meaning of desire.

He could be that man. He wanted to be that man despite his original intention to drive her away. And so went the last of his wisdom.

He surveyed her face from forehead to chin and centered on her mouth. "You've never been so attuned to someone that when you enter a room, that person is all you see? You've never wanted someone so desperately that you would risk everything to have them?"

She drew in a shaky breath. "Not that I recall."

"I cannot imagine you would have voluntarily missed out on all that lovemaking has to offer."

Her eyes took on a hazy cast. "What makes you think I have missed out?"

He traced her lips with a fingertip. "If you had, you wouldn't be so quick to dismiss the existence of phenomenal sex."

He expected her to argue the point. He predicted she would back away. He wasn't prepared when she gripped the back of his neck and brought his mouth to hers.

All her untapped passion came out in the kiss. He could taste the mint on her tongue, could sense any latent resistance melt when he tightened his hold on her. He had no doubt she could feel how much he wanted her when he streamed his hands to her hips and nudged her completely against him.

He should halt the insanity before he carried her to his bed, or dispensed with formality and took her down where they now stood. Yet stopping didn't appear to be an option—until she stopped.

Madison wrested out of his arms, looking stunned and well kissed and quite perturbed. "What was that?"

Zain leaned back against the wall and dared to smile. "That was uncontrolled passion. I suppose I shouldn't be surprised you didn't recognize it."

She backed up a few steps and tugged at the hem of her blouse. "I tell you what that was. That was a huge mistake on my part. That was too much talk about that darn baby-making mountain."

When she spun around and listed to one side, he clasped her arm to prevent her from falling. "Perhaps it was the tea," he whispered in her ear from behind her.

"Perhaps I'm just an idiot." She pulled away again and spun around to face him. "I'm going to bed now."

"Do you wish some company?" he asked as she backed toward her room.

"Yes... No, I don't wish any company."

With that, she turned and disappeared through the glass door, leaving Zain alone with a strong urge to follow her, and an erection that would take hours to calm.

Now that he'd sampled what Madison Foster had to offer aside from her political expertise, he didn't want her to leave yet. He wanted more. He wanted it all.

She wanted to scream. She wanted to pull the covers over her head and forget what had happened the evening before. She wanted to tell the person who was knocking to go away and come back in day or so. Maybe by then she would be over her mortification enough to make an appearance.

Instead, Madison shoved the heavy eggplant-colored spread aside, left the bed and put on her robe on the way to answer the summons. If she happened to encounter the reason behind her current distress, she just might have to give him another piece of what was left of her mind. Or invite him in...

She yanked open the door to discover Elena once again standing on the threshold, tray in hand and a cheerful smile on her face. "Good morning, Miss Foster. Did you sleep well?"

"Like a rock." Like the dead or better still, the drunk. "What was in that tea, Elena?"

She breezed into the room and set the tray on a table near the glass doors. "Chamomile and a few other things."

Madison tightened her robe. "What other things?"

Elena straightened and swept a hand through her silver hair. "Some herbs and honey and schnapps."

Schnapps. That explained a lot. "You should have warned me. I drank three cups and had to take a twenty-minute shower to sober up before I could find the bed."

"My apologies, *cara*. I only wanted to aid you in relaxing."

"I was definitely relaxed." So much so she'd melted right into Zain's mouth.

Elena pointed in the direction of Madison's chin. "I have a special balm that will help with that irritation."

Confused, Madison strode to the mirrored dresser to take a look. Not only was her hair a blond Medusa mess from going to bed with it wet, she had a nice red patch of whisker burn below her bottom lip. "I used something new on my face, so that must be it. I'll be avoiding it from now on." Avoiding Zain's seduction skills, even if she couldn't avoid him.

"Would this something new be tall, dark and have a heavy evening beard?"

She met Elena's wily smile in the reflection. She hated to lie, so she'd simply be evasive. Turning from the mirror, she gestured toward the tray holding a silver pot and a plate of pastries. "I hope that's not more tea."

Elena shook her head. "No. It's coffee. Very strong

coffee. I decided you would need some caffeine for your meeting with Prince Zain."

She didn't recall scheduling a specific time. Then again, last night's details were a bit fuzzy, except for the blasted kiss. "When does he expect me?"

"Now. He's is in the study, waiting. And he seems to be in a somewhat foul mood."

Lovely. "Do you know the reason behind his foul mood?"

Elena tapped her chin with a slender finger and looked thoughtful. "Perhaps it is because he has tried something new on his face and he would like more of the same."

Madison internally cringed. If she kept backing herself into corners, she'd soon be folded in half. "Elena, seriously, this is just a rash. I have very sensitive skin."

"Yes, *cara,* and I am the Queen of Italia. I can tell when a woman has been kissed, and kissed well. And of course, I know Prince Zain is the culprit. He is a charmer, that *diavoletto.*"

Little devil was an apt description of Zain Mehdi. *Sexy little devil.* "Okay, if you must know, we shared a friendly kiss. Thanks to your special tea, I had a temporary lapse in judgment."

Elena laughed softly. "Prince Zain's powers of persuasion are much stronger than my tea. I only caution you to take care with your heart."

Madison held up her hand as if taking an oath. "I promise you there will be no more kissing, friendly or otherwise. I'm not one to bend the rules, much less break them."

Elena smiled. "I wish you much luck with that." She headed for the door and paused with her hand on the knob. *"L'amore domina senza regole,"* she muttered before she disappeared into the corridor.

Love rules without rules.

Who said anything about love? She wasn't in love with Zain Mehdi. In lust maybe, but that fell far from love.

Regardless, she didn't have time to ponder the woman's warning or the kiss or anything else for that matter. She needed to prepare to see the future king.

After she completed her morning ritual, Madison applied some makeup and twisted and secured her crazy hair at her nape. She dressed in brown slacks and sleeveless beige silk turtleneck that she covered with a taupe jacket, intentionally making certain she bared no skin aside from her hands and face. Wearing gloves and a veil would probably be overkill. She chose to nix the pastry but paused long enough to drink a cup of black lukewarm coffee. Even if she was somewhat hungry, she didn't dare feed the butterflies flitting around in her belly.

Those butterflies continued to annoy her as she grabbed her briefcase and headed downstairs to the second-floor office. Surprisingly she found the door partially ajar, but no guards and no prince in sight when she entered the vacant study. Only a few seconds passed before Zain emerged from what appeared to be an en suite bathroom.

Aside from one wayward lock of dark hair falling across his forehead, he looked every bit the debonair businessman. He wore a pair of black wool slacks and a white shirt with a gray tie draped loosely around his neck. The light shading of whiskers surrounding his mouth led Madison right down the memory path toward that toe-curling kiss.

She shoved the thoughts away and put on a sunny smile. "Good morning."

Without returning the greeting, Zain crossed the room

to the coat tree to the right of the desk and took a jacket from one hanger. "Did you have breakfast?" he asked.

He was so absolutely gorgeous she'd love to have him for breakfast. And lunch. And dinner… "I didn't have time. But I did have the most important staple—coffee."

He turned, slipped the coat on and nailed her with those lethal dark eyes. "I'll have the chef prepare you something you can eat while you wait."

"Wait for what?"

"I am about to address my royal subjects."

Several key concerns tumbled around in Madison's mind. She'd begin with the first. "Best I recall, you're not scheduled to do that for another two days."

He slid the top button closed on his collar. "Apparently the masses did not receive the memo."

Apparently. "Where is this going to take place?"

He gestured to his right. "Outside on the terrace where my father and my father's father have always spoken to the people."

Madison set her briefcase on a chair and immediately walked to the double doors to peek through the heavy red curtains. She saw a substantial stone balcony containing a podium with a skinny microphone as well as several stern—and heavily armed—sentries standing guard. As she peered in the distance, she caught a glimpse of an iron fence, also lined with guards, holding back the milling crowd. And in that crowd stood a few respectable correspondents, along with more than a few pond-scum tabloid reporters.

After dropping the curtain, she faced Zain again. "Do you know what you're going to say?"

He rounded the desk, leaned back against it and began to work his tie. "I am your new king. Accept it."

Her mouth dropped open momentarily from shock. "You can't be serious."

"It is simple and to the point." His smile was crooked, and so was his tie.

"Perhaps a little too simple and too pointed."

"I am not yet prepared to speak on all my plans."

"But are you prepared for the questions that are going to be hurled at you by reporters?"

He buttoned his coat closed. "Rest assured I've handled the press before."

"Even paparazzi?"

"Especially paparazzi."

Considering his notorious way with women, she supposed he probably had encountered more than his share of media stalkers. However, she still worried he could get bombarded by a few queries that could trip him up. Hopefully he'd learned how to ignore those. Too bad his tie was too askew for her to ignore.

Without giving it a second thought, Madison walked right up to him to fix the problem. The memory of her mother doing the same thing for Madison's dad settled over her. Was she in danger of becoming her mother? Only if she professed her undying love to Zain and promised to follow him throughout the world. He wasn't the undying-love kind, but he certainly did smell great. Nothing overpowering, just a hint of light, earthy cologne. Or maybe it was the soap he'd used in the shower. Never before had she aspired to be a bar of soap, but at the moment she did. How nice it would be to travel down all that slick, wet, fantastic male terrain, over muscle and sinew and hills and valleys. Definitely hills…

"Are you finished yet?"

Zain's question jarred Madison back into the here and now. "Almost." She smoothed her hand over the gray silk tie and straightened lapels that didn't need straightening. Just when she was about to step back, he captured her hands against his chest.

"I am curious about something," he said, his dark eyes leveled on hers.

"Sage-green satin. Matching bra, if you must know." Heavens, she was volunteering underwear info before he'd officially asked.

"Actually, I was about to inquire about your night and if you slept well."

Now she felt somewhat foolish and confused as to why she hadn't tried to wrest her hands away from his. "I slept well, thank you, although I did have a few odd dreams."

He raised a brow. "Sexual dreams?"

"Strange dreams. I was climbing up a mountain chasing a snake."

His smile caught her off guard. "Some believe climbing denotes a craving for intercourse. Need I say what the mountain and snake symbolize?"

That phallic mountain would be her Waterloo if they didn't stop discussing it. "Spoken like a man. I'm sure you could make a dream about doing laundry all about sex."

"Perhaps if it involved washing your lingerie."

She tried to hold back her own smile, without success. "Right now you should be concentrating on your speech, not sex dreams."

He raised her hand and kissed her palm before setting it back against his chest. "It's difficult to concentrate with this ongoing chemistry between us."

She couldn't argue that, although she would. "Don't be ridiculous."

"Don't be naive, Madison. You feel it now."

She admittedly did feel a bit warm and somewhat tingly. Maybe a little lightheaded, but then that could be some lingering effects of the tea. She managed to slip from his grasp and take a much-needed step back. "If you're referring to what happened last night, that was a mistake."

"You're going to deny that you wanted to kiss me? That you want to kiss me now?"

She could deny—and lie—in the same breath. "I want to get back to the issue at hand, namely your speech. In my opinion, it's important that you appear to be a strong yet compassionate leader. Be decisive but not forceful."

"I have come to one important decision now."

She folded her arms beneath her breasts. "What would that be?"

He moved closer, rested a hand on her shoulder and brought his lips to her ear. He whispered soft words that sounded lyrical, sensual, though she couldn't begin to comprehend the message, at least not literally. She could venture a guess that the missive was sexual in nature.

When Zain pulled back and homed in on her gaze, she released a slow, ragged breath. "Do you care to interpret what you just said to me?"

"Later, when we have complete privacy."

That sent Madison's imagination straight into overdrive and would have quite possibly, had it not been for the rap on the door, sent Madison straight into Zain's arms.

"Enter," he said, his voice somewhat raspy and noticeably strained.

Madison smoothed a hand down her jacket then over her hair as Deeb stepped in the room, looking every bit the humorless assistant. "You are cleared to proceed, Emir."

Zain rubbed a hand over his jaw. "The shooters are in place?"

"Yes. Four positioned on the roof, two in the tower."

The reality of Zain's importance suddenly hit home for Madison. So did the reality of what she'd almost done—kiss the king for the second time in less than twenty-four hours. Yet she didn't have time to think about it as two bodyguards swept into the room, pulled back the curtains and escorted Zain onto the terrace.

Madison stood to one side slightly behind the drapes while Mr. Deeb took his place beside her. When Zain positioned himself behind the podium, a series of shouts ensued above the murmuring crowd. "What are they saying?" she asked Deeb.

"They are calling him a turncoat."

Ouch. She wished she could see Zain's face, gauge his reaction, but she could only see his back and his hands gripping the edge of the wooden surface, indicating he could be stressed. But no one would know that, she realized, the moment he began to speak in words she couldn't begin to understand.

"What's he saying?" she asked Deeb who remained his usual noncommittal self.

"He is telling them he is honored to be their leader and he looks forward to serving them."

So far, so good. But then she heard the sounds of disapproval and didn't feel nearly as confident. "What now?"

"He claims he is not his father and that he will rule differently," Deeb said. "He is also speaking of positive changes he wishes to make, such as improvements to the hospital and the schools."

As Zain continued, Madison noticed the temporarily dissatisfied crowd had quieted and many people, particularly women, seemed to hang on his every word. And although she couldn't interpret his words, she could certainly appreciate his voice—a deep, mellow voice that went down as smoothly as a vintage glass of wine.

After an enthusiastic round of applause, she turned to ask for clarification from Deeb, only to hear someone suddenly shout in English, "Is it true you fathered a child with Keeley Winterlind?"

Though she'd been aware of Zain's liaison with the supermodel, Madison was seriously stunned by the query, and thoroughly appalled that someone would interrupt a king's speech in search of a sordid story. Worse, was it true?

Zain ignored the question and continued to speak to the throng that seemed to grow more restless by the minute. Then another reporter demanded he address the pregnancy issue, prompting shouts from the masses.

Although Madison still couldn't see Zain's expression, she did notice his hands fisted at his sides. She had no clue what he'd muttered, but it didn't sound at all friendly and, considering the crowd's angry reaction, it wasn't. Amid the show of raised fists and verbal condemnation, Zain turned and stormed back into the study. He didn't afford her or Deeb a passing glance, nor did he hesitate to make a swift exit, slamming the door behind him.

Madison waited for the sentries to leave before she sought confirmation or denial from her only immediate source of information. "Is it true about the baby?"

Deeb's expression remained emotionless, but she saw a flicker of concern in his eyes. "I am afraid, Miss Foster, you will have to ask the emir."

And that's exactly what Madison intended to do. First, she had to find him, and soon, before all hell broke loose.

Four

"Did you find your meal satisfactory, Your Wickedness?"

Zain looked up from his barren plate to see Maysa Barad—*Doctor* Maysa Barad—standing in the doorway wearing a bright purple caftan, her dark hair pulled back into a braid. He returned her smile, though that was the last thing he cared to do. But she was his friend, and she had opened her home to him as a temporary sanctuary. "It was very good. My compliments to your chef. He has a masterful hand."

"*She* is a master," Maysa said as she pulled back the adjacent chair and sat. "I made your dinner after I gave my chef the night off. However, since I still have household staff on the premises, we should continue to speak English to ensure our new king has his privacy."

At the moment he preferred not to be reminded of

his duty. "My position will not be official until the coronation."

"You were king the moment your father passed. My sympathies to you, though I know the two of you did not always see eye to eye."

That was an understatement. "Thank you for that, and for allowing me to arrive virtually unannounced."

"You are always welcome here, Zain." She rested her elbow on the table and supported her cheek with her palm, sending the heavy bangles at her wrists down her arm. "And you have always been the official king of mischief."

"And you are still as pretty as you were the last time I saw you."

Her smile expanded. "But are you still the little devil who attempted to frighten me with toads?"

She had been the sister he'd never had. "You were never really frightened, were you?"

"No. I was simply playing along until Rafiq came along to rescue me."

Zain had always suspected that to be the case. Maysa had been in love with his brother for as long as he could recall. He wondered if she still was. "Speaking of Rafiq, will you be attending the wedding?"

She straightened in the chair, her frame as rigid as the carved wooden table. "I received an invitation, but do not wish to witness that charade."

Yes, she was still in love with Rafiq. "I agree it might not be the best match."

"A match made in misery. Rafiq will never be happy with a woman whose heart belongs to another man."

"What man?"

Zain saw a flash of regret pass over her expression.

"I would rather not say. In fact, I have already said too much."

"Can you tell me if Rima has returned this man's affections?"

"Yes, she has."

He tried to contain his shock. "Does Rafiq know?"

She lifted her shoulders in a shrug. "If he does, he has chosen to ignore it. Regardless, it is not my place to tell him, and I would hope you keep it to yourself, as well."

He did not like the thought of concealing the truth from his brother, yet he doubted Rafiq would believe him. "It would not matter, Maysa. Rafiq is all about duty, regardless of the circumstance. He has every intention of honoring the marriage contract."

She flipped her hand in dismissal. "Enough talk about your brother and his bride. Tell me about California. I did not have the opportunity to visit there when I was in medical school in the States."

Los Angeles had only been his home base and little more. "I traveled a good deal of the time."

"Then tell me about that. I am sure you met many interesting people and saw many interesting sights."

He had seen devastation, drought, famine and disease. Sights he never cared to see again, especially in his own country. "I'm certain my experiences do not compare to yours as a physician."

She shook her head. "My experiences have been challenging since my return to Bajul. I am the only female doctor and the only one who will treat those who can pay very little, if at all. The others cater to the wealthier population."

That came as no surprise to Zain. "Your commitment is admirable, Maysa. Once I am fully in charge, I will make certain the hospital undergoes renovations and medical offices are added. Perhaps then you can receive pay for your services."

"I do not need the money as much as the people need my help," she said. "Fortunately, my father has allowed me to live in his palatial second home regardless that I have failed him as a daughter. He is also kind enough to provide the funds to keep the household going, though I despise taking even one riyal from him."

Zain could not imagine a father considering his daughter a failure after she had established a successful medical career. But then Maysa's father had always been an ass. "Does the sultan come to visit often?"

She released a bitter laugh. "Oh, no. He is either in Saudi or Yemen with my poor mother, building his fortune so that he may provide for his many mistresses."

Maysa had the same issues with her father as Zain had always had with his. "I believe I recall you were bound to a betrothal at one time. I take it that did not come to fruition."

"Actually, it did. Two weeks after the wedding, I realized that contrary to our culture, a woman does not need a man to survive. It took some effort to obtain a divorce, but I managed it. And Father has not forgiven me for it."

"I'm certain it hasn't been easy on you."

She shrugged. "I realized there would be those who would shun me because of my decision, yet I refused to let that deter me. No man will ever dictate my future."

Zain couldn't help but smile when he thought about Madison. She and Maysa were very much alike. Yet he felt more than brotherly fondness for Madison.

"Do you find me amusing, *Your Highness?*" Maysa asked.

"No. You reminded me of someone else I know."

"Someone special?"

Perhaps too special for his own good. "Actually, she is a political consultant Rafiq hired to save me from myself."

"She has a huge task ahead of her then."

"Believe me, she is up to the task. She is also very headstrong, and extremely intelligent. Fortunately, she has a sense of humor, as well. Sometimes I find her frustrating, other times extremely intriguing."

"Is she attractive?"

"Yes, but her attractiveness goes well beyond her physical appearance. She is one of the most fascinating women I have ever encountered."

She inclined her head and studied him. "You have feelings for her."

Maysa's comment took him aback. "She is an employee."

"An employee who has hypnotized you, Zain. Perhaps the sheikh has met his match in more ways than one."

"That is absurd," he said without much conviction. "I have only known her a few days."

"Yet it is those immediate connections that at times make a lasting impact on our lives."

From the wistfulness in Maysa's tone, Zain recognized she spoke from experience. "Even if I did develop these feelings you speak of, we both know a permanent relationship with an outsider could never happen."

She drummed her fingertips on the tabletop. "Ah, yes. We are back to the antiquated tradition of marrying our own kind. You have the power to change that."

"I have other changes to make that are more important. Changes that will affect the future of this country."

"And you are not concerned about your own future?" she asked. "Would you give up a chance at finding love for a tradition that should have died long ago?"

He was too tired to defend his decisions, which led to his next request. "Would you have an available room where I could stay the night?"

"I have twelve bedrooms at your disposal," she said. "But will you not be missed?"

He would, but he did not care. "Deeb knows where I am."

"Zain, although it is truly not any of my concern, you cannot hide away when times become difficult."

He tossed his napkin aside. "Then you've heard about the latest accusations."

"I was there when you spoke this morning. You had everyone in the palm of your hand until that *himar* intruded."

Zain had considered calling him something much worse than a donkey. "For your information, I am not hiding. I am only taking a brief sabbatical to gather my thoughts."

She frowned. "Forgive me for pointing this out, but you have always been one to withdraw from the world when you lose control. The role you will soon assume requires continuity. Are you certain you are willing to bear that burden?"

Though he did not appreciate her commentary, he reluctantly admitted she was partially right. "I have prepared for this opportunity for many years. Once I am established, I will commit fully to my duties."

She smiled and patted his hand. "I know you will. Now if you will follow me, I will show you to your quarters for the evening, where you can rest and fantasize about that special consultant who has obviously earned a little piece of the king's heart."

Maysa knew him all too well, yet she was wrong

about his feelings for Madison. She did not—nor would she ever—have any claim on his heart.

After Zain's twenty-four-hour absence, Madison finally located him on the palace's rooftop. He sat on the cement ground with his back against the wall, hands laced together on his belly, one long leg stretched out before him, the other bent at the knee. He seemed so lost in his thoughts, she questioned whether she should give him more alone time. Regrettably, time was a luxury they didn't have. Not when she required answers to burning questions in order to circumvent the gossip. Provided it *was* gossip.

Before moving forward, she paused a few moments to ponder his atypical clothing. The standard white tailored shirt, Italian loafers and dark slacks had been replaced by a fitted black tee, khaki cargo pants and heavy brown boots. He reminded her of an adventurous explorer ready for travel—and in some ways dressed to kill. His rugged appearance was unquestionably murdering her composure.

Madison shored up her courage, walked right up to him and hovered above him. "I see the sheikh has finally returned."

He glanced up at her, his expression somber. "How did you know where to find me?"

"Elena mentioned you might be here. She said you and your brothers used to hide from her up here when it was time for your lessons."

He smiled but it faded fast. "I should have known she would give my secrets away."

Madison wondered what other secrets he might be keeping. "Mind if I join you?"

He gestured toward the space beside him. "It's less than comfortable, but be my guest."

She carefully lowered herself to the ground and hugged her knees to her chest, taking care to make sure the hem of her dress was properly in place. "The next time you decide to do a disappearing act, do you mind letting me in on it?"

"I assure you, it will not happen again."

"I hope I can trust you on that. You wouldn't believe how frantic everyone was until Mr. Deeb told us you were safe."

"I was never in danger," he said as he continued to stare straight ahead. "I stayed with a friend at a house in the foothills."

She could only imagine what that might have entailed if that friend happened to be female. "How did you get there? And how did you manage to evade your body-guards? Rafiq is still furious over that."

"I took one of the all-terrain vehicles, and Deeb was aware of my departure. Guards are not necessary when I take care to disguise myself."

She noticed a camouflage baseball cap resting at his side. "So that's the reason for the casual clothes?"

"They serve me well in hiding my identity."

They served him well in highlighting his finer points, and that sent her straight into a fishing expedition. "And this friend had no qualms about concealing the future king?"

"Maysa understands my need for privacy. She made certain I was not disturbed."

As she'd gathered—a woman friend. "Does this friendship come with or without benefits?" She hated that she sounded like some jealous lover.

"Without benefits," he said before adding, "although I do not expect you to believe me."

He sounded more frustrated than angry. "I never said I didn't believe you."

He sent her a sideways glance. "Then you are in the minority. Most people choose to believe the worst of me."

She lowered her legs and shifted slightly to face him. "Since it seems you don't have an official press secretary, I spent the day sending out releases stating you vehemently deny fathering Keeley Winterlind's child. The question is, did I lie?"

"No."

She released the breath she didn't know she'd been holding. "Not even a remote possibility?"

"No."

She truly wanted to believe him, but… "I do remember seeing photos of the two of you a couple years ago."

"That means nothing." Now he sounded angry.

"It means there's proof you had a connection with her."

"A platonic connection," he said. "I came upon her ex-lover threatening her at a social gathering and I intervened. We remained in contact because she needed someone to set her on the right path. However, she was young and impressionable and immature. The last I heard, she had reunited with the boyfriend because I could not convince her that the controlling bastard wasn't good for her."

If what he'd said was true, then in essence he was a champion of women. "Do you think she's the one claiming you're her baby's father?"

"No. She contacted me this afternoon and assured me she had nothing to do with the speculation, and I trust her. She also confirmed the ex is the father."

"I'm relieved I told the truth when I denied the speculation."

"As if that will do any good."

He seemed so sullen, Madison felt the need to lift his spirits. "Have you seen the news footage of your speech?"

"No, and I refuse to watch it."

No surprise there. "Well, you looked incredibly debonair and poised." And absolutely gorgeous. "I'm sure you'll start receiving requests for invitations from a slew of queen candidates."

"I highly doubt they would be interested in light of the recent attacks on my character."

Her efforts to cheer him up were on the verge of becoming an epic failure. "Hey, if they could see you in your adventurer's gear, they wouldn't care about your character."

She'd finally coaxed a smile from him. A tiny smile, but at least it was something. "I fail to understand how I could charm a woman with clothing not fit for a king."

"Then maybe you don't know women as well as you think you do. Of course, it doesn't hurt you're the ruler of a country, and your house isn't too shabby, either."

For the first time since her arrival, he gave her his full attention and a fully formed smile. "You are looking quite beautiful tonight."

She couldn't immediately recall the last time any man had called her beautiful. Her shapeless aqua sundress certainly wouldn't qualify. "Thank you, but this outfit is designed solely for comfort, not beauty."

"I was not referencing your clothing." He lightly touched her cheek. "You are beautiful."

When Madison contacted those dark, mysterious eyes, that spark of awareness threatened to become a flame. With little effort, it could blaze out of control. Yet she recognized Zain was only attempting to divert attention from the seriousness of the situation, and possibly cover his internal turmoil. She truly wanted to provide him with a diversion, but the last thing Zain needed was a potential scandal involving his political consultant. The last thing she needed was to venture into personal involvement with him. She'd already started down that slippery slope.

She shored up her wavering willpower. "Now that we have engaged in sufficient mutual admiration, we should probably go inside and discuss how we're going to handle any other problems that might arise. I'd also be happy to listen to what you have planned for the council meeting tomorrow."

"I prefer to stay here with you."

And she wanted to stay with him, honestly she did, but to what end? "If we stay much longer, we could make another mistake."

He searched her face and paused at her mouth before returning to her eyes. "I have made many mistakes in my lifetime, but spending time with you will not ever be a mistake."

Her foolish heart executed a little flip-flop in her chest. "Flattery will get you everywhere."

"Everywhere?"

One more sexy word out of his incredible mouth and she'd be too far gone to stop any madness that might occur. "The only place we should be going is into your office, and repairing your reputation is the only thing we should consider."

He studied the stars and sighed. A rough, sensuous and slightly irritated sigh. "You are right. Business

should always come before pleasure, no matter how re-
volting that business might be."

Madison was admittedly somewhat disappointed that
he conceded so quickly. "You will get through this, Zain.
It's only a matter of time before you earn your country's
trust. You are destined to be a great leader."

"I sincerely appreciate your faith in my abilities."

He both looked and sounded sincere, causing her spirits to rise. "Now let's get some work done before dawn."

When Zain came to his feet and held out his hand to
help her up, Madison wasn't quite prepared for the sharp
sting of awareness as they stood. She wasn't exactly
surprised when he framed her face in his palm. But the
sudden impact of his mouth covering hers nearly buckled her knees. The kiss was powerful, almost desperate,
yet she didn't have the will to stop him. Every argument
she'd made against this very thing went the way of the
warm breeze surrounding them.

She somehow wound up backed against the wall with
Zain flush against her. Even when he left her mouth to
trail kisses down her neck, lowered one strap and slid
the tip of his tongue slightly beneath the scoop neck of
her dress, she disregarded the warning bells sounding
in her head. Even when he worked her hem up to her
waist, slipped his hands down the back of her panties
and clasped her bottom, she couldn't manage one protest. And as he kissed her again, pressed as close to her
as he possibly could and simulated the act she'd been determined to avoid with both his body and tongue, stop
became go and thinking became an impossible effort.

Separated only by silk and cotton, Madison felt the
beginnings of a climax, prompting an odd sound bubbling up from her throat. She was vaguely aware of the

rasp of a zipper, very aware the no-return point had arrived and extremely aware when Zain abruptly let her go.

She closed her eyes and waited until her respiration had almost returned to normal before she risked a glance to see him facing the wall, both hands raised above his head as if in surrender. "It appears we're suffering from restraint issues."

He straightened and redid his fly. "Suffering is an apt description."

She pushed the strap back into place while struggling for something more to say. "Out of curiosity, why did you stop?"

He leaned back against the stone and stared straight ahead. "You deserve better than frantic sex against a wall."

"Honestly, it was the hottest few moments of my life and frankly out of character for me."

"Leave, Madison."

The command caught her off guard. "We still have to go over—"

"We'll meet in the morning."

"But you need—"

"I need you to go before I am tempted to carry you to my bed and complete your climax before giving you another while I am inside you."

Madison understood that, loud and clear. She couldn't remember ever having such a heated physical reaction to a man's words. Then again, no man had ever said anything remotely close to that to her. "I'm not leaving until I make myself clear. Whatever this thing is between us, it's going to take a lot of strength to ignore it. I'm not sure that's going to happen, so we have two options. One, we accept we're consenting adults and just do it and get it out of our system. Or I bow out gracefully before I cause you more problems."

He finally looked at her. "The second option is out. The first will not be possible until I am assured you can give me what I need."

Surely he wasn't suggesting… "Are you questioning my lovemaking abilities?"

"No. I need to know I have your respect and above all, your trust."

With that, Zain turned and disappeared through the opening leading to the stairway.

Madison sank back onto the ground and pinched the bridge of her nose from the onset of a tremendous headache. She did respect Zain and his ideals. Did she trust him? At the moment, she wasn't sure.

"My apologies for disturbing you, Emir."

Zain tossed his notes onto the side table to acknowledge Deeb, who had somehow entered his suite without his notice. But then he'd been distracted since he'd left Madison on the rooftop an hour ago. "What is it, Deeb?"

"I wanted to know if you required anything before I leave for home."

He needed the woman in the bedroom next door, but he could not have her. Not yet. "You are dismissed."

Deeb nodded and said, "Have a restful evening, Your Highness."

That was not a likely prospect. When Deeb retreated toward the door, Zain reconsidered and called him back. "I have a few questions for you." Questions he had intentionally failed to ask for fear of the answers.

Deeb pushed the glasses up on his nose. "Yes?"

Zain shifted in the less-than-comfortable chair. "How long have you been employed by the royal family?"

"Fifteen years last December."

His thoughts drifted off topic momentarily. "And you never thought to marry during that time?"

"I am married. I have been for fifteen years."

He was surprised Deeb had not mentioned that before, but then he had never inquired about his private life. "Children?"

A look of pride passed over the man's expression. "I have six children, four boys and two girls. The oldest is nine, the youngest three months."

As far as Zain was concerned, that was quite a feat for several reasons. "You were with me in the States for seven years, so I find that rather remarkable."

"If you recall, you allowed me to return to Bajul during your travels."

Clearly the man impregnated his bride every time he'd been home. "And your wife did not take exception to your absences?"

Deeb hinted at a smile. "If that were true, we would not have six children."

Zain could not argue that. "Are you still happily wed?"

"Yes, Emir."

Zain tented his fingers beneath his chin. "To what do you attribute that happiness?"

"Patience and tolerance. Most important, sustained passion. When you choose your mate, it is best to always remember this."

He could not agree more, especially when it came to the passion. "I appreciate the advice."

"You are welcome, Your Highness. Now if that is all—"

"It is not." He had to pose one more question. An extremely difficult question. "Do you know if the rumors of my father's infidelity are true?"

Deeb tugged at his collar as if he had a noose around his neck. "I feel compelled not to betray the king's confidence."

As suspected, he did have information. "You need not conceal my father's secrets any longer, Deeb. You answer to me now." He despised sounding so harsh, but he was that desperate for confirmation.

"I know of only one woman," he said after a brief hesitation.

"Who is this woman?"

"I will only say that she is above reproach. She was only doing the king's bidding."

Zain sensed that Deeb was protecting more than the king's secrets. He could very well have a connection with the mistress, which led him to believe she could have been a former staff member. At the moment, he was too exhausted to press his assistant for more details. "That will be all, Deeb."

"As you wish." Deeb turned to leave before facing Zain again. "If I may speak candidly, I would like to add that some things are not as they seem."

He'd said that to Madison on more than one occasion. "Perhaps, yet you cannot deny that my father dishonored my mother?"

"Again, every situation is unique and at times not for us to judge."

Zain could not help but judge his father. The man had caused him to doubt himself on many levels, the least of which had to do with personal relationships. "Thank you for your candor. You may go now."

"Before I take my leave," he said, "may I speak freely?"

"You may." For now.

"If it is any solace, I firmly believe you are nothing like the king."

With that, Deeb left the room, leaving Zain in a state of disbelief. He learned tonight how little he knew about his assistant, yet the man seemed to know much about him.

Feeling restless, Zain paced the room for a few moments, growing angrier by the minute as he thought back to Deeb's confirmation of his father's infidelity. He strode to the shelf housing several books, picked up the photo of the king posing with a U.S. president and hurled it against the far wall. The glass shattered and rained down in shards to the carpeted floor.

Despite Deeb's insistence there were extenuating circumstances, Zain could never forgive his father. Not when his ruthless behavior had dealt his mother the worst fate. Death.

Five

The second she walked into the conference room, Madison felt as if she'd entered Antarctica. With their immaculate black suits and impeccable grooming, Rafiq and Zain Mehdi could be corporate raiders involved in a business debate, not two brothers engaged in an ongoing war of wills.

"Good afternoon, gentlemen," she said as she pulled out a chair across from Zain, sat and scooted beneath the massive conference table.

"Do you have anything to report on the latest scandal?" Rafiq asked, while Zain seemed more interested in the view out the window at Madison's back.

She set her briefcase at her feet and folded her hands on the table. "I do, actually." A report that wouldn't go over well with Zain. "I spent most of the morning on the phone tracking down Ms. Winterlind's publicist. I finally heard from her a few moments ago."

Zain finally looked at her when she hesitated. "And?"

"She told me that Ms. Winterlind did in fact leak the initial claim that you're the father of her baby."

Anger flashed in Zain's eyes. "Impossible."

"I'm afraid it's not. She did send her apologies to you through the publicist and is in the process of retracting the claim."

"It seems your faith in the model was misplaced, Zain," Rafiq said.

If looks really could kill, Zain had just delivered a visual bullet, right between his brother's eyes. "She had her reasons."

"What would those be, brother? She has her sights set on trapping a king?"

Zain muttered something acid and probably insulting in Arabic. "She is not like that, Rafiq."

Time for a much-needed intervention on Zain's behalf. "Actually, Prince Rafiq, she made the claim to protect her son from her ex, who is a known batterer. Fortunately, he's currently incarcerated on assault charges."

Zain's gaze snapped to hers. "Did he beat her?"

Evidently he still cared about the model, maybe even more than he'd let on in their previous conversations. "No. He beat up some guy in a bar and nearly killed him. He'll be going away for a long time."

"Good riddance," Zain muttered.

"Are there other women who will surface with similar claims?" Rafiq asked Zain, venom in his tone.

Zain's eyes narrowed. "The women with whom I have been intimately involved are trustworthy."

"I believe the model contradicts that assertion."

"I was not intimate with her."

Rafiq raised a brow. "Then it would seem those whom

you have bedded and spurned would be more likely to lie."

Zain looked as if he might bolt out of the chair. *"Izhab ila al djaheem, Rafiq."*

Madison had no idea what Zain had said to his brother, but she did feel she needed to defuse the situation, possibly at her own peril. "Look, Your Highness, Prince Rafiq does have a point. We need to know if there is even a remote possibility a woman might come forward with some scandalous claim, unfounded or not."

Zain's expression turned cold. "My former lovers should not be a concern, unless perhaps one is interested in the extent of my sexual experience."

His attitude, and the pointed comment, shredded her already thinned patience. "I don't need a list, only a number. Less than five? More than ten? Fifty?" Now *she* sounded like a scorned lover.

"I assure you, my past will not affect my ability to lead," he said. "Many married leaders worldwide have openly engaged in affairs and continued to rule."

Madison had known more than her fair share. Some came through it unscathed. Others had not. "Any scandal could influence your people's trust in you if it rears its ugly head again."

He kept his gaze centered on hers. "Does that include your trust in me, Madison?"

"Trust is earned, *Zain.*"

She regretted the informality faux pas the minute she glanced at Rafiq and saw the suspicious look in his eyes. She could only imagine how the exchange sounded—like lovers engaged in a spat.

Rafiq checked his watch and stood. "The meeting begins in ten minutes. You can continue this discussion later."

Madison might receive an emphatic no, but she had to ask. "I'd like to sit in on the meeting."

Rafiq looked as though she'd requested to run naked through the royal gardens. "That is not permitted."

"I will allow it," Zain said. "You may observe from the gallery. I'll have Deeb interpret for you."

She wasn't sure if Zain had granted her request because he wanted her there, or because he wanted to one-up his brother. It didn't matter as long as she had a ringside seat where she could watch him in action.

When Zain failed to stand, Rafiq nailed him with another glare. "Are you coming now, or should I have the guards escort you?"

"I will be along shortly," Zain said. "I need to speak privately with Ms. Foster."

"I have no doubt you do." With that, Rafiq strode out of the room.

As soon as the door closed, Madison directed her attention to Zain. "This is exactly what I feared would happen. My stupid miscue with your name wasn't lost on your brother. There's no telling what he thinks is going on between us."

"Let him believe what he will," he said. "He would have assumed the worst whether I had touched you or not."

Oh, but he had touched her. "If you're not concerned about Rafiq, then why did you need to speak to me in private?"

He looked all too serious. "First, I want to apologize. My problem is with Rafiq's attitude, not yours. Second, I need to know if you're all right after last evening."

She shrugged. "I'm fine. It happened, it's done and it's over."

He inclined his head and studied her. "Is it truly over?"

If only she could say yes without any reservations. Trouble was, she couldn't. "Right now you need to concentrate on what you have to propose to the council."

He reached across the table and took her hand. "How can I concentrate when I know you're upset?"

"I told you, I'm fine." She came to her feet and grabbed her briefcase. "I'm sure you'll regain your full concentration once you're in the meeting. Now let's go before Rafiq calls out the guard."

As Zain stood, Madison started toward the door. But before she made it more than a few steps, Zain caught her arm and turned her to face him. "Do you recall what I said to you last night?"

She recalled every detail of last night. "Yes, and I meant what I said to you a few minutes ago. You're going to have to prove you're trustworthy."

"At times trust requires a leap of faith."

If she leaped too quickly, she could land in an emotional briar patch. "Faith has failed me before."

"You are not alone in that. Yet whatever my faults might be, I am a man of my word."

She really wanted to believe that. "Speaking of words, you've never told me what you said to me the day you addressed the crowd."

He rubbed his thumb slowly back and forth down her arm. Not only could she feel it through her linen jacket, she could feel it everywhere. "You really wish for me to tell you now?"

"Yes, I do." Although she had a feeling she might regret it.

As he had the first time he'd whispered words she

hadn't understood, he rested his lips against her ear. "You should never have kissed me."

He had to be kidding. "That's it? You're saying the kiss was all my fault?"

"No. It was my fault for baiting you. I simply did not believe you would take the bait. However, if we had never shared that first kiss, I would not be lying awake at night fantasizing about all the ways I would make love to you. I would not want you so badly that I would gladly reschedule this meeting and take you away from here."

He released her then, walked to the door and left the room, while she stood still as a statue, cursing Zain for his uncanny knack of keeping her off balance. She didn't move an inch until Deeb summoned her into the hallway.

Madison followed the entourage down the corridor, watching as Zain walked ahead with overt confidence. Several times she had to tear her gaze away after trying to sneak a peek at his notable royal butt. Once they reached the end of the hall, Zain walked through double doors while Deeb showed Madison to his right, where they descended a short flight of stairs, and into the glass-enclosed gallery.

Madison took a seat in the front row of chairs beside him and looked down on the scene. Several men were seated at a large round table—eleven by her count—all dressed in high-neck button-down white robes, various colored sashes draped around their necks, and white kaffiyehs with bands that matched the sashes. The chairs flanking either side of Rafiq were noticeably empty, one most likely reserved for Zain. She leaned toward Deeb and asked, "Who's missing, aside from His Highness?"

"The youngest emir, Adan," he said. "He is excused today due to the importance of his mission."

Madison doubted Zain would be afforded the same

courtesy if he'd decided not to appear. As the minutes ticked off, she began to worry he might have taken that route. And considering the way the council members kept looking around, she assumed they were worried, as well.

A few seconds later, the doors opened to the future king, prompting the men to stand. He wore the same white robe with a gold-and-black sash draped around his neck, but nothing on his head. She didn't know if he was intentionally bucking tradition, or if someone had forgotten his headdress. Frankly, that was fine by Madison. She'd hate to see even one inch of that pretty face concealed from her view.

When Zain lowered himself into the chair, the men followed suit while Deeb reached forward and flipped a switch to the intercom. Zain began to speak in a language that Madison regretted not learning. She'd only mastered a few official greetings and the all-important request for the ladies' room. Perhaps she would ask Zain to teach her more. She imagined he could teach her quite a bit from a nonlinguistic standpoint, and she would happily be a willing student.

Madison forced her attention back to the meeting and wondered what she'd hoped to gain by observing when she couldn't understand a word.

Deeb demonstrated that he understood her confusion when he said, "They are currently discussing economic concerns. Rafiq is the minister of finance."

"And Adan?" she asked.

"He is the head of the military."

That made sense. Unfortunately, nothing else did.

As the discourse continued, Madison became focused on watching Zain's hands move as he spoke. Strong, steady, expressive hands. Skilled hands. Her thoughts drifted back to the night before when she'd experienced those hands on her body. She'd wanted to experience more of them in places that he'd obviously avoided. The sudden, unexpected rush of heat caused her to cross her legs against the sensations. She felt as she might actually start to squirm if she didn't get her mind back on business. Easier said than done.

Hormone overload, pure and simple. What else could it possibly be?

You've never been so attuned to someone that when you enter a room, that person is all you see? You've never wanted someone so desperately that you would risk everything to have them?

Yes, she wanted Zain, with a force that defied logic. Even more now after what he'd said only minutes ago.

I would not be lying awake at night fantasizing about all the ways I would make love to you.

Graphic, detailed images of making love with Zain filtered into Madison's mind when she should have been focusing on the meeting. She shifted her crossed legs from restlessness and pure, undeniable desire for a man who shouldn't be on her sexual radar. But he was, front and center, sending out signals that she urgently wanted to answer.

The sound of raised voices jarred Madison out of her fantasies and back into reality. She regarded Deeb, who appeared impervious to the disruption.

"What's happening now?" she asked.

"The emir is explaining his water proposal. Sheikh Barad has taken exception to it."

"Which one is he?"

"To the right of Prince Rafiq."

Madison honed in on a fierce-looking man with a neatly trimmed goatee and beady eyes. "Is he a relative?"

"No. He is a childhood friend of Prince Rafiq's. His sister, Maysa, is a physician."

Maysa. The woman Zain had visited the other night. "He doesn't appear to care for Zain."

"He does not care for the emir's plan, nor does he care for the emir's demand that he halt any plans for drilling."

Obviously oil and water truly didn't mix in this case. "Is this going to be a problem for Zain?" Not again. "His Highness?"

Deeb didn't seem at all disturbed by her second informality screwup. "That depends on how he chooses to handle the matter."

Zain chose to handle it by rising from the chair and slamming his palm on the table. He then launched into an impassioned diatribe that seemed to silence everyone into submission.

"He is telling everyone that he is the king," Deeb began. "His word is the law, and those who go against him will be summarily dismissed and tried for treason."

Apparently Zain was dead serious. "What does that entail?"

"If found guilty, a firing squad."

Madison wondered if that held true for unsuitable women who overstepped their bounds and slept with the king. She preferred not to find out.

Zain reclaimed his seat but continued to speak, this time in low, more temperate tones. Deeb explained that he spoke of the people, their needs and the importance of their future, the evils of profiteering and raping the land, as well as his commitment to bringing the country into the twenty-first century. "If there are those who do not support his vision," Deeb continued, "they may relinquish their positions immediately."

As Zain continued to address the men, Madison found

his absolute control, his sheer air of power, as heady as a hot bath. Funny, she had never been turned on by authoritative men. Then again, she'd never met anyone like Zain before. Not even close. In the five years she'd lived with her former boyfriend, not once had Jay ever made her feel as if she might climb out of her skin if she didn't have him. Not once did she spot him across a crowded room and feel an overwhelming sense of passion.

Without warning, Zain abruptly stood, did an about-face and strode out of the room, leaving the men exchanging glances with each other, their mouths agape. Everyone but Rafiq, who looked more angry than shocked.

"I guess the meeting's over," Madison said as the rest of the members began to exit, one by one.

"Yes, it is," Deeb said solemnly. "Unfortunately, the emir's problems have only begun."

Madison understood that all too well. Her respect for Zain had risen tenfold, but so had the realization that his position required his undivided attention. He couldn't afford any distractions, and that included her.

Feeling a headache coming on, Madison left the gallery and headed straight for her quarters. She vowed that from this point forward, she would avoid being alone with Zain.

"I must commend you on your success, brother."

With only a brief glance at Rafiq standing at the study door, Zain tossed the robe onto the sofa and claimed the place beside it. "I am pleased you have finally realized I am quite capable of handling my duties."

Rafiq strolled into the room and took the opposing chair. "I am not referring to your duty. I am referring to Ms. Foster. It has taken you less than five days to bed her. However, that is still two days more than the new cook's assistant ten years ago."

He should have known his sibling would never congratulate him on his success with the council meeting. "And if my memory serves me correctly, you slept with the gardener's daughter the day you met her, brother."

Rafiq presented an acerbic smile. "True, but that young woman did not have the power to destroy my reputation."

"Neither does Ms. Foster, and for your information, I have not slept with her." Not beyond his fantasies.

"All signs point to the contrary."

"And your imagination is out of control."

"I did not imagine the way the two of you looked at each other earlier today," Rafiq said. "Nor did I imagine your talk of trust."

"She was referring to trust in regard to my recent disappearance." Only a partial truth. "You always have, and always will, assume that I have no self-control when it comes to the opposite sex."

"I would be joined by the rest of the world in that assumption."

With effort, Zain kept his anger in check. "Perhaps that is why you hired Ms. Foster. You were setting me up to fail because of the temptation she poses."

He presented a self-satisfied smile. "Then you admit you are tempted by her."

More than his brother knew. "And you are not?"

"I am to be married in two weeks' time."

"You are still a man, Rafiq, and you are marrying a woman who does not support your libido, only your foreign bank account."

Rafiq came to his feet. "I have no time for this. But mark my words, should you give in to temptation with

Ms. Foster, you are taking a risk that could destroy what little standing you have left among our people."

Zain refused to comment as his brother exited the room. Yes, Madison posed a tremendous temptation. And yes, any intimacy with her would come with considerable risk. But she had become one of his greatest weaknesses in the past few days. Perhaps one of his greatest weaknesses ever.

Feeling restless and ready to run, Zain decided he needed some space. He knew exactly where he wanted to go, and he did not intend to go alone.

"Change into some comfortable clothes and shoes, and come with me."

Madison remained at the open veranda door, determined to stand her ground with Zain. "After today, running off together is the last thing you need. In fact, I've decided it's best we aren't alone together again."

"We will not be alone for long on this journey."

Evidently they'd be accompanied by a contingent of guards, which would be for the best—if she decided to go with him. "Where exactly do you plan to take me?"

"It's a surprise."

She planted her fists on her hips and refused to budge. "I'm not too fond of surprises."

He leaned a shoulder against the doorframe. "You will enjoy this one. We do need to hurry to reach our destination on time."

"Which is?"

"On the outskirts of the village. It will take us a while to arrive there."

Could he be any more vague? "As far as I know, the village is only a mile or so from the palace, which is about a two minute drive. Are we going by camel?"

He had the gall to grin. "No. We are going by foot."

He'd evidently lost his royal mind if he honestly believed she'd agree to traipse down a mountain in the dark. She was basically a klutz on level ground in broad daylight. "You're proposing we walk down to the village at dusk."

"Yes, and if you will stop talking and start dressing, we might be there before dawn."

He apparently wouldn't give up until she gave in, and she wasn't quite ready to do that. "I refuse to go unless you give me details."

He streaked a hand over his chin. "All right. I want you to see the village with me serving as your guide. I want you to know the people and understand why my position as their king holds great importance."

"Why didn't you just say that in the first place?"

"Because you are quite beautiful when you are not in control."

And he was quite the cad. An incredibly sensual cad. "I'll go, but only on one condition."

He released a rough sigh. "What would that be?"

"You say please."

He took her hand and gave it a light kiss. "Would you please do me the honor of allowing me to show you my world?"

How could she refuse him now? "Fine. Just give me a few minutes."

"Wear a waterproof jacket, since rain is predicted for later tonight."

Great. "You expect me to walk back up the mountain in the dark all wet?"

He grinned. "There is no guarantee you will be wet, but chances are you very well could be, whether it rains or not."

The innuendo wasn't lost on Madison, or her contrary libido. "If you don't behave, I'm staying here."

His smile faded into a frown. "I will arrange transportation for our return if that will satisfy you."

"That will." She could only hope he made good on his word. "Wait here while I change."

"I may not come inside and wait?"

How easy it would be to say yes, but if she did, they might forgo their little expedition for a different kind of journey. In bed. "No, you may not wait inside."

"You still do not trust me."

"Not when my underwear happens to be involved."

After closing the door on him, Madison piled her hair into a ponytail then quickly changed into a T-shirt, jeans, her lone pair of sneakers and an all-weather lightweight coat. Probably not the best in the way of hiking clothes, but they'd have to do.

She returned to the veranda to find him leaning back against the wall, a military-green jacket covering his black tee and beige cargo pants, the camouflage baseball cap set low on his brow. For all intents and purposes, he could be an ordinary man on a mission of leisure. Yet there was nothing ordinary about those pensive dark eyes.

He held out his hand to her. "Are you ready for an adventure?"

That depended on what kind of adventure he had in mind. Only one way to find out. "As ready as I'll ever be."

After Madison clasped his offered hand, Zain led her down the side stairs leading to the labyrinth of courtyards on the ground level. He came to a small iron gate and opened it to a rock path that led away from the rear of the palace. The stone soon turned to dirt, and the trail soon took a sharp downward descent.

"Are you sure this is safe?" she asked when they reached a rocky place that looked way too precarious to go forward.

Zain released her, stepped down and then signaled her forward. "Take my hand and I'll assist you."

She would rather ride down on his back but that could be a bit awkward. "Okay, if you say so."

Slowly, steadily, they navigated the pathway until they finally reached firm footing, and not once had Zain let her go. She began to relax as they continued on, knowing he would do his best to keep her out of harm's way. But then he came to an ominous-looking boulder pile and started to climb.

"Follow me," he said over one shoulder.

Madison remained at the bottom and glared up at him. "Excuse me, but I thought we're supposed to be going down, not up."

"First, you must see the view from here before we continue."

Her gaze wandered up to the plateau. "You can describe it to me."

"You have to witness it firsthand."

"I can't see it if I break my neck."

He scurried down and gestured toward the formation. "I will be immediately behind you offering support should you need it. Trust me, I will not let you fall."

She did trust him, at least in this case. "Okay, I'll do it, as long as you keep your eye on the goal and not on my butt."

He smiled. "I cannot promise I will not look, but I will try to refrain from touching you."

And she'd try to refrain from requesting he touch her, though she couldn't promise that, either.

One foot in front of the other, she silently chanted as

she began the ascent. Truth was, she'd hiked before in similar terrain, just not in a long time. Yet her confidence grew knowing Zain would catch her if she stumbled. And with only moderate effort, she made it to the top just in time to catch the view of the valley washed in the final rays of the setting sun.

"Unbelievable," she muttered when Zain came up behind her. "I can see so much more here than on the veranda."

"I told you it was not to be missed." He rested his hands lightly on her shoulders. "If you look closely, you can see the lake right beyond the base of Mabrúruk."

She spotted a patch of cerulean-blue on the horizon. "I see it. Is that a hotel on the cliff above it?"

"A resort," he said. "It's owned by the Barad family and managed by Shamil Barad."

"Maysa's brother," Madison replied. "Mr. Deeb told me about him."

"Maysa is nothing like him." He sounded and looked irate. "Where she cares about the people, Shamil only cares about padding his fortune at any cost."

"Believe me, I've met his kind. And I'm positive you'll keep him in his place."

He leaned and kissed her cheek. "I truly appreciate your confidence in me."

As Zain continued to point out the landmarks, Madison found herself leaning back against him. And when he slipped his arms around her waist, she didn't bother to pull away. She simply marveled at the passion in his voice when he spoke about his people, and relished the way he made her felt so protected.

A span of silence passed before Madison looked up at him. "You really love your country, don't you?"

"Yes, I do," he said as he stared off into the distance.

"That is why I cannot fail, yet the burden to succeed at times seems too heavy for one man to bear. Especially a flawed man like myself."

She sensed making that admission had cost him, and that alone made her appreciate him all the more. She turned into his arms and gave him a smile. "But you will succeed, Zain. You have too much conviction not to see this through."

"I am certainly going to try." For a moment he looked as though he might kiss her but surprisingly let her go. "We'd best be on our way, otherwise we will be walking in the dark."

"If we must."

Zain led the way, his hand firmly gripping hers as they made their way down the slope. Once at the bottom, he took her by the waist, lifted her up and set her on her feet. "I am so glad I made it without breaking something," she said as she tightened the band securing her hair.

"I would never let you fall, Madison."

Oh, but she was in the process of falling for him, and he couldn't be her human safety net. In a matter of weeks, she would leave him behind, and she'd have only the memories of a man who was beginning to mean too much to her. So tonight, she would make more good memories that would remain long after they'd said goodbye.

Six

"How much farther is it?"

Zain glanced back at Madison, who was trudging up the drive slowly. "Only thirty meters or so."

"My metrics suck, Zain," she said, sounding winded. "And apparently so does my stamina. But at least you were kind enough to stop for food, however rushed the meal might have been."

He'd feared being identified in such a public place. Fortunately, they'd somehow escaped recognition. "We are almost there."

As they rounded the bend, the three-quarter moon provided enough light to illuminate the small flat-roofed structure that had been a second home during his youth. He paused and pointed. "It is right there."

She came to his side and squinted. "Who lives here?"

"My friend Malik. He owns the surrounding land and raises sheep."

Madison knelt to retie her shoe. "Does he know we're coming?"

"No, but he will be glad to see me." Or so he hoped. Seven years had come and gone since their last contact, but they had been the best of friends though they lived on opposite sides of the social dividing line.

She straightened and secured the band in her hair. "Let's get going, then, before my legs give out completely. If that happens, you'll have to carry me the rest of the way."

He saw no reason not to do that now. Without giving Madison warning, he swept her up, tossed her over his shoulder and started toward their destination.

"Put me down, you royal caveman."

Had she not been laughing, he would have complied due to the insult. "I am not a caveman. I am a gentleman."

"A gentleman Neanderthal."

"I am the Neanderthal who is coming to your rescue, therefore you should refrain from complaining."

"My hero."

Ignoring her sarcasm, he continued until he made it up the single step and onto the small porch before he slid her down to her feet. "Are you sufficiently rested now?"

She adjusted her clothing and sighed. "I'm probably a mess."

"You are a beautiful mess."

She smiled. "You are a wonderful liar."

He reached out and touched her flushed cheek. "It is unfortunate you do not realize the extent of your beauty, yet is it also refreshing. I have known too many women whose beauty is only superficial. Yours is far-reaching."

She laid her palm on his hand. "You are determined to say all the right things tonight, aren't you?"

He also wanted to do all the right things, avoiding any missteps along the way. That alone prevented him from kissing her now, though he desperately wanted to do that, and more. "I am only trying to give you an enjoyable evening."

"So far, so good, expect for the marathon walk. Now, do you think you might want to knock before your friend goes to bed?"

"That is probably a good idea." He reluctantly dropped his hand from her face and rapped on the door.

Several minutes passed before Malik answered the summons. "Yes?"

Zain removed his cap. "Do you have water for two weary travelers, *sadiq?*"

The initial confusion on his friend's face quickly dissolved into recognition. "Zain, is that you?"

"Have I changed that much?"

Malik greeted him with a stern expression. "No, you have not changed. You are still the *kalet* who always appears unannounced."

Sadly, he had mistakenly believed he would be welcome. "Perhaps I should return another time."

"I prefer not to wait another seven years before I can beat you at a game of Tarneeb." He opened the door wide and grinned. *"Marhaban, sadiq."*

The warm greeting lifted Zain's spirits and concerns. He entered the house and accepted his friend's brief embrace before he remembered Madison was still waiting outside.

He turned and gestured her forward. "Malik, this is Madison Foster. Madison, Malik El-Amin."

"It's a pleasure to meet you, Malik," Madison said as she offered her hand to Malik to shake.

"Come and sit." Malik gestured toward the familiar low corner sofa covered in heavy blue fabric.

Before they could comply, a dark-haired child bolted into the room and immediately hid behind Malik. She smiled up at Zain as she twirled a long braid and rocked back and forth on her heels.

"Who have we here?" Zain asked.

"This is Lailah," Malik said as he nudged her forward. "She is six and our oldest."

"She's beautiful," Madison said from behind Zain.

Malik smiled with pride as he swept Lailah into his arms. "She fortunately resembles her mother, as do the rest of our daughters."

When a sudden, bittersweet memory filtered into Zain's mind, he pushed it aside. Yet he couldn't quite dismiss the regrets over losing touch with his friend. "How many children do you have?"

"Three more," Malik said as he set Lailah on her feet, prompting her to exit as quickly as she'd come into the room. "Badia is five and Jada is four. Ma'ali is our youngest. She arrived three months ago."

Zain patted his back. "Congratulations. It appears Mabrúruk has been good to you."

Malik frowned. "Perhaps too good."

He looked around for signs of his friend's wife. "Is Helene so exhausted she has already retired for the evening?"

"She is putting the baby to bed."

"Unfortunately, I have not been successful in that endeavor."

Zain turned his attention to the former Helene Christos, who breezed into the room, her thick brown hair flowing over her shoulders, a swaddled infant nestled in the crook of her arm. He immediately went to her and kissed both her cheeks. "You have not changed since the day you wed Malik." A somewhat controversial wedding between an Arabic farmer and a Greek-American restaurant owner's daughter. Clearly they had survived that controversy.

She frowned. "And you are forever the royal charmer, Zain Mehdi. But then I suppose I should be calling you King now. Forgive me for not bowing. I have my hands full."

He decided not to point out he was not the official king yet. "Clearly Malik has his hands full as well, since you have given him four daughters. I suppose he deserves that much."

She patted his cheek. "As do you. I wish for you many daughters and much grief protecting them from rogues like you and Malik."

"I'll second that," Madison added.

Zain felt bad for not including Madison in the conversation. Without thought, he took her hand, pulled her forward and kept his palm against the small of her back. "This is Madison Foster."

Helene eyed her for a few moments before she handed the sleeping infant over to her husband. "Are you a souvenir Zain brought from Los Angeles?"

Madison shook her head. "Not hardly. I'm currently serving as a consultant during his transition from prince to king."

"Helene's family owns the restaurant where we dined tonight," Zain added.

"The tapas were wonderful," Madison said. "I haven't found anything remotely as good in the D.C. area."

Helene's expression brightened. "You're from D.C.? My family is originally from Baltimore, although I haven't lived there since my father saw an opportunity and opened his restaurant here fifteen years ago." She reclaimed the baby from Malik before gesturing toward the sofa. "Have a seat and tell me what's the latest in spring fashion in America."

When the women settled onto the sofa to converse, Malik nodded to his right. "Let us escape before we are asked our opinions on footwear."

Zain followed Malik into the modest kitchen that had been fitted with modern appliances. "I see you have made some improvements."

Malik leaned back against the counter and folded his arms. "After my mother passed four years ago, I felt the need to make Helene feel more welcome in our home."

"I was not aware of your loss." A loss to which Zain could relate. "My sympathies. She was a good woman."

"She was a hard-working woman. She was forced to be the sole support following my father's death. I do not wish Helene to endure such hardship if I can prevent it."

Yet Malik had turned down Zain's loan offer several years ago. "Is the farming going well?"

"It has been for the last few years. After I married Helene, we were shunned by a few traditionalists but fortunately accepted by those who have blended, multi-cultural families. Those people kept us afloat until we finally gained acceptance."

He felt a measure of guilt that he hadn't been around to offer moral support. "I am sorry it's been so difficult for the two of you, Malik. My wish is for your continued success and a prosperous future for your family."

"You can assist us with that, Zain."

Finally, the man would let go of his pride and accept help. "How much money do you need?"

"I am not speaking of money," Malik said. "The local madrasa is in great need of funds for supplies and books. We cannot afford a private school and we want our daughters to have the best education."

Only one more change he would need to make among many. "Consider it done. I will add that to the budget now under consideration." And hoped he would not face another battle with the council.

"I appreciate whatever you can do." Malik inclined his head and sent him a curious look. "What is your true relationship with this Madison Foster?"

That happened to be one question he wasn't prepared to answer, perhaps because he was still uncertain. "As we previously explained, she is a contracted employee."

"Is serving as your lover one of the requirements?"

The question took Zain aback. "She is not my lover."

"Yet that is precisely what you are wishing for, *sadiq*."

"I did not say that." He sounded too defensive to support a denial.

Zain was certain Malik saw through his guise after his friend laid a hand on his shoulder. "When you escaped the palace to play with the local boys in the village streets on the day we met, I recognized you were destined for greatness. And when you became the chosen successor to the throne, I knew that would come to pass. Are you willing to give up your destiny for a woman who would not be deemed suitable?"

Zain tamped down his anger for the sake of friendship. "Are those not the words of a hypocrite, Malik? You did not let suitability sway you when you chose Helene."

"Yet I am not the king with an entire country following my every move."

He reluctantly acknowledged his friend had a point. "The people of this country should not be allowed to dictate my personal life or who I choose to be with."

Malik narrowed his eyes. "It is apparent this woman

means more to you than another conquest to add to all the others."

He felt the need to be truthful. "I am not certain what she means to me. I do know she seems to understand me in ways no one has before. When she's not in my presence, she is constantly in my thoughts. When I am with her, I dread the moment she has to leave me. Have you felt as if you had known someone your entire life, yet you've only known them for a few days?"

"Yes. Helene. And you, *sadiq,* are in the throes of love."

He had to believe that his current state was only the result of unrequited lust. "I cannot afford those emotions, Malik. I do know I can only consider the time we have now before she returns to America."

"And when will that be?"

"Following the coronation." The time had come to pose a request, one his friend could adamantly refuse. "Do you have a vehicle I could borrow for the evening? I will see that it is returned to you tomorrow morning."

"You did not arrive in an official car?" Malik asked.

"We walked into the village so that Madison could see the sights. Tonight I desire to be only a man with no responsibility other than being with a remarkable woman."

His friend scowled. "Yet you are a king with no car and obviously no guards."

"I do not need guards where I have been, or where I am going."

"Where would that be?"

"I wish to show Madison the lake."

Malik gave him a good-natured grin. "You wish to show her more than that, I fear. Perhaps you need protection not from guards, but from the powers of Mabrúruk."

"I only need a vehicle." In terms of lovemaking, the

protection issue would warrant discussion only if the situation arose once he had Madison alone. "Will you accommodate me, or will I need to go door-to-door to make the request?"

Malik walked to the back entrance, took a key hanging from the hook on the wall and returned to offer it to Zain. "This is to my truck. It is old and it has no rear seating, but it runs and it does have fuel, as well as two blankets for your comfort. Please return it in the same condition."

Zain pocketed the keys. "I am eternally in your debt."

"You may repay me by proceeding with caution. But then you have always been the master of escape, which leads me to believe you have a plan."

He planned only to leave as soon as possible before he had to endure more of his friend's counsel. "If you are finished with the advice, we need to be going before the night is over."

"I only have a few more words to say." When Zain opened his mouth to protest, Malik held up a hand to silence him and continued. "I understand your need to hurry, but I urge you to think before you head down the path of no return. And after some consideration, you may keep the blankets as a memento."

They shared in a hearty laugh as they returned to the living area to find the women still engaged in conversation. Zain was surprised to see Madison holding the baby against her shoulder and rocking slowly, back and forth.

She seemed very natural with the child, yet he saw a hint of sadness in her eyes when she glanced at him, and perhaps longing. That telling sign led Zain to believe she had not been honest when she'd firmly stated she had no interest in having a family. Perhaps she had not found the right man to father her children. He could be that man.

The thought came to him clear and concise, rendering him mentally off balance. He could not wish for the unattainable. He would not subject her to years of regret by wanting more from her than he could give her. But he could give her this night. A night she would not soon forget.

"Are you sure this thing is going to make it?" When Madison failed to receive a response from Zain, who had his eyes trained on the treacherous road, she gave up trying to talk to him. Between the vehicle's squeaks and groans, and the whistling wind, which had picked up steam, conversation was out of the question.

She'd climbed into the monstrosity on the assumption they were returning to the palace. She soon realized she'd been wrong when they headed away from the village and started toward the massive mountain.

Madison gripped the top of the windowless door as Zain guided the truck on a downward trek through a narrow passage comprised of boulders on both sides. She decided in this case ignorance was truly bliss and closed her eyes. She stayed that way until they came to a teeth-jarring stop.

The moon and the headlights provided enough illumination for her to view the shimmering lake spread out before them. Zain rounded the car, opened the passenger door, held out his hand and helped her climb down.

"So this is it?" she said as soon as she had her feet on solid ground. "I just wish I could see it better."

"I promised to bring you here before your departure, and with the upcoming chaos, I felt tonight would be the best time."

She didn't want to think about leaving Bajul, about

leaving him, so she wouldn't. "I'm glad we survived the drive so I could see it." Or see as much as she could.

She did spot a path leading to the shore, and immediately saw relief for her aching feet. Without another word, she took off toward the lake and, after arriving on the sandy beach, toed out of her sneakers and socks and rolled up her jeans. The minute her toes hit the cool water, she sighed at the sensations. A soothing balm for her sore soles.

"Take care of the piranha."

Madison spun around and did a little dance out of the water. When she heard the sound of Zain's laughter echoing over the area, she glanced up to see him standing above her. She considered sending him a dirty look but doubted he could see it, so she chose to give him a verbal lashing. "That was not funny at all, Zain Mehdi. It's bad enough that you took me on a dangerous joyride to get here, and now you're trying to scare me with killer fish."

He slipped his hands in his pockets. "My apologies for frightening you."

She snatched up her shoes and started toward him. "I take it there are no flesh-eating fish?"

"There are fish, but they do not crave flesh."

"Good to know, after the fact," she said when she reached him. "What now? Midnight scuba diving? Underwater basket-weaving?"

"Whatever you wish to do."

What Madison wanted to do and what she should do were two different animals. She stared up at the mist that had formed over the looming mountain, and the clouds gathering in the distance. "Since it looks like it's about to rain, we should probably head back to the palace."

"Are you afraid of rain?"

She turned her attention to Zain, specifically his eyes, which seemed darker than midnight. "I'm afraid of what might happen if we stay."

"You fear we'll make love."

"Yes, I do. I told myself I wouldn't be alone with you where anything was possible. And here we are."

He moved a little closer. "And I have told you I have certain conditions before that will happen."

"You want me to say I trust you." And if she didn't, that would be the end of it.

"Do you trust that I would never hurt you?"

Not physically, but he could hurt her in so many other ways. "I know that."

"Do you trust that what has been said about my relationships with women is not the truth?"

"Do I think your sexual exploits are overblown? Probably." Though she wasn't sure how exaggerated they might have been.

He reached out and touched her face. "Most important, you may trust that whatever happens between us tonight, I will not take it lightly. And I will not tell a soul. I only want to prove that you are a desirable, sensual woman. With that said, do you trust me?"

Call it instinct, call it crazy, but she did. "Yes, I do trust you. I'm not sure I trust myself around you."

He took her shoes, dropped them on the ground, slid her jacket away and tossed it down to join her sneakers. "I will teach you to trust your own sexuality." He shrugged out of his jacket and added it to the pile. "I only ask that you let go of your inhibitions."

That could be a test for her normally cautious self, and she wondered if going forward would be worth the risk. Yet when he pulled her into his arms and lowered his mouth to hers, she began to believe she could meet the challenge. He kissed her gently at first, just a light tease of his tongue against hers. Then he held her tighter, kissed her deeply, thoroughly, until her pulse started to sprint. The rain had begun to lightly fall, but she didn't care. Didn't care that before this was over, she would be soaked to the skin. Come to think of it, they could be down to only skin very, very soon.

Madison started to protest when Zain pulled away and stepped back. But all arguments died on her lips as he tugged his shirt over his head and tossed it aside. Due to the limited light, she could barely see the finer points of his bare chest. However, she could make out the width of his shoulders, the definition of his biceps and the light shading at his sternum. She was dying to touch him, investigate the extremely masculine terrain. As if he'd read her mind, he moved forward, leaving little space between them, and flattened her palms against his chest immediately below his collarbone. She took a downward path over his damp skin and when she circled his nipples with her fingertips, she heard the slight catch of his breath. When she slid her hands to his abdomen, she thought he might have stopped breathing. She kept going, using a fingertip to trace the thin trail of hair that disappeared into his waistband.

But that was as far as he allowed her to go. He clasped her wrists, lifted her hands and kissed each palm. Then without fair warning, he pulled her T-shirt up and over her head. She wore only jeans, a pink floral bra and a blanket of goose bumps that had nothing to do with the weather. She predicted he would soon relieve her of the rest of her clothes. Instead, he claimed a boulder to take off his boots and sent her a *What are you waiting for?* look.

"No inhibitions," he said when she failed to remove her bra.

The time had come to kick the self-consciousness to the curb. She sucked in a deep breath, undid the clasp, slipped the straps from her shoulders and added her bra to the clothes heap. "No inhibitions."

The words seemed to shred Zain's control, apparent by the way he pushed off the rock and engaged her in one deep, deadly kiss. After a few moments, he shifted his attention to the column of her throat with light kisses. When his mouth closed over her breast, Madison feathered her hands in his hair in order to stay somewhat steady against the sensual onslaught. So caught up in the pull of his mouth, the feel of his tongue swirling around her nipple, she was only vaguely aware that he'd unfastened her jeans. She became extremely aware when he pushed her pants down her hips, along with her underwear, until both dropped to her ankles.

"No inhibitions," he whispered. "No turning back."

She couldn't turn back if she wanted to, and she didn't. Not in the least. Taking his cue, she used his broad shoulders for support and stepped out of the jeans. Now she was completely naked, while he was still dressed from the waist down. Normally that might make her feel extremely uneasy. Instead, she was incredibly hot, especially when he kissed her again, his hands roving over her bottom, his fingers curling between her thighs.

She wanted him as naked as she was. She wanted him more than she'd wanted anything in quite some time. And it appeared she would get what she wanted when he swept her up into his arms, carried her to the ancient truck and set her on the tailgate. She glanced over her shoulder to discover the bed had been conveniently cov-

ered by a colorful quilt, but all her attention soon turned
to Zain as he stood in front of her, his hand at his fly.

She was in the buff and barely breathing and drenched.
Everywhere. She was also overcome with impatience
when Zain failed to remove his slacks.

"Birth control," he grated out as he continued to lower
his zipper.

She didn't want to reveal why it wasn't a problem, or
burden him with the truth—the chance she could become
pregnant was slim to none without medical assistance.
This was not the time for sadness or regrets and, most
of all, sympathy. "It's not an issue."

"Are you certain?" he asked.

"You're going to have to trust me on this."

That seemed to satisfy his concerns as he took little
time shoving his pants down and kicking them away.
Now they were both equally undressed and she was extremely impressed. Despite the fact that he'd left on the
truck's parking lights, she still wished she could see
him better. But even if the sun made an unexpected appearance, Zain wouldn't have given her the chance to
assess the details. He hoisted himself onto the tailgate
and in a matter of seconds, had her on her back on the
makeshift bed.

He hovered above her, his hand resting lightly on her
thigh, his gaze leveled on hers. "Do you still trust me?"

Right now, she'd say anything if he'd just get on with
it. "Yes."

"Then roll to your side away from me."

Madison wasn't sure where this might be heading,
yet she complied because she did trust him. Trusted him
not to hurt her. Trusted him to take her on an unforget-
table ride.

Zain fitted himself against her back, pushed her

damp hair aside and pressed his lips to her ear. "Clear your mind and think of nothing else but us together." He streamed his hand down her thigh and lifted her leg over his. "Enjoy these moments." He slowly slid his palm down her abdomen. "Pretend this is the only time you will feel this good—" he eased inside her "—again."

The moment Zain hit the mark, Madison shuddered from the sensations. He seemed to time his movement with the stroke of his fingertips, and she responded as if she never had felt this good, because she couldn't recall when she had. He kept a slow, steady pace with both his touch and his body, yet her own body reacted as if they were on a sexual sprint. If she could prolong the involuntary release, she would, but that all-important passion had led to this moment when her body claimed all control. The orgasm arrived quickly in strong spasms, wave after wave of pleasure that seemed to go on forever, though not nearly long enough.

Zain muttered something in Arabic that sound suspiciously like an oath, then pulled out and turned her onto her back. He entered her again, this time not quite as carefully as before, but as promised, he didn't hurt her. He did fuel her fantasies as he rose up on his arms and moved again, harder, faster, his dark gaze firmly fixed on hers. Madison found his powerful thrusts, the continuing rain and the fact they were out in the open highly erotic. And so was the way his jaw went rigid, his eyes closed and his body tensed with the force of his climax that soon came sure and swift.

When Zain collapsed against her, Madison savored the feel of his solid back beneath her palms, even his weight. She didn't exactly appreciate what he had done to her—coaxed her into crossing a line she had never intended to cross. A dangerous boundary that could cost them both if anyone found out.

But even in light of that possibility, she truly believed that this first experience with the king—the *only* experience she could afford—had been absolutely worth the risk.

Unfortunately, it was the last risk she would allow them to take.

Seven

Had it not been for the deluge, Zain would have made love to her again. And again.

Instead, he had carried Madison and set her in the cab. He re-dressed in soaked clothing and gathered hers, only to return to find her wrapped in the dry blanket. Not long after they'd left the lake, she'd settled against his side, her head tipped against his shoulder, and fallen fast asleep. Even when he navigated the rugged terrain, she hadn't woken. But during that time, and since, he had been very aware that she was still naked beneath the blanket. Whenever she stirred, his body did the same. Tonight's brief interlude had not been enough. If he had his way, they would enjoy more of the same, and often, in the upcoming days.

When Madison shifted slightly, Zain glanced at her to see she was still sleeping, looking beautiful and somewhat innocent. She brought out his protective side, though she did not need his protection. She was fiercely independent, fiery and intractable, everything he admired in a woman. Tonight she had proven she possessed an untapped passion that he needed to explore further. She also made him want to right his transgressions and prove to her he owned a measure of honor. He wanted to toss away convention and be with her after the coronation. And that was impossible. Eventually he would be required to marry, and he would not relegate Madison to mistress status. She deserved much better, and so would his future wife. So had his own mother.

That did not preclude him from being with her until the day she left.

When he hit a bump in the road, Madison raised her head and gave him a sleepy smile. "How much longer until we're at the palace?"

"Approximately ten minutes."

She straightened and sent him a panicked look. "You should have woken me earlier," she said as she sorted through the clothes at her side.

"Dressing is not necessary." He preferred she remained naked, as he planned to take her to his bed as soon as they arrived.

"I'm not walking into the royal abode wearing only a blanket." A blanket she tossed aside without regard to her nudity or his discomfort.

He became mesmerized when she lifted her hips and slid her panties into place, followed by her jeans. She picked up her shirt, shook it out, allowing him an extended look at her breasts, the pale pink nipples...

The sound of grating beneath the tires forced his gaze to the road that he'd inadvertently left during his visual exploration. He jerked the truck back onto pavement immediately before he ended up in some unsuspecting citizen's front yard.

"Are you trying to kill us, Zain?"

"I was avoiding a goat."

Madison laughed softly. "An imaginary goat."

He frowned. "It is your fault for distracting me."

"It's your fault for not keeping your eyes on the road."

"I am a man, Madison. You cannot expect me to ignore your state of undress. You should know that after what we shared tonight."

"You're right, and I'm sorry."

He sent another fast glance in her direction to find her completely clothed and smiling. "Are you more comfortable now?"

"I'm very wet."

That prompted a very vivid fantasy, and a return of his erection. "If you will remove your pants again and come over here, I will remedy that."

She shot him a sour look. "You are such a bad boy. No wonder all those women fell all over themselves to be with you."

"Two women."

"Excuse me?"

He finally recognized that she could trust him freely only if he freely gave her accurate information. "I was involved with two women during my time away."

Her blue eyes widened. "You're saying that out of all those highly publicized photos of you escorting various starlets and such, you were only involved with two?"

The disbelief in her voice and expression drove him to disclose the details. "The first woman was older," he continued. "I met Elizabeth through business contacts about a year after I arrived in L.A. My father released only limited funds to me and she assisted with my investments. I owe the majority of my second fortune to her."

"How long were you together?"

Too long for his comfort. "Almost three years."

"What about the second woman?"

This explanation would prove to be more difficult, and much more revealing. Yet for some reason, he wanted Madison to know the facts. Facts few people knew. "Her name was Genevieve. I met her in a café in Paris. I was there for business, she was on sabbatical."

"Then it was only a brief fling?"

"No. I joined her in Africa."

"Africa?" Madison sounded stunned by the revelation. "How long were you there? *Why* were you there?"

"Eighteen months in Ethiopia and, after a three-month break, fifteen months in Nigeria. Genevieve is a humanitarian aid worker. I assisted her with the relief effort by delivering supplies and building temporary shelter."

"Did anyone know your true identity?"

"Only Genevieve." He smiled with remembrance. "She introduced me as Joe Smith."

"That name definitely encourages anonymity," she said. "And to think that all this time, people believed you were holed up with some supermodel, while you were less than a thousand miles away from Bajul being a really stellar guy. Unbelievable."

"Genevieve convinced me I needed to learn the reality of the situation in order to be a better leader." And he had not been prepared for that reality. "I have never seen such desolation. Violence brought about by unrest and ignorance. Famine, starvation and disease brought about by drought and insufficient food and water distribution."

"And that's when you decided to develop your water conservation plans."

He started up the road leading to the castle, relieved that the conversation would soon have to come to an end. "I vowed when my opportunity to rule arrived, I would do everything in my power to prevent the possibility of that devastation in my country. I had not expected the opportunity to arrive so quickly. My plans were to return to Bajul to present my proposals when I received word of my father's death."

"So he never knew about your ideas."

"No." Even if he had, his inflexible father would have rejected them because he had the power to do so. "Regardless, I will never be able to repay Genevieve for forcing me to open my eyes to the possibilities. The experience changed me. She changed me."

"She sounds like a very special woman."

"She was caring and committed and possessed all the attributes I had never acquired." And she'd been much too good for a man whose character had been questionable up to that point in time.

Madison laid a hand on his arm. "But as you've said, you've changed for the better. Not many men in your position would have personally taken on those challenges, and dangerous ones at that. Most would have written a check and returned home."

He appreciated her praise. He greatly appreciated her willingness to listen without judgment. "At times I wish I could have accomplished more, especially when it came to the children."

She sighed. "I know. I remember traveling with my parents to some of the worst poverty-stricken places in the world. The children always suffer the most, even in America."

The memories came back to Zain with the clarity of cut glass. Memories he had never shared with one soul since his return. "I met a special child there. She was around four years of age and an orphan. The workers took charge of her care until a relative could be located. For some reason, she attached herself to me. We spoke different languages, yet we found ways to communicate. Perhaps she appreciated the treats I gave her."

"Or maybe she recognized someone she could trust."

The sincerity in Madison's tone temporarily lifted his spirits. "Her name was Ajo. It means *joyful,* and that suited her. Yet I saw no joy in her when they took her away." He would never forget the way she held out her arms to him, or her tears. The images still haunted him, and at times he felt he had abandoned her.

"Do you know what happened to her?" Madison asked.

He arrived at the gate and raised his hand at the confused guards who, after a slight hesitation, allowed him entry. "Genevieve has been kind enough to keep me apprised of her situation and to deliver the funds I send monthly for Ajo's care. Fortunately, her aunt and uncle see to it she is safe and secure."

"That's wonderful, Zain. But what about your relationship with Genevieve?"

A complex relationship that was never meant to be. "I returned to L.A. when she was reassigned. I had my responsibilities, and she had hers."

"Were you in love with her?"

He was surprised by the query, and uncertain how to answer. He'd cared a great deal for Genevieve, but love had not entered into it. "We both understood from the beginning that our relationship could only be temporary.

We agreed to enjoy each other's company while the opportunity existed."

Madison shifted back to his side and rested her head against his shoulder. "I'm sorry I misjudged you. I bought into the whole 'superficial, arrogant, rich playboy' assumption, just like everyone else did. It's nice to know that couldn't be further from the truth. Despite your issues with your father, it's clear he raised you to be an honorable man."

Anger broke through his remorse. Anger aimed at his patriarch, not at Madison. "My father knew nothing of honor, and he did little to raise me. You may thank Elena for that. I would never take a mistress and force my wife to have a child she did not want. As far as I am concerned, he was responsible for her death due to his careless disregard."

"What happened to her, Zain?"

The strong urge to halt the conversation overcame him. He had already said too much. But Madison's expectant look proved too much, as well. "She was found below the mountain, not far from the lake. Some believe she slipped and fell. Many believe she took her own life due to my father's infidelity. I suppose we will never know the truth."

"I'm so sorry, Zain."

So was he. Sorry that he had almost ruined the evening with regrets. That ended now.

He tipped her face up and kissed her. "We will return to the veranda the same way we left, only we will stay in my room tonight."

She pulled back and slid across the seat away from him. "We're going to walk in the front door, otherwise we'll look guilty. And we're going to stay in separate beds, tonight and every night until I leave."

That would not suffice. "I would prefer you sleep in my bed the majority of the night after we make love. As long as we've parted by morning, no one will be the wiser."

She folded the jacket's hem back and forth. "We can't take the risk that someone will find out. I had a wonderful time tonight, but we can't be together in that way again."

How many times in his youth had he said something of a similar nature to a woman? "That is unacceptable. How to you expect me to pretend I do not want you when I do?" More than she knew. More than he realized until he faced the prospect of not having her.

"We're going to limit our alone time together."

"You've said that before."

"This time I mean it, Zain. I am not going to be responsible for a scandal that could ruin all the work we're doing to restore your image."

Zain gripped the wheel and stared straight ahead. "Then you lied when you said you trust me."

"I do trust you, and so should your people. I admire and respect you even more now. But when I said I didn't trust myself, I wasn't talking about sex. I've already blurred the personal and professional lines and I can't afford to become more emotionally involved with you than I already am. Now we need to go inside before they come looking for us."

Before Zain could respond, she was out the door and walking toward the path leading to the front entrance. He left the truck and caught up with her in the courtyard flanking the front steps. After clasping her arm, he turned her to face him. "I will honor your wishes. I will allow you your blessed distance, but not before I give you this."

He crushed her against him and kissed her with all the desperation he experienced at the moment. He expected her to fight him, and when instead she responded, he realized she wanted him as much as he wanted her. As much as he needed her for reasons that defied logic. He agreed with her on one point—this was not only about sex.

Then she wrested from his grasp, looking as if he'd struck her. "Don't make this more complicated than it already is, Zain."

Madison hurried around the corner and by the time he reached the stone steps, she had already disappeared through the doors.

Once inside, he was met by a security contingent and Deeb. "You are all dismissed," he said in Arabic. "No harm has come to me to warrant this attention." Not the kind of harm they would assume.

He ascended the stairs only to have Deeb stop him on the second-floor landing. "Your brother asked me to summon you to his study upon your return."

Confronting Rafiq was the last thing he needed. "I have no desire to speak to him."

"What shall I tell him, Emir?"

Tell him to go to hell. "I will see him in the morning."

Zain arrived at the corridor leading to his quarters in time to see the door to Madison's room close, shutting him out.

Perhaps she could easily dismiss him and what they had shared tonight, but he would wager she would suffer for the decision to avoid him. So would he.

But he would do as he had promised and hoped she decided they should take advantage of what little time together they had left. In the meantime, he would prepare to spend the first of several long, sleepless nights.

* * *

Ten days had passed since Madison had enjoyed a decent night's sleep, and she had Zain to thank for that. Not only had he upheld his promise to give her space, he'd downright ignored her. He'd avoided all eye contact when they'd been together, and he'd only spoken to her when she had spoken first. The two times they'd briefly found themselves alone following one of his myriad meetings, not once had he mentioned their night together, nor had he delivered even the slightest innuendo. He hadn't joined her and Rafiq for dinner, but at least she'd had a chance to get to know the older brother, who was highly intelligent and not quite as serious as she'd once assumed.

She truly didn't know if Zain was simply pouting, or proving a point. Either way, she admittedly missed their intimate conversations. Missed kissing him, as well. She definitely missed her former common sense, which had apparently followed the rain out of town.

Zain had been right to remain in strictly business mode, and business was exactly what she needed to focus on today, and each day until the coronation.

Madison sought out Elena and found her in the kitchen, where the wonderful scents permeating the area caused her stomach to rumble even though she'd had enough breakfast to kill an elephant. Evidently she'd been making up for the lack of sex by eating her way through the kingdom.

"That smells marvelous," she said as she approached the metal prep table holding a platter full of puffed pastries.

Elena smiled and gestured toward the fare. "Please try one. The chef prepared the samples for Prince Zain's

approval, but he refused. He said he did not care if they
served water and wheat at the wedding reception."

Clearly His Royal Pain in the Arse had forgotten
they'd added guests to the list, who could be beneficial
to his reign. But hey, if he didn't want to try the goodies,
she certainly would. "Thanks, I believe I will take a bite
or two." Or three, she decided when the flaky crust and
creamy filling practically melted in her mouth.

After Madison had consumed five of the canapés, she
looked up to meet Elena's quizzical look. "Tell the chef
he's hit a home run with this." As if the guy would understand a baseball analogy. "Better still, tell him they're
perfect."

"I will pass that on," Elena said. "I will also tell him
to prepare double for you."

Great. She'd demonstrated she had serious etiquette
issues. "That's not necessary. I eat when I'm nervous,
and this whole reception has me on edge. I hope we're
doing the right thing by not having a separate gathering
prior to the coronation."

"Have you consulted the new king about forgoing
that honor?"

"Actually, it was his idea. He's not being all that cooperative these days. Maybe he's a bit anxious about officially becoming His Majesty in less than two weeks."

"Or perhaps he is being denied something he wants
more than the crown."

Madison faked ignorance. "A new sports car?"

Elena raised a thin brow. "You may fool the rest of
the household, *cara,* but you are not fooling me. I know
you and Prince Zain stole away without notifying anyone of your departure, and returned in wet clothing."

The palace apparently had spies in place and gossip down to a science. "He wanted to show me the lake

and we got caught in a storm." A firestorm. "That's all there was to it."

"Are you certain of that?"

She knew better than to try to lie to a wise bird like Elena. She also knew not to reveal too much, even if she thought she could trust her with the truth. "Wise or not, we have developed a friendship. He's even begun to confide in me about his past and, most important, his goals. That's been beneficial for me, since I've been preparing the speech he'll deliver next week." A speech he would probably reject.

She couldn't miss the concern on Elena's face. "What has he said about the king and queen?"

"Since he took me into his confidence, I don't feel I should say more." She'd already come down with foot-in-mouth disease to go with the voracious appetite.

"Anything you could say to me, *cara mia,* I have already heard in the many years I've been here. The staff talks about things they know nothing about, and most is not true."

She did have a point. "He mentioned something about the king having mistresses, and that he believes that was directly related to the queen's death."

Elena grabbed the platter and took it to the counter next to the massive industrial sink. "Go on," she said, keeping her back to Madison.

The fact Elena didn't deny the conjecture was very telling. "He also said that the queen was forced to have a third child against her will."

Elena spun around, a touch of anger calling out from her amber eyes. "That is not true. The queen would have done anything to have another child. And furthermore, the king was the one who only wanted two children, yet he was so devoted to her, he gave her what she desired. Sadly, Adan did not aid in her happiness."

"Was she so unhappy that she took her own life?"

"I would not begin to speculate on that, and neither should you."

Madison held up her hands. "I'm sorry I've upset you. I was only repeating what Zain told me." Darn if she hadn't done it again—called him by his given name.

Elena sighed. "It is not your fault, *cara*. And I beg of you to please not repeat what I have said."

She found it odd that Elena would want to conceal the information from the boys she had practically raised. "Don't you think the princes have a right to know the truth?"

"Some secrets are best left in the past." Elena picked up a towel and began to twist it, a sure sign of distress. "Did you require anything else from me? If not, I have some work to attend to."

Madison knew not to press the matter any further. She needed Elena as an ally, not an enemy. "Actually, I was wondering if you had a final guest list for the reception. I want to go over it with His Highness." Provided he didn't toss her out on her posterior, injuring her pride.

"Yes, I do." Elena walked into the office, emerged a few moments later and handed her two pages full of names. "You'll see that I have made a separate column for the prospective queen candidates and their fathers. I thought you would find that helpful."

She found it appalling. "I suppose Prince Zain will appreciate that information. He can come prepared for when they converge upon him."

Elena surprisingly patted Madison's cheek. "Do not worry, *cara*. He will find none of them to his liking as long as you are here." With that, the woman smiled, returned to the office and closed the door.

Obviously no one could pull the wool over Elena's eyes, and that could present some complications if Madison didn't remain strong in Zain's presence.

Not a problem. The way things were going, she'd be lucky if he ever seriously spoke to her again, let alone touched her.

Eight

He wanted nothing more than to touch her. Only a slight touch. Or perhaps not so slight at that.

Since Madison's arrival in the study, Zain had engaged in several fantasies that involved taking her down on the sofa where she sat reciting names that mattered not to him.

"Who is Layali Querishi?" she asked. "That sounds familiar."

He fixated on Madison's blue blouse, which could easily be unbuttoned, allowing access to her breasts. "She is a sultan's daughter and a popular singer."

"And gorgeous." She crossed her legs, causing the skirt's hem to ride higher on her thighs. "I remember seeing an article about her Australian tour."

"I do not recall her looks." Nor did he care about them. He only cared about running his hands up Madison's skirt as a reminder of what they had given up for the sake of professionalism.

"Do you think that's a good idea?"

Madison's question startled Zain into believing he might have voiced his thoughts. "What are you referring to?"

"Pay attention, Your Highness."

He had been paying attention—to her. "My apologies. I have a lot weighing on my mind." And a heavy weight behind his fly.

"I said do you think it's a good idea to seat all these women together at the same table? That's grounds for a queen candidate catfight."

He could not hold back his smile. "Some might find that thoroughly entertaining."

"Or thoroughly in bad taste. I suggest we separate them to avoid bloodshed."

He started to suggest they discard the list and move on to something much more pleasurable, when a series of raps sounded at the door. Familiar raps that readily identified the offending party.

Madison consulted her watch. "It's late. I can't imagine who would be stopping in this time of night, unless it's Mr. Deeb."

"It's not Deeb."

"Then who is it?"

"My brother."

Thankful his coat sufficiently hid his current state, Zain rounded the desk and opened the door to Adan wearing his standard military-issue flight suit and a cynical smile. He made a circular sweeping gesture with his arm and bowed dramatically. "Greetings, His Majesty, king of the surfing sheikhs."

He had not mentioned that pastime to Madison, but she definitely knew now. He wanted to send Adan on his way but instead gave him the required manly embrace. "When did you arrive?"

"I flew in a while ago." Adan leaned around him. "And who is this lovely lady?"

"I'm Madison Foster." Zain turned to see her standing in front of the sofa. "And you must be Prince Adan."

"The one and the only." Adan crossed the room, took Madison's hand and kissed it. "Are you one of my brother's California conquests?"

"She is a political consultant," Zain added in an irritable tone. "Which means she is off-limits to you."

Adan released her hand but offered up a devil-may-care grin. "I have only honorable intentions."

She returned his smile as she reclaimed her seat. "You also have a very British accent."

"He has an aversion to authority," Zain said. "He spent most of his formative years in a military boarding school in the U.K."

Adan attempted to look contrite. "I have since learned to respect authority and take orders, as long as they are not delivered by my brothers."

Zain wanted to order him out of the room. "Considering the lateness of the hour, I am certain you are ready to retire."

"Actually, I am wide-awake." He had the audacity to drop down beside Madison and drape his arm over the back of the sofa. "How long will you be here?"

"Ms. Foster will be with *me* until after the coronation," Zain answered before she could respond. "And we still have much to accomplish tonight."

"We can take up where we left off tomorrow," Madison said as she came to her feet. "I'm sure you two have a lot of catching up to do after all these years."

Adan clasped her wrist and pulled her back down

beside him, sparking Zain's barely contained fury. "I visited Zain in Los Angeles less than six months ago. In fact, I was his guest at least once a year during his time there."

Many times an unwelcome guest, as he was now. "For that reason, he should return to his quarters so that we might resume our tasks."

Adan ignored him and took the pages from Madison. "What is this?"

"We're going over the guest list for the upcoming wedding reception," she said.

He leaned closer to her. "Am I on it?"

She seemed unaffected by his nearness, and that only served to anger Zain more. "Since you're in the wedding party, there's no need to add your name."

Adan perused the pages for a few moments. "Ah, I see we have a bevy of prospective brides in attendance. Najya Toma's much too young. Taalah Wasem is too stuffy. And I had hoped to claim the third one as my own. No one would turn down a chance to bed Layali Querishi." He winked. "Of course, she is not quite as beautiful as you."

Zain had had quite enough. "If you are finished with your attempts to seduce my employee, I suggest you retire to your quarters now so that we may resume our duties."

Adan reluctantly came to his feet. "You are beginning to sound like Rafiq. Did you leave your sense of humor in the States?"

"Did you leave your sense of decorum in your jet?"

"Women are quite taken with my jet."

Zain pointed at the door. "Out. Now."

Adan had the audacity to laugh. "I can take a hint, brother. And I certainly understand why you would want

Ms. Foster all to yourself." He regarded Madison again. "It has been a pleasure, madam. Should you need protection from this rogue, feel free to notify me immediately."

She needed protection from his rogue brother. "I assure you, Adan, Ms. Foster is in good hands and does not require your assistance."

Adan sent Madison another smile. "Then I will bid you both good-night."

After Adan thankfully left, Zain closed the door and tripped the lock. He turned back to Madison and launched into a tirade on the heels of his anger. "Although you obviously enjoyed my brother's attention, you should know that he is a master of seduction. Stay clear of him."

"That's rich, coming from you." She tossed the papers aside and sighed. "Not to mention he's practically a baby, and he seems perfectly harmless."

He took a few steps toward her. "He is five years my junior. That makes him twenty-eight, and a man."

"And he's three years younger than me, so in my eyes, that makes him cougar bait."

He had not realized she was over thirty, but then he had never asked her age. "Adan would not care if you were twice his age. He recognizes a beautiful woman, he is anything but harmless and he has designs on you."

She rolled her eyes. "Stop playing the jealous monarch, Zain."

He was not playing. "I am only concerned about your well-being."

She tossed the pages aside. "Really? For the past few days, you haven't seemed at all concerned about my well-being, or anything else, for that matter. You've barely given me the time of day."

And it had nearly destroyed him. "I am giving you space as you've requested."

"You're giving me the cold shoulder, and I don't deserve that."

"And you believe I deserve this torture?"

"What torture?"

He slid his hands in his pockets and took two more slow steps. "Each time you are near me, I can only think about touching you. Ignoring you is my only means of self-defense."

"You could at least be civil."

When he reached her, he took off his jacket and draped it over the back of the sofa. "Civility is the last thing on my mind when you're dressed as you are now."

She looked down before returning her gaze to his. "It's a plain blouse and knee-length skirt, Zain, and I've been dressing this way since we met. It's more than decent."

Decent yes, but his thoughts were not. "And I have suffered because of your choices."

She rested her elbow on the back of the sofa and rubbed her forehead. "Fine. I'll wear a full-body burlap sack from now on."

"It would not matter what you are wearing. I would still imagine you naked."

"And that makes you just like every other man who comes in contact with a female."

He leaned forward and braced his palms on the cushions on either side of her hips. "Is that what I am to you, Madison? Only one more man who wants you? Was our lovemaking nothing more than a diversion?"

Unmistakable desire flashed in her eyes. "It was... It was..."

"Remarkable?"

"Unwise."

He brushed a kiss across her cheek before nuzzling her neck. "Tell me you do not want to experience it again, and I will leave you alone."

"You're asking me to lie."

He touched his lips to hers. "I am asking you to admit that you still want me. I want to hear you say that you are as consumed by thoughts of us as I am."

"Stop making it so hard to resist you, Zain."

Using the sofa's back for support, he lifted her hand and pressed it against his fly. "You are making it hard on me, Madison."

She rubbed her thumb along the ridge. "That sounds like a very personal problem to me."

He kissed her then, a kiss hot enough to ignite the room. But when she tried to pull him down beside her, he resisted and straightened.

She glared up at him. "I get it now. You're teasing me and then you're going to walk out of here just to punish me."

"I promise I have no intention of punishing you." He lowered to the floor on his knees to fulfill his greatest fantasy. "Unless you consider absolute pleasure a form of punishment."

When he reached beneath her skirt and slid her panties down, she released a slight gasp. And when he parted her legs, she trembled. He kept his gaze leveled on hers as he kissed the inside of one thigh, then the other, and prepared for a protest. Instead, she remained silent as her chest rapidly rose and fell in anticipation.

"Unbutton your blouse and lower your bra," he said, though he realized she might not answer his demand if she believed he had gone too far.

Yet she surprised him by releasing the buttons with

shaking fingers before reaching beneath the back of the blouse to unclasp the bra.

Seeing her eyes alight with excitement and her breasts exposed was almost his undoing. As badly as he wanted to dispense with formality and seat himself deep inside her, he had something else in mind. Yet before he sought his ultimate destination, he had one final question. "Tell me you want me to keep going."

She exhaled slowly. "You know I do, dammit."

The first curse she'd ever uttered in his presence served to excite him even more. "Then say it."

"I want you to do it."

That was all he needed to hear. He pushed her skirt up to her waist for better access, slipped his hands beneath her hips and lowered his mouth between her trembling legs. He watched her face to gauge her reaction as he teased her with the tip of his tongue, varying the pressure to prolong the pleasure.

When her eyes momentarily drifted shut, he stopped and lifted his head. "Look at me, Madison. I want you to see what I am doing to you."

She blinked twice as if in a trance. "I don't think I can."

"Yes, you can, and you will."

When their gazes locked, he went back to his exploration, more thoroughly this time. She gripped the cushions and lifted her hips to meet his mouth, indicating she was close to reaching a climax. And as she tipped her head back and released a low moan, Zain refused to let up until her frame and expression went slack.

After her breathing slowed and her eyes closed again, he rose to his feet. Leaving her now would be difficult, but he felt he had no choice. He turned and started toward the door, only to halt midstride when she asked, "Where are you going?"

He faced her to find she was clutching her blouse closed, a mixture of ire and confusion in her expression. "I am going to bed, and you should, as well. You should be relaxed enough to enjoy a restful sleep." He regrettably would not. He would lie awake for hours, aching for her and wondering when he would have her again. If he would ever have her again.

"Oh, no, you don't," she said. "You're not going to just leave me here alone after you've somehow managed to turn me into some sort of wild animal in heat."

"I know you, Madison, and this wildness is the part of you that you've kept concealed from the world, and from yourself. You have simply never met a man who encourages that side of you before now. I am that man."

She released the blouse, allowing it to gape open. "A real man would come over and finish what he started."

It took all his resolve not to answer her challenge. "From this point forward, you will have to come to me. But mark my words, we will finish this."

Mark my words, we will finish this...

To this point, Madison hadn't given Zain that satisfaction, although he'd given her plenty during their little office interlude. She'd managed to afford the same courtesy he had shown her by turning the tables on him. She'd made a point to avoid him the past three days, but unfortunately, she couldn't avoid him tonight.

While she claimed a corner of the banquet hall, nursing a mineral water and a solid case of jealousy, the imminent king stood at the front of the room, basking in female attention. Who could blame them? He was a tall, dark presence dressed in a black silk suit, light gray shirt and a perfect-match tie. Both his looks and his status had earned him more than his share of attention. She'd basically been relegated to wallflower status, after she'd made the required rounds among the dignitaries and diplomats she'd personally invited. Normally she didn't like being invisible, yet tonight she didn't care if she blended into the background. It didn't matter one whit if no one noticed her.

"You are looking exceedingly lovely tonight, Ms. Foster."

Madison glanced to her left and met the dimpled baby Mehdi's charming smile. She still couldn't get over his lack of resemblance to his older brothers, who could almost pass as twins. Where their eyes were almost black, Adan's were golden and his hair was much lighter. That didn't make him any less gorgeous in a boyish sort of way. "Thank you, Your Highness."

"Tonight you should refer to me as Adan." He took a step back and studied the crimson cocktail dress she'd chosen instead of the black one Zain had requested she wear all those weeks ago. "Red certainly becomes you."

She smoothed a hand over the skirt. "I worried it might be overkill."

"Your beauty has almost killed some of our elder statesmen. You'll know who they are as they are holding their ribs where their wives have landed elbows throughout the evening."

She couldn't hold back a laugh over that image. "Don't be ridiculous."

"I am only being observant." He nodded toward Zain. "My brother the king has certainly noticed. He has watched your every move all night, and he's presently staring at us, the fires of hell in his eyes."

Madison turned her attention to Zain and confirmed

he had one heck of a glare leveled on them. "He's too involved with his admirers to care about me."

"He cannot give them his proper attention when you are all that he sees."

"That's ridiculous."

"That is the truth." He leaned close to her ear. "Right now he believes I am propositioning you, and if he knew that for certain, he would come over here and wrap his hands around my throat."

She couldn't believe he would even think that about Zain, let alone voice it. "He wouldn't do that. He's your brother."

Adan straightened and smiled. "He is a man obsessed with a woman. I have no idea what you have done to bewitch him, but your spell has effectively created a monster. I have never known Zain to be so possessive. Perhaps he is caught in a web of love and he has no idea how to free himself."

A web of lust, maybe, but Madison didn't buy the love theory. Anxious to end the troubling conversation, she opted for a topic change. "The wedding was nice, although I didn't understand one word of the vows." She also didn't understand how a bride could have looked so sad on her wedding day.

"You did not miss much," Adan said. "It was a merger. The culmination of a business arrangement born out of obligation. An obligation I will eventually face. But since I have no direct claim to the throne, I intend to enjoy my freedom until I am at least forty. Regrettably, Zain is not as fortunate. He will be expected to marry a suitable bride as soon as possible."

Madison didn't need to be reminded of that, nor did she need to encourage more discussion about Zain by commenting on the antiquated tradition. "Speaking of the bride and groom, I haven't seen them in a while."

"They have retired to the marriage bed," Adan said as he snatched a glass of fruity punch from the roving waiter's tray. "And by now Rafiq has confirmed that his bride is not a virgin. Of course, he will not care as long as she spreads her legs in an effort to produce the mandatory heir."

She frowned. "That's rather crass, and how do you know for sure she isn't a virgin?"

"Because another Mehdi brother had her first."

Surely not... "Zain?"

Adan downed the rest of his drink and set the glass on the nearby side table. "Yours truly."

Madison did well to hide her shock. "You slept with your brother's wife?"

"Future wife," he said. "And I did not instigate it. I had recently arrived home from the academy to celebrate my seventeenth birthday at a friend's house. Rima came by after having argued with her true love. She was looking for consolation wherever she could find it. I happened to be searching for a willing woman to give me my first experience. I tried to refuse but, alas, I succumbed to her charms. It was, as they say, the perfect storm."

A perfect mess, in Madison's opinion. "And Rafiq never wondered where she'd gone after they argued?"

He sent her a practiced smirk. "I said she argued with her true love. I did not say she argued with Rafiq."

She had somehow become embroiled in a real-live Arabian soap opera. "Then who is it?" Reconsidering the question, she raised her hands, palms forward. "Never mind. I don't want to know."

When Madison noticed one young woman standing on tiptoe and whispering in Zain's ear, she'd seen enough.

Her feet hurt and her heart ached. She only wanted to crawl into bed and throw the covers over her head. That probably wouldn't stop the images of the king taking another willing woman into his bed.

She set her glass next to Adan's and smiled. "Since the crowd seems to be dwindling, I'm going to head to my quarters now. It's been nice talking to you." And very, very interesting.

He lifted her hand for a kiss. "Should you require a man's undivided attention, I am on the second floor in the room at the end of the hall."

She tugged her hand away and patted his cheek. "You, Adan, are too charming for your own good, and I'm really much too old for you."

"As was Rima."

She wasn't going to jump into that sorry situation again. "Good night."

Without waiting for Adan's reply, she hurried through the expansive ballroom and bore down on the double doors that led into one of the many courtyards. Since the building was separate from the palace proper, she found the surroundings seriously confusing, particularly when only dimly lit by random lights alongside the various pathways. Deeb had accompanied her to the reception, but he had long since left, and now she was on her own. That shouldn't present a major problem. She had a master's in political science, a good sense of direction and she'd always excelled at geography. Give her a map and she could find her way anywhere. Too bad she didn't have a map of the jumbled of walkways.

Madison chose the most direct path and immediately arrived at an intersection. She couldn't remember whether to go right or left and wished she'd paid more attention on her way there. She could see the looming palace, but had no clue how to get there. Maybe she should flip a coin—heads, right; tails, left. Maybe she would end up in Yemen if she took a wrong turn.

Luckily she heard approaching footsteps behind her and pivoted around, expecting to see a security guard who could show her the way. She wasn't prepared to see Zain walking toward her instead.

She refused to do this, her prime motivation for taking off down the hedge-lined brick path to her immediate right. At the moment, she didn't care if she wound up seeking shelter in a caretaker's cottage, as long as she could escape before she did something totally foolish, like taking the pretty prince down into the hedges and having her wicked way with him.

"Madison, wait."

She didn't dare look back. "No."

"You cannot continue."

"Yes, I can. Watch me."

"You are about to hit a dead end."

No sooner than he'd said it, Madison did it—almost ran smack dab into a brick tower with a nice little water feature set off to the side of a small bench.

She had no choice but to face the music, or in this case, the monarch. "Go back to your guests, Zain," she said when she turned around.

He loosened his tie and collar. "The guests have all departed."

She folded her arms beneath her breasts. "You couldn't entice even one of those nubile young creatures into your bedroom?"

He slipped the single button on his coat. "They did not hold my interest."

If he made one more move to undress, she would have to resort to hedge-diving. "I'm sorry to hear that. Now if you would kindly point me in the right direction, I'll be on my way."

When he stalked forward, she retreated, once again finding herself backed against a wall. "I am not letting you leave until you understand that being without you is killing me," he said.

"You seemed quite alive to me tonight."

"Those women meant nothing to me." He braced one hand above her head and used the other to slip the wide strap down her shoulder. "Seeing you in this dress made matters worse, as did watching you with Adan. Had he touched you again, I would have crossed the room and wrapped my hands around his neck."

She almost laughed when she recalled Adan had said those exact words. "You can't go around beating up any boy who pays attention to me while I'm here. And I won't be here much longer."

"Precisely," he said before he leaned down and kissed her bare shoulder. "Our time together is limited and I do not wish to waste more than we already have."

"What happened to me coming to you?" Better still, what was happening to her determination to resist him?

"My patience is in tatters. We have been playing the avoidance game long enough. It's time to release our pride and admit that we need to be together. I *need* to be with you."

And heaven help her, she needed to be with him as much as she needed air, which seemed to leave her when he streamed his hand over the curve of her hip.

If he wanted to finish this once and for all, then they would finish it, even if it meant going out in a blaze of glory. "If you need me that much, stop talking and kiss me."

He did, with enough power to light up the country.

Before Madison knew it, Zain had her bodice pulled down, his mouth on her breast and his hand between her legs. Somewhere in the back of her mind, she realized she should tell him to stop and take it to the bedroom before they went any further. But she was too weak with wanting and too far gone to halt the madness.

And madness it was when he pushed her panties down and did the same with his slacks before he wrapped her legs around his hips and drove into her. His intense thrusts blew her mind and propelled her to the edge of orgasmic bliss. That one-time foreign sound began to form in her throat, only to be halted when Zain planted his palm over her mouth.

At that point, she heard the nearby voices, saw movement between the break of the trees. Knowing that could get caught only heightened the dangerous pleasure, and brought about a climax that shook her to the core. She could tell Zain had been affected, too, by the way he tensed and released a guttural groan in her ear, followed by that same single harsh Arabic word.

The sound of their ragged breathing seemed to echo throughout the area, and Madison hoped the passing party had moved out of earshot. Zain loosened his hold, allowing her legs to slide down where she fortunately found her footing. She still felt as if she were on shaky emotional ground.

For that reason, she had to get away from him. "We need to return to our respective rooms before Deeb sends out a posse and they catch you with your pants down."

He planted both palms on the wall and rested his forehead against hers, his eyes tightly closed. "When I think about you leaving me, even only for a moment, it sickens me."

She could relate to that. "We knew my leaving was

inevitable, Zain. The more time we spend together, the harder it will be to say goodbye." At least for her.

He raised his head, some unidentifiable emotion in his eyes. "Stay with me tonight, Madison. All night. I want to wake in the morning to find you beside me."

And that seemed like a recipe for disaster when it came to her heart. "But—"

His soft kiss quelled her protest. "I am begging you to stay."

Madison had stayed with Zain that night, and every night for the past week. They had grown so close, and she had become so lost in him, she'd begun to believe she didn't know where he ended and she began. And that frightened her, but not enough to stop sleeping in his bed, and waking up every morning to his wonderful face. This morning was no exception.

When a ribbon of light streamed through a break in the heavy curtains covering the window, Madison rolled to her side, bent her elbow and supported her cheek with her palm. She took a few moments to capture a good, long look at the beautiful sleeping prince. The prince who would become king in two days.

His dark lashes fanned out beneath his closed eyes and his gorgeous mouth twitched slightly, as if he might smile. The navy satin sheet rode low on his hips, exposing the crease of his pelvic bone and the stream of hair below his navel. Her face heated when she remembered following that path last night with her lips, causing Zain to squirm when she kept right on going.

She realized she was only a shell of her former self—the woman who had repressed her sexual nature for fear of losing control. Lately, losing control had been preferable when it came to making love with Zain, in many

ways, and in many different places—in the study at
noon, in the shower several times, in the tunnel leading to the lower-level grounds and on the veranda after
midnight, even knowing extra guards had been posted at
the corners of the building on all levels. Yet some of the
most memorable times came when they took walks in
the garden, holding hands and stealing innocent kisses.
And the long talks had meant the world to her, conversations about politics and policy and sometimes their pasts.
Zain had even reluctantly admitted he harbored some
guilt over not having the opportunity to say goodbye to
his father, and that made her ache for him.

But the one defining moment in their relationship happened two mornings ago, when she'd awakened alone
in his bed, with an orchid on her pillow and a note that
read, "You make my days, and my nights, worthwhile."

She'd realized she loved him then. Loved him more
than she ever thought possible. Yet none of that mattered.
In forty-eight brief hours, he would enter a new era as
the king, signaling the end of theirs.

But she still had today—an important day for Zain—
so she shook off the downhearted thoughts and kissed
his bare shoulder. When he didn't respond, she pressed
another kiss on his unshaven jaw, then propped her chin
on his chest. "Time to get up, Your Sexiness."

His eyes drifted open and his lips curled into a smile.
She would store that smile in the memory bank to get
her through the lonely days to come. "I am up," he said
in his sexy morning voice.

Madison caught his drift and lifted the sheet. Yes,
he had definitely arisen to the occasion, as usual. "I'll
rephrase that," she said as she dropped the covers back
into place. "You need to get out of bed, get dressed and
get ready to address your subjects. On that note, I don't

know why you won't give my speech suggestions even a little bit of considera—"

He rudely interrupted her light lecture when he flipped her onto her back and rubbed against her. As far as bedside manners went, she couldn't complain. "My royal staff yearns for your attention," he said as he buried his face in her neck.

She had to laugh over that one. "Aren't we just the king of bad euphemisms this morning?"

He lifted his head and grinned. "I have more descriptive ones, if you'd like to hear them."

Before she could object, he had his lips to her ear and her body reeling with possibilities when he recited a litany of crude, albeit sexy, suggestions. When he looked at her again, she faked shock. "Oh, my. Did you minor in dirty words in college, or have you been watching too much cable TV?"

His cupped her breast in his palm. "You bring out the savage in me."

She could say the same for him. He made her want to growl, especially at the moment when he set his hands in motion all over her bare body.

Right when he had her where he wanted her—hot, and bothered and almost begging—the bedside phone began to ring. He eased inside her at the same moment he picked up the receiver. Madison marveled over his ability to multitask, then became mortified when she recognized Rafiq's voice on the other end of the line.

"I am currently occupied," Zain said. "However, when I am able to pull myself away from this most pressing matter, I will be downstairs in the study."

After he hung up, Madison laughed. "You are so bad."

He frowned. "Last night you told me I was very good."

"No. That's what you told me."

The teasing quickly ended as they concentrated on their lovemaking, on each other with a familiarity normally reserved for longtime lovers. But they were so attuned to one another now, it seemed as if they had been lovers forever. And in the aftermath, when Zain's gentle, whispered words of praise floated into Madison's ears, she started to cry. For some reason, she'd done a lot of that lately, but never in front of him.

As he folded her into his arms and stroked her hair, he didn't question her about the tears. He only held her close to his heart until they finally subsided.

"I'm sorry," she said after she recovered from the meltdown. "I guess my leaving is starting to sink in."

"I am trying not to think about it," he said. "Otherwise, I might not get through my duties today."

She wanted so badly to tell him she loved him, but what would be the point? Nothing had changed. Nothing would. She was still the unsuitable American, and he was still the Arabian king steeped in tradition, destined to choose one of his kind.

So she raised her head and gave him her sunniest smile, even though she wanted to sob. "Speaking of your duties, the time has come for you to impress the masses, the way you've continually impressed me."

His dark eyes were so intense, it stole her breath. "Madison, I..." His gaze drifted away with his words.

"You what?"

When he finally looked at her again, he seemed almost detached. "I want to thank you for all that you've done. I would not have gotten through this process had it not been for your support."

That comment was as dry as the desert, and not at all what she wanted to hear. "And to think you almost sent me packing that first night."

"I am glad you fought me on that, and I will never forget our time together."

Funny, that sounded a lot like an early goodbye. Maybe he was just doing some advance preparation, and she should take his cue. "You're welcome, Your Highness. Now that the party's over, it's time to take care of business."

Nine

He had arrived at this first of two monumental moments with a certain confidence, and he had not managed that alone. Unbeknownst to Madison, he had every intention of taking her advice and speaking from the heart. If only he had been able to do that this morning. The one word he had not been able to say—had never said to any woman—had stalled on his lips. Committing to that emotion would only complicate matters more. She was bound to leave, and he was bound to duty as the leader of his country.

"They're ready for you, Emir," Deeb said as he opened the doors to the veranda.

"Good luck, Your Highness," Madison said from behind him.

Since their last conversation that morning, a certain formality had formed between them. Yet he could not consider that now, nor did he dare look at her and meet the sadness in her eyes. "Thank you," he said as he left her to deliver the most important speech of his life.

He moved onto the balcony containing enough guards to populate a military installation. After taking a few moments to gather his thoughts, he stepped behind the podium, and the cameras began to flash. Zain surveyed the masses spread out on the grounds as far as the eye could see. Among those in the immediate vicinity, he spotted a few familiar faces—Maysa, Malik and his family, as well as several childhood friends—and that served to further bolster his self-assurance. Many of the others looked both eager and somewhat suspicious, most likely because they were waiting for him to fail. He refused to fail.

He pulled the pages containing the prepared speech, then on afterthought, set them aside. He also ignored the teleprompter that Madison insisted he have so he wouldn't falter. If his words did not come out perfectly, so be it. His country would then know he was not perfect, and that suited him fine. He had his flaws, but he had the best of intentions. Now he had to convince the country of that.

After adjusting the microphone, Zain began to speak, immediately silencing the restless crowd. He began with outlining his water conservation plan, which garnered minor applause. He continued by insisting that education was the key to prosperity, and he vowed to fund school improvements. He went on to talk about the importance of family, his love for their country and his commitment to its people. He spoke about his father in respectful terms, highlighting all that the former king had accomplished during his forty-year reign, and that he would proudly serve by his example. That earned him a roar from the crowd and shouts of approval. Perhaps he had finally arrived.

Yet as he remained to acknowledge their support, he could not help but wish Madison was at his side. Wish that he had the means to change tradition and choose his bride by virtue of her attributes, not her dowry. But that would present the possibility of rejection not only by the council, but also the traditionalists who expected him to marry one of their own. And even if he could successfully lobby for that change, would he subject Madison to this life? Would he risk destroying her sense of independence in exchange for assuming the role of his queen? A role that had left some women emotionally broken, including his own mother. He then recalled when Madison had said she would never give up her life for any man, and he could not in good conscience ask that of her, even if the thought of letting her go sickened him.

When he felt the tap on his shoulder, he turned to find Deeb, not Madison, as he had hoped. "The press is waiting in the conference room, Emir."

One hurdle jumped, yet another awaited him— answering intrusive questions. "I will be along shortly." First, he planned to seek Madison's approval, a move he would have never made before her, and not because he lacked respect for women. Because he had been that inflexible. She had changed him more than he realized. More than any woman had, even Genevieve. Madison had served as his touchstone for the past month and, in many ways, had given him the strength to survive the chaos. Her opinion mattered to him. She mattered to him, much more than she should.

With a final wave, Zain returned to the study to find Madison seated across the room in front of the corner television, watching the international analysis of his address. He approached the chair and laid a hand on her shoulder to garner her attention. "Did Deeb interpret for you?"

When her frame went rigid, he removed his hand. "Yes, Deeb translated, and you did a remarkable job. For the most part."

When he moved between her and the TV to ask what she hadn't liked, he noticed she did not look well. Her skin was pale and a light sheen of perspiration covered her forehead. "Are you feeling all right?"

"I'm fine," she said as she abruptly stood. "It's a little warm in here."

When she swayed, he clasped her arm to steady her. "You should sit down again."

She tugged out of his grasp. "I said I am perfectly fine, Your Highness. I'm just going to…"

Her eyes suddenly closed, her lips parted slightly, and as she began to fall, Zain caught her in his arms and carried her to the sofa. He had never felt such concern, such fear and such anger over his staff's failure to immediately act.

He turned his ire on Deeb. "Do not stand there like an imbecile. Summon Dr. Barad. Now!"

Madison came awake slowly, feeling somewhat confused and disoriented. She had no idea how she'd ended up on Zain's office couch, although she did recall being dizzy and starting to free-fall. After that, nothing but a big, black void.

When she raised her head from the sofa's arm, an unfamiliar female voice said, "Stay still for a few more moments, Ms. Foster."

The owner of that voice finally came into focus—an exotic woman with dark almond-shaped eyes and long brown hair pulled back into a braid. "Who are you?" Madison asked in a sandpaper voice.

"Maysa Barad." She lifted a stethoscope from a black bag set on the coffee table. "I'm a local physician and friend of the family."

She was also the woman Zain had visited a few weeks ago, and darn if she wasn't gorgeous. "Where's Zain?" she asked, not caring if she hadn't used the proper address.

"He left and took the goons with him after I told him I couldn't do a proper examination with an audience."

Why not? She'd done a swan dive in front of one. "Any idea what happened to me, Dr. Barad?"

"You fainted. And please, call me Maysa." She pressed the metal cylinder against Madison's chest, listened for a few minutes and then pulled the stems from her ears. "It's definitely not your heart."

She wouldn't be surprised if it was, considering it was close to shattering. "That's good to know."

"Your blood pressure's stable, as well. I took it when you were passed out."

"Just wish I knew why I passed out."

"Are you eating well and getting enough rest?"

She'd been eating like a pig at a trough. "Yes on the eating, not so much on the rest. It's been fairly stressful around here." She didn't dare mention that Zain had been the primary cause of her lack of sleep.

Maysa dropped the stethoscope back in the bag and sent her a serious look. "When was your last menstrual cycle?"

An odd question since she'd never passed out from a period. "Honestly, I'm not sure, because they're not regular. I was born with only one ovary, and my doctor isn't convinced it functions all that well."

"Then you've been diagnosed as infertile?"

This was the complicated part. "Not exactly. I have been told that my chances of getting pregnant without medical assistance are remote and, even then, not guaranteed."

"How long ago was this?"

Madison had to think hard on that one, when all she wanted to do was go back to sleep. "I had an ultrasound ten years ago, but I always go for my annual checkups."

"Then you have no way of knowing for certain if perhaps your ovary is in fact functioning."

"I suppose that's accurate."

"Have your breasts been tender?"

Come to think of it, they had. Then again, they were Zain's favorite toys of late. "Maybe a little, but they get that way right before my period."

"That leads to my next question. Have you had sexual relations in the past month?"

She'd had sexual relations in the past few hours. "Why is that important?"

"Because your symptoms indicate you could be pregnant, provided you have been exposed."

Had she ever, and often. But pregnant? No way. "I'm really not sure how to answer that."

Maysa laid a gentle hand on her arm. "I promise you that anything you tell me will be held in the strictest of confidence. We also adhere to doctor-patient privilege in this country."

As long as Madison didn't have to reveal who she'd been having relations with, she might as well admit it. "Yes, I have been exposed, but I truly can't imagine that I could be pregnant."

"There is one way to find out," she said. "I'll have a pregnancy test sent over in the morning."

Madison felt another faint coming on. "Can you make sure to be discreet?"

"I will." Maysa rose from the sofa and smiled down on her. "In the meantime, I want you to rest here awhile longer, and then retire to your room for the remainder of the evening. If you have any more spells, don't hesitate to have Zain call me."

She mentally nixed that suggestion. "Thank you. I appreciate that."

"Also, even if the test is negative, you should stop by my office and I'll draw some blood to be more certain. It could be you've eaten some tainted food."

Lovely. She hated needles about as much as she hated being viewed as fragile. "I'll let you know as soon as I know."

Maysa reached the door, paused with her hand on the knob and then faced Madison again. "You might want to forewarn the father."

She couldn't even consider telling Zain now. "Believe me, he wouldn't want to be bothered."

Maysa sent her a knowing smile. "He might surprise you."

With that, the doctor left, and Madison tipped her head back on the sofa and stared at the ornate chandelier on the ceiling. She never dreamed she would prefer food poisoning over pregnancy, but considering the poor timing, and the circumstance, a baby was the last thing she needed. Definitely the last thing Zain needed.

Of course, she was leaping to large conclusions without good cause. She'd had unprotected sex with Jay for five years, and that had never resulted in a bun in her oven. Of course, Jay hadn't owned a magic fertility mountain, either.

Ridiculous. All of it. She didn't know why she'd fainted, but she highly doubted pregnancy had anything to do with it.

The day had started off like any other day. Madison had awakened that morning after sleeping almost sixteen hours straight, taken a shower, picked out her clothes—and peed on a stick. Now it had suddenly become a day like no other.

She stared at the positive results for a good ten minutes before it finally began to sink in. She was going to have a baby. Zain's baby. A baby she'd always secretly wanted but convinced herself she would never have.

Myriad thoughts swarmed in her head, followed by one important question. How was she going to tell Zain? More important, should she even tell Zain?

He did have a right to know, but he also had the upcoming coronation hanging over his head. He had an entire country counting on him, too. A country that had finally begun to accept him. A scandal—any scandal—could ruin everything.

Right then she wanted to crawl back under the covers and cry the day away, as well as weigh her options. But when someone knocked on the door, and if it happened to be Zain, she might be forced to make a snap decision.

She tightened the sash on her robe, secured her damp hair at her nape, convened her courage and opened the door.

"Good morning, *cara*," Elena said as she breezed into the room, a tray in her hands and something white tucked beneath her arm.

After taking one whiff of the food, Madison began to feel queasy. "Thanks, but my appetite isn't up to par."

Elena faced her with concern. "Are you still not feeling well?"

She dropped down on the edge of the bed. "I'm still a little weak."

"Then I will give strict orders you are not to be disturbed. But you need to eat something to regain your strength. Perhaps I should bring you some tea."

"No," she belted out. "I mean, schnapps probably wouldn't be good for an upset stomach." Definitely not good for a developing baby.

"I would bring you ginger tea to help with the nausea." She removed the cloth from beneath her arm and held it up. "I have also brought you fresh towels should you decided to take a long bath later."

"I appreciate that," she said, before it suddenly dawned on her Elena was heading into the bathroom, and the blasted test was still on the counter.

She could try to distract her. She could tackle her. Or she could accept that it was already too late, because the minute Elena came back into the room, she could tell the secret was out by the look on the woman's face.

"I see you have confirmed you are with child," Elena said in a remarkable matter-of-fact tone.

"Looks to be that way, but it's possible to have a false positive reading." Her last hope, and a remote one at that.

Elena looked altogether skeptical. "It is possible, but not probable when a Mehdi and a mountain are involved."

She'd drink to that, if she could drink. "You're making a huge assumption. How do you know I didn't have a torrid night with the chef?" *Dumb, Madison, really dumb.*

"The chef is nearing seventy years of age, and he can barely stand. I also knew from the beginning you would not be able to resist Prince Zain, and he would not be able to resist you."

Madison couldn't prevent the waterworks from turning on again. "I swear I never meant for this to happen," she said as she furiously swiped at the tears. "I have never crossed professional lines and I have never been so weak. I also never believed I'd be able to conceive a child."

Elena perched on the edge of the bed and took her hand. "You have never met a man like Prince Zain."

That wasn't even up for debate. "He is one in a million. An enigma and complex and very persuasive."

"He is his father in that respect."

Madison had the strongest feeling there could be a personal story behind that comment. She didn't have the strength to delve into more high drama. "And tomorrow, he's going to replace his father. He doesn't need this complication."

"He does need to see that you are all right. He has been so consumed with that need, he has taken to ordering everyone around like a petulant child."

That was news to her. She figured he'd gotten so caught up in the precoronation activities, she'd been the last thing on his mind. "Then why hasn't he stopped by?"

"Because Dr. Barad ordered him to stay away from you for at least twenty-four hours."

She experienced a measure of satisfaction that he was concerned, but she also feared his reaction when she lowered the baby boom. If she decided to make the revelation.

"Have you given any thought to when you are going to tell him?" Elena asked, as if she'd channeled her concerns.

That's all she'd been thinking about. "I have no idea.

I'm not even sure I should tell him." She held her breath and waited for a lecture on the virtues of honesty.

"Some would say it would be wrong to withhold such important information from Prince Zain," Elena began. "But I know the seriousness of the people's expectations when it comes to their ruler. You could be viewed as an outsider and unworthy of the king. You could be shunned, and so could your child. And Prince Zain's standing could forever be tarnished beyond repair."

She knew all those things, but that didn't make it easier to hear them. "And that's my dilemma, Elena. I wish I were better emotionally equipped to handle it, but I'm not. I'm worried that if I do tell him, he'll be angry and he'll send me immediately packing." That would solve her problem, but it would hurt to the core.

Elena squeezed her hand. "When the rumors surfaced about the paternity issues involving the Prince Zain and the model, I knew they were not true. He would never abandon his child, nor would he abandon the woman he loves with all his heart."

"He's never said he loves me, Elena." But then she had never told him, either.

"He is like any other man, afraid to say the word for fear he will swallow his tongue and never speak again, among other things."

They shared in a brief laugh before the seriousness of the situation settled over Madison again. "If what you say is true, then I would be asking him to choose between me and his child, and his country. And if he does choose us, he might regret that decision the rest of his life, and in turn resent me."

"That is possible."

Madison fought back another onslaught of tears. "Please tell me what to do, Elena."

"Only you can decide, *cara*. And you must ask yourself two important questions. Are you strong enough to stay, if that is what he wants from you, and do you love him enough to let him go if you decide not to ask that of him?"

She did love him enough to choose the latter. She couldn't ask him to choose and risk he'd hate her for it. She'd rather part as friends, and live on a lifetime of memories. As far as what she would tell their child, she'd have to figure that out later when she had a clearer head and a less heavy heart.

Elena brushed a kiss across Madison's cheek before she stood. "Whatever you decide, please know I believe you are more than worthy of Prince Zain's love. If the situation were different, I would welcome you as the daughter I was never fortunate enough to have."

Madison came to her feet and gave her a long hug. "And I would be proud to be your daughter-in-law, Elena." If things were different, which they weren't. "I can't thank you enough for you advice and support."

"You are welcome, *cara*," she said with a kind smile. "And should you be in need of a governess after the baby's birth, please keep me in mind. I would be happy to raise another Mehdi son or daughter."

She appreciated the offer, though she couldn't imagine Elena ever leaving this place. "I will definitely keep it in mind."

"And I will be praying for a bright and happy future for you both."

After Madison saw Elena out, it became all too clear what she had to do. She crossed the room, picked up the phone and pounded out Deeb's extension. When he answered with his usual dry greeting, she dispensed with all pleasantries. "This is Madison Foster. Could you please reschedule my flight for first thing in the morning?"

A span of silence passed before he responded. "You do not wish to attend the coronation?"

She couldn't very well tell the truth, so she handed him a partial lie. "I'm really disappointed I can't attend, but I have a job offer and they want me to start immediately."

"Should I inform the emir you've had a change in plans?"

"No. I'll tell him." Or not.

"As you wish."

After she hung up, Madison curled up on the bed to take another nap. She needed more rest to regain her strength before she took the last step. A step that she didn't want to take—the final goodbye to the man she loved.

When Zain opened the door and saw the sadness in Madison's eyes, he knew why she had arrived unexpectedly in his quarters. She was not there only to wish him well, though she probably would. She was not there to spend one final night in his arms, though he wished she would. She was there to say her goodbyes.

"May I come in?" she asked, sounding unsure and unhappy.

He opened the door wide. "Please do."

Once inside, they fell into an uncomfortable silence before she spoke again. "I went by your office first but Mr. Deeb said you'd retired early, so that's why I'm here. I hope it's okay."

"Of course. You have been here before."

"I know, but never through the front door."

That brought about both their smiles, yet hers faded

fast. "Come and sit with me awhile." *Stay with me forever.* The thought arrived with the force of a grenade. A wish he could not fulfill.

After he cleared several documents from the sofa, Madison took a seat on the end, while he claimed the chair across from her. "You look much better than you did the last time I saw you. Are you feeling better?"

"Much better. I've had plenty of sleep."

He could not say the same for himself. "Did Maysa determine why you fainted?"

"It could be a number of things, but all that matters now is I'm fine."

She sounded less than confident, and that concerned him. "I am happy to hear that. I've been very worried about you since I had to catch you during your fall."

"You caught me?" She both sounded and looked taken aback.

"I would never let you fall, Madison." And he would never forget those moments of intense fear. "Do you not remember?"

She shook her head. "No. I just remember being dizzy, and then I woke up on the couch."

"I was furious when Maysa demanded I leave you alone." He still was.

"Elena told me you were not in the best of moods. I'm sure my little mishap, coupled with the upcoming ceremony, didn't help. So are you nervous about tomorrow?"

No, but she was. He could tell by the way she folded the hem of her causal blue top back and forth. "I am ready for it to be over." Though that meant they would be over, as well.

"I'm sure you are. But it's the realization of your dreams, and that has to make you happy."

Holding her would make him happy. Having her as a

part of that dream would be the ultimate happiness. He felt he could do neither. "You should be happy to witness the fruits of your labor when I am officially crowned."

Her gaze faltered. "I didn't do that much, Zain."

He would strongly disagree. "You managed to mold me into the king I was meant to be, and that was no small accomplishment." She'd managed to steal his heart in the process.

She presented a sincere smile. "Yeah, you were a challenge at times. But I wouldn't take a moment of it back."

Nor would he, and he could not let another minute pass without being closer to her. He pushed off the chair and joined her on the sofa, much to her apparent dismay when she slid over as far as she could go.

"You need not be concerned," he said. "I am not going to touch you unless you want me to do so."

She sighed. "I would love for you to touch me, but that would only make it harder to leave you tonight."

He took a chance and clasped her hand. "Then stay with me tonight. Better still, stay with me after the coronation."

She pulled her hand from his grasp. "And what would my duties be, Zain? Your staff consultant, or your staff mistress?"

He experienced the resurgence of the anger he had harbored all day. "I am not my father. I have never viewed you as my mistress."

"But that's exactly what I would be when you choose your proper royal wife. Of course, you could send me on my way when that happens. And that would probably be best since I couldn't stand the thought of some other woman in your bed."

He could not stand the thought of any other woman in his bed aside from her. "I wish I could promise we could have an open relationship, but that is not possible. We would both suffer for it."

"Then I guess we will just have to suffer through a permanent goodbye."

When she came to her feet, Zain stood, as well. "I am asking you not to go, Madison. I am begging you to stay."

She lowered her eyes. "What would be the point?"

He framed her face in his palms, forcing her to look at him. "Because I care for you, and I want your smile to be my last memory before you leave."

When she laid her hands on his, he expected her to wrench them away. Fortunately, she did not. "If you really cared about me, you wouldn't do this. You'd realize this is tearing me up inside."

"And you would realize it is killing me to say goodbye tonight. I promise I only want to hold you, and to know you are beside me in the morning on the most important day of my life."

"You are asking so much from me, Zain. Too much from us."

Desperation drove him to continue to plead his case. "I am asking you to give us this final night together."

"But I'm not strong around you."

When he saw the first sign of tears in her eyes, he tipped his forehead against hers. "You are strong, Madison, and you have given me strength when I have needed it most." He pulled back and thumbed away the moisture from her cheek. "You said you trusted me before. Trust me now."

"I'd keep you awake with my crying."

"I will gladly provide my shoulder."

He seemed to wait an eternity for her to speak again. "Do you promise not to steal the covers?"

His spirits rose at the sight of her smile. "I promise I will do my best."

"Then I'll stay." She pointed at him. "You have to wear clothes, and you can't try to seduce me."

He held the power to do that, but her faith in him was paramount. "I will remain dressed, and I will be on my best behavior." While battling the clothing constraints and his ever-present desire for her.

"Okay." She hid a yawn behind her hand. "Then let's get on with it before I pass out again."

His worry returned. "Do you feel that you might faint?"

"No, but I might fall asleep on my feet."

As she entered the bathroom, Zain retrieved a pair of unused pajama bottoms from the bureau and ignored the top. He had promised he would remain dressed, but he hadn't said how dressed he would be.

In an effort to hide his bare chest, he climbed into bed, pushed the wall switch that controlled the overhead light and covered up to his chin. She soon emerged from the bath and snapped on the nightstand lamp to reveal she was wearing one of his shirts. Clearly she meant to torture him.

She stood by the bed, a hand on her hip and a frown on her face. "Are you wearing anything, or have you already gone back on your word?"

He reluctantly lifted the sheet. "I am covered from the waist down and I feel that is a good compromise. You know I tend to get warm at night."

"Fine. Scoot over."

After he complied, Madison slid onto the mattress and snapped off the light. When she remained on her side, away from him, normally he would fit himself to her back. Tonight, he felt compelled to ask her permission. "May I hold you?"

"Yes, you may," she answered without looking at him.

He settled against her, slipped one arm beneath her and draped the other over her hip. The scent of her hair, the warmth of her body, sent him into immediate turmoil. After a while, when he heard the sound of her steady breathing, he began to relax. Knowing she was there with him, if only for tonight, provided the comfort he needed. His eyes grew heavy and he soon drifted off.

He had no idea how long he had been asleep when he was awakened by the feel of Madison's soft lips on his neck.

Not knowing if her affection stemmed from a dream, Zain remained frozen from fear of making the wrong move. But when she whispered, "One more memory," he knew she was fully awake.

She was already undressed, and she made sure he joined her in short order. With nothing between them but bare skin, they kissed for long moments, touched with abandon. And when those kisses and touches led to the natural conclusion, Madison took the lead, and he let her. She straddled his hips, rose above him and guided him inside her.

Zain acknowledged this was her means to maintain some control, by leading him into the depths of pleasure, and he gladly followed. He watched her face as she found her climax, and realized he had never seen her look so beautiful. Yet his own body demanded release, and it came, hard and fast.

When Madison stretched out on top of him, their bodies still joined, he rubbed her back gently. He had never felt so deeply for anyone, and he had never cherished her enough until that moment, knowing that she had given him this final, lasting gift of lovemaking. He wished they could suspend time and remain this way indefinitely, but that was impossible.

He refused to consider that now. Refused to take away from this time with her. And when he felt her tears dampen his shoulder, he held her closer and wished he could do more. If wishes were coins, he'd have enough to fill the entire palace. Yet he would never be able to fill the empty place in his soul when she left him. At least he would have some time with her tomorrow, and that thought helped him sleep.

Zain was sound asleep when Madison left his bed right before dawn. She hated to depart without his knowledge, but she didn't want to wake him. She was afraid to wake him. Afraid because he could easily persuade her back into bed and back into his arms. Maybe even persuade her to stay for the coronation, and even longer.

As it stood now, she had a plane to catch at the airstrip in an hour, a car coming in twenty minutes before that, and she still had to take a shower and finish packing. She hurriedly re-dressed in the bathroom, and when she returned to the bedroom, she thankfully found Zain sleeping like a baby.

A baby...

She couldn't think about that now or she'd start crying again, even though she felt all cried out. But she wasn't stupid enough to believe there wouldn't be more tears in her future. A lot of tears, along with a bucketful of regrets. Regret that he couldn't be a part of their child's life. Her life.

Madison took a chance and quietly approached the bed even though she risked waking Zain, but she couldn't leave just yet. The first signs of daylight allowed her to take a mental snapshot of him to help her remember these last moments. He looked almost innocent with that dark lock of hair falling over his forehead. And because he was stretched out on his belly, with his head toward her on the pillow, she could see his eyes move behind closed lids. He was probably dreaming about becoming king, but to her he would always be a desert knight with a winning smile and a hero's heart. Maybe he hadn't rescued her, but he had given her the most precious of gifts.

On that thought, she lifted his arm that was draped over the side of the mattress, and pressed his hand lightly against the place where their baby grew inside her. Someday, when their child's questions about his or her father inevitably began to come, she would simply say *Daddy loves you,* because she inherently knew he would.

As the tears began to threaten, and Zain slightly stirred, she released his hand and placed it on the empty space she had occupied so many nights. Then she leaned down and kissed his cheek. "Good night, sweet prince. I love you."

She walked away, praying she didn't hear him calling her name. But she heard only silence as she left his room for the last time. She experienced relief knowing she could leave before he even realized she was gone.

Ten

"What do you mean she is gone?"

Zain could swear Deeb physically flinched, the first sign of a crack in his unyielding demeanor. "She called yesterday evening and asked me to arrange for her flight to be moved to this morning."

He'd mistakenly believed that when he awoke to the empty space in his bed, she had left to dress for the coronation. "Did she say why she needed to depart early?"

"She mentioned something about a job offer that required her immediate return to the States."

Madison had never mentioned that to him. In fact, she had led him to believe she would be in attendance at his crowning. He wondered what other lies she had told him.

Driven by fury, he grabbed the ceremonial robe from the hanger behind his desk, slipped it on and began buttoning it with a vengeance. "If that is all, you may go."

"Prince Rafiq requests a meeting with you before the ceremony."

His brother should be on his honeymoon, not hovering like a vulture. "Tell him to meet me here in ten minutes, and I will allow him five."

Deeb bowed. "Yes, Your Majesty."

"Will you allow your former governess some of your precious time?"

At the sound of the endearing voice, Zain looked across the room to see Elena standing in the doorway, dressed in her finest clothes, her silver hair styled into a neat twist. "You may come in and stay as long as you wish."

She swept into the room and gave Deeb a smirk as she passed by him. After Zain took a seat behind his desk, Elena claimed the opposing chair. She folded her hands in her lap and favored him with a motherly smile. "I do not have to tell you how proud I am of your accomplishments."

The anger returned with ten times the force. "At least I have your support. Unfortunately, I cannot say the same for Madison, who took it upon herself to leave without telling me."

Elena practically sneered at him. "Remove your *testa* from your *culo*. You have no one to blame but yourself for her actions."

He did not appreciate being blamed for something beyond his control, especially by the one woman he could always count on. "I did not tell her to leave early."

"But did you ask her stay, *caro?*"

He forked both hands through his hair before folding them atop the desk. "I did, yet she refused me."

"How did you ask her?"

"I requested she stay on after the coronation, and then she accused me of asking her to be her mistress."

"If your request was not accompanied by a marriage proposal, then she was justified in her accusation."

He had no patience left for her lecture. "She knows that marriage between us is not possible. There would be severe repercussions."

"Then you are saying you would marry her if the situation were different?"

He did not know what he was saying at this point in time. He only knew he had already begun to miss her, and she was barely gone. "I see no need to speculate on impossibilities."

She leaned forward, reached across the desk and took his hands. "You must ask yourself now if sacrificing love for the sake of duty will be worth it."

"I have never claimed to love her."

"Then tell me now you do not."

If he did, he would be lying. He chose to cite a truth. "I am committed to ruling this country, as it has been ordained by the king."

She let go of his hands, leaned back and laughed. "*Caro,* you never cared about your father's wishes before. You must assume this responsibility because it is right for you, not because he challenged you or because he issued a royal command in an attempt to keep you reined in."

"Do you truly believe that was the intent?"

"Yes, I do. He saw so much of your mother in you. She was also a free spirit and fiercely independent. Since he could not control her, he was determined to keep you under his thumb by making unreasonable demands."

He had never heard her mention his mother in those terms. "I assumed he believed I was the most suitable son to answer the challenge. I should not be surprised he had other motivations, or that he never believed in me."

"He was somewhat calculating, Zain, but he was not a stupid man. He would never have designated you as his successor if he did not think you up to the challenge. And I personally believe you would make a magnificent king, but the demands could suffocate you in the process. I do not want you to live your life regretting what might have been had you chosen a different path."

He felt as though he were suffocating now. "Then I shall prove you both wrong."

Rafiq entered the room, a folder beneath his arm and a solemn expression on his face. He leaned down and kissed Elena's cheek. "The ceremony is set to begin. I have reserved a seat in the front row for you."

She smiled up at him. "Thank you, *caro mio.* And I want you to know that I believe you would make a good king, as well."

Elena quickly rose from the chair and leveled her gaze on Zain. *"Il vero amore e senza rimpianti."*

Real love is without regret....

The words echoed in Zain's mind as Rafiq pulled up the chair where Elena had been seated. "What was that all about?" he asked.

"Nothing." He had no reason to offer a valid explanation for something Rafiq would not understand. He did have a pressing question to pose. "Were you aware of Ms. Foster's early departure?"

Rafiq opened the notebook and studied the page. "No, but her absence is favorable today. You do not need any distractions."

Zain could argue she meant much more to him than a distraction, but he would only be met with cynicism. "How is Rima?"

"She is well," he said without looking up.

"Is she not disappointed that you are here and not on a wedding trip?"

Again, Rafiq failed to tear his attention away from the documents. "My wife understands the importance of my duties, and today my duty is to see that the transition goes smoothly." He finally looked up. "You have a full schedule. The press conference begins immediately following the ceremony, then you will be expected to attend a luncheon with several of the region's emissaries. This evening, you have the official gala."

He would rather eat lye than spend an evening suffering through another barrage of sultans attempting to foist their daughters off on him. "How many people will be in attendance?"

He closed the notebook. "Several hundred. I have to commend Ms. Foster on her assistance with the attendees. She somehow arranged for the U.S. vice president to be there, along with the British prime minister."

"She did not mention that to me."

"She wanted to surprise you."

Zain was surprised to learn the news, but not surprised she pulled it off. He checked his watch to see that he had little time before the ceremony, and found his thoughts turning to Madison. He wondered where she was at this moment, if she happened to be remembering their night together, or attempting to forget him. Perhaps he would call her later, or perhaps not. After today, he could offer her nothing more than a conversation that could cause them only longing, and pain.

He rose from the chair, removed the royal blue sash from the box on the corner of his desk—the sash that his father and his father's father had worn during their reign—and placed it around his neck. "I am ready now." Was he ready? He had no choice but to be ready.

"Before you go," Rafiq began, "I want you to know that although we do not always see eye to eye, I am proud of your accomplishments thus far, particularly your water conservation plans. I have lobbied the council members and I am happy to report all but one are now on board."

"Who is the holdout?"

"Shamil, and that is because I have not been able to reach him since my wedding that he did not bother to attend."

Zain found that odd since Shamil had been Rafiq's closest friend, the reason why Shamil had been appointed to the council. "Perhaps he is traveling."

"Perhaps, but that is not a concern at the moment. Let us away before we are late."

As Zain walked the corridor leading to the ceremonial chamber, with Deeb and Rafiq falling behind him, each step he took filled him with dread. Not dread over assuming the responsibility, but dread over making a mistake he could not take back. When they passed the area lined with attendees held back by braided gold ropes, he could only see visions of Madison. The remembrance of Elena's parting words overrode the burst of applause.

Il vero amore e senza rimpianti...real love is without regret.

And when the doors opened wide, revealing those who had received a special invitation to witness the ceremony, he stopped in his tracks.

"What are you waiting for, brother?"

Zain had been waiting all his life not for this moment, but for a woman like Madison Foster. Nothing else mattered—not his birthright, not duty, only his love for her. He would live with constant regret if he did not at least try to win her back, and that was much worse than the fallout from his next decision.

He turned to Rafiq, slipped the sash from his neck, and placed it around his brother's. "The crown is yours, Rafiq, as it should have been from the beginning. Wear it well."

Confusion crossed Rafiq's expression. "Are you saying—"

"I am abdicating."

"Why?"

"If I told you, you would not understand. Suffice it to say that I have learned commitment must come from the heart. Though I will remain committed to my country and intend to see my conservation plans implemented, my true commitment lies elsewhere."

Rafiq scowled. "You would give up your duty for a woman?"

"I am giving up my duty for love."

"Love is inconstant, Zain. It drives men to weakness."

"You are wrong, brother. It drives men to honor." Zain laid a hand on Rafiq's shoulder. "I am sorry you are so trapped in your love of duty that you will never know real love."

With that, he turned on his heels and left, ignoring the silent, esteemed guests who apparently had been rendered mute from shock.

When he reached the study, he stripped out of the robe, tossed it aside and began to mentally formulate a plan.

"Is there anything I can assist you with, Emir?"

He should have expected Deeb to come to his aid, as the faithful assistant had for years. "Call the airstrip and tell them to ready the second plane for immediate departure. After that, ask one of the staff to pack my bags."

Deeb moved into the room and stood at attention. "Where will you be going and for what length of time?"

He unlocked the drawer containing his passport. "I will be going to Washington, D.C., for an indeterminable about of time." He would only be there a matter of hours if Madison tossed him out on his *culo*.

"If you are going after Ms. Foster, she has not yet departed."

Zain's gaze snapped from the folder to Deeb. "Why is it that you are only now telling me this?"

"I assumed the plane would have taken off by now. It seems the pilot has delayed the flight due to inclement weather."

Zain peered out the window and as predicted, the sun was shining. "The rain stopped hours ago."

"Yes, Emir, it did," Deeb said.

The pilot must be an imbecile, or overly cautious, but either way, Zain was pleased. "Call the airfield and make certain the plane remains as it is."

"As you wish, Emir. Shall I accompany you?"

Zain pocketed the passport, rounded the desk and placed his hands on Deeb's shoulders. "No. You shall go home to your wife and children and spend a lengthy sabbatical in their company. I will make certain you are paid your wages until you resume your duties as my brother's assistant."

Deeb smiled, taking Zain by surprise. "I truly appreciate your consideration, Emir, and I hope that we meet again soon."

Perhaps sooner than he would like if he did not hurry. "Now that we have finalized my arrangements, I am off to see a woman about my future."

Delays, delays and more delays.

Madison leaned back in the leather seat and muttered a few mild oaths aimed at the idiot responsible for the three-hour wait on the tarmac. Unfortunately, she had

no idea who that idiot might be, since she couldn't understand a word of the offered explanations.

But she couldn't complain about the service she'd received in the interim. She been plied with food and drink
and even shown the onboard bed by the flight attendant.
She preferred to nap in the seat, belted in, until they were
safely in the air, hopefully by next week.

She checked her watch for the hundredth time and
confirmed the ceremony should be over by now. Zain
was probably being presented to the press as the newly
crowned king of Bajul. She was happy that he had finally realized his dream, and sad that she couldn't play
a part in it. Even sadder that he wouldn't be a part of
his child's life.

When someone knocked on the exterior door at the
front of the plane, Madison hoped someone had arrived
either to inform them of takeoff, or to explain why they
couldn't seem to get airborne. She watched as the attendant pulled down the latch, and then the woman bowed.
Madison wondered if some dignitary had delayed the
flight in order to hitch a ride. If so, she hoped he or she
didn't expect a friendly reception from her.

But when she saw the tall, gorgeous guy step into
the aisle, she realized she'd been wrong—very wrong.

As if he didn't have a care in the world, Zain flipped
his sunglasses up on his head and dropped down in the
seat beside her.

"What are you doing here?" she asked around her
astonishment.

He presented a world-class grin. "I've decided you
could use some company on your journey."

He had lost his ever-lovin' royal mind. "You can't do
that. You just became king. They're not going to toler-
ate you running out on your obligations on a whim."

He lifted her hand and laced their fingers together. "This is not a whim. This is a plea for your forgiveness."

"I forgive you," she said. "Now leave before they oust you from the palace on your royal behind and strip you of your crown."

"They cannot do that."

"Maybe not, but since you've worked so hard to re-store your reputation as a non–flight risk, don't you think it would be beneficial to actually prove that is the case?"

"My reputation is no longer a concern."

Had she taught him nothing? "It should be, Zain, if you're going to be an effective king."

"I am not the king."

Her mouth momentarily opened before she snapped it shut. "If you're not the king, then who is?"

"I abdicated to Rafiq."

She took a moment to sort through the questions running through her brain at breakneck speed. "Why would you do that when this has been your dream forever?"

He brushed a kiss across her cheek. "It was my fa-ther's dream, or perhaps I should say his ploy to keep me under his control, according to Elena, who told me that this morning. Being with you is my real dream, al-though I did not know that until I was faced with what I stood to lose if I lost you."

Alarm bells rang out in Madison's head. "What else did Elena tell you?"

"She told me that if I chose the crown over you, I would only live with regret, and she was correct. I want to be with you as long as you will have me."

She was still stuck on his conversation with Elena. "And that's all she said?"

He frowned. "Should there be more?"

"I guess not." She felt relieved that he appeared to be

in the dark about the pregnancy, and thrilled that he had returned to her without that knowledge. But still… "I'm worried you're going to regret this decision to give up everything you've worked for and what you still have left to achieve. Not when you've made it so clear how much you love your country."

"I love you more."

She couldn't quite believe her ears. "What did you say?"

"I said I love you more than my country. More than my wealth and more than my freedom."

After his declaration began to sink in, Madison said the only thing she could think to say. "I love you, too."

He gave her the softest, most genuine smile. "Enough to marry me?"

Not once had she let herself imagine that question. "Zain, we haven't known each other that long. In fact, we've never really dated. Maybe we should just start there."

He lifted her hand for a kiss. "A wise woman recently told me that an immediate connection to a person leaves a lasting impact."

"Elena's words?"

"No. Maysa's. She told me that when I talked nonstop about you the night I went to see her. And she is right. I have felt connected to you since the day we met, and I want to make that connection legal and legitimate in everyone's eyes."

If he was willing to take that leap of faith, why wouldn't she jump, too? After all, they had a child to consider—information she needed to reveal, and soon. But before she could force the words out of her mouth, the door to the cockpit opened, and in walked none other than Adan, wearing his military flight suit and his trade-mark dimpled grin.

Zain shot out of his seat and moved into the aisle. "What are you doing here?"

Adan responded with a grin. "I am flying the plane, of course, and you should thank me. I'm the reason why we have yet to take off."

"I do not understand, Adan."

Neither did Madison, but she couldn't wait to hear the youngest Mehdi's explanation.

"I delayed our departure because I suspected you would come to your senses and realize you could not let a woman like Madison leave."

"You came upon that conclusion on your own?" Zain asked in a suspicious tone.

Adan looked a little sheepish. "All right, I admit that Elena formulated the plan, and I agreed to it. And if it had not worked, I planned to whisk Madison to Paris, which by the way is where we will be stopping for the night to refuel."

"You have a woman waiting for you there," Zain said.

Adan grinned again. "That is a distinct possibility."

Zain pointed to the cockpit. "Fly the plane."

"That is my plan, brother. And feel free to utilize the onboard bed during our flight."

"The plane," Zain repeated.

After Adan retreated, Zain returned to Madison and clasped her hand once more. "Let's marry in Paris."

Oh, how she wanted to say yes. But first, she had a serious revelation to make. "Before I agree to marriage, there's something I need to tell you."

"You are not already married, are you?"

She smiled. "No, but I am pregnant."

He stared at her for a moment before comprehension dawned in his stunned expression. "You are serious?"

"Yes, I am serious. I wouldn't joke about a thing like that." But she wasn't beyond using humor to defuse his possible anger over the secret. "And that's the reason why I fainted. It wasn't bad food or your overwhelming charisma, although that does make me want to swoon now and then."

When he failed to immediately comment, Madison worried that her attempts at levity hadn't worked. That brought about her explanation as to why she had withheld the information. "I wanted to tell you, Zain, but I didn't want you to have to choose between the baby and your obligation to your country. And I also need you to understand that it's not that I didn't want a child, I just thought I could never have one. I never wanted to deceive you, but—"

He stopped her words with a kiss. "It's all right, Madison. I could not feel more blessed at this moment."

Neither could she. "Then you're okay with it?"

"I will be okay when you say that you will marry me."

Madison held her breath, and finally took that all-important leap. "Yes, I will marry you."

Any reservations or hesitation melted away with Zain's kiss. In a few months, she would finally have the baby she'd always wanted and thought she would never have, with the man she would always love.

Epilogue

"Here are your babies, Mrs. Mehdi."

After the nurse placed the bundles in the crooks of Madison's arms, she could only stare at her son and daughter in absolute awe. Not only had her lone ovary functioned well, it had worked double time. She only wished their father had been there to see them come into the world.

As if she'd willed his presence, Zain rushed into the room sporting a huge bouquet of red roses and an apologetic look. "The damn plane was delayed because of the rain," he said as he set the flowers down and stripped off his coat.

No surprise to Madison. Wherever there was rain, there was Zain. "It's okay, Daddy. Just get over here and see what you've done."

He slowed his steps on the way to the hospital bed, as if he were afraid to look. But when he took that first glance at his babies, his eyes reflected unmistakable joy, and so did his smile. "I cannot believe they are finally here."

Neither could Madison. "After fourteen hours of labor, I was beginning to wonder."

He leaned over to softly kiss her. "I regret I was not here with you to see you through this."

"That's okay. Elena stayed the entire time and held my hand, worrying like a mother hen."

"Where is she now?"

"I sent her back to the condo. She mentioned something about napping beneath the California sun so she could work on her tan."

He smiled as he brushed a fingertip across their daughter's cheek. "She is beautiful, like her mother."

Madison pushed the blanket away from their son's face to give his father a better look. "And our baby boy is so handsome, just like his uncle Adan."

That earned her a serious scowl. "You are determined to punish me for my late arrival."

"No, I'm just trying to cheer you up, but I guess under the circumstance, that's not going to be easy to do."

"No, it is not." He scooped their daughter into his arms with practiced ease, as if he'd been a father forever, not five minutes. "Holding new life in your arms helps ease the sadness."

It had definitely been a time of sadness back in Bajul, as well as a week full of unanswered questions. "How is Rafiq doing?"

"It is hard to tell," he said. "He seemed all right at the funeral, but he is not one to show any emotion."

Madison had learned that firsthand. During the the two times she and Zain had returned to Bajul, she couldn't recall seeing Rafiq smile all that much. Then, neither had his bride. "I wish I had known Rima better. Do they have any idea what happened with the car, or why she was even in it alone that time of night?"

When the baby began to fuss, Zain lifted their daughter to his shoulder. "No true explanations have emerged thus far. As it was with my mother's death, we may never know."

For months Madison had considered telling her husband about the conversation with Elena involving his mother, but she'd decided to put that on hold for the time being. Today should be about the joy of new beginnings, not sorrow and regrets.

The nurse returned to the room and when she caught sight of Zain, Madison thought the woman might collapse. It didn't matter if they were seventeen or seventy— and this woman was closer to the latter—females always responded the same way to Zain. "Is this the babies' daddy?" she asked.

No, he's the chauffeur, Madison wanted to say but bit back the sarcasm. "Ruth, this is my husband, Zain."

When Zain stood to shake her hand, Ruth grinned from ear to ear. "It's a pleasure to meet you. Is it true you're a sheikh?"

"Yes," Zain said. "But today I am only a new father."

Madison couldn't be more proud of that fact, or the way he pressed a soft kiss on his daughter's forehead. She was definitely going to be a daddy's girl.

The nurse lumbered over to the bed and took Madison's baby boy out of her arms, much to her dismay. "Where are you going with him?"

Ruth patted Madison's arm. "Don't worry, Mommy. He'll just be gone for a little while. Now that he and his sister have warmed up a bit, it's time for their first bath."

She was a little disappointed to give up her children

so soon after their birth, but it would allow her and Zain some time to reach one important decision.

After Ruth carted off the twins, Madison scooted over, gritted her teeth against the lingering pain of childbirth and patted the space beside her. "Come over here, you sexy sheikh."

He turned his smile on her. "Is it not too soon to consider that?"

She rolled her eyes. "I just gave birth to the equivalent of two five-pound bowling balls, so what do you think?"

"You have a point." He kicked off his Italian loafers, climbed onto the narrow bed and folded her into his arms.

"We need to decide on their names," she said as she rested her cheek against his chest. "We can't just refer to them as 'He' and 'She' Mehdi indefinitely, although it is kind of catchy."

"How do you feel about Cala for our daughter?" he asked.

Zain had never suggested that name before now, but Madison supposed his trip home to mourn after the end of a young woman and her unborn child's life had somehow influenced his choice. "It's perfect. I'm sure your mother would have loved having a granddaughter named after her."

"Then we shall call her that. And our son?"

She lifted her head and smiled. "Why not settle for what we've been calling him the past five months?" The nickname they'd given him the day they'd learned the babies' genders during the ultrasound.

He grinned. "Joe?"

"Short for Joseph, which just happens to be my great-great-grandfather's name."

"Joseph it is."

Now that they had covered that all-important decision, she needed to address one more. "Do you have any regrets about giving up the crown and leaving Bajul?"

"Only one. We never made love on the rooftop."

She elbowed his ribs. "I'm serious."

"I have a beautiful wife and two perfect children. How could I possibly regret that?" His expression turned somber. "Do you regret that you have put your career on hold for me?"

Something Madison had sworn she would never do, but then she's never imagined loving a man this much. And during the last conversation with her mother, she'd actually admitted it. "I haven't put my career completely on hold. I'll be doing some preliminary consulting for the senator's campaign the first of the year."

"And you do not mind traveling to Bajul in a few months and staying for a time?"

"As long as we wait until my parents come for their visit, I'm more than game. Besides, I've told you that I feel it's important that our children know their culture, and you still have important work to do on your conservation plans."

He planted a quick kiss on her lips. "Good. While we're there, we will return to the lake and relive our first experience."

The experience that had brought them to this day. This new life. This incredible love. "That sounds like a plan. You bring Malik's truck, and I'll bring my overactive ovary. We might even get lucky a second time."

"I cannot imagine feeling any luckier than I do now."

"Neither can I."

When the nurse returned their children to their waiting arms, completing the family they had made, Madison and Zain settled into comfortable silence, as they'd done so many times since they had taken that giant leap of faith, and landed in the middle of that sometimes treacherous territory known as love.

Madison felt truly blessed, and it was all because of one magical mountain, and one equally magical man. A man who might not be the king of his country, but he was—and always would be—the king of her heart.

* * * * *

Have Your Say

You've just finished your book.
So what did you think?

We'd love to hear your thoughts on our
'Have your say' online panel
www.millsandboon.co.uk/haveyoursay

- Easy to use
- Short questionnaire
- Chance to win Mills & Boon® goodies

Visit us Online

Tell us what you thought of this book now at
www.millsandboon.co.uk/haveyoursay

YOUR_SAY

The World of Mills & Boon®

There's a Mills & Boon® series that's perfect for you. We publish ten series and, with new titles every month, you never have to wait long for your favourite to come along.

Blaze.
Scorching hot, sexy reads
4 new stories every month

By Request
Relive the romance with the best of the best
9 new stories every month

Cherish™
Romance to melt the heart every time
12 new stories every month

Desire™
Passionate and dramatic love stories
8 new stories every month